Also by Howard W. Lewis

The Daedalus Rimes Saga

Daedalus Rimes I
Essence

Daedalus Rimes II
Afterdeath

Daedalus Rimes III
The First Galactic War

Daedalus Rimes – ESSENCE

es·sence \ the individual, real, or ultimate nature of a thing esp. as opposed to its existence

Book-1 of the Daedalus Rimes Saga

A Novel by

Howard W. Lewis

Published by Howard W. Lewis / May 5 2013; Daedalus Rimes - Essence
Cover / Chapter Art by Fantasio Fine Arts

DAEDALUS RIMES - ESSENCE

PRINTING HISTORY
AuthorHouse / August 2009; the Essence of Daedalus Rimes

Visit our website at
www.authorhwlewis.com

ISBN: 978-0-9887504-2-5

Acknowledgements

For my family, friends, editor and illustrator whose support and encouragement has helped me through the long process of bringing this story to life.

Prologue

The beginning of the third millennium of the Christian calendar was marked by the general acceptance that life beyond the confines of our planet, and even our solar system, is possible. Still, when possibility became reality, the entire world reeled with the shock that we share our universe with others.

4:20 PM Friday

News teams across the Eastern seaboard of the United States filmed an object entering the earth's atmosphere over the Atlantic Ocean. The object was first reported as a flaming meteor. However, seconds prior to what seemed an imminent impact off the coast, the object slowed, leveled off at a few thousand feet above the water, and continued west at supersonic speed, leaving a thick contrail of vapor in its wake. Within fifty miles of New York City, the object turned southwest and disappeared with an instantaneous burst of speed. Within seconds, the object shot two hundred miles down the coast, passing over Philadelphia and Baltimore, and approached Washington, DC. Decelerating at the same incredible rate as it had accelerated, it appeared in the darkening afternoon sky at the northeastern edge of the city.

The object was officially designated a UFO on its approach to New York City, and as it entered the restricted air space above Washington, DC, the airborne terrorist response forces sprang into action. Military forces rushed to the rooftops of government buildings with shoulder-launched missiles and high-powered rifles. American fighter planes scrambled from neighboring military bases, vectoring in from all directions. The contrails of the approaching aircraft looked like spokes in the sky with Washington, DC as the hub. Sonic waves from approaching jets rattled windows across ten states. Before the jets could reach their target, the object abruptly dropped down through the gray haze hanging over the busy city and leveled off less than a hundred feet over the stunned commuters.

Clearly visible to everyone on the ground, the bizarre craft silently passed over the Capitol Building, giving throngs of tourists an unexpected photo opportunity. It stopped and hovered momentarily before gliding noiselessly forward. At over sixty miles per hour, the object raced over the National Mall and banked tightly around the Washington Monument. It stopped suddenly, emitting a loud hum that scattered the crowds of tourists below, and slowly descended to the grass of Lafayette Park, across Pennsylvania Avenue from the White House. It was 4:24 PM.

Shaped like an elongated beetle, the wingless, windowless object was approximately sixty feet long, twenty four feet wide, and eighteen feet high. The front, wider than the rear, possessed a large oval opening that resembled the intake of a jet engine. The opening ran side-to-side six feet high and twenty one feet wide, giving it the appearance of a gaping mouth. The rear of the vessel had small, thin indentations running up and down the last six feet in evenly spaced rows. The smooth surface was a dull slate gray, and the object had no other visible markings or doors.

The initial panic among nearby civilians quickly passed. Many who had fled in terror just moments before returned and stood within a dozen feet of the craft, recording the event with cellphones and camcorders. The military and police, however, descended on the scene with an amazing ferocity and clarity of purpose that surprised those unfortunate enough to be caught within the quickly established perimeter.

Before the area could be cleared of civilians and the recording devices confiscated, a news team with a live feed aired the event on a local network. Although intense efforts to censor the release of information were brought to bear, the footage was released nationally within minutes and internationally in less than an hour.

The camera coverage, although rough and often shaky, provided clear details of the landing, the appearance of an opening in the side of the object, and the disembarking of several alleged extraterrestrials who were followed out of the craft by a group of humans. The news team jostled its way through the growing crowd and was able to briefly record comments made by the released humans. They indicated that they had been abducted some time ago and were now being returned to Earth. The audio was lost when the surging crowd knocked the microphone off the camera. Within seconds of losing audio, the video feed was cut, and the news crew was taken into custody along with thousands of other civilians trapped within the protective military perimeter. Within hours of the landing, the military implemented the most intense media blackout and most extensive quarantine in American history.

The departure of the DC-ET Spaceship, as the media dubbed it, was videotaped late that evening by hundreds of network news teams that had formed a media city outside the military perimeter. The president addressed the nation shortly thereafter, offering assurance that the situation was under control and that there was nothing to fear from this historic first contact with extraterrestrial beings. Although the president spoke for over half an hour, he never mentioned the humans that had arrived with the aliens, the quarantine, or the media blackout. His speech repeated the theme that the extraterrestrials were friendly, and that the first meeting had gone well. In closing, the president requested that the nation remain calm and asked citizens to obey the police and military, making it clear that irresponsible reporting or profiteering by businesses or individuals would be dealt with severely.

Surprisingly, the national impact of the event was only slightly more intense than the first few days of the Gulf War. Most people returned to work the following Monday and life went on as usual. With few exceptions, everyone, everywhere, at home or at work, was riveted to the news. There were reports of alien attacks, alien abductions, and alien vessels coming and going from military installations. These were followed by government press releases categorically denying any abductions and attacks, but neither confirming nor denying any related activity at military installations.

Without any solid information to work with, news networks filled the gaps in their broadcasts with often-inflammatory but carefully-voiced speculation and commentary. Political hopefuls, trying to further their careers, attacked the current political methodology that was being used to handle the situation. Theologians argued over the effect the event would have on religious doctrine, while at the same time, numerous religious organizations began to unite under the common belief that this event signaled the approach of the apocalypse.

Using footage from the landing, the press identified several people exiting the spacecraft as Americans who had been reported missing. Using this information, news teams from across the nation and around the world descended on the families and friends of these missing persons, hoping for interviews with anyone who knew anything about them. The government declined to comment on the existence of these individuals or their identities, and no interviews or information was forthcoming. On a nationally televised talk show, audio specialists and lip readers analyzed the footage of the landing and concluded that one of the abducted had said “a war” and “attacked by.” Shortly after the show aired, the FBI placed key network executives under arrest for “journalistic terrorism”. Around the country, gun sales hit an all-time high, people began to hoard food, the stock market plummeted, and CNN covered it all on their 24-hour “Alien Watch.”

1 - The Visitor

Dark blue-gray skies dappled with low clouds were all that remained of the moonless night. The sun was just starting to light the eastern sky with a colorless, dismal glow, and a heavy mist, not quite a drizzle, gave the cold morning air a penetrating chill. A caravan of four black vehicles with dark, tinted windows proceeded unnoticed down the sparsely populated freeway. A late model black sedan led the way, followed by a limousine and another black sedan, with a full-size van bringing up the rear.

The helicopter overhead would have been undetectable if not for the faint “whoop whoop whoop” made by the rotating blades. The pilot had high-definition radar-enhanced night vision on a heads-up display, providing visibility far superior to daylight. Two snipers in black jumpsuits and flat black helmets sat behind the pilots and faced their respective sides of the helicopter, high-powered rifles poised and ready. The snipers wore powerful infrared scopes that defined the terrain by temperature. The heat of the engines in the vehicles below glowed white-hot and the bodies of the occupants were orange; even the birds perched in the trees appeared as little white dots of light on the branches.

Moving as a single entity, the vehicles exited the freeway and proceeded into a lower–middle class suburban neighborhood. The homes were modest tracts, identical in shape with only the minor twists of color and décor differentiating one from the next. It was 6:00 AM Monday morning, four weeks and two days since the first contact, when the group of vehicles pulled up in front of an unimposing tan and brown stucco home with a low white picket fence and a For Sale sign in the front yard. The long, sun-parched grass needed mowing. If not for the lights in the front window, the home would have appeared unoccupied, but its occupancy had been assured and verified.

The timing of this visit had been strategically planned to ensure that the resident would be home and awake, and the likelihood of any other activity in the neighborhood remote. A black van, identical to the one in the arriving group, was parked across the street. The van had been there since 4:00 the previous afternoon. The individuals in the back of the van had monitored and reported the arrival and activities of the occupant of the house for the last fourteen hours.

Like a choreographed dance, the doors of the two sedans opened and eight agents wearing identical black suits, white shirts, and black ties exited and took up their assigned positions:

two men across the street, two on the sidewalk by the lead vehicle, two on the sidewalk by the following sedan, and two agents, one male, one female, at the front door of the house. Standing on either side of the door, the agents waited for the order to continue. The street was silent except for a dog barking in the distance and the nearly imperceptible whoop of the helicopter overhead. The order came via concealed radio receivers tucked into the agents' ears. On cue, the female agent on the right rang the doorbell. A dog barked and scratched at the door. The porch light came on and a female voice quieted the dog.

"Who is it?" the woman queried from behind the bolted door.

"Federal Bureau of Investigation, Ms. Rimes," the female agent answered. "We have information regarding your husband."

The deadbolt made a click-clack as it was retracted and the door opened quickly, stopping with a bang as it hit the end of a security chain. The loud noise resonated in the silence of the dawn, causing the two agents at the door to tense and the other agents in the group to scan for threats among the shadows. The door quickly closed again, and a fumbling with the security chain could be heard. Again the door opened, this time more slowly. A woman in her late forties to early fifties in a modest business skirt, blouse, and jacket peered out the door. Her graying light-brown hair was neatly combed and she wore a minimal amount of makeup. The smell of coffee, perfume, and hair spray wafted out of the door.

"Where is he? Is he alive?" she asked.

"The … individual who can answer your questions is waiting in the car," the female agent said.

Julie Rimes opened the door to look at the limousine parked out front. When she did, the dog bolted past her, causing the two agents to instinctively assume defensive positions.

"Don't be frightened," Julie chided. "She doesn't bite," adding quickly, "unless I tell her to."

Julie's dog, a mature fawn boxer, ran down the walkway, eagerly greeting each of the agents by the car in turn and then jumping up on the back door of the limousine. Its little stub of a tail and whole rear end wiggled wildly with excitement. Julie stepped toward the car, but the two agents blocked her path.

"Get out of my way!" she shouted impatiently.

"Please, Ms. Rimes; your husband is not in the car. The individual who wishes to speak with you insists on talking to you here, in your house. If you will let us verify the house is secure, our client will enter and answer all your questions," said the female agent with brusque, emotionless precision, making it clear that pleasantries were merely a formality.

Julie Rimes looked at the black limousine and then at the two intensely serious agents in their nondescript suits and ties, surreal in their mist-speckled dark glasses and short-cropped hair that glistened under the amber porch light. *Why wear sunglasses before daylight?* Julie wanted to ask. Under other circumstances she would not have hesitated to challenge their authority. Sensing that she had no other options, she acquiesced.

"Yes, of course," she replied with a sarcastic bite. "Come into my house and verify it's secure so I can find out if my husband is alive or dead." A tightening in her throat, a lump of expectant anguish, choked off any further comment. She backed into the house, her eyes blurring with tears she thought had long run dry. Her worst fears resurfaced as logic reasoned that by not answering the question of Dade's welfare, they had confirmed the negative.

Julie glared at the male agent as he entered the house and watched intently as he began a systematic check and electronic scan of the rooms, windows, and exterior doors. She couldn't fathom why the security of her house was of any concern and was mentally preparing a barrage of questions for the female agent, when the agent by the limousine took the wiggling boxer by the collar and led it back to the house, where he turned it over to Julie. The dog pulled against her grip, eager to return to the limousine. Wiping the tears from her eyes, Julie abandoned her plan to question the agent and stared at the limousine as if she could somehow extract the answers she sought.

"No weapons, no surveillance." Julie heard the agent in the house say into a concealed microphone on the collar of his shirt. Taking a position at the back door, the agent cued the next action with his final comment. "The house is secure."

The front doors of the limousine opened and two more agents in black stepped out. Once they were in position, a figure in a long hooded cloak emerged from the back door. All three proceeded up the walkway where Julie was waiting. Both agents continually scanned the adjacent bushes and shadows for threats. At the front door, the female agent directed Julie to the side as the lead agent and cloaked figure entered the house. When the female agent closed the door, the last man took up his position outside.

Julie scrutinized the cloaked figure, trying to see its face.

"My God!" she whispered, catching only a glimpse of the clawed, paw-like hand that carried a thin black briefcase.

"It's one of *them*. The aliens." She released the dog's collar, backed up, and froze against the wall.

She had seen clear pictures of the strange creatures on the news and recognized their featureless faces, protruding fangs, thin sinewy bodies and clawed hands. This, she was certain, was one of them.

Without hesitating, the cloaked figure walked through the kitchen and stopped by the table. The dog ran through the kitchen, dodging the agent who tried to grab it, and jumped up on the alien with its front feet, its tail and haunches wiggling as they had at the limousine. The alien stepped back and eased the dog to the floor. Bending over, it gently rubbed and scratched the dog's ears with its clawed hand. The alien looked up. In the cold fluorescent light of the kitchen, its mottled skin and expressionless black eyes were visible from within the shadows of the hood. In a rasping voice punctuated with odd clicks and wheezes, the cloaked figure spoke.

"Please. Come sit with me, Julie, and I will tell you what has happened since your husband left." Setting the briefcase on the table, the alien slowly removed the cloak, as if doing so would somehow relieve the shock of its unusual appearance. The alien draped the cloak over the back of a chair and bowed slightly at the waist with its hands open before it, its palms up.

At full height, the creature was considerably shorter than the FBI agents escorting it. Standing no more than five feet tall with the build and stature of an adolescent, it did not present a physically frightening presence. It wore a floor-length, sky-blue gown cinched at the waist with an intricately engraved metal band with a ringlet of metal on one side. The smooth, glossy exposed skin on its arms and face was a translucent bone-white, mottled with light gray and brown irregularly-shaped patches. The face, having the same size and proportions as a human, possessed unusual features. Where a nose should have been, there were star-shaped slits. The mouth had no lips and seemed tightly stretched between two canine fangs that protruded a little more than an inch from its upper jaw. Where ears should have been, only small, semicircular indentations the size of a normal ear canal could be seen. The eyes were glossy black orbs in thin slits, and the fold of each eyelid ran back to the top of each ear indentation. The top of the head was bare and slightly conical near the back, and something that looked more like thin wet noodles than hair grew in a sparse ring around the crown. A strip of the same blue fabric as the gown was used to tie the odd noodles into a ponytail that extended to the creature's narrow shoulders.

"Don't be frightened, Julie. I will not hurt you," it rasped as it sat down at the end of the table. The dog immediately put its head in the alien's lap, and the alien continued to massage the dog's ears with the claws of its gnarled fingers.

"Come here, Candy!" Julie demanded.

Turning briefly to look at Julie, the dog put her head back on the alien's lap and nudged the clawed hand.

"It looks like I have at least one friend here," the alien said, the corners of its mouth turning up in what appeared to be a smile.

Julie inched her way toward the table, stopping about five feet away.

"Do you know where my husband is? Is he alive?" she somehow managed to choke past the lump in her throat. Hearing the distress in Julie's voice, Candy ran over to her, licking and nuzzling her tightly clenched fist.

The alien leaned forward and implored her. "I know everything that has happened, but there is no quick or simple answer to your question. You must hear for yourself what I have to say. Please, sit down. This will take less time than you may imagine."

Julie moved closer to the table. Leaning over and reaching with the full length of her arm, she pulled out a chair, maximizing the distance between her and the alien. She dropped into the chair, emotionally exhausted.

"Is Dade alive? Can you at least tell me that, please?" Julie pleaded.

From the sleeve of its smock the alien produced a round silver box about five inches in diameter and two inches deep. With reverence, it set the box down on top of the thin black briefcase, leaving its clawed hands resting on either side. The alien looked down at the box and took a long, deep breath, and its black eyes disappeared as the folds of its eye slits closed. After an uncomfortable pause, the alien began to speak.

"When your husband left for work that morning, he was running late. He didn't have time for his morning cup of coffee and forgot to put the garbage out for collection; however, despite the argument of the night before, he did attempt to kiss you goodbye and told you he would call when he got to work."

Julie opened her mouth to speak and then closed it. She had told the police everything she could remember about that morning: the time that Dade had left for work, everything about the car, what Dade was wearing, and that he was running late. But she never mentioned the argument or the thwarted kiss good-bye. There was no need; it couldn't have been relevant. Until now, she hadn't even thought about the coffee, or the fact that the garbage didn't make it to the curb for another two weeks.

The alien opened its eyes slightly and focused on Julie. The telepathic nudge Julie felt as the alien entered her mind was immediately lost as the alien began to relay the story in a way that involved much more than the sound of its rasping voice.

2 - Abduction

The motion light came on as the garage door opened. Beyond the perimeter illuminated by the small bulb, it was pitch black. Low clouds hid a sliver of a moon and blanked out the stars that would have provided at least nominal visibility. It was not cold out, at least not to the point that Dade was inclined to button up his coat. As he backed out of the driveway, the headlights of his car illuminated the garbage cans lined up in front of several houses down the street.

"Damn it," he said, stopping halfway down the driveway. He shifted his driving glasses to the top of his head and tilted his watch back and forth in an attempt to read it. In the darkness, he couldn't read the LED face without pressing one of the buttons, and he could never remember which one to press.

"The garbage will have to wait until next week," he grumbled, knowing he was already running late. Repositioning his glasses, he thought, *I should have gotten the bifocals so I wouldn't have to keep screwing with these things.* He released the brake and continued toward the freeway, hoping he could make up some time. There were few cars on the road this time of the morning, so Dade didn't feel overly guilty about speeding, but he was concerned enough to keep a wary eye on the rearview mirror for the flashing lights that might make him even later for work.

Twenty minutes later, he glanced at his watch beneath a streetlight and noted with satisfaction that he was back on schedule. At the bottom of the freeway off-ramp he turned right onto a two-lane road that would take him ten rural miles to the new industrial center where he worked. He was the supervisor of equipment maintenance for a company that manufactured aftermarket car parts and accessories. Demand was growing faster than the company could produce, and the move to this new industrial center was the first of several planned expansions.

Dade liked to get an early start to make sure everything was ready to go when the maintenance crew arrived. At least then his department would not be the target of the owner's trite criticisms. Plans were in the works for a night shift so equipment maintenance could have less of an impact on production, and Dade groaned at the thought of trying to divide his time between night and day crews. He had been told in his initial interview that he'd seldom have overtime, which was important to him; salaried supervisors were excluded from overtime pay. Unfortunately, with the small company stretched to the limits of its manpower and resources, ten- and twelve-hour days had become commonplace, and Dade was waiting to see his performance review next month before placing his demands regarding work hours and pay. Or at least, that was the excuse he kept giving Julie as the long hours at work grew longer and more frequent.

The fatigue at home was affecting the time they were able to spend together. The situation had finally worked itself to a head the day before when a crisis on one of the automated press's hydraulic systems caused Dade to work late and he missed their anniversary dinner. The ensuing argument, his angry outburst, the flood of tears it caused, his pathetic apology, and now Julie's cold shoulder caused the knot in his gut to tighten.

"I didn't hit her! All I did was yell!" Dade shouted at the dark road before him, his spittle glistening on the windshield.

"I haven't hit anyone in years. Can't I vent a little steam?" he continued weakly, feeling self-conscious of his voice.

Two years in jail, six years of anger management, two jobs, one failed marriage and now, with a little stress, the burning knot that formed within his gut was back. He had yelled—no, he had raged at Julie, the one person who made his otherwise shitty life worth living. He had given her the voice and the look that signaled he was one step away from inflicting bodily harm. Dade shook his head violently in an effort to dispel these thoughts and tried feebly to shift his concentration to the day's work schedule.

There were no cars behind him and no cars ahead, just the way he liked to drive a winding road. There was nothing he found more irritating than driving behind a law-abiding road slug, one of those drivers who really did the suggested twenty miles per hour on turns and always obeyed the posted speed limit. He was in sync with the road, coasting into turns and accelerating out of them, when he noticed low clouds in the otherwise pitch black sky being illuminated from below just over the next rise. Dade was still four or five miles from the industrial center, so he was certain it couldn't be lights from its buildings.

I hope it isn't another accident. He remembered a fatal collision several months earlier in a pocket of fog near this very spot. The highway patrol had closed the road for several hours while the dead and injured were removed by ambulance and damaged vehicles were towed away. As he crested the rise, he bumped his high beams down to prevent blinding whomever might be on the other side. The glow of the clouds vanished like a light bulb had been turned off, leaving nothing ahead but darkness.

"What the hell was that?" he said.

Beyond the range of his headlights, there was only darkness and the occasional silhouette of a tree or barbed wire fence off the side of the road. In this remote area, there were no homes or streetlights, and on this particular morning the clouds blacked out the sky so that not even a star could be seen. He bumped his headlights back to high and slowed down, wary now that something was not right. He was certain that he had seen something—but what? Ahead of him in the distance, he could see a vehicle's red taillights in the road. The lights were not on; they just reflected the beams of his headlights.

This could be one of those highway robberies. He recalled the disturbing stories he had read in the news lately. He and Julie had left urban Detroit years earlier to get away from the crime and the emotional baggage of a life he wanted to forget. In those days, he had carried a loaded snub-nose .38 to and from work, against Julie's wishes and in violation of the law. Having the gun with him had provided him with a sense of security then; a feeling he didn't have now.

As he approached the vehicle he continued to slow down. The vehicle was a large American SUV, significantly larger than the Japanese compact he drove. Almost unconsciously, he toggled the switch to lock the doors, but the resounding "ker-chunk" of the solenoids gave him little solace. The vehicle ahead of him was stopped in the center of the lane with both the driver's and passenger's doors open. There were no lights on, not even the inside courtesy light.

Dade slowed his vehicle to a crawl as he came up behind the car in the road. He noticed that it was steaming, like cars will on a cold morning when the sun begins to heat the damp surface of painted metal. But there was no sun, and nobody in or near the car. The hair on the back of his neck stood up in warning; something was wrong, very, very wrong. He was trying to decide whether to stop, speed by, or turn around, when the area around his car suddenly lit up with an intense bright light. His lights went out immediately and the engine stalled. Dade found himself unable to move or breathe. The bright light faded to inky black as the tense feeling of paralysis dissolved into physical and mental numbness.

3 - Escape

It was the fetid odor Dade first noticed when he awoke. Something unclean, a nauseating combination of sweat, vomit, feces, urine, and something else—something sour and rank. His stomach was upset, a feeling like driving fast over dips in the road combined with a spinning sensation. He choked involuntarily and dry heaved several times, receiving the bitter taste of bile in his mouth. If he had drunk his morning coffee, it would have ended up all over the wall in front of him. *Wall or ceiling?* He felt as though he was lying down and standing at the same time. *It must be a wall,* he reasoned, noting that it was clean and smooth above his head and crusted and splattered with—he wasn't sure what—from about chest level to the floor. In the dim light, he could see what he believed was the floor. It was littered with debris and more of the crust that was on the wall. He dry heaved again and spit the bile from his mouth. He watched as it arced across the distance in front of him, hitting the surface of the wall at about waist level to join the layer of crust approximately six feet away.

That should have hit the floor.

He heard someone else choking and vomiting near him, and he tried to turn and look but found himself held flat against the surface behind him by a rubbery sheet that extended from his chest to just below his knees. He was in a sort of tray or a shallow open box made from the same smooth slate gray material as the wall. Like the wall and the floor, the tray was also crusted and filthy. When he turned his head in either direction, he could only see the edge of the tray's lip. And when he struggled, the rubbery sheet tightened like shrink-wrap. He again heard someone vomit, this time to his right, and at about the same time someone started to cry on his left.

"Who else is here?" Dade asked in as normal a tone as he could muster. His voice reverberated around the room like a shout during Sunday mass.

"I am," a whispering female voice answered from the left.

"So am I … uh … William, uh … Bill Jacks, Rivers Bend, California." boomed a deep baritone voice from the left and what must have been the tray next to his. Dade visualized him as a middle-aged black man.

"Hello, Bill, my name is Dade. I live near Rivers Bend. Were you driving on Mill Road this morning?"

"Yeah. Going to work. I'm a security guard at the Mill Valley Industrial Center."

"Where are we, Bill?" Dade asked.

"Dunno. I just woke up a little while 'fore you. I don't feel real good, sick to my stomach an' all."

"They're demons," came the whispering female voice. "I've seen them. They collect the dead and take them to hell."

"Oh, great," Bill muttered under his breath.

"What's your name, Miss? Where are you from?" Dade asked, trying to sound calm and reassuring.

"Rebecca. I'm from Oregon," she whispered.

"What do these demons look like, Rebecca?" Dade asked.

"They are ugly, hideous little monsters with glowing eyes. They float across the ground. I've seen them bringing in dead people," whispered Rebecca, barely loud enough for Dade to hear.

"I don't think they were dead, Rebecca. I'm not dead, and you're not dead. I don't think what you saw were demons," Dade said.

"Aliens," Bill muttered. "Yeah, aliens. And we're in their flying saucer."

From Dade's right came a new voice. This one sounded like a young man. "I knew it, I knew it! I knew it was a spaceship, man. I should've ran. I knew I should've ran. We're all gonna die, man. They're gonna cut us apart and study us!"

The young man began to choke, and Dade saw the arc of vomit hit the wall to his right as the man voided his stomach. It was now obvious to Dade what the source of the crust was, and in that realization came the understanding that this group was not the first to be held here—wherever *here* was.

"Holy crap!" Bill exclaimed.

It was the fear in Bill's voice more than what he said that caused Dade to turn his head and look. Someone or, more appropriately, something was standing in front of Bill. The creature was a little over waist-high, maybe four feet. Dade could only see its back and left side. It was wearing dark brown coveralls, probably black, but very dirty or dusty. The exposed skin of its hand and head was a greenish brown, like swamp water, and appeared to have a leathery, heavily creased texture.

The creature turned and glided in front of Dade and was joined immediately by another alien. An acrid smell assailed Dade's nostrils. It was apparent that the sour smell came from these alien creatures. Their foul odor in close proximity was so strong that it nearly drowned out the other rank smells saturating the air. The pair of aliens stood in front of him as though they planned to have a three-way conversation. The young man to the right of Dade began to hyperventilate. Forcing control of his panic, Dade prayed the young man wouldn't start yelling again.

The aliens' heads were almond-shaped, large in comparison to their slender torsos. They had two large oval iridescent eyes, like those of a dragonfly, only these eyes radiated light rather than reflecting it. The eyes constantly changed colors in shades of blue, green, and yellow moving patterns. If it were not for the intense fear and helplessness that Dade felt, he would have been amused. It wasn't the eyes that Dade found to be amusing, but the crease that ran from just below their eyes to where their heads were attached to their torsos.

"You look like butt heads," Dade sneered defiantly. The taunt, recalled from his childhood, actually applied to these creatures.

As though responding to his comment, one of the aliens reached up toward Dade's face, causing him to involuntarily recoil and turn his head to the side in revulsion. The alien's limb stopped just below Dade's chin and moved across his chest and down his left arm. It was not a normal hand or arm; it was an orb with six thick tentacles in constant motion on the end of another, thicker tentacle. The arm, orb, and fingerlike tentacles all seemed boneless, flexing in a rubbery, snakelike fashion that alternately stretched and shrank. The tentacles of the hand pressed and poked painfully with much more force than Dade would have expected from so slight a creature.

"What do you want?" Dade asked, fear and panic apparent in his voice. Without answering or making any sound at all, the creatures turned to face one another for a moment and then moved off to his right. Dade could see why Rebecca said they floated. They glided along using the motion of the tentacles on their lower limbs, as if they were carried on snakes.

The aliens stood at the tray to the right of Dade, repeating the inspection or examination of the young man in the same manner that they had examined him. The young man began to hyperventilate again. A scream pierced the silence, and the young man began to shout. "Don't touch me! Keep your filthy hands off me, man!" There was a brief silence and then the alien nearest Dade moved to the side and reached between the two trays. Dade heard a click, and the young man's tray slid forward at the bottom, moving from a vertical position to a horizontal one, and dropped to floor level.

"No! No! Please not me! Not me, man!" the young man screamed hysterically over and over. Behind Dade, someone choked and vomited. *How many others are there?*

Once the tray was horizontal, he could see that the young man was pinned to the surface with the same type of rubbery sheet as his. The young man looked to be Caucasian, in his mid- to late twenties, a bodybuilder, not tall but very physically developed. Dade noted that the man's intense struggling was causing the sheeting to press deeply into his flesh at the shoulders and shins.

The two aliens, one pushing and the other pulling, moved the cart with little effort down along the wall to Dade's right and then exited through an opening he had not previously noticed in the dim light.

The man shouted and cursed in the adjacent compartment until he let out a bloodcurdling scream that lasted for his entire lung capacity, then followed it by another and another, each rising in pitch to shrieks of agony.

My God, they are dissecting him! Dade struggled impotently in his bindings.

The other prisoners began shouting and screaming in fear. He pitied those who were just waking up in this fetid place, their senses assaulted by foul smells and horrific sounds. Taking a deep breath, Dade concentrated on relaxing his muscles and calming his thoughts. He recalled a session of anger management where the counselor described the relationship between fear and anger. "If you can control fear, you can control anger, and in turn control the emotions that would otherwise control you." For the first time, Dade truly understood.

Relaxing his muscles, he tried to move his arm up slowly. The sheet tightened before he was able to move it more than a fraction of an inch, but he did manage to move it. Encouraged, he tried again, and again it tightened after the slightest movement. He considered the distance from his waist to his chest and calculated that it would take hours before he would be able to get one arm free. His hands were at his sides over the pockets of his pants. He could feel the change he had grabbed that morning for lunch money. He could also feel the outline of his pocketknife, a gift Julie had given him on his birthday after they were married. The knife, like his wallet, was something he always carried with him. It was a Swiss Army knife, the type with blades, screwdrivers, scissors, and such. He called it his pocket toolbox.

Closing his eyes, he focused his concentration on moving the knife little by little toward the top of his pocket. His wrist and forearm soon began to ache and cramp from the exertion, and he found that he could not raise his shoulder any higher and any attempt to bend his elbow was met with a painful tightening of the sheet.

Beads of sweat formed on his forehead. The drops joined together and ran off his face, forming rivulets down his neck that soaked the collars of his shirt and jacket. His continued effort was finally rewarded when the knife cleared the top of the pocket. Unfortunately, the knife was now pinned between his wrist and waist. Folding his painfully cramping fingers into his palm, he slowly worked the knife down his wrist and into the palm of his hand using the tips of his index and middle finger. At last, he held the closed pocketknife in the palm of his hand.

Dade realized that it had grown quieter now. The shrieks and screams had quieted to a hoarse rasping and gurgling. With the exception of Rebecca's murmured prayers and some soft whimpers behind him, there was nothing to distract him from his task.

Since he was now the last on the front row of trays, he believed he would be next in line for dissection. Trying to clear his mind of unpleasant possibilities, he concentrated on slowing his racing heart and returned to the challenge of opening the blade of his pocketknife. He knew every bump and line of the knife, and his thumbnail had no problem finding the recess cut into the edge of the smallest blade. He reasoned that it would be easier to open that one, plus it was much sharper than the large one, which had received the most use.

Every time he began to pull the blade out with his thumbnail, the thumbnail slipped out of the recess in the blade and the blade snapped shut. He tried over and over again, moving the knife this way and that in unsuccessful attempts to open the blade. Cursing aloud, he struggled in his wraps and received a painful squeeze for his efforts. Again, concentrating to regain his composure, he slipped his thumbnail into the recess in the blade and drew the blade outward. This time, however, he slipped the tip of his index finger between the blade and the case of the knife. His thumbnail slipped out of the recess, and the razor-sharp blade bit deeply into the flesh of his fingertip. Ignoring the burning sting, he slid his fingertip slowly between the blade and the case to force the blade open. He could feel the blade dragging across the bone of his finger, and warm, greasy blood soaked his hand and leg. The blood added a beneficial lubricant that improved the movement and progress of opening the blade. After a few painful minutes, the blade locked open with a snap.

He could no longer feel the tip of his index finger and realized that he had probably severed the nerve. The slippery effect of the blood combined with the numbness in his finger now made it difficult for him to get a grip on the knife handle. Wedging the butt of the knife against his thigh and pulling the sharp edge of the blade up, he pressed the tip of the blade into the rubbery sheet. Even with the knife pushing straight out from his body, it still wouldn't cut through the rubbery membrane. With sweat burning his eyes, he looked down at the blade; the membrane was stretched so tightly around it that he could see its every detail, yet it was still unable to penetrate. Angry at his failure, he thrashed in frustration and the wraps tightened painfully in response. But as they tightened, the knife blade cut through the membrane with an audible pop.

The sheet on either side of the slit immediately relaxed, creating a loose ridge the width of the knife blade across his hips. He tried moving the blade with an in-and-out sawing motion but failed to open the hole any larger. He forced the sharp edge of the knife into the membrane at a 45-degree angle, stretching the rubbery surface with as much force as he could muster, and then purposefully struggled to get the rubbery surface to tighten. The blade pulled up straight as the membrane tightened, cutting a quarter of an inch and loosening another section of the wrap. He repeated the process several more times, finally freeing his hand, which made the act of bracing and moving the blade easier. Once both hands were free, he was able to use their combined strength to lever the blade up under the sheet, stimulating the tightening and cutting action. After cutting the last strip at the top of his chest, he was able to work downward from his pocket to just below his knees.

Leaning forward in the tray to get a better angle on the lower end of the sheet that held his legs, Dade could see into the tray on his left. He recognized the large black man as one of the security guards that manned the gate at the industrial park. The man was watching him intently. Dade stopped cutting and nodded at him.

"You ain't got time to take in the scenery," the man whispered. "Get back to work."

The absence of sound from the next room gave credence to Bill's comment. Once they finished with the young bodybuilder, the aliens would likely come for their next victim. As soon as the final strip across his shins had been severed, Dade stepped forward, intending to turn and step over to Bill's tray. Instead, he bounced up off the floor, turned a pirouette in midair, and struck the vomit-crusted wall across from his tray. Seeing Bill's terrified expression, Dade whispered, "Low gravity. Gotta watch that first step."

Leaning forward and pushing like an ice-skater with the insoles of his feet, Dade moved to Bill's tray. He could see Rebecca to Bill's left. She was short and wide at the hips, and wore an ankle-length green dress that clashed with her very unnatural, bright red hair that was brushed into one of those big hair styles, heavy on the hairspray and flipped up into a curl at the shoulders. Rebecca's eyes were closed, and her head was back as far as she could move it. She continued her ceaseless murmur of prayers.

Bill was soaked with sweat that beaded up in little puddles in his closely cropped hair and ran down his face in streams. The large man's thick neck muscles stood out clearly from his exertions. Dade looked around the side of Bill's tray for the controls the alien had used to lower the tray. He was certain that if there were controls for raising and lowering, there would be controls for releasing the bindings.

"What you doing? Cut me outta here, would ya," whispered Bill.

"There are some controls on the side here. Let me try them," responded Dade.

"Just start cutting. You know that works," pleaded Bill.

Ignoring Bill's pleas, Dade inspected the side of the tray. Under the back edge, about midway between the top and bottom, he felt a series of indentations; there were six in all, situated in pairs. He pressed the top indentation, feeling his fingertip press into its soft center, but nothing happened. He pressed the next indentation, and with an audible click, Bill's tray started to lower horizontally like the bodybuilder's had. He pressed the next button, and the rubbery sheet tightened.

"Damn it, man. I told you to cut it!" Bill said.

Dade pressed the fourth indentation, and the rubbery sheet loosened considerably.

"Here we go," Dade whispered as he pressed and held his finger down. The rubbery sheet continued to loosen until the overlapping sheets rolled back, first from one side and then from the other, releasing Bill from the tray at about the time it had finished lowering him horizontally to the floor. Bill sat up as soon he was free and Dade helped him to his feet. Bill looked authoritative in his blue security guard uniform with the shoulder patch and badge.

"Wouldn't by any chance have a gun, would ya?" queried Dade.

"Sure do," answered Bill.

"Excellent. We're probably going to need it," Dade let out a sigh of relief.

"That'd be fine, 'cep' it's unloaded and locked in the back of my Explorer, where I can get to it in an emergency."

"Damn it! How 'bout a knife, pocketknife, slingshot? Anything that remotely resembles a weapon?" Dade shot back.

"Nope, only these," Bill said, holding out his large hands and making them into impressive fists. "And I think they'll work just fine on them oogly li'l buggers."

"Let's hope so," Dade said.

Showing Bill where the controls on the trays were, they made plans to release the other prisoners to improve their odds of overpowering the aliens and perhaps finding someone else with a weapon. Dade went to Rebecca and Bill went in the other direction. Dade noticed an opening just to the right of Rebecca's tray and approached the corner slowly, using the skater- shuffle again. He was so tense and agitated by fear and flowing adrenaline that he had to concentrate intently on slowing his movements to avoid overshooting the corner in the low gravity. He peered around the corner into the next chamber. The room was semicircular, about fifteen feet to the far side where three dish-shaped seats stood about three feet apart in front of an angled control panel. Above the control panel was a large, elongated oval window through which he saw nothing but blackness.

Dade inched his head through the opening just enough to see around the corner. He could see three aliens and the tray that held the young bodybuilder. Two of the aliens bent over the tray with their heads down near the man. The third alien, its eyes glittering shades of blue and green, was standing near the opening on the far end of the wall through which they had brought the young man in the tray earlier. One of the aliens lifted its head slightly and then poked it down again. Dade could make out a bluish-black tube that extended from just below the alien's eyes. A faint sucking and slurping sound emanated from the tray. *My God, they're eating him,* Dade realized, his face contorting with disgust.

Dade heard someone running behind him. Pulling his head back, he turned just in time to see Bill stumble backwards with his arms flailing at his sides toward the opening on the far end of the dividing wall.

Falling into a seated position, Bill bounced and slid backward through the opening and into the chamber with the aliens. Dade looked back around the corner in time to see the alien by the door stretch and grow taller, its eyes flashing white light as Bill slid to stop less than three feet away. Bill scrambled to his feet with a terrified look on his face.

"Dade! Dade!" Bill shouted. "Attack now!

With his knife already in hand, Dade leaned forward and dug into the floor with the insoles of his feet, propelling himself toward the nearest alien, which was still bent over the tray.

Rolling onto his knees, Bill pressed his heels into the corner of the floor and wall behind him and catapulted himself from a crouched position toward the alien standing a few feet away. Like a switchblade, the alien's bluish-black tube-shaped proboscis snapped up out of the crease in its face and spewed a jet of black, viscous fluid directly into Bill's face. The fluid splattered across his face, covering his eyes and nose from temple to temple. With a scream of pain that rivaled the roar of a lion, Bill blindly finished his lunge and successfully tackled the offending alien.

Having propelled himself forward much more efficiently than he had planned, Dade slammed into the crouching alien and drove the four-inch blade of his pocketknife into the back of the alien's leathery head. As he tumbled headfirst over the alien and the tray, his face passed within inches of that of the man inside. His face was a pallid, whitish gray, his lips curled over blood-stained teeth, his mouth and eyes wide open in a death mask of agonizing pain. With the blade of his pocketknife firmly embedded in the leathery flesh of the alien's head, the handle was wrenched from his grip as he tumbled into the back of the third alien.

Dade grabbed the alien by the head and neck as he tumbled forward onto the floor and pulled it down with him. Its tentacled appendages reached backward, grabbing Dade by the throat, wrists, and one leg, and squeezed with incredible force. The alien was trying to pull Dade's hands off while twisting in its own leathery flesh to bring its proboscis around to bear. Inches from Dade's face, it sprayed a jet of black fluid into the right lens of his glasses. The deflected fluid splashed onto his forehead, temple, and ear. The immediate and intense burning was so severe that Dade managed to choke out a scream of agony even as tentacles crushed his throat.

Compelled by pain that felt like a blowtorch to the face, Dade found the strength to twist the alien's head enough to send the next jet of acid spewing away from him. The crushing force of the tentacles was beginning to loosen Dade's grip and had effectively choked off his ability to breathe. Knowing that he was losing the fight and would soon lose consciousness, Dade desperately slammed his head into the side of the alien's.

Trapped between Dade's pounding skull and the floor, the soft leathery head of the alien was compressed nearly flat with each blow. Dade slammed his head down with as much force as he could, each blow growing weaker until he lost his grip on the leathery flesh and reeled on the verge of unconsciousness. Instinctively, Dade pulled at the tentacles wrapped around his throat, and much to his surprise he pulled them free. Sucking in a much-needed breath of air, he continued to pound the alien's head with his fists. A substance that looked like blue cottage cheese and grape clusters oozed from the ruptured eyes of the alien. Dade pushed himself up off the limp creature and struggled to his feet, trying to wipe the burning fluid from his face. His hands immediately began to burn and he hastily wiped them on his jacket.

Across the room, Bill was screaming, cursing, and slamming the other alien up and down with one hand like a rag doll and slapping at his face with the other. Dade looked at the tray. The alien he had stabbed was slumped over it with the red handle of his pocketknife protruding from the back of its head. Removing his glasses and jacket, he used the sleeve to wipe the burning substance from his face and ear. To his horror, pieces of dissolving skin and fragments of his ear wiped off onto the jacket. Dabbing carefully at his raw flesh, he stumbled over to where Bill knelt over the battered remains of his alien.

"My eyes! Oh my God, my eyes," Bill sobbed as he swayed forward and back on his knees, his hands tightly clasped over his face.

"Here. I've got something to help wipe that crap off," Dade said between gasps.

"The others? You get 'em?" Bill asked.

"All dead," Dade answered.

Bill slowly removed his hands and turned his head in the direction of Dade's voice. Dade choked and swallowed hard, fighting the urge to vomit. Bill's face was gone. From just above his upper lip to his hairline and from temple to temple, bare skull was visible, whitish-yellow with streaks of blood. Bare muscle and shreds of connective tissue lay exposed. A piece of cartilage hung over the cavity where Bill's nose had been, and collapsed sacks that were once his eyes hung from the gaping sockets. The palm and fingers of both his hands were stripped of skin and flesh in the same fashion as his face. Dade gently dabbed the wounds on Bill's face and hands to remove the remaining acid, leaving raw, ragged flesh around the perimeter. Fortunately, there was very little bleeding. Dade reasoned that the fluid must be some kind of powerful digestive enzyme that inhibits bleeding while dissolving soft tissue.

Bill didn't make a sound while Dade tended his wounds. The only outward indication that he was in pain was the tensing of the muscles in his neck and powerful arms. Dade removed his white shirt and tore off the long sleeves, folded one sleeve into a pad and put it over the exposed flesh of Bill's face and tied the other around Bill's head like a blindfold to hold the pad in place. Tearing strips from the remains of the shirt, he bandaged Bill's hands and then covered his own aching wounds. His adrenaline spent, his body bruised and burned, Dade stumbled back to where the other prisoners were still bound in their trays.

There were two more rows with four trays each. The remaining nine prisoners were all women, ranging in age from their twenties to late fifties. As soon as they realized what had happened, they all started to shout questions at the same time. "Who are they?" "What do they want?" "Where are we?" Dade didn't have any answers for them, and after the frustration of attempting to explain that to the first few he released, Dade shouted for them to shut up. He repeated himself over and over, each time louder than the last, until with the exception of a young girl who was crying hysterically, he finally had their attention.

Speaking loudly so that all could hear over the hysterical sobbing, he said, "My name is Dade. I don't know who they were, what they wanted, or where we are. All I know for certain right now is that they are dead, and I am not. Now, once everyone is loose, I intend to start getting some answers. Until then, try to remain calm." Although he was demanding it of the others, remaining calm was something he wasn't quite sure he could do himself. Even when the women had calmed down and lowered their voices, most continued to ask questions, hoping to make sense of the nightmare they found themselves in.

In an effort to assess the skills and abilities of the group, Dade asked each person her name and occupation as he released the bindings. There was Rebecca McCabe, a fifty-something religious missionary; Margaret Heckart, a thirty-five-year-old elementary school nurse; and Beth Porter, a rather gruff-looking businesswoman with cold, pale blue eyes in her late forties. There was also Ruth Tuman, a quiet but very serious-looking electrical engineer in her late twenties; Ann Moore, a tiny woman who ran a day care facility; and Crystal Santos, Cathy Purcell, and Marsha Clarke, members of an all-girl metal band, all young and pretty. Cathy and Marsha appeared as he would expect—scared shitless; however, the band's leader, Crystal, had the hardened look of a kid who had been raised on the street. Although pretty, she had several scars that notched her left eyebrow and one on her cheekbone. He thought they were probably obtained in fistfights, like the ones on his own face. If she was frightened, she didn't show it.

In the last tray was Tiffany Steiner, a performing arts undergrad suffering from severe emotional trauma. She had been camping with her fiancé, Jimmy Bourke, a physical education major at USC, and was awake when Jimmy was taken by the aliens. She had listened for an eternity while he screamed in agony. Rambling on dazedly, she kept talking even after Dade had helped her to her feet in the low gravity. She continued to recount to the others odd, disconnected, irrelevant details.

Letting instinct and habit take control, Dade tried to get the group working as a team, something he did every morning with his maintenance crew. Pairing up weak with strong, he assigned tasks that would keep them busy and preoccupied.

"Margaret, I'd like you and Ann to help Tiffany and Bill. Bill's out in the other compartment and has severe wounds on his face and hands. See if anybody has any pain medication, do what you can to keep them calm, and treat them both for shock." Leaning close to Margaret, Dade quietly added, "Keep Tiffany back here for now, until I can do something to cover her fiancé up." Margaret nodded gravely.

"Beth, come here," Dade said, addressing the stern-faced woman, and motioned for her to join him.

"Ms. Porter," he was quickly and gruffly corrected. The woman glared at him without making any effort to respond to his request.

Visibly tensing, Dade straightened to his full height. He shifted his weight to the balls of his feet, marched aggressively over to the woman, and stepped well inside what he thought Ms. Porter might consider her personal space.

"Beth, Bethany, Ms. Porter, hey you! Listen, lady, I don't have time to worry about being politically correct, and I don't have time to remember the approved names people go by. So if I'm looking at you and my mouth is moving, you're going to listen without giving me a ration. Do I make myself clear?" Dade said. Without raising his voice, he had clearly and evenly enunciated each word with exaggerated clarity as he moved his face within inches of hers for effect. The slight opening of her eyes was the only indication that his chastising had made an impression.

"Sir, yes sir. Loud and clear, sir!" Beth answered after an unpleasantly long silence, shouting her answer in mock boot camp style without moving her face away from his.

"Grrreat," Dade replied, narrowing his eyes. He knew from a wealth of experience that he was going to have trouble with this woman. "I would appreciate it if you would keep an eye on Rebecca. Try to keep her from further compounding the already complex situation that we are in by stirring up the others with her fanatical religious ideas," Dade said, trying to smooth their rocky start by attempting to sound a little less demanding.

"Is that all?" Beth responded dryly, as though the request lacked significance.

"Anything else you can think of that will help this situation would be greatly appreciated," Dade said.

Beth snapped a salute, pivoted on her toe and heel, and marched over to where Rebecca knelt, reciting scripture about the apocalypse. Dade studied her stocky muscular frame as she walked away. At slightly less than six feet, she was at least as tall as he was, in better shape than him, and outweighed him by ten to twenty pounds. *Not a woman I would want to slug it out with,* he thought, noting her well-developed biceps.

"All right, you three, the all-girl band," Dade said, pointing at the young women standing around the alien Bill had killed. "I would like you three to look for some weapons, or anything we can use for weapons. Can you do that?"

"Weapons? Freaking-A!" Crystal, the greasy-haired band leader replied, giving the alien a kick. The alien's head rolled around, twisting at the neck as it flopped toward Marsha and Cathy. The girls screamed and jumped out of the way. Crystal laughed derisively at them and gave the head another kick.

"Ruth, you're with me. Let's see if we can figure out how to fly this thing." Dade gestured for the electrical engineer to follow him. He headed toward the control panel, using the skater walk that seemed to be the most efficient form of locomotion in the low gravity. Ruth stumbled along behind.

"Figure out how to fly … what? Are we …? Who's flying it now?" Ruth stammered as they walked.

Dade picked his coat up off the floor where he had dropped it. The enzymes had eaten holes in the fabric and it looked more like a tattered shop rag than the neatly pressed suit coat it had been only a few hours before. He went to the tray where the tortured remains of Jimmy lay like a centerpiece and draped the coat over Jimmy's ghastly face. The only parts of his body that hadn't been stripped to the bone were his head, extremities, and torso from the groin to just below the chest. The rest, with the exception of a few strands of tendon, were stripped down to bare yellowish-orange bone. A puddle of brown-black slime filled the bottom of the tray. Ruth stared wide-eyed with her hands over her mouth while Dade pushed the tray into a corner away from the group. Even though the tray did not require much effort to move, Dade was exhausted. Taking a moment, he stood and leaned against the wall next to the tray. The wounds on his head and face throbbed intensely. He pressed the side of his head with a bandaged hand in a futile effort to stop the ache.

"Are you going to be all right?" Ruth asked through the fingers she still held over her mouth.

"I don't think I'm ever going to be all right," Dade said, straightening up and wiping his raw hands on the sides of his pants. "But I'll worry about that later, so let's see what other obstacles we have to overcome."

Dismissing the hopelessness that formed the core of his exhaustion, Dade moved with confident strides toward what he presumed must be the controls of the alien spacecraft.

4 - Lost

Dade's initial assessment of the spacecraft's construction did not find it particularly alien. Upon closer examination, though, he noted that the floors, walls, and ceilings were constructed of a slate gray material that had neither the touch nor feel of metal or any other identifiable material. The floors seamlessly curved into the walls and the walls into the ceilings. Even around the windows, no seam or joint could be found. The seats, the panels, everything looked as though they were manufactured and molded as a single piece. There were no doors, vents, or drains—nothing to indicate a way in or a way out.

The controls consisted of three stations with obviously different functions. The first station on the left faced what Dade presumed was forward. This station had an oblong, faceted screen that echoed the shape of the aliens' eyes, with another smaller screen just below it. Both screens were dark. Keyboards ran along both sides of the lower screen, but instead of keys, they had indentations like the controls on the trays. To either side of the large screen was a series of lights that slowly pulsed shades of blue and purple.

A triangular screen illuminated the center console with a soft, pale blue light. In the center of the screen was a three-dimensional image of a dark purple sphere marked with black lines, similar to the latitude and longitude lines on a globe. To the left side of the triangular screen was an outline dotted with an array of little purple lights that appeared to represent the spacecraft and its interior compartments. Under the screen were two sets of keyboards like those at the first station, only with fewer indentations. At the top of the triangle on either side were two sticks with more indentations arrayed evenly around their circumferences.

The last station, also illuminated in a soft, pale blue light, had a round screen with eight evenly spaced lines running from the outer edge toward the center, stopping at the perimeter of a small square outline. On the left side of the screen was a dark horizontal bar. On the right side, a vertical bar was shaded from white at the bottom to violet at the top. The violet light pulsed slowly. Like the other stations, this one had keypad indentations below the screen.

In front of each station, concave stools rose up from the floor on thin round stalks that grew wider at the top. The seats were clearly not designed for human comfort. Dade sat down at the center console.

"This is where the pilot sits," he said, placing his hands in his lap. Ruth took the seat to his right.

"I think that must be communications over there," Ruth said, indicating the station to the left. "And this must be navigation." Just then, white lights flashed atop all three stations. The little outline of the spacecraft and its compartments went from light to dark blue, and a bright white light flashed at the side.

"I didn't touch anything," Dade said.

"Nor I," Ruth added, turning around to find the spot in the vessel that the light indicated. She saw Crystal, Catherine, and Marsha looking at a flashing white light on the wall, about six feet off the floor. Dade's ears popped as the atmospheric pressure dropped rapidly.

"Stop! Stop whatever you're doing!" Dade leapt from his seat and stumbled headlong toward the three girls. Crystal reached out and tapped a spot on the wall, and the white light changed to soft purple and then went out. Sliding to a stop next to Crystal, Dade could feel the pressure building again. He worked his jaw to equalize the pressure in his ears.

"Sent us out to look and see. Guess what we found behind door number three?" Crystal moved to the rhythm of her voice as she pointed at the wall.

Dade looked. The outline of a door faded and disappeared. To the right of it were two indentations, one above the other.

"You could have killed us all!" Dade shouted.

"We were doing what you asked!" Crystal shouted back, raising her voice. Her dark, defiant eyes met his. "We looked for weapons as you bid, and what you said is what we did. Looking for trouble all around, and trouble, trouble, trouble is what we found." Glancing around to ensure she had an audience, she shifted from rhythmic verse to the voice and gestures of a game show host.

"Which brings me to . . . what we have found so far!"

On cue, Marsha held out what looked like a short baseball bat with a dish on the thick end.

"A very coool flashlight!" Crystal announced. She took the device from Marsha and pointed it toward a dark area in the rear compartment. She pressed an indentation near the handle, and the device hummed and flared. Intense light lit up the back corner of the ship, illuminating Ann and Tiffany, who stood just inside the sphere of light. Neither woman moved. Crystal turned off the light and faced Dade triumphantly.

"It be light, and it be bright! Bitching flashlight, huh?"

Dade stared into the dimly lit corner where Ann and Tiffany stood motionless. He could barely see them from where he stood.

"I don't think that's a flashlight. I think it's a weapon. Do not, I repeat, do not turn it on again," Dade said. Crystal's smirk faded along with whatever rhyme she had planned to say next.

"Yeah, sure. Whatever you say," Crystal said.

Dade shuffled toward Ann and Tiffany, pointing a bandaged hand at the girls.

"You three, don't move. Don't touch *anything*. I'll be right back."

Dade stopped next to Ann and placed his hand on her shoulder.

"Ann, are you all right? Can you hear me?" He gave her a gentle shake. She remained motionless. Her eyes stared blankly and she did not appear to breathe. Dade glanced around, looking for help. He caught Margaret's eye as she knelt near Bill and motioned for her to come over. She rose to her feet and shuffled over to where he stood.

"I'm just a school nurse . . . I put bandages on skinned knees, for Christ's sake . . . I can't . . . I can't help Bill. He needs a hospital. He needs experts!" Margaret stammered.

Dade placed his hands on Margaret's shoulders and looked directly into her eyes. "You are the closest thing we have to a doctor. Do what you can; that's all I ask. Now help me sit these two down." He nodded toward Ann and Tiffany.

"What happened to them?" Margaret asked, wiping the tears from her eyes with the sleeve of her blouse.

"I think they're just temporarily paralyzed. The girls thought it was a flashlight. I think it's some sort of immobilizing weapon, probably the same thing they zapped us with when we were taken," Dade said as he lifted Ann's arm from Tiffany's shoulder.

"They're going to be all right, aren't they?"

"I think so. Now you hold onto Tiffany while I move Ann into a sitting position."

He bent Ann at the waist as if he were positioning a mannequin and lowered her into a seated position with her back against the wall. He placed her hands in her lap and carefully closed her eyelids. Margaret helped him repeat the process with Tiffany.

"They should wake up after a while, just like we all did after we were abducted. Keep an eye on them and help them when they do," Dade said. Leaving Margaret to care for Ann and Tiffany, he returned to where the three girls were waiting.

"Give me that!" Dade demanded, pointing at the bat. Crystal handed it to him, looking past him to where Margaret knelt beside Ann and Tiffany.

"I didn't know it wasn't a flashlight. How was I s'pose to know?" Crystal asked.

Dade cradled the object in his hands as he examined it. "This is not a joke. We are not on a ride at an amusement park. A man has died, and before this is over more of us may die. We are on unfamiliar ground. Anything we do could accidentally result in the death or injury of one or all of us. I can't be everywhere and do everything. And even if I could, there is no guarantee I would make the right choices. We must be able to count on each other to proceed with extreme caution with whatever we do."

Looking up into their faces, Dade continued more forcefully. "The reason I asked you three to look for weapons is because you have controlled your fear well. I know you're frightened. Hell, I'm terrified, and so is everyone else. But if we are going to survive, we are going to have to control our fear and act as a team.

"You're a band, right?" Dade asked.

"Yeah, the Metal Maidens," responded Crystal, nervously brushing greasy strings of her jet black hair over her eyes in an effort to inhibit the intense glare she was getting from Dade.

"Good." Dade nodded. "You have experience working together as a team. Jimmy's dead. Big Bill is out of action, and I'm damaged. You three are young, fit, and look like you have some street smarts. Do you think you can handle a fight, if and when it comes down to it?"

Marsha and Catherine looked at Crystal, who gave an almost imperceptible nod. The girls turned to Dade and answered in a questionably serious chorus. "Freaking A," they chimed, snapping to a pathetic interpretation of attention and giving a single-fingered New York salute.

Dade shook his head woefully. In other circumstances, he would have been angry. In this case, though, he reasoned that the trio of misfits was actually paying him respect in its own twisted way.

He handed the weapon back to Crystal and addressed them with a dead serious demeanor. "Freeze ray—for use on aliens only. Okay?" The girls nodded in unison as Crystal cautiously took the weapon from Dade's hands.

"What else did you find?" Dade asked.

The smirk returned to Crystal's face. She raised an eyebrow, looked at the bat, and then nodded at the wall.

"Not just one. Not just two. As you can see, we got three." On Crystal's cue, Marsha reached over and placed her finger in an indentation on the wall. Seconds later, an oblong door opened. The grey material of the door flowed outward from the center into the adjacent wall, revealing two more bats in recessed racks within a small compartment.

"Isn't that, like, so cool," Crystal said. Reaching in, she removed a bat and handed it to Catherine. Removing the other, she handed it to Marsha.

"There's a big compartment in the back," Marsha said, "filled with a bunch of stuff they must have swiped when they nabbed us. I found this in a small case." She pulled a 9mm semiautomatic from where it was tucked at the small of her back. Dade took the pistol and slipped it under his belt.

"If there is a fight, it will probably be at this door. See if you three can come up with a plan to defend against a forced entry. Maybe set up some of those trays to use as a barricade."

Marsha saluted with her left hand, this time without her middle finger, and the three girls strode off together. Dade shuffled back to the control panel where Ruth was studying the controls.

As he sat down again at the center console, Ruth began to explain her theories on the control panel's functions.

"Purple is green. White is red. If we screw something up, like with the door, we get an alarm, or white light, which would be like a red light."

Dade nodded agreement, and Ruth continued. "We must be traveling on some sort of autopilot. The reason we can't see anything out the window is because we must be traveling near the speed of light, or through some kind of fold or rift in space."

"So how dangerous do you think it would be to turn this tub around and head for home?" Dade asked, holding his hands over the keyboard to size up the reach to each indentation.

Ruth pointed to the purple lights. "The lights should tell us when we screw something up, like with the door. Still, dangerous as hell. But do we have a choice?"

"Of course we have a choice. We could let this thing fly us to wherever it's going and hope that whoever is there won't be pissed that we killed the crew. Or, we could fumble with these controls and, by some miracle, actually figure out how they work. Then, by an even greater miracle, if we find our way home, and if we don't burn up in the atmosphere or carve out a crater on the Earth's surface, and if our own military doesn't blow us to pieces, we'll bc fine. If we don't, we're screwed. If we do, odds are we're screwed. Listen, if it was just me, I know what I would do. But—"

"But nothing! Take us home, Dade," Bill's voice boomed from behind them.

"Yeah! Hooommme," came a chorus from the Metal Maidens.

"Home," nodded Margaret, who was sitting with Bill.

"I think we have better than even odds. Let's try," Ruth said, smiling.

"What about everyone else?" Dade said, feeling the burden of responsibility suddenly resting heavy on his shoulders.

"You make six, and that's a majority," Ruth pointed out.

"You make seven," Beth announced from the entrance to the rear compartment. "And if I recall, you made it perfectly clear that this was not a democracy. So, tough guy, the voting is over. Now quit being a weenie and make the hard choices. You're the one with the balls, right? Sir," she added. Without waiting for a response, she snapped a perfect heel-to-toe 180-degree turn and marched back where she had come from.

"What a bitch," Ruth muttered.

Dade needed no additional prodding. Placing the heels of his palms on the surface of the control console and positioning his fingers over the indentations, he paused and took a deep breath. "Okay, people, fasten your seatbelts," he called out loudly. Then, very softly and under his breath, he added, "Bend over and kiss your ass goodbye."

The panel had six indentations on each side with two long grooves running vertically between them. Dade reached up, hesitated, then pressed the far left indentation. He looked at Ruth, who shrugged her shoulders and said, "Try another." He pressed another, and nothing happened. And another, still nothing happened. He kept trying until he had pressed all twelve of the indentations without any noticeable changes. There were eight more indentations, four on each side near the top of the triangular screen around the two sticks. Dade tried pressing those indentations and moving the sticks. Still, nothing happened.

"See if the screen is touch-activated," Ruth suggested. Dade reached out and touched the middle of the purple triangle. The triangle immediately turned yellow and the whole room began to vibrate rapidly. Dade jerked his hand back and held his hands above the panel, hoping for some insight into what to do next. The vibration reduced in pitch, and the inky blackness outside the window changed to smoky blotches of gray on black. As the vibration slowed to a rhythmic rumbling, the view outside the window came into focus, revealing a vast, starry expanse. The oblong screen to Dade's left lit up and a cascade of colored lights began to play across it. The two vertical grooves at the bottom of Dade's triangular screen turned red. The color dropped like mercury in a thermometer, only when it got to the bottom of the groove, it turned orange. It dropped again and turned yellow. It continued in the same manner until, after purple, it went out. At that point, the rumbling stopped. Dade looked at Ruth and nodded at the star-filled window.

"You recognize any of these stars?" he asked.

"I never studied astronomy. I have trouble recognizing the Big Dipper on a clear night," Ruth said.

Dade turned around to find everyone in the room looking over their shoulders.

"Anybody recognize these stars?" he asked.

Beth stepped forward, scanning the window from one side to the other. She held up her hand and gestured toward the window.

"Damn! It's so thick with stars I can't get a reference. Can you turn this thing so I can see more than just this area?"

Dade turned and placed his hands back on the console.

"I'll give it my best shot," he said as he pressed an indentation on the left. The left-hand groove below the screen turned purple, and a faint humming sound like high-power lines could be heard all around them. Dade pressed the next indentation. A green bar appeared below the purple groove, and the horizontal lines on the sphere around the triangle began to move down. Dade continued to experiment with the controls. He was able to determine that the lower left-hand keypad controlled forward speed, and the stick and indentations at the top controlled the rotation up, down, left, and right. The right-hand keypad controlled vertical or horizontal speed, with the stick controlling the direction. The two bars indicated speed, and the triangle on the screen was some sort of visual dimensional reference for direction of travel and speed.

After repeated scans in all directions, Beth identified several familiar constellations. There was one exceptionally bright star that she believed was the best candidate for the solar system of Earth.

Dade lined the ship up on the star and set the controls for the best possible speed using the left lower keypad.

The star seemed to hang in front of them without a change in size or appearance. Without any change to offer a point of reference, it seemed as though they were standing still. If it weren't for the speed indicator, Dade would have been certain they were not moving.

"It could take months, or even years, at this speed to reach that star," Dade said to no one in particular. "Ruth, any ideas on how to get back to the speed we were at before I shut it down?"

Ruth put her hands onto her console. "The course would have to be plotted. It would have to be timed or programmed, or you would fly past your target area. This looks like a navigation station; let me see what the controls do."

Ruth began to press the indentations on the lower pads and discovered that they controlled the size and position of the square box indicated on the round screen. Buttons on the top right controlled the adjacent rainbow-colored vertical bar, raising or lowering the color spectrum. The first button on the left turned the horizontal bar purple, and the second button caused it to run through the colors of the spectrum until it was solid red. When Ruth pressed the third button, the area outside and below the window was illuminated with a bright light that grew in intensity for about three seconds before pulsing a sharp beam of intensely bright light out into the infinity of space with a crackling sound that caused the whole ship to shudder.

Dade blinked his eyes repeatedly in a futile attempt to clear his vision of the spot he now saw wherever he looked. Gesturing to Ruth's console, he stated, "I don't think that's navigation, I think it's a fire control station for the ship's weapons."

"Damn, that light was bright!" Ruth rubbed her eyes and nodded in agreement. Pointing to the bar on the right of her console, she explained, "I believe this indicates the charge you intend to use. We just shot the whole wad, both barrels, if you will. Right now, it's recharging. With a less powerful shot, it would probably recharge faster."

She pointed to the horizontal bar on the left as she continued, excited yet analytical, in control of her discoveries. "This bar indicates the firing sequence: energize, arm, and fire."

"Make a note of that for future reference, and if we have to use it, remind me to duck. I feel like I have a sunburn," Dade said, pressing a finger experimentally to the end of his nose. Now that his vision was returning, he noted that Ruth's complexion was red and blotchy.

Dade continued to work the controls of the console, trying various combinations to get the ship to accelerate further. Frustrated by his failure, he stopped and glared at the panel.

"Try touching the screen again, but at different spots," Ruth suggested.

Dade touched the triangle and nothing happened. He reached up to the top of the screen where three bars in different shades of purple formed their own little triangle at the top, and pressed the lower bar. The bar turned green and the vessel began to vibrate, slowly at first and then picking up in pitch as the lower bar moved through the colors of the spectrum and stopped at red, at which point the vibration stabilized.

"Look at the stars!" Ruth cried. No longer sharp and clear, they were now fuzzily out of focus, like comets all headed in the same direction.

"Okay! Now we're getting somewhere," Dade said as he pressed the next bar. The bar changed colors again and the ship accelerated. As the pitch of the vibration intensified, the star field appeared as gray and black blotches. When he pressed the topmost bar, the colors changed again, the view outside the window slowly faded to pitch black, and the vibration rose in pitch to such a high frequency that it was almost imperceptible.

"Excellent!" Dade shouted. "Damn the torpedoes. Full speed ahead." The group behind them clapped and cheered. Ruth, however, didn't look particularly pleased with their accomplishment.

"What's the problem?" Dade asked quietly so that only Ruth would hear. Ruth plucked at the back of her hand and answered softly.

"We don't know where we are going or how long to stay at this speed. And if, big if, we get to Earth, how will we land this thing?"

"Just look," Dade said, gesturing across the panels. "These controls are designed for simplicity and automatic function. If they weren't, we would have killed ourselves in the first five minutes. I'm confident the star we're heading toward is ours and that when we get there, together, we will be able to land this thing safely. We're going to be heroes," he said, grinning and silently hoping that the fear and hopelessness he felt would not be perceived by this truly courageous and intelligent woman.

"All right, hero, how long at this speed?" Ruth queried, tapping the face of her watch.

Dade looked at his watch, not a particularly expensive watch, but not a cheap one either. The face of the LED readout was black. He pressed the illumination button and nothing happened. He pressed the remaining buttons without results.

"My watch is broken. What time do you have?" Dade asked, giving the useless device several forceful thumps on the lens. She held her watch out for him to see.

"My watch is mechanical. Yours is electrical. My watch stopped at 4:37 AM, approximately the time I was abducted. I'll bet we don't have a functional watch in the group."

Checking with the others, Dade confirmed Ruth's deduction. They had no way to tell time. Dade rubbed his chin, feeling the stubble of whiskers.

"I'm guessing it's been about twelve hours," he said. "I can count off four hours, then slow down, get our bearing, and proceed again for four more hours, or less, depending on how close we look."

Ruth didn't look happy. "Okay, it's a plan, better than anything I can think of," Ruth said, taking a small notebook from her pocket. "I'll count out the first four hours, keeping track in this. You try to sleep. You look like hammered shit."

"Thanks!" Dade replied sarcastically, smiling at her unexpected use of profanity. He didn't argue with her. It made sense, and he really did feel exhausted.

He paced around for a few minutes, trying to find a clean spot on the floor. He finally gave up and lay on his back, crossing his arms on his chest. He closed his eyes and slowly drifted off into a fitful sleep filled with horrific, all-too-recent memories.

5 - Evasion

"All right, sleeping beauty, it's time to get up," Ruth said, gently tapping Dade on the shoulder.

Dade lurched upright, swinging his clenched fists wildly. Ruth jumped back, narrowly escaping a blow to the face.

"Dade, wake up! It's me, Ruth, remember?"

Dade rubbed his eyes, which were sore, gritty, and irritated.

"Yeah, I remember. I was just hoping it was a bad dream," he said as he rose to his feet.

He stretched his back and rotated his head, trying to relieve the pain and stiffness from his earlier exertions and injuries, but the movements only caused his wounds to ache with renewed intensity.

"Damn, I'm too old for this kind of shit," Dade moaned in protest.

"Aren't we all," Ruth replied flatly. "Now, let's get this done so I can get some sleep. I feel like I'm going to drop in my tracks."

Dade sat down at the console and touched the screen, causing the ship to decelerate until the star field came into focus again.

There, in the center of the screen, was the bright star, perceptibly brighter than before.

"In case this thing doesn't have automatic brakes or something, I think we should aim just a little to the right or left so if we overshoot the target, we go by it and not through it."

"Makes sense to me, Skipper. Do it," Ruth replied.

Dade was aligning the ship with an open area next to the bright star when he noticed movement in the cluster of stars near the edge of the screen.

"Look there." He pointed to three points of light growing brighter and moving at an angle toward them.

"I see them," Ruth responded. "It looks like we have company, and— Hey! Look at my screen!" she cried.

The right hand of her screen was filled with a cluster of white dots, coming in slowly at about three o'clock and moving toward the center.

"I don't like the look of this. Ruth, see if you can't get them boxed up with that targeting thingamajig," Dade said as he turned the ship toward the approaching vessels and boosted the low-speed setting to maximum.

Dade counted nine objects coming directly at them. The dots of light moved up and down, right and left, like a cluster of anchovies with a barracuda swimming through it.

"Dade, every time I put the targeting box on these guys they move out of it like they can tell I'm targeting them."

"That's because they can," Dade said. "Look at the sphere on my screen." The round globe that encircled the triangle on Dade's screen had white sections on the forward right-hand side. As Dade maneuvered the ship around, some of the sectors would go out and others would come on. Dade turned the ship back toward the star.

"We need to get the hell outta Dodge. Let's go back to high speed," he said, punching the lower bar of the acceleration triangle. The vibration of acceleration began to increase.

Suddenly the vessel rocked hard to the left and the screen illuminated with an intense bright light. Dade and Ruth should have been thrown from their seats, but a gravitational force was automatically generated at the control stations, proportional to the force that had sent the craft tumbling out of control. The others were not so lucky and ended up slamming into the walls and each other. Screams and shouts from the confused and frightened group filled the air.

Dade jabbed the top of the acceleration triangle, bypassing the middle bar. The whole ship shook with such intensity that Dade bit his tongue. As the ship quieted down and the screen went black, Dade spit the blood from his mouth and turned to look at the group behind him.

"Anybody hurt?" he asked.

He limped over to help untangle the pile of people that had landed against the wall. There were no serious injuries, just bumps and bruises. Dade suggested that they move back to the trays and try to use the restraints as seatbelts so they wouldn't be thrown around again. Although no one particularly liked the idea, they agreed to do it.

The flash of light that rocked the vessel had worsened the already tender skin on Dade's face and made his eyes feel sandy. He asked if anyone had sunglasses. Marsha, Crystal, and Catherine had matching pairs. Crystal's turned out to be broken and Marsha couldn't find hers, but Catherine's were present and intact.

Returning to the console, Dade could see blisters forming on Ruth's nose and cheekbones, and her eyelids were beginning to swell.

"Looks like you got a pretty severe flashburn, kiddo," Dade said, sitting down and looking Ruth over for additional injuries.

"You look a little overdone by the sun yourself, Skipper."

"Listen, there's no point in both of us taking this heat. We're outnumbered and outgunned. You're never going to get a lock on any of those ships before they smoke us. The most we can hope to do is outrun them, and right now I don't even know what direction we're running."

Ruth swallowed nervously before speaking. "We have to slow again soon, don't we?"

"Yeah, so why don't you go back there and strap in."

"I'm not leaving you up here alone, Dade," Ruth said, placing her hands on the console in a manner that suggested he would have to drag her away.

"Don't get me wrong. You're not being excused for the rest of the trip, if that's what you're thinking. Chances are, if we take a couple more hits and this ship isn't destroyed, I will be. Since you're the only other person who knows how to fly this thing, there's a good chance you'll be pulling my dead or incapacitated butt off this seat and taking over. Does that make you feel any better?"

"No, not really. I just don't think you should have to do this alone."

"I'm not alone. I have my Metal Maiden shades to protect me," he said, pulling the studded chrome sunglasses with batlike wings on the sides out of his pocket and snapping them open. After removing his wire-rim glasses, he slipped on the sunglasses with an aristocratic flourish and made the motion of shooing Ruth away.

"Okay, but I'm coming back out between jumps," Ruth said as she shuffled into the rear compartment.

"Hurry up and get strapped in, and I'll get us back on course."

Once Dade felt he had given Ruth enough time, he actuated the controls to reduce speed. When the ship had reached normal space, there was no sign of the hostile ships. Before Dade could get lined up on the star, though, they started appearing all around the ship. This time he didn't hesitate to punch the high-speed bar first. Clenching his teeth for the bumpy acceleration, he braced himself while the ship shook with an intensity much more severe than before. The shaking was so violent that he feared the ship would break into pieces, and he was about to decelerate when the ship settled into smooth, black-windowed flight again.

Dade moved to the weapon's console. He adjusted the targeting window to its largest size and centered it in the round screen. Next, he energized the firing circuit as he had seen Ruth do and charged the weapon to full power. Moving back to the control console, he adjusted the sunglasses on his painfully blistered nose, took a deep breath, and touched the screen, bringing the ship out of black space.

The ship slowed back to normal space with an ominous moan that Dade did not recall hearing before. As soon as the controls would respond, he increased the maneuvering speed to maximum, reached over to the weapon's console, and pressed the fire button. As the crackling surge of energy built in preparation for the discharge pulse, Dade turned the ship hard to the left and pointed it in the direction of the hostile ships' last appearance. As the front window illuminated just before firing, three ships appeared in the distance. Dade put his head down in anticipation of the light pulse. The deck under his feet shuddered as the pulse discharged. Dade felt the heat of the flash on the top of his head and shoulders.

Looking up, he saw the center ship breaking into pieces, emitting orange and red flashes of light. The two other ships tumbled slowly away. Four other ships appeared and Dade saw their pulse weapons begin to illuminate. Without delay, he pressed the top bar to take the ship back to black space. The entire vessel began to pound up and down as it had before, only many times as severe and for much longer. Held in his seat by the gravitational field it generated, his upper body hammered against the panel with the violent shaking. Unable to escape the beating, he attempted to shield his face, at the very least.

Everything went black outside the window again as the ship settled into smooth flight, with the exception of an uneven metallic whine that seemed to come from all around. Dade's face felt numb and rubbery, and the quantity of blood dripping off his chin told him that he had been pretty badly injured during the acceleration. Gingerly examining his face, he noted that his nose was probably broken, and he felt cuts on his cheekbones and lips. He explored the inside of his mouth with a finger and found his upper and lower front teeth missing. Although it didn't hurt yet, he was well aware that his face was going to start to hurt very soon.

The panel before him had flashing white lights all over it. The triangle was red and yellow with white diamonds flashing brightly on the bottom and sides. The three light bars at the top of the screen that controlled the jump to black space were flashing white also. The metallic whine Dade had noticed earlier slowly increased in intensity. Reaching over to the weapons console, he reset the pulse weapon as he had done before. Feeling fragments of teeth in his swelling, blood-filled mouth, he leaned over and tried feebly to spit the offending mass onto the floor, but it ended up drooling down his chin and onto his chest.

The metallic whine intensified to an ear-splitting roar as the whole ship began to vibrate violently. Dade's curses were an incoherent, drunken rant as he slapped his one good hand onto the flashing triangle. The ship immediately dropped out of black space with a screeching hiss like an amplified fingernail on a blackboard. He increased the maneuvering speed as soon as he reached normal space, initiated the weapons firing sequence, and turned the ship hard to the right, holding it in a tight turn. Two ships appeared in his wake; this time, farther away than before.

Dade centered the front window on the hostile ships just as the pulse weapon fired. Looking up after the flash, he saw the two ships still there; one tumbled out of control and the other was corkscrewing away. He had begun to initiate the firing sequence again when the ship rocked hard to the side and the compartment filled with a blinding flash.

His face and arms stung from the flashburn, Dade again tried to initiate the pulse weapon. Once again, the impact of enemy fire rocked the ship. Dade's arm was up, shielding his face from additional flashburn when the second blast hit, but the heat was so intense that it left the back of his arm smoking. Trying once more to fire the ship's pulse weapon, he found the screen and indicating bars flashing white. He pressed the fire bar and nothing happened. Looking up, he saw the ship he had fired on earlier was still out of control and that the distance between them was closing fast. Working the steering controls, he turned the ship into a converging course with the tumbling craft.

"Ramming speed!" he croaked through mangled lips as the two ships collided, sending his bruised and battered face once again slamming into the panel.

Struggling to focus, Dade saw the stars rotating in the window. His attention was drawn to the brightening light of a pulse weapon on an enemy ship. He reached up and pressed the jump speed bar on the control panel and covered his face. The ship shook violently and an instant later the compartment was filled with a blinding flash. Dade screamed in pain as the bandage and hair on the top of his head burst into flames. Tearing the rag from his head, he slapped at his burning hair. The shaking of acceleration stopped and was replaced by a diminishing whine as the ship slowed to normal space.

Dade grabbed at the controls with his smoldering hands. Finding his fingers numb and unresponsive, he pressed his seared flesh into the panel's indentations as he fought to maneuver the damaged vessel. His right eye was completely swollen shut, which forced him to cock his head to the side to see out the narrow slit of his rapidly swelling left eye. An enemy ship appeared extremely close off to the left. Dade twisted the controls, rolling his vessel into a collision course with the enemy ship as its pulse weapon began to glow.

"No time!" he croaked as he accelerated his vessel, closing the distance between the two ships in an instant. The impact and discharge of the enemy ship's weapon were simultaneous, slamming him once again against the control console and mercifully knocking him unconscious.

Dade dreamt he was walking through the snow-covered fields he had played in as a child. It was a happier time, the longest he had spent with a foster family. Before the bad times, before he was sent to the city. In the distance, he could see the house. The warm glow from the kitchen window promised reprieve from the biting wind that whipped across the field. But the farther he walked toward it, the farther away the house seemed to be, until finally he could no longer see it at all. The cold wind cut like a knife into his very soul. When he reached to button his jacket, he found that he wasn't wearing one.

I'm going to freeze to death, he thought, straining his burning eyes in the wind. He hoped to see the elusive glow of the kitchen window; instead, he saw only darkness.

Dade's head ached with the intensity of a supreme hangover. He tried without success to open his eyes and found them swollen tightly shut. When he tried to reach up to his aching head, a hand gently closed on his wrist.

"Don't move, Dade," he heard Ruth say. "You're hurt pretty bad. Margaret is trying to bandage you up."

He tried to ask what had happened but only managed an incoherent gurgle. Anticipating his questions, Ruth gave him a status report.

"The consoles are all dead. The overhead light is out as well. What gravity we had earlier is gone now. You, Margaret, and I are floating near the center of the control room. Everyone else is still strapped in their trays. Our ship is tumbling end over end. The enemy ships are still out there, but for some reason they're shooting at each other now, not us. At least, not yet."

"Cold," Dade croaked, the word sounding more like "code."

"Yes, it's been getting colder and colder since the lights went out. Things being what they are, it doesn't look very promising, Skipper."

There was a clanking and scraping on top of the ship. The stars outside the window quit spinning and Ruth could see six enemy craft in front of the ship. They all moved slowly away and then, one after another, disappeared with a flash of light. The hull began to vibrate, the stars blurred, and as the view faded to black, the interior was plunged into complete darkness. People began to scream in the back compartment.

Ruth let out an ear-piercing whistle and a thundering "Shut up!" that belied her quiet demeanor. Speaking loudly and projecting more confidence than she felt, she attempted to calm the growing panic.

"We lost the battle, people, but we haven't lost the war. Not yet. And as long as we stay focused and remain calm we have a chance. Give up, and we're dead. We're being towed somewhere right now. Try to stay warm and get some rest. I don't know how long this ride is going to last."

Clinging together in the weightlessness, there was no way for them to determine how long they traveled through the blackness. Dade drifted off several times from exhaustion, waking to a nagging thirst, the dull ache of hunger, and the sound of Ruth's teeth chattering. The cold actually felt soothing to his burned and aching body. The women held him close in a feeble effort to keep him and themselves warm. Dade would have complained if he hadn't felt obligated to share the warmth of his body.

The changing pitch in vibration alerted Ruth that the ship was slowing. The window appeared in the darkness, a gray patch that grew brighter as stars came into focus and the ship settled into normal space. Dimly illuminated by the external light, the compartment seemed bright after the total darkness. Ruth unwound Margaret's arm from hers and let go of Dade, who appeared to be unconscious. She worked her way to the window.

The inside of the window was covered with ice crystals that distorted the stars and shapes outside. Scraping away at the ice with her thumbnail, she peered through a small patch.

This wasn't normal space; the stars all around appeared fuzzy. They were being carried toward a massive cylindrical object that was surrealistically clear in the blurred star field. The group of ships ahead looked like specks as they entered projections in the midsection of the cylinder. Gauging the size of the cylinder with the smaller craft for reference, Ruth estimated the vessel to be well over six thousand feet in diameter and least four times as long.

Beth came forward from the rear compartment, gliding from one location to the next with unexpected grace until she reached the front window.

"Hurry up!" Beth barked toward the rear compartment.

Crystal appeared in the entryway to the right, one arm stroking the air like a swimmer, the other holding onto a pulse weapon. She tumbled clumsily head over feet into the forward compartment.

"This sucks!" Crystal lamented, wiggling in midair, making little forward progress.

Beth kicked off and grabbed Crystal by the foot as she glided by, and the two continued together to the far wall, where Beth turned and tucked like a swimmer. Bracing her feet against the wall, she put an armlock around Crystal's waist and pushed off the wall in the direction of the front window. Beth grabbed the left seat at the control console with her free arm and looped to a stop between the seat and the console.

"You take your position here, and don't fire until I say so," Beth said.

"I'm going to float away," Crystal whined.

"Wrap your legs around the base of this seat and quit your sniveling," Beth ordered.

The compartment went dark as their vessel was carried into an opening in the larger alien vessel. There was a thump and a scraping sound. Then, without any warning, gravity was restored. Everyone who was caught in midair slammed to the floor. This was not the same as the low gravity they'd had earlier: this was intense, stronger even than then Earth's gravity.

"Girls, are you in position?" Beth's voice boomed.

Three barely audible voices answered, "Yes," from the darkness.

"What happened to 'Freaking-A'?" Beth shouted. There was no response.

"You girls are tough. You are bad. You're the meanest bitches these little bastards are ever going to have the misfortune to meet. Now, ARE YOU READY?" Beth shouted with a deep resounding confidence the situation did not inspire.

"Freaking-A!" the girls shouted back in unison.

"The rest of you get in the back. We'll take it from here," Beth ordered.

Ruth crawled to where she hoped to find Margaret and Dade.

"Margaret? Dade?" Ruth called out when she didn't find them.

"Back here. I'm back here," Margaret answered.

Ruth crawled in the direction of Margaret's voice.

Dade pulled himself up against the wall, turned, and leaned back against it in a sitting position. The pull of gravity on his tortured body felt as though it would rip the burned and bruised flesh from his bones. From the voices of the others, he figured he was about midway between the front and back of the forward compartment, directly across from where he believed the access hatch was located. He pulled the bandages from his hands with shattered teeth. It was impossible to determine which hand was more damaged, but he managed to fumble the 9mm pistol from his belt. He could still feel the fingers of his left hand, so laying the gun on his leg and holding it down with the wrist of his right arm, he pulled back on the slide mechanism to chamber a round. His fingers verified that the safety was released. Wrapping his useless right hand around the grip of the pistol, he held it in place with his left hand, finally slid his left forefinger slowly onto the trigger, exercising care not to accidentally discharge a round. He hoped he would remain conscious long enough to be of some use in the impending battle.

There was a hiss and a change in air pressure. Dade could feel air move over his sensitive skin.

"Now!" Beth shouted. There was a crackle of pulse rods and Dade saw brilliant white light through his closed eyelids.

Numerous pops and flashes of orange immediately followed the initial illumination. To his right, Crystal's scream was interrupted by a grunting exhalation as the air was knocked out of her lungs. Dade raised the pistol, trying to target the orange flashes he saw through swollen eyelids, and pulled the trigger. The pistol barked in response, and he kept pulling as fast as he could, the reports overlapping like the burst of a machine gun.

Dade felt himself crushed back against the wall by a powerful impact. The back of the pistol hit him in the forehead and flew out of his hands. His head reeled from the blow to his forehead. Unable to breathe, he rolled onto his side. Before he blacked out, he thought he could hear Beth shouting obscenities and the growl and hiss of an angry beast.

6 - TEELA20.10127

Teela was spending her first off-shift in the quiet privacy of the Archives section reading and viewing the ancient records. The patrol reports from earlier campaigns were among her favorites. She was fascinated with the logs of the pilots and ground troops that gave individual accounts of battles with the Kahshinki clone forces. She had, of course, heard the victory stories during her training period, but these individual logs gave details of defeats, bitter requests for support, and frightful reports of injuries and damage. The stories she had been told had failed to mention these types of details.

When she didn't want to read, Teela reviewed the most ancient of all the logs: visual records of artifacts recovered from the ruins of the Korlah home world after the Kahshinki were defeated there. Consisting mostly of carvings, statues, and painted pictures, the logs depicted an exciting time when the Korlah were a primitive warrior race. Both males and females wore long robes very similar to the tahs now worn by the birthing units, except that the males' garments were much more ornate and elaborate.

Her favorite archive record was a painted sculpture of a male and female. The male, much smaller and shorter than the female, made up for his slight proportions with a stout muscular build accentuated by a sleeveless robe gathered with an ornate belt, hung with two large bladed weapons at each hip. The tender way their arms were entwined as they faced each other, their foreheads touching, indicated a deep affection. Teela often stared at this log during her off-shifts, fantasizing about the two unknown Korlah and imagining what their lives must have been like before the Kahshinki invasion.

The visual records were the ones that first entertained her before she taught herself to read. Birthing units usually didn't learn to read until they were many cycles older than Teela; they didn't need to. When they weren't birthing, they were taking care of the infant and adolescent shells. The older birthing units assigned to administrative and management functions of the Shell section were the only ones that received reading instruction. Teela had learned to read while she served as an assistant to a Technical section instructor, indoctrinating young shells into their new duties. The shells were easily frightened and often developed behavioral problems that the birthing units were better at dealing with than their instructors.

During that indoctrination period, she had paid close attention to the lessons and practiced reading in the archives. Eventually, she became quite adept at researching the old logs and learned how to locate the more exciting and descriptive accounts of battles. She was deeply engrossed in a particularly interesting log involving a hand-to-hand fight with Kahshinki duplicates in a swamp on some distant world when she was interrupted.

"Teela! I thought I would find you in here. How can you stand it in this dirty place? It must be crawling with scrum beetles."

The source of the irritating distraction was Manalla, a sister birthing unit who had been directed to find her. Teela did not particularly like Manalla, and considered her lazy and prone to exaggeration.

"This is my off-shift, Manalla. Can't you please find someone else?"

"No, Teela. The section supervisor has demanded that you report immediately. She has received an order from Director Gremensh that calls for your transfer to the Biotech section. Everyone is looking for you!"

Unable to repress her fear, Teela's crown tendrils wilted and blanched. She stumbled as she rose to her feet. Manalla moved in quickly to support her. Holding her close, she pressed her face against Teela's to comfort her.

"It's probably nothing. A mistake, I'm certain. Don't be frightened." Manalla offered the lies in a hopeful attempt to reassure her terrified birth sister.

Hands shaking, Teela removed the log bar from the reader and placed it back in its storage tray with exaggerated care. Without speaking, the two exited the archives and sealed the door.

Teela's legs were weak as she walked down the corridor to the transit spoke that would take her back in toward the Shell section. She clenched and unclenched her hands, trying to stop shaking.

The order is finally going to be executed, she thought. It had been several cycles since she had seriously worried about the order for her reclamation. For over ten cycles, it had sat in a pending status, neither executed nor revoked. Pending what, she was not certain, but she feared she would soon find out. She tried to convince herself that reclamation was just the inevitable end of an eighteen-and-three-cycle delay. She wished she had died with the others during the Kahshinki attack and been spared the countless shifts hiding her injuries from the leaders. Damaged units were repaired based on skill: either valuable experience or knowledge. The unskilled, inexperienced, and untrained were used as spares to repair those more important, and their remains were fed into the biomatter reclamation units in the Biotech section.

Teela had been barely five cycles old when the attack occurred. She and her birth sisters were taking a midshift nap when an explosion shattered the Nursery. She awoke in a pile of wreckage. Pierced by a shard of wall panel from her upper abdomen to the inside of the opposite inner thigh, she was literally pinned to her sleep mat. Around her in the twisted wreckage were her shellmates, over two hundred in this Nursery alone. She could hear the others crying in pain.

Lying in the semidarkness, she saw the hand of another shell under the rubble near her. She wanted so much not to be alone, and struggled against shooting pains to reach it. She finally grasped it and squeezed to reassure her sister that she was not alone. There was no response; the hand was cold and lifeless.

It seemed like a very long time before salvage workers made their way to her. The crying around her had long since stopped, and bad odors now plagued her crown tendrils. When the scraping and banging of workers removing the debris grew near, she tried to call out, but her mouth was so parched that she had no voice. Finally, the wall beams and panel were lifted off of her.

A huge warrior unit in a dusty black uniform looked down at her with one functional eye. The other eye was missing; a wound ran across its face from its chin to its eye socket, disappearing into dry blood and dust-caked crown tendrils. Unfrightened by its gory face, Teela smiled broadly, holding up her arms as if to a section mother. The warrior instead put its foot on her chest, grabbed the end of the panel shard, and jerked it from her body. Teela screamed in surprise and pain, but her scream was nothing more than a silent exhalation. The warrior grabbed her and the limp body next to her by the arms, lifted them up, carried them impassively into the next compartment, and threw them without ceremony onto a large pile of decaying corpses.

Teela pushed the legs of her dead sister off of her chest so she could drag herself off the pile, her arms pulling the dead weight of her legs toward the corridor. She knew the area well, and crawled down to the next section compartment where the birthing mothers slept. It was not so long ago that she had slept there as well, but she was too old now that she had been weaned. Still, on occasion, she would sneak back and crawl into bed with one of the mothers.

Struggling with agonizing pain in her abdomen and legs, she forced herself to continue, frightened that the one-eyed warrior would return and throw her back in with the corpses. She crept through the door of the resting chamber and, after checking many pads, finally found one occupied by a sleeping mother. Weak, exhausted, and aching, Teela tried to climb up onto the sleep pad. Unable to do so, she fell to the floor, and for the first time since she was injured she began to cry. Her high-pitched croaks echoed plaintively in the large, darkened chamber.

Nerhala energized the light bar at the head of her sleep pad to see what was making such an awful noise and suppressed a scream upon seeing the filthy, blood-soaked child wailing on the floor. She checked to make sure no other mothers were awake, then turned out the light and lifted Teela onto the bed, kissing and cajoling her into silence.

Nerhala consulted no one when she took Teela to the old archives. Few ever went there; Nerhala often hid there from section mothers doling out unwanted assignments. This time, though, she had a job: she was going to save this shell, something she had been unable to do for the ones killed or hurt in the attack. Armed warrior units had come into the Shell section for the injured shells; Nerhala had helped to calm the frightened children and load them into transport carts. It wasn't until later that she had found out that they weren't being taken for repair, but for reclamation. In spite of her innocence, she was deeply ashamed of her complicity.

Nerhala obtained bandages and healing supplies from the biotechs under the guise of treating the salvage workers' cuts and scratches. Teela's injuries were much more severe than those of many sent for reclamation. Able to provide only superficial aid for Teela's severe abdominal pain and swelling, Nerhala feared the child would cease. For thirty or more workshifts, Nerhala updated Teela's log bar as though she were still in the Nursery, removing it at the end of each shift so that it wouldn't be included in the bed count.

As Teela recovered, Nerhala told her over and over that she must learn to hide her limp, that she could not let anyone see her scars, and that if anyone ever found out, they would both be taken by warrior units and cease to exist. Teela didn't require much convincing; she was plagued with nightmares of the one-eyed warrior unit coming to take her away. These nightmares would haunt her for the rest of her existence.

When the main chamber's repairs were complete, Nerhala slipped Teela in with the shells that were being relocated from other temporary care centers. The ruse was successful; Teela was accepted back into the Nursery as though she had never been gone. Remaining inordinately attached to Nerhala after the ordeal, Teela was less inclined to play with the other shells; instead, she emulated the birthing unit mothers and assisted Nerhala whenever she would let her. When it came time for the shells to be assigned duties at ten cycles, Teela ended up as Nerhala's assistant. For several cycles now, she had worked happily and without worry for her favorite birth mother.

The aftermath of the attack resulted in severe conditions throughout the vessel. Because they were underway at the time, they could not draw raw materials from any planetary bodies to facilitate repairs. The attack had damaged food processing, repair and fabrication facilities, and the Shell section, and had disabled portions of the propulsion system, causing the ship to secure the light drive units.

The leaders established harsh measures to recover from the situation. The dead and injured were reclaimed and a rationing system was established based on a section's contributions toward repair and recovery. All birthing operations were halted and work rounds of two shifts on and one off were implemented, instead of the usual two off and one on. Birthing units were relegated to the lowest positions on the ship, performing janitorial duties and receiving only a single nutriment loaf and measure of water each work round. Mothers who couldn't find a patron to provide additional rations for special services grew thin.

Four cycles passed before the ship's propulsion was repaired, and another three went by before the subsistence rationing of the

Shell section improved and mothers were ordered to resume birthing.

By this time, Teela was over twelve cycles old and had been directed to report with the other birthing units for implantation. The process went quickly. At numerous stations in the Biotech section each birthing unit placed her log bar into a recorder, removed her gown, and lay down on a table. A biotech lowered a dome-shaped device over her lower abdomen, held it in place for a few seconds, and then removed it. The birthing unit would then get up, take her log bar, and leave.

When it was Teela's turn, instead of removing her gown, she pulled it up just above her abdomen to avoid exposing the scar on her torso. The biotech pulled Teela's log bar from the recorder and compared it to the sabat marking on the left side of her face.

"You are small for twelve cycles," the technician stated, examining the log bar again.

"Yes, many of us have not grown as large as normal on the reduced rations," Teela answered, hoping the half-truth would be accepted. The biotech nodded, noting how thin she was.

If the biotech noticed the jagged scar on Teela's leg, nothing was said. Down came the dome and the tech held it in place, paused, tapped some controls on the side of the device, and then cocked her head to one side, a confused look on her face. Calling over another biotech, the two examined the device and finally lifted it off.

Teela tried to get up to leave, but they directed her to remain on the table. Together, they examined the scar on Teela's inner thigh. They traced the scar tissue in the underlying flesh up across her groin and abdomen and lifted her gown to find a matching scar just below her upper right breast.

The techs stepped away and conferred quietly. Teela tried to think up a plausible explanation for her scars, but when the technicians returned, none was requested. One of the technicians tapped something into a console on the end of the table, pulled out Teela's log bar, and handed it back. Teela slid off the table and smoothed her gown. Her eyes remained downcast to avoid eye contact with the other birthing units as she left. She walked slowly down the corridor, the log bar in her trembling hand, recalling Nerhala's warning over ten cycles ago that the warriors would take her if her injuries were discovered.

The nightmare of discovery had now emerged from the dark shadows of her past, and she found herself being escorted by security guards down a corridor toward an uncertain future. She opened her perspiring palm and looked at the log bar that documented her existence. Like the logs in the archives that fascinated her, she wondered whether someone would ever read the reports on this bar and find it as meaningless and futile as her existence now felt.

So many times Teela had imagined herself as a warrior, fighting desperate battles against insurmountable obstacles. If she had been born a warrior now, into the generation that would wage the Campaign, she would have had the opportunity to die in battle, leaving a log bar of honor instead of the pitiful life of a sterile birthing unit. A life that ended not in glorious battle, but in forced dismemberment of a damaged unit for usable parts, the remains ground into worm and beetle food.

"Stop! Wait one bit," someone called from behind.

Challmara, a senior technical unit Teela saw regularly as an off-shift customer, came running from an alcove just behind them. Teela found most of her paid relationships to be empty, businesslike arrangements. With Challmara, however, there seemed to be more. Challmara was always kind and never bickered about prices of Teela's personal services. And because she was many cycles older than Teela, at times she felt a comfort and security with her that reminded her of Nerhala. In this relationship, she had been able to enjoy a modicum of the emotional sustenance she so desperately craved but seemed unable to obtain anywhere else.

"Where are you taking this birthing unit?" Challmara demanded of the armed guards.

The ranking guard responded out of respect for Challmara's considerable rank. "To the director of Biological Maintenance and Repair." His emphasis on the rank of the order initiator implied that Challmara had no authority in this matter.

"Spare parts, most likely," the other guard added callously, nudging Teela forward.

As they continued down the corridor, ignoring Challmara's protests, Challmara followed closely behind them and addressed Teela when she realized the guards would no longer speak to her. "Why are they taking you? What have you done?"

"I don't know," Teela squeaked. Her voice choked with shame and fear; she did not want to acknowledge the obvious, did not want to admit her secret even now.

"Don't be afraid, little mother. I will find out. Everything will be all right." And then, for the benefit of the arrogant security unit, she added, "I have several directors who owe me." Turning, Challmara raced back down the corridor, sliding around the corner into the alcove she had come from. Her behavior was uncharacteristic of someone of her rank.

The escorts stopped at the entrance to the Bio section director's cubicle. The senior biotech administrative assistant at the long, curved workstation held out her hand, and Teela placed the log bar in it. As if burned, the assistant immediately dropped it onto the counter. She looked with disgust from the sweat- and blood-covered log bar to Teela's hand. In clenching the log bar so tightly, Teela had punctured her palm with her own claws. The assistant drew a wipe from a panel behind the station and cleaned off the log bar and counter. She pushed the soiled wipe across the counter toward Teela.

"Here. Clean off your hand and go in. The director has been waiting over three sets for you."

Teela slipped silently into the director's office, her nursery slippers gliding across the floor without making a sound. She had developed this technique over the cycles, making herself small, quiet, and unseen. Now, more than ever before, she did not want to be seen.

Gremensh, the Bio section director, stood beside Khranga, the Warrior and Pilot section senior director, who sat before a console. They were intently watching a visual display on a log reader with their backs to the door. Khranga pointed at the screen.

"We have examined the remains. They were Kahshinki, and they died as recorded here. This could not have been staged. They would never sacrifice their own. Watch again how they attack. There, you see? The creature had no idea that the

Kahshinki was going to lace it. Now look how the smaller one kills these two. On the first, it uses a little blade, since it has no claws. And then it kills the other Kahshinki in contact combat after getting severely laced as well. This truly would have been a contest worthy of a Spectacle Event."

Khranga continued in a more analytical tone. "It was shortly after they dropped out of hyperlight that they were first detected. The controls were configured for the four limbs of a Kahshinki, and this creature mastered them in less than a set. It wasn't until they discharged a high-power, tight-focus weapons pulse that our patrol detected them. Scanning the area of the pulse, the patrol found the hyperlight trail, and we projected the course the vessel was on and determined that it was attempting to return to this system here." Khranga stood and pointed to a spot on a star chart displayed on the wall.

"Isn't that beyond the current projected location of the Kahshinki forces?" Gremensh asked.

"Precisely. Which would mean that this ship represents a collection run for the next target system. We not only know where they are, we now know where they intend to go next!" Khranga jabbed the chart with an extended claw for effect.

"And what of this creature, the one Afron has selected? Why is it so valuable to our plans?" Gremensh asked, sitting in the chair and replaying the visual log.

"Not being a warrior or a pilot, I can't expect you to appreciate this. But this one creature killed two Kahshinki with its bare hands and then went on to fly this cargo ship in a running battle against ten Kahshinki long-range fighters. Even though the Kahshinki fighters were of a minimal weapon and armor class, it was still an unimaginable challenge. The recordings from the vessel's log and those from our patrol's scanners provide an accurate account of how this primitive beast managed to pilot a cargo vessel, destroy one fighter and damage two others with a single pulse blast, and disable another with a pulse blast and then destroy it by ramming it. The freighter was damaged by numerous pulse blasts and operating with minimal control when it rammed and disabled the fighter. Our training patrol was under strict orders to observe and not to engage, but the young pilots were so moved by the desperate efforts of this unknown pilot that was about to be destroyed at the hands of the enemy, several broke formation and engaged the remaining fighters, thus preventing the vessel's destruction.

"You must understand, Gremensh. If this creature were Korlah, it would be celebrated as both warrior and pilot, a distinction no Korlah has attained in ninety cycles. Besides, these are sentient beings, very much like us. Afron is convinced this species is the key to her plans. Should we succeed with this experiment, we could then use that success and the resulting information to—"

Teela! The voice came from the doorway, a few feet behind where Teela stood, but it was not a voice in the usual sense: it was an intense thought placed directly into Teela's mind.

Teela jumped and turned, nearly falling as her legs twisted together. Standing in the doorway was Afron, member of the Council of Elders and leader of Tactical Affairs. Afron represented the living memory of an eminent Korlah leader believed to have been alive at the time of the revolution against the Kahshinki. The leader's memories had passed through more than fifteen shells before settling in the body that now stood before Teela in a single-piece white suit with a loose-fitting gold vest. Teela knelt, her arms at her sides with the palms up, and bowed her head in the traditional display of respect for a high-ranking official.

"How long have you been standing there?" boomed Khranga, hearing the scuffle of Teela's feet but not Afron's telepathic voice.

Ignoring Khranga, Afron knelt in front of Teela and brought her outstretched hands together between her own.

Teela, my tender little mother, why are you shaking so? No one here is going to hurt you. Afron's thoughts, kind and reassuring, were delivered as if to a frightened child.

Look at me, don't you remember me? Afron imparted to her as their gazes met.

Teela looked up into the young face. Barely sixteen cycles, Afron still had the appearance of a child. Afron stroked a little scar above her right eye with the claw of her outer thumb.

I remember the day I got this on the play floor of the Nursery; the other mothers scolded me for crying and being so upset. But you kissed my tears and told me how dignified the scar would make me look, how it made me different from the others, how I would now have a battle scar that I could wear with pride, a testament to my honor so that I would always remember how hard I had played that day.

"Yes, I do remember," Teela replied, casting her gaze to the floor. Afron had repeated her words almost exactly as Teela had spoken them ten cycles ago.

Then we are old friends, and old friends do not lie to each other, do they? Afron stood, pulling Teela to her feet.

"I would not lie your Eminence. I have not lied!" Teela gasped, horrified.

No, no, of course not. How foolish that would be. It is what I have to tell you that is not a lie. Please, old friend, let me show what I can do for you today.

Afron pulled a log bar from the pocket of her vest and showed it to Teela; she had taken the log bar of Teela's existence from the assistant in Gremensh's office. The leader walked over to the console, pulling Teela along, and with a thought discernable only through the intensity of her gaze instructed Gremensh to vacate the seat. Gremensh scrambled to her feet, apologizing as she backed away. Afron snapped Teela's log bar into the recorder and called up the order for Teela's reclamation onto the screen.

Is this what you are so upset about? Afron asked, tapping the screen with an extended claw.

Teela was quaking with fear now, barely able to acknowledge the question.

I am so sorry. I wish I had known about this sooner and could have taken care of it. Here, look. Teela watched as Afron changed the order from "pending" to "revoked," authenticating the order with a coded entry and signing it, BY ORDER OF AFRON, LEADER OF TACTICAL AFFAIRS.

The screen went blank and Afron pulled the log bar from the terminal, holding it out for Teela to take. Teela's hands were over her face in an attempt to repress the sobs of relief she could no longer restrain.

Afron stood and took Teela by the shoulders and guided her into the seat. For the first time since entering the room, she spoke audibly.

"There, there, now. You just sit down here and relax. Everything has been taken care of. You need not ever concern yourself with that little problem again. You have my personal word." Gremensh and Khranga stared in disbelief at the attention that this high-ranking leader was lavishing on a lowly birthing unit.

"I'm … so … sorry. I have … been afraid … so long. Thank you … Afron. Thank you," Teela squeaked out between sobs.

"Yes, yes, of course you have, but you need not be afraid any longer. I am so glad that I have been able to help you with this problem. You see, I have a little problem of my own that I need help with. I need someone with your knowledge and skills. I need you, Teela. You will help me, won't you?"

If she hadn't been seated, Teela would have fallen. She knew how the bargaining process worked. Favors were not offered or given without the expectation of favors in return. Although Afron was in a position of ultimate power, she had just negotiated an arrangement that, regardless of what was requested, Teela had no alternative but to accept. This made the action voluntary and devoid of political criticism, an arrangement the leaders liked to set up when there was a potentially bad decision at risk.

"Yes, Your Eminence. Whatever you wish," Teela responded, bowing her head and turning up her palms.

Afron lifted Teela's head to meet her penetrating gaze. "This is not an order. I am asking you as an old friend to help me willingly. Will you?" Afron asked, her voice devoid of the warmth her thoughts had delivered earlier.

"Yes," Teela squeaked, looking into intense, deeply knowledgeable eyes that seemed out of place on such a young face.

"Very good. We have no time to waste," Afron announced to Gremensh and Khranga. "Set it up immediately. Teela and I will meet you in the Transfer Chamber."

"Yes, Your Eminence." They bowed in unison and rushed out of the room.

"Transfer Chamber?" Teela whispered, more to herself than as a question for Afron.

"Yes, Teela. The very same one you brought my current shell to four cycles ago. Do you remember?"

Teela acknowledged it ruefully, shamed by the thought. It had always seemed wrong to deliver innocent young shells for transfer, their minds to be absorbed into the collective memories of a ranking official—no longer a child, no longer innocent.

"I remember it like it was only last shift," Afron said. "You told me not to be afraid, that everything would be fine as long as I performed as you had taught me. You said I would be gifted with many wonderful memories, and that I would become a respected and honored leader. You did not lie! Everything you told me was true. What I am asking of you is very similar to what you asked of me then. I want you to trust me. Do not be afraid."

"I am too old to be a shell. I am damaged. I … I have too many memories," Teela blurted out, interrupting Afron.

"No, you are the perfect age, and for this transfer we need you to have memories."

Tapping the log cube in her hand, Afron added, "And I know about your damage. Your utilization will no longer require the capacities of a functional birthing unit, so your damage is of no consequence."

"I will be reassigned … with rank … and title?" Teela pressed, negotiation a natural response because of her routine dealings with clients.

"Of course, with rank and title," Afron responded, laughing at the guile of this seemingly naive birthing unit. "But that can wait until later. We have no time to waste. Come with me."

Afron drew Teela to her feet, and interlocking her arm with Teela's, drew her as close as a friend and escorted her from the office.

7 - Death

Dade woke to the sound of someone pounding on metal and the low murmur of voices. His head and body throbbed with every heartbeat. Barely able to breathe through his swollen nose and mouth and unable to open his eyes, he tried to sit up. Excruciating pain tore through his burned and bruised chest and abdomen; he choked out a surprised yelp.

"Take it easy there, Slugger." Dade recognized Margaret's voice.

"Looks like we lost this battle, too," she said, "but if it's any consolation, I counted four bad guys being hauled off. You all put up a courageous fight, especially Beth."

"Baat?" Dade struggled to enunciate the name with his ragged mouth.

"Beth, oh my, yes! What a spectacular fight. She was in the Marines, a sergeant or something. From what I could see during the light flashes, all heck broke loose when the girls fired those flashlight guns. Apparently, they had no effect on the boarding party and the girls were mowed down in seconds by the return fire. Whatever kind of weapon it was, it knocks the heck out of whomever it hits. But you found that out, didn't you? We were losing fast and badly, but when you opened fire with that pistol, I think they must have been caught off-guard. You nailed the bad guy in front, and he fell back into the others. When they all started blasting you, Beth ran right through all the shooting and jumped into the middle of their group. They couldn't shoot without hitting each other.

"Well, she karate chopped and kicked the crap out of the whole bunch before they finally knocked her down. They beat her up pretty bad, but she's going to be all right. Oh yes, *these* aliens are different, big ugly suckers with fangs and long hair that looks like wet noodles. They are about the same size as us, have pointed heads and walk on their tiptoes."

"Hey there, Skipper, I was getting worried about you. You've been out for quite a while," Ruth said, joining Margaret next to Dade.

Dade tried to lick his lips but found his tongue thick and dry.

"Ow da udtors?" Dade mumbled, attempting to speak.

"How are the others?" Ruth interpreted. Dade nodded his head.

"Fine, except for some cuts and bruises, and, of course, dehydration. Beth has been trying to get them to bring us some water for a while now. That's her pounding on the door. She should be sitting down. I think she's got some broken ribs, and she could probably use a few stitches. I've never seen someone wake up so pissed off before. I thought she was going kick my ass next."

"Weah … ah … weh?" Dade asked.

"We are in a really, really big spaceship. You should have seen this thing; it is enormous, a mile in diameter and maybe three miles long. And I think we are traveling near light speed, 'cause when we came aboard the stars were all fuzzy, like when we were speeding up to black space. They put us in this hot, stuffy little room with no water or bathroom. Some of us had to pee in the corner; fortunately nobody has had to go number two yet."

"Ow … eh … peoh?" Dade said. Ruth was trying to decipher the question when Bill answered.

"Ah've been better," Bill said. "Don't be worrying bout us, you got to concentrate on getting better, cause we all gonna...."

Dade heard a hiss and the sound of a door sliding open. The banging sound stopped.

"Water. Do you ugly bastards understand drink? We need water." Beth was pantomiming drinking from a glass to the pair of armed aliens that had opened the compartment door.

One of the aliens centered its weapon on Beth. Beth stepped back, not wanting to feel the crushing blow again. Four more aliens filed into the small room and leveled their weapons on the group. Someone stifled a scream. Rebecca started to recite the Lord's Prayer. Margaret screamed. Dade felt himself being grabbed by the feet.

"Let go of him!" Beth shouted just before the crackling whump! of an alien weapon's discharge. Dade felt himself being dragged out the door. The sounds of screaming faded with the hiss and click of the closing door. He could hear the aliens speaking a language that sounded like low growling and clicking. He groaned in pain as he was gripped and lifted by his arms and legs and sensed that they were placing him onto—no, *into* something. Into a tray like the one he had first been restrained in.

"No!" Dade screamed through split lips.

The aliens held him down and secured him with the wrapping. He grabbed at the pockets of his trousers for his knife, but it was gone.

Afron and Teela walked all the way to the Transfer Chamber without speaking. The technicians inside bowed deeply as Afron entered, but she seemed oblivious of their presence. Walking to the center of the room, Afron turned and sat on the edge of a long table and telepathically directed Teela to join her. She directed her thoughts only to Teela so that the others would not be privy to their full conversation.

"We have recently recovered an injured warrior pilot who has courageously defeated many Kahshinki. We need to know what this warrior's home world is like and how technologically advanced their species is."

"Home world? Species? This warrior is not Korlah?" Teela asked incredulously.

"An intelligent, sentient species, with amazing similarities to us. At first, we thought they must be Kahshinki duplicates that escaped, but they are not. These are individual, genetically different beings of the same species, eleven of them in fact. But this one, the one that is injured and will soon die, was their leader. If you can successfully accept a transfer from it, you will be gifted with many wonderful memories, and I will be able find out what they are."

Afron took Teela's hand and gave it a reassuring squeeze. The gesture did not reassure Teela, though; instead, it evoked memories of the young shellmates she had tried to soothe before sending them off for transfer, knowing she would never speak to them again. Afron remembered the young child that she had delivered to this room; she was certain that child no longer existed.

"I … I have heard … that a shell's mind is taken during the transfer. That … that … if a shell has too many memories, the transfer will damage the mind," Teela spoke quietly, carefully avoiding eye contact with Afron.

"I have never heard such things," Afron replied, her thoughts dripping with sincerity. "The reason a shell's memories are kept to a minimum is to reduce duplication. If two similar individuals are joined in transfer, it becomes difficult to differentiate the memories, which can be confusing for those involved. But I have never heard of any resulting damage to the mind. Since it is not likely for you and this being to have any similar memories, I do not expect there to be any confusion. And haven't I already proven to you, old friend, that all the memories from before transfer will be part of your memories afterward?"

Their conversation was interrupted when the door to the Transfer Room slid open to admit Khranga and Gremensh. Behind them was a procession: four armed warriors, two warriors with a transfer gurney, and then four more armed guards. The crowd blocked Teela's view of the gurney, but the mournful howling of its occupant caused her great discomfort.

"As ordered, Your Eminence," Khranga announced, bowing in unison with Gremensh.

Afron nodded an acknowledgment to her directors and slipped off the table, drawing Teela with her to the far end of the chamber, away from the new arrival.

"Place it on the table and ready it for transfer," Afron commanded coldly.

The biotechs ran to the table and began to prepare the restraints. Six warriors bent over the gurney and released the creature's restraints. It lurched forward and was immediately slammed back down by six sets of clawed hands.

Be careful, you oafs! If it dies before transfer, I will have you all reassigned for reclamation! Afron shouted, causing the warriors to wince from the intent and intensity of her telepathic directive.

Twelve hands gripped the howling and struggling creature as they lifted it from the gurney to the table, where the waiting biotechs quickly fastened and secured its restraints. Khranga directed the ten warriors to take up positions around the room, their weapons at the ready. Afron drew Teela by the hand toward the table and she got her first good look at the mutilated head flopping from side to side, its black tongue wagging between pitiful wails. She stopped, resisting Afron's pull.

"No … no … I can't. Not this … Please, Afron, please!" Teela pleaded, hiding her face with her hands.

You ... will ... look! Afron barked, the intensity of her thoughts causing Teela to jump with each word. Without any attempt at gentleness now, she jerked Teela over to the edge of the table.

"This is a real warrior, damaged beyond recognition and injured beyond possible survival, and yet it continues to fight and struggle. Did you see? It took six of our warriors to hold this one pitiful, wretched beast. Such courage, such determination—these are the characteristics that permitted the Korlah to overthrow the Kahshinki parasites. And now you would refuse this incredible opportunity to join with greatness? Allow the honor of this warrior to cease?" Afron had chosen her approach carefully, teasing out the hidden hopes and desires from Teela's subconscious.

Teela looked at the struggling beast and tried to visualize herself as a warrior in such a situation.

"Have you tried to calm it, to show it kindness?" Teela asked, feeling more pity than fear for the injured creature.

Afron and Gremensh looked at Khranga.

"How can you show kindness to something that attacks you?" Khranga hissed.

"How many of your warriors have been killed?" Teela asked as she gently and nervously placed her hand on the creature's shoulder.

"One has injuries that will require repair, and three were knocked senseless," Khranga replied.

"None killed. That's good." Teela gently stroked the creature's shoulder while she loosened its restraints.

"What are you doing?" shouted Gremensh.

"Showing kindness to an injured warrior. There must be trust and acceptance for transfer to succeed; otherwise, there is no point in proceeding. If you are frightened, then you should move somewhere where you will feel safe."

Afron laughed at Gremensh's injured expression, but cautiously stepped behind the line of warriors shortly after Gremensh did.

Teela was resigned to her fate. She felt amazingly calm after all the distressing events she had just gone through. This hideous creature no longer frightened her. She felt sorry for the suffering it must be experiencing and hoped she could soothe its pain and fears. She spoke softly to it and continued to stroke its shoulder and arm, as she would a frightened child. The creature stopped struggling and turned its face toward hers.

She continued to speak to it in a low voice as she released and removed the restraints. The creature sat up abruptly and grabbed her feebly by the shoulder with its mutilated hands. Ten pulse rifles energized in unison, filling the room with the crackling hum of their powered-up pulse chambers.

Teela stopped talking, her eyes tightly shut, as she continued to stroke with her shaking hand. She opened her eyes slowly. The gruesome face was inches away from hers, its breath bubbling out of its shredded mouth. Turning first in one direction and then another, the creature was apparently ascertaining the locations of the humming pulse rifles. Teela began to talk softly again. She reached up and put her hand onto the one gripping her shoulder. She carefully pulled the hand off her shoulder and held it between both of hers. The back of the hand was burned and blistered, but on its underside she could see clear, smooth skin.

Perhaps undamaged, these creatures are not so hideous, she thought, trying to imagine the grisly face with smooth skin.

Releasing the disfigured hand, she put one of her arms behind the creature's back for support and gently pushed on its chest. It relaxed with a deep sigh and allowed Teela to lay it down. As soon as she began to replace the restraints, though, the creature started to struggle again. She stopped and continued to caress its arm and murmur reassuringly, and eventually the creature allowed her to replace the restraints.

Teela climbed up onto the other side of the long table and lay down with her crown touching the creature's.

"We are ready," she announced with feigned confidence.

Squeezing past the guards, the biotechs rushed to fasten Teela's restraints and position a boxlike enclosure over the creature's head, followed by a cylindrical device that covered both their heads. The technicians stood on each side of the table and looked to Gremensh.

"Begin," she directed.

The biotechs tapped controls on the enclosure that caused the box to fill with a slow-acting lethal gas. The creature began to struggle and the restraints tightened in response. The struggling turned into convulsions. The spasms of the lower limbs were so violent that one of its shoes flew into the air, landing at the feet of a nearby warrior.

"What are you doing to it?" Afron shrieked, sounding like a frightened child.

"Thc cuthanizing gas mixturc is not corrcct, but thc cffcct will be the same," Gremensh responded.

"This has the appearance of another of your many failures. If you weren't such a loyal servant, I would find myself a replacement," Afron hissed to Gremensh, who ignored the comment. She was relieved to see the convulsions reduce to mere tremors, one foot jerking to the side before finally lying motionless.

Teela calmed herself and tried to clear her mind. She concentrated in the way she had been instructed, and as she had in turn instructed so many shells, and called with her mind. "I am the light. I am the path. I am the receptacle for new life. Bring forward your first memory and follow it to me." She repeated the line with her thoughts, over and over, opening her mind to accept the memories of the dying creature.

My god, I'm being served up as the next meal, Dade thought as he twisted and struggled, hoping to find a vulnerability in the wrap. Anything that would grant him an escape from the horrors he envisioned. He was being bumped and jostled around corners, and could hear many footsteps and the growling and clicking sounds these aliens made. Margaret had said that they had fangs. He wondered if he was to be ripped apart rather than dissolved slowly. Neither prospect sounded inviting.

So Goddamned weak and helpless. This is no way to die. No way! Working himself into a panic, he ranted incoherent curses and threw his head from side to side, reopening the wounds on his mouth and face. He hoped desperately to make himself black out again so that he might be spared a death like the one Jimmy had suffered.

The tray stopped moving. Dade could hear the grunts, hissing, and growls of their speech. There was movement and muttering over him and he could feel their breath on his sensitive skin. Suddenly his wraps were being loosened.

This is it. This is my last chance to go out swinging, he thought, panicked beyond reason. As soon as the last wrap was removed, he lunged upward with his head and chest, the effort bringing sharp pains to his bruised abdomen.

He had hoped his head would strike whoever was leaning over him, but before he could raise his good arm, his limbs were gripped painfully and he was brutally forced back into the prone position. It felt as though the hands were ripping holes into his burned and bruised flesh, and he screamed in agony when they lifted him into the air. Struggling impotently to break the torturous grip, his mind raced with visions of his own death.

I'm being torn apart. This is my punishment for resistance. God forgive me if I've brought this on the others. Dade choked with fear and his bladder voided. It wasn't much, in his dehydrated state, but it was enough to send a wave of shame rippling through his already-anguished mind.

They lay him down and put the restraining wrap on again. He sensed that he was on a platform of some sort, and that the group was moving away from him in all directions. He reasoned that he was on display in the center of a room. Shamed by his loss of control and composure, he tried to calm himself and rationalize what was happening to him. He reasoned that if they were just going to kill him, he would be dead by now. If they were going to eat him, they must like playing with their food. This was looking more and more like either experimentation or vivisection. Or possibly both.

Something touched his shoulder. The blistered skin still stung from recent handling and was exceptionally sensitive to even this light touch; an alien standing next to him was making soft purring sounds and gently stroking his arm. Turning his head toward the sound, he struggled to open his swollen eyes.

It's trying to communicate, he reasoned. Running a thirst parched tongue over his lips, Dade noted the metallic taste and greasy slickness of fresh blood in his mouth and cursed his inability to speak. His wraps were being loosened again and his heart raced. Where had the others gone? Was he alone with this one? What should he do? What could he hope to do? In the instant it took to conceive the thought, he made his choice. He would fight. There was no benefit he could imagine in making this easy for them.

As soon as the wraps were removed, he lurched forward and grabbed feebly at the creature next to him, his mutilated hands catching it in a weak embrace. The electrical crackling of alien weapons energizing caused him to freeze. The recent memory of that sound, the crushing impact of their discharge, and the shooting pains he felt even now in his chest and abdomen warned him of the agony he was inviting. The hum of the weapons seemed to come from all around; he was definitely not alone with this creature. The alien removed its hand from his shoulder and took his hand, very softly. It began to quietly purr again while gently attempting to tug his arm from its shoulder. Dade could feel the alien's hand and shoulder trembling.

It's shaking with fear. I've frightened it. They may be trying to show me they mean no harm, and I'm attacking them. The events leading to his capture raced through his memory. Ruth had said that the alien ships had started to attack each other. *Why would they do that? It didn't make any sense, unless they were attacking the aliens that were attacking us. These aliens are different than the ugly little toads Bill and I killed. Margaret said we killed four of them when they boarded our ship. My God, what have I done?* Dade thought. Waves of doubt flooded his mind, challenging the decisions he had made and settling as an uncomfortable chill in the pit of his stomach, as they always did whenever he made a serious, irreversible mistake.

Dade released his grip, and the alien set his arm back at his side, gently nudging him to lay back. He didn't resist. His mind was drowning in the possible consequences of attacking these creatures if they had, in fact, rescued them. If they had, and were attacked for their trouble, why should they show him any kindness at all?

He felt the wraps being put back on and instinctively struggled against them. The gentle touch and soft purring convinced him that no harm was intended, and he relaxed, allowing himself to be bound. He resigned himself to whatever fate awaited him.

The alien that had been touching him moved away. Dade could hear their animalistic speech. Something was placed over his face, not touching it, but close. It surrounded his head and muffled the sounds in the room. A few minutes later, he heard a hiss, followed by a bitter smell and burning sensation in his nose and mouth. He began to suffocate, and convulsed involuntarily in an effort to escape.

A soft, dark pillow further muted the sounds around him, enveloping his head and mind. His pain disappeared into the creamy, thick darkness that swallowed him into its warm embrace. A voice spoke to him from somewhere in the blackness. No, not a *voice*, but rather a *thought*. He felt weightless, without physical form, gliding through the black void. The voice was inviting him to follow, asking for his first thought.

What is my first thought? he wondered. Not thought; memories. *What are my first memories?*

His earliest memories were of a tricycle he rode when he was three or four. The image came to him with incredible detail and clarity. He could smell the damp pavement and hear the rustle of wind through the leaves in trees overhead as he *experienced,* more than merely remembered, riding the tricycle down a sidewalk made rough by the roots of trees pushing up the slabs of concrete. Following this experience came others, each with sensory perceptions that were crisp and clear in their recollection: the taste of oatmeal with butter and brown sugar as he sat eating breakfast with his foster sister and mother. More memories appeared and passed, coming faster and faster. The stream of memories blended into a river, then into a thundering cascade of images, smells, and sensations that made up the biological recording of his life that had been etched into the electrical matrix of his brain. It flowed around and through him and ended as it had begun, in the black void of nothingness where souls begin, and perhaps end.

8 - Rebirth

The creature on the table arched its back against the restraints and lct out a long, rattling brcath. Thc biotcchs made a few checks on their panels and indicated to Gremensh with a gesture that the creature's life function had ceased.

For the first time since Teela had loosened the restraints, Afron approached the table, waving the biotechs away.

"Khranga, have your warriors wait in the corridor. Gremensh, dismiss the technicians," Afron said, standing alongsidc the table where Teela lay motionless. With a glance from Khranga, the warriors quickly filed out of the room. The technicians didn't wait for direction from Gremensh and disappeared into an alcove near a row of counters and consoles on the opposite side of the chamber. Gremensh and Khranga approached the table, exercising care not to encroach on Afron's space.

"Has she ceased?" growled Khranga.

"No," Afron said. "Not physically. This shell now contains the essences of two mature minds. At this moment, a battle is being fought, a struggle for control. It's a struggle between the blended memories, a fight to make sense of their combined meanings. If this experiment is successful, in the next few bits the essence of one will vanquish the other, and she will wake up. Of course, she could end up catatonic, babbling like an infant, or violently insane. This has never succeeded with any of the alien species in the past, so the possibilities are endless."

"But you said … she wouldn't …." Khranga stopped, feeling the blade of Afron's cold, hostile thoughts stab into her brain with an intensity intended to punish.

"I say what needs to be said for the success of our Mission and the greater glory of Korlah," Afron said without looking at her subordinates.

Gremensh and Khranga bowed their heads, either in respect, or more likely, in the conditioned and politically appropriate response to the long-touted Mission goals. And in fear of Afron's ability to revoke her opponents' ranks and titles, if not their existences.

"I … think … what … Afron meant … was … that … she lied," Teela said, her words uttered with a barely audible mechanical detachment.

"Teela?" Afron spun around and stared at the small birthing unit. Still bound to the transfer table and unmoving, her eye slits shut and mouth partially open, Teela looked dead.

"Teela, tell me of your thoughts," Afron whispered, emanating emotional warmth and friendship.

Teela remained motionless with her eyes closed. After a long pause, her mouth trembled as though she was struggling to speak. She finally answered in the same disconnected, trancelike manner.

"Happy. I am happy. Many … many thoughts, strange … thoughts? Or memories … I think," she whispered, drawing Afron closer.

"Why are you happy, Teela? Tell me about these thoughts." Afron attempted unsuccessfully to probe the chaos of images and emotions whirling through Teela's conscious mind.

Teela opened her eyes suddenly in response to the mental invasion, locking an icy glare on Afron. Surprised, and uncomfortable with this uncharacteristic behavior by a lowly subordinate, Afron broke her mental probe and stepped back cautiously.

"I am happy … the warriors … were not killed." Teela blinked her eyes as though trying to clear her vision and looked around the room. Setting her gaze on Khranga, she continued, her voice stronger and more confident. "How is the warrior that was injured boarding the Kahshinki cargo ship?"

"The warrior's injuries are of no consequence," Afron answered for Khranga. "Tell me why you are concerned about the warrior?"

Ignoring Afron, Teela kept her eyes on Khranga, waiting for an answer. Khranga looked to Afron for help.

"Tell her, Khranga, and do not attempt to deceive. I sense that this unit is intolerant of deception," Afron said, visibly angered.

"The warrior will recover. A few broken bones and a badly bruised throat from a primitive projectile weapon, that fortunately lacked the velocity necessary to fully penetrate the warrior's armor."

"Why do you ask this question?" Afron was tense, bordering on hostile.

"Armor. Of course," Teela smiled, but her smile faded when she turned her head toward Afron. "You know why." Teela locked her eyes on Afron's, a blatant challenge to her authority.

"Thought harm was meant. Thought enemies. Didn't know. Glad no deaths." Teela spoke without emotion, looking directly into Afron's eyes and emanating a violent hostility that made her uneasy.

"I know what you really want to know," Teela said, "You want to know if your experiment worked, or whether you wasted a perfectly useless birthing unit." Teela paused, watching the Council leader's face flush with embarrassment at the accusation of manipulating the situation.

Khranga charged forward. Afron stopped Khranga with a thought, causing the obese warrior to stumble midway through what would have been a painful blow to Teela's head.

Afron stepped over to Teela and grabbed her roughly by the throat with one hand and the top of her head with the other. She pressed her forehead against Teela's and thrust her mind deep into Teela's subconscious.

Feeling as though her skull would explode, Teela tried to scream, but she was only able to whimper. Afron ripped through the details of her combined memories like the blades of a blender.

"It worked!" Afron said, releasing Teela's throat and backing away.

Teela sucked in a lungful of air and choked convulsively.

"We have its essence and can communicate with it," Afron exclaimed. "It worked!" she shouted at Gremensh. "It worked!" she shouted at Khranga. "It really worked!" Placing her hands on her waist, she stood over Teela and looked down at the tightly-bound birthing unit as though she had just received a new and greatly anticipated gift. She turned to Khranga and directed the warrior to bring the other damaged beast to the Biorepair section, then directed Gremensh to prepare to perform repairs on it using the remains of this one for spare parts. Her telepathic instructions were only heard by their intended recipients.

"Would you please release my restraints? They are really quite uncomfortable," Teela said, avoiding eye contact and keeping her tone very respectful, in the manner of a lowly subordinate.

"Yes, of course. Just one moment," Afron replied as she called five warriors back into the room with her mind. As Khranga left, the armed warriors took positions around the room with their weapons at the ready. Afron backed away from the table and locked her gaze intently onto Teela.

"I sense the essence of this human in your mind," she said. "It is weak, hiding in the shadows like frightened braddle. You must keep its memories and expel its essence, Teela. It is imperative for your survival." Afron shifted her gaze to Gremensh.

"Release the restraints," she said once she was safely beyond the circle of warriors. Gremensh nervously scanned the room for a biotech. Finding none to delegate the task to, she approached the table, looking to Afron for confirmation.

The leader gestured impatiently for her to proceed. Gremensh released the bindings and rushed back behind the ring of guards without waiting for them to fully retract.

Teela pushed off the wraps and sat up on the edge of the table. Leaning slightly to one side and resting on one arm, she rubbed her bruised throat with her free hand. Suddenly, she pulled the hand away from her throat and held it in front of her face. Turning it over, she extended and retracted her claws, watching with rapt interest the way the claws slid in and out of the fleshy folds of her fingertips, razor-sharp talons gleaming malevolently in the brightly lit room. For the first time that she could recall, she thought of them as weapons. Conscious all at once of the frightening and disquieting emotions this line of thought provoked, she closed her hand and looked almost dreamily around the room. Then she hopped off the table.

The ring of warriors, the directors, and the leader nervously jumped in unison, and two warriors energized their pulse rifles.

"What's the matter? What's wrong?" Teela asked, confused by the defensive postures and serious expressions of the warriors surrounding her. She looked around and behind, half expecting to find something horrible enough to elicit fear in armed warriors.

"Why are you frightened? Are you frightened of me?" she demanded, looking down to confirm that she was still who she thought she was. A long, uncomfortable pause followed while she studied the faces around her. She recognized one of the warriors. Young and nervous, it pointed its energized weapon at her with trembling hands. Holding her arms out, palms up in a display of surrender and submission, she turned slowly around, making it clear that she had no weapons. She stopped when she faced the young warrior again. She placed her hands on her hips and leaned forward, forcing the warrior to withdraw the energized weapon slightly or risk burning her.

She spoke as she would to a misbehaving adolescent. "Am I so fearsome a birthing unit that you need a pulse rifle to protect yourself?"

The warrior's tendrils blanched with embarrassment as a chorus of chuckles from the other warriors echoed around the room. Switching the rifle off, she swung it grudgingly back to the ready position.

"Thank … you … Maul," Teela said, using her Shell section name and omitting the "lauh" designation that would have recognized her warrior clan status. This resulted in a roar of laughter from the others. The tension in the room eased visibly as the posture of the warriors relaxed.

A chill swept through Teela's heart as she looked back at the table. The scuffed shoe, soiled pants, and odors of sweat and urine were both familiar and foreign to her. This thing was now part of her. Thoughts she could not yet understand raced through her mind with dizzying clarity. With limbs that felt numb and unresponsive, she stumbled back to the table. She lifted the gas hood from the head, allowing it to fall to the floor with a jarring crash that silenced the room.

She stared at the empty shell of what had been a living being, intimately realizing what and who it once had been. Afron had told her that she must dispel the remaining essence of this being, but she feared Afron's deception more than the essence that she felt within her own mind.

Don't leave ... Don't leave yet, she implored, directing the thought deep into her own mind toward something she felt there, something that was projecting emotions that were well beyond mere memories. She knew she needed to remember something, to do something, something important, something she didn't yet understand but needed desperately to come to grips with. If she allowed the essence to remain, would it take control? Could she control it completely? She didn't know the answers, but knew she would have to guard her thoughts from Afron's prying mind.

So engrossed with inner turmoil, Teela barely noticed when Afron cleared the room, leaving only a single warrior and Gremensh. She released the restraints around the human corpse and then painstakingly removed them, as if she was afraid to cause additional harm.

The sight of the body's smashed and disfigured features released visions of a life now shared with hers. Closing her eyes for a moment, she could see beyond the damage. She envisioned a face like a reflection in a mirror—a face without injuries. She felt as if it were her face, but knew that it was not.

She touched the collar of his once-white T-shirt, now crusted black with blood, and remembered removing the neatly folded shirt from the top drawer, unfolding it, and putting it on. She caught a scent of bleach as the T-shirt passed over her head, but it wasn't her head that emerged. She cocked her head to the side, thinking about the differences in perception.

They smell through the holes in their faces. I cannot see color; everything is black and white, hot and cold.

She couldn't think of a Korlah word for color, but the word fit smoothly into her thoughts. She saw the glimmer of a medallion, a Saint Christopher, one that Julie had given her—no, him,—as a gift. And although he wasn't religious, he had never taken it off. He had worn it always, a reminder that she loved him despite the rough times they had managed to overcome.

Releasing the clasp, she pulled the medallion and chain from the neck of the corpse and fastened it around her own. She lifted his hip with considerable difficulty and tugged a worn wallet from his rear pocket. Although the wallet was damp with urine, the pictures inside were dry. She flipped through them.

"Julie," she said aloud in English, noticing how strange it felt to articulate the name.

She slid the wallet into the slip pocket of her tah and proceeded to unfold the corpse's clenched left hand. She was struggling to remove a modest gold band from the grotesquely disfigured hand when Gremensh interrupted.

"What are you doing?"

Teela looked up, giving Gremensh a blank stare. Afron answered for her.

"Collecting memoirs from a past life; it's nothing to fear. It's normal after transfer."

Apparently confident that Teela was not going to be a threat, Afron moved closer to better observe the gruesome contest for the ring. With a look of disgust, she took hold of Teela's hands and pried them off the hand of the corpse.

Let me have Gremensh remove that for you later. There is nothing here for you to do. Once the essence is completely gone, these objects will lose their importance. Let me take you to someplace more ... appropriate, she said, imparting great concern and compassion for Teela's distress.

With Gremensh holding one arm and Afron the other, Teela was reluctantly led from the Transfer Chamber. Teela looked back as though she were forgetting something important, but she could not recall exactly what that something could be.

They walked through the Bio section's examination and repair areas on their way to Gremensh's private examination room. Afron and Gremensh led while Teela, a subordinate, followed closely behind with the armed guard. Teela halted and watched in amazement as two biotechs grafted facial tissues onto an injured worker. Perturbed by her resistance, Afron jerked Teela by the arm.

"Could you do that to humans?" Teela pointed excitedly.

"What are hu-mons? What are you babbling about?" Gremensh demanded.

"Your technicians, the ones there. Do you think they could repair … the other damaged creature? They are called *humans*."

"I intend to find out," Gremensh answered cautiously.

"What about genetic differences? Aren't these humans all genetically different?"

"How would you know that?"

"I remember you saying it." Teela turned and looked toward Gremensh expectantly.

Afron, who had been silent during the exchange, injected herself into the conversation.

"I'm certain this is all new and very exciting for you, Teela, but I really need to begin a formal dissemination of your new memories, and this is neither the time nor place."

"No!" Teela shouted, suddenly remembering what was almost forgotten. "This is the time and place for this, and it cannot wait. Gremensh, what about genetic differences?"

Gremensh, perplexed by the audacity of this lowly birthing unit, was silent, looking to Afron for guidance.

"Why is this so important, Teela, that you would tax the patience of your superiors in this manner?" Afron demanded, the cold, cutting edge back in her voice.

Knowing that it would be futile and likely fatal to make demands of this arrogant leader, Teela adopted a posture of respect.

"I am sorry. I have forgotten my place, Your Eminence. But one of the humans was severely laced by the Kahshinki during the battle for control of the cargo ship, and is in need of repair or it may cease. If we were to fail to make an attempt at repair, we would miss an opportunity to demonstrate respect for one that has killed a Kahshinki in unarmed combat, and thus lose honor."

Afron was silent for a few seconds. Although she fully intended to repair the damaged human, her motivation to do so was completely different. She realized that she had just been presented with a controversial political challenge. Under the rules and laws of Korlah, no official may knowingly fail to honor any who has achieved victory in an unarmed contest with a Kahshinki. By presenting an acceptable and achievable form by which to bestow honor, Teela challenged her to comply or lose honor in failing to do so.

Afron threw her head back and laughed loudly, drawing a look of amazement from Gremensh. She put her arm around Gremensh and shook a finger at Teela.

"We can learn a few things from this one, this new one. She is not likely to have learned the laws of Korlah as a result of transfer; therefore, she is apparently much more educated than you led me to expect, and it is when something is unexpected that you find yourself surprised." Turning her attention to Teela, Afron projected her thoughts; her mood was dark and threatening.

If human physiology is as similar to that of a Korlah as I have been informed, I am certain our processes can arrest any tissue rejection that may occur, regardless of any genetic differences between the tissues. I have already directed the repair of the other damaged human. Khranga has been sent to bring it to the repair facility, and the ceased human unit is being preserved for use as spares. So you see, I have already planned to honor its courage and have no need for you to remind me of my responsibilities or obligations.

Afron focused her cold black eyes on Teela's and projected her icy thoughts deep into Teela's mind. *We will get to know each other better, Teela, if I may call you that. You are definitely not the harmless, milk-sacked, vacuous birthing unit that Gremensh described to me. Now, combined with the memories of this human, you have presented me with more surprises than I have had in many lifetimes. Let me assure you, it would be wise for you to get to know me and my capacity for patience.*

Recognizing the dangerous proportions to which the situation had escalated and fearing Afron would sense her deceptions,

Teela dropped to her knees and bowed her head in supplication in an effort to break the mental assault.

"Please, Your Eminence, forgive me for these indiscretions. My mind is racing with thoughts of vital importance to Korlah, this ship, and you. I … I … will try to … think … about what I am going to say, before I say it."

Pulling Teela to her feet, Afron softened her acid tone slightly. "I'm not sure I want you to start thinking about what you're going to say. You're dangerous enough already. Now what was it you were going to tell me? You said it was … something of *vital importance*?"

"The humans have been crowded into a small, poorly ventilated cell without food, water, or waste reclamation facilities. They are dying of thirst and are growing desperate. You will find that humans are quite innovative and extremely dangerous if they feel they have nothing to lose."

"That idiot, Khranga!" Afron shouted. "I'll have the cretin cleaning floors with her crown tendrils."

Grabbing Teela by the hand, Afron took off at a pace so rapid that Teela had to run to keep from being dragged.

Beth woke up coughing violently; she spit to clear her mouth of a thick ball of mucus and blood. Ruth knelt cautiously beside her, careful not to be inadvertently attacked as Beth regained consciousness.

"You've been out a long time, Beth. I think this last time you may have punctured a lung. Margaret said if you take another hit, it could kill you," Ruth pleaded.

"Then the rest of you better get off your asses and do something to help me!" Beth shouted, bringing on another set of ragged coughs.

"We did, and we still lost!" Marsha said. "I took a friggin' shot in the gut and so did Ruth, and while you've been napping, we made a plan for escape that will work better than your dumbass idea of charging armed guards." Marsha glared down at Beth.

"You're right. It was a stupid, impulsive move." Beth pushed herself painfully to her feet. Flexing slowly to gauge the full extent of her injuries, she looked at the troubled and frightened expressions of those around her.

"What can I do to help with this escape plan of yours?" she asked Marsha.

"Not my plan, man; it's Ruth's," Marsha said. "But it's a good plan, really good. Ruth found a panel by the door and figured out how to open it. She thinks she can hotwire the door and make it open. But I don't think you should fight. Ruth is right; you don't look good. I think you're hurt pretty bad."

Before Beth could respond, the compartment door hissed open. Two armed guards with charged pulse rifles stepped in, followed by two more. The group immediately retreated from the guards. Failure to give them room in the past had led to punishing blasts from their pulse rifles.

"Do nothing. Wait until they leave," Ruth said, hoping the guards wouldn't notice the open panel by the door. The guards stood shoulder to shoulder across the small chamber like a firing squad. Through the doorway, an alien entered that was not armed or dressed like the others. This one was rather large, even fat, as indicated by rolls of flesh around its neck and waist. Its uniform was refined and covered with insignias and emblems.

"We have ourselves a superior officer here, folks," Beth said, studying the new arrival.

The officer pointed to Bill and said something. The guards herded the group to one side away from Bill. Two unarmed guards came in and began to drag Bill from the room.

"Don't worry, Bill. They won't get you far. We're going to come out in a few seconds and surprise them," Ruth said, her voice weak and unsure.

"Ahm not 'fraid," Bill said. "Don't ya'all worry 'bout me. Take care of yourselves. Get the hell out if ya can."

The fat officer stood there for a minute, the guards resuming their line across the room. Studying them intently, it finally held its hands out with palms up and bowed its head, turned, and walked out the door. The guards cautiously backed out, and the door slid shut once they were gone.

"Positions, everyone!" Ruth shouted as soon as the door closed.

Marsha and Crystal took positions in front of the door like sprinters at the starting line. Catherine and Ann took positions behind them, followed by Margaret, who looked more like a terrified child than the attack soldier she was supposed to be. Beth pushed up alongside Margaret, spit onto the floor, and smiled a bloody grin at her, an attempt at reassurance that unnerved the already-frightened nurse.

At the open panel, Ruth worked with the contents. There was a crackling and a flash of light, followed by a loud pop.

"Shit!" Ruth shouted, jerking her hand out of the panel. Holding her burned and smoking fingers in the palm of her other hand, she looked up at the disappointed expressions of the group.

"All things are relative," Ruth said. "This door is electromechanical. I'm just unfamiliar with the details of this configuration. There's more power here than I thought. These aren't like wires; they're more like tubes or pipes. I *can* do this!" She wrapped her hand with cloth for insulation. "I know I can do this. Give me a minute."

"Oh dear God," Rebecca prayed from the back of the room where she was crouched on her knees, her hands clasped before her face. "We beseech you to guide Ruth's hands so that we might escape our bonds and rescue our brother Bill."

"Amen. Now shut up!" Beth said, in hopes of ending the prayer before it had a chance to roll into another sermon.

There was another crackling sound, followed by another flash of light and a pop. This time, however, the door slammed open with a deafening clang.

Khranga's deputy director nearly knocked Afron over when she came running out of an alcove from an outer spoke. Out of breath, the warrior dropped onto her knees and spoke with an urgency bordering on panic.

"Your … Eminence, … there has been an … incident!" The deputy glanced from Teela to Afron.

"Proceed," Afron directed.

"The beasts have escaped. Khranga … and three others, maybe more, dead. They have … weapons … and have switched them to lethal pulse."

"Why has no one sounded the alarm? You idiots! Sound the alarm. I want every warrior not manning a critical station to cordon off the forward area. I want fighters standing by to launch if they try to steal a ship. I want any ship that launches without orders destroyed before it clears the hold."

"Yes, Your Eminence!" The warrior turned and ran.

Seething, Afron rotated her head in slow circles on her stiff neck. She tightened her grip on Teela's hand, turned, and narrowed her eye slits to creases to emphasize the seriousness of her inquiry.

"What other items of *vital importance* should I know about?" she asked.

9 - Guests

The alarm klaxon sounded, a deep electronic thrum that vibrated throughout the vessel. The corridors filled with warriors responding to messages on the communication panels. Afron and Teela moved with the flow, not quite keeping up. When they arrived at the forward area of the isolation zone, Afron directed a warrior to force a path through the crowd and pulled Teela behind her. Reaching the forward perimeter of the crisis area and spying Khranga's first lieutenant, Afron demanded the status of the incident, the intensity of her telepathy evident in the large warrior's wince and cocked head.

"Khranga went in with four armed warriors to bring out the damaged beast you sent for. They removed the beast from the holding cell and were in the process of securing it for transport when the door to the holding cell opened without direction from the controls. The other beasts poured from the cell and overpowered Khranga and three guards. When my support group arrived, they were driven back with weapon fire. They now hold the subcorridor from the main access to the transit tubes."

"Didn't you fire back? Didn't you charge their position?"

"Yes, Your Eminence, but they have Khranga and have threatened her existence if we charge them."

"Threatened Khranga's existence? They understand rank and speak our language now?" Afron barked.

"No, Your Eminence, but they fired lethal pulse blasts and then held Khranga out where we could see her with a pulse rifle directed at her head."

"It's a pity they didn't end her existence and save me the trouble."

Pushing Teela against the wall, Afron leaned close and spoke into her mind. *If this situation is not resolved immediately, you and your new memories will be of no use to me! Demonstrate your value by getting the beasts to surrender. They must not learn of our ability to transfer. If you tell them of this, you and they will cease to exist.*

Without waiting for a response, Afron jerked Teela roughly forward and shoved her at the lieutenant.

"This birthing unit thinks she can get these beasts to surrender. If she succeeds, provide them with food, water, and a secure, well-ventilated compartment with at least one waste reclamation unit. If she fails, you will attack. If this is necessary, terminate Khranga and the other idiots that were captured with her, but the beasts and this birthing unit must not be damaged beyond repair. I don't care how many of your worthless tit-suckling warriors have to throw themselves into lethal fire; I want this incident resolved by the end of this shift, or I will personally escort you and your entire subsection to the nearest reclamation unit."

"Yes, Your Eminence!" the lieutenant shouted, and grabbed Teela around the waist before Afron could add another insult, lifting her off her feet. She spun around and took off at a full run through the crowded corridor.

At the bend in the corridor where the escape attempt had reached a standoff, the warrior stopped and dropped Teela onto her feet. The lieutenant held her roughly by the arm and hissed into her face.

"You have fifty bits until I order a full assault. I may not be allowed to end your existence, birther, but the damage you will suffer will challenge the skills of the biotechs to repair you to acceptable utility."

The lieutenant passed Teela to a field warrior who pulled her to the edge of the corner. Before leaving her alone and unarmed, the field warrior informed her that the beasts were shooting at anything that moved beyond that point.

Teela surveyed the turn in the corridor. The wall before her and to her right was cratered by full-charge pulse blasts. Having decided on a course of action, she was pulling her arm into the sleeve of her tah to use as a flag of truce when she was suddenly shoved out into the open. Falling onto her face and chest, she slid into the corner. Three pulse blasts hit the wall over her head as she fell, one so close that her crown tendrils stung from the heat.

Slowly turning her head to look down the hall, she found her vision blocked by the end of a lowered gurney. She raised her sleeve cautiously above the edge of the tray and waved it back and forth, hoping she would not be shot at. She strained to find the human words for what she wanted to say. Each word came with great difficulty.

"Doe ahn't shoe hoot … I ham na-hot armed," she managed to croak out, knowing the English was poorly articulated.

"Show us your hands, asshole." Teela recognized Crystal's accent.

She rolled onto her back and raised one hand; when it didn't vaporize, she raised the other. She sat up and looked back down the corridor to find the warriors glaring defiantly at her.

Turning slowly, she scanned the narrow corridor. She could see thermal outlines of three shooters crouching in the darkness, aiming their weapons from the safety of alcoves and doorways in the distance. Bill was strapped into the gurney. With the exception of his bandaged face and hands, he appeared uninjured.

"Yoh … okay, Pill?" Teela asked as she released his restraints. Bill turned his head toward Teela as though he were straining to see her through his bandages.

"What's happening? Is that you, Dade?"

"Noh, … but heh whan me to help, ahn I whan to."

Teela laced her arm around Bill's elbow. Together they stood and began to walk down the narrow corridor into the seemingly impenetrable darkness. At the first alcove, Crystal stood in the shadows, the glowing tip of her charged pulse rifle pointed at her. There were no sounds except for the soft hum of energized weapons and the brittle crunch of broken glowlamps under their feet.

"In here," a low voice directed from inside the hatchway of a darkened compartment. Teela was certain it was Beth. She could clearly see the thermal images of Khranga and two warriors lying on their backs at the far end of the room. From their heat signatures, Teela knew they were still alive. Auras of heat radiated from each side of the door inside the room, and the strong odors of sweat and urine engulfed her crown tendrils in thick, noxious waves. Teela anticipated the ambush just inside the doorway.

"I haf no we-pons," she stated softly as she led Bill into the compartment.

Marsha grabbed her by the arm as she passed through the door and swung her into the wall. Teela didn't resist as she was pushed to the floor and her arms pulled behind her back. The compartment glowbar was energized, and the small cell slowly illuminated with pale radiance.

Teela lay motionless as Marsha and Beth bound her arms with strips of cloth that had been torn from their clothing and braided into a crude rope. Searching her for weapons, Beth pulled Dade's wallet from the pocket of her tah.

"What the hell are you doing with this?" Beth asked, tapping the floor in front of Teela's prone face with the wallet.

"Proof … tatt Dade … haas com … comun-ick-hated wit meh." Teela's breath sent the dust on the floor rolling away from her face in little puffs. Her position and discomfort made the words even more difficult to pronounce. Using her foot, Beth rolled Teela onto her back and stood over her, pointing a pulse rifle at her face. Teela turned her head to the side to escape the weapon's heated tip.

"Start talking, Squirt."

Teela spoke slowly, trying to enunciate the words as clearly as possible. The difficulty of making the foreign sounds caused her to contort the muscles of her mouth and expose her teeth in a most disquieting display.

"Dade, han now hu Beth, haf mede seer-ee-ohs errors in judge-mont. You haf rep-eat-deadly at-hacked dose who haf sought to rescue you. We haf been tri-hing to protect ourselves wit-out har-mink you. The … communik-ation took longer than expected, and we—"

"Wait a minute! You didn't rescue us; we rescued ourselves, and at no small cost." Beth spat out the words with unrepressed vehemence.

"Yes, han noh. Hu librated the vessel fum da Kahshinki, but den yur vessel wahs dis-sabled by de at-hacking craft, han woot haf been destroyed hat we not inter-veened. If we hat not brought you aboard when weh dit, you would haff frozen or suff-cated in a short time. Finding you waahs a surprize. We hex-pected hescaped Korlah to be on dah vessel, han we dit not hex-pect to be ah-saulted."

"And what about locking us up in here to die of thirst?"

"Wit-out communik-hating, how could weh know your needs or coin-vince you that we mean you no haaam. Had you not staged dis escape attempt, Bill woot be get-hink med-cal help by now an duh rest huf you would be getting da food, water an a larger room wit a toilet, as I, … uh, as Dade had quest-ted."

"I don't believe this bullshit. I want some proof. How about some water, right now!" Beth demanded, her voice rasping from exertion, injury, and lack of water.

"Did you notice how I entered the hallway?" Teela asked, her voice losing its gentle, apologetic poise as she grew angry. With anger came clarity. The words flowed more easily, without straining.

"Yeah, you jumped. So what?"

"I wahs pushed. Da soldiers there were hoping you woot shoot me, thus releasing them from their orders to wait until I was given a chance to negotiate your surrender. You see, if I fail, and I wasn't given much time to succeed, they will pour down that hallway with a vengeance that you cannot imagine. They are saying that you have killed these three. That gives them considerable leverage to kill every one of you without reprimand, and every one of them that dies in the process will be celebrated with honor."

"Your buddy, the fat one over there," Beth said pointing to Khranga, "I know that's a general or something from that fancy uniform and the way the others kiss his fat ass. If your soldiers charge us, he'll be the first one fried."

"He's a she, and it was her troops that saved your lives by bringing you aboard. She is likely the only one of them that truly respects your heroic efforts. Now, pay attention. The orders are, if I fail, the attacking troops will hammer all of you and me to bloody pulps. They will kill her and the two soldiers to spare them the dishonor of failure. We're running out of time. You're in charge now, so make a decision! And keep in mind; you're making it for all of these people. Decide now!"

"I think it's telling the truth," Marsha pleaded from behind Beth. "I … I don't wanna fight these things again, not if we don't have to. Please, Beth."

"I got a feeling bout this one here, Sarge. I trust um. No good reason, jus' a gut feeling. Sides, ahm too good looking ta get beat up any mo'." Bill rumbled smoothly from the darkness.

"Go get the others. And stay in the shadows," Beth ordered, sending Marsha rushing off into the hallway.

"Darkness gives you no advantage, Beth. We see heat, and we can see you in the shadows as clearly as in the light," Teela explained with casual disregard for divulging strategic content, hoping to encourage Beth to surrender.

Switching the pulse rifle off, Beth leaned it in the corner by the door. She bent over, grabbed Teela under the arms and lifted her to her feet. Spinning her brusquely around to face the wall, she began to remove the bindings. She leaned in close as she loosened the last wrap and whispered a warning into Teela's ear. "You damn well better be telling the truth. 'Cause if you're lying—"

The rest of the group filed back into the small compartment, sparing Teela the remainder of Beth's threat. The group crowded into the room but remained as far away from Teela and the other Korlah as the cramped quarters permitted. Beth shoved her way over to the door as the last of the group arrived.

Her hands untied, Teela turned and faced the group. Those who weren't looking expectantly at Beth watched Teela with a mixture of anger and disgust.

"I'm so damn tired I can't fight anymore anyway. What now, Squirt?" Beth asked.

Beth's complexion was a waxen gray, and dark rings under her eyes emphasized the bruises and contusions on her forehead, nose, and chin. All vestiges of the robust strength she had once radiated were gone. The group as a whole looked beaten and defeated.

"This was a misunderstanding," Teela said, speaking to the group. "It was not a battle. You have not lost, and they have not won. I know that you have no reason to trust me—but try. Everything will be all right. I give you my word."

The group stood mute, their eyes glazed from exhaustion and thirst. Teela knew she had to end this soon.

"All right, Reverend," Beth said, placing her hand on Rebecca's shoulder, "this looks like a good time for another one of those prayers of yours."

Rebecca, who had been hunched over in the corner with her long, stringy crimson hair hanging over her face, straightened up, pushed her hair back, and smiled at Beth.

"Yes, it is. It certainly is. We will have a prayer circle. Everyone join hands. Everyone, please," Rebecca said, her typical expression of worry replaced with an enthusiastic smile.

The group joined hands in a tight ring, and Rebecca began a fire and brimstone prayer for salvation from evil.

Teela watched as they joined hands. Glancing at her own clawed hands, she suddenly felt excluded and awkward. She cautiously made her way around the group of humans to get over to Khranga, who was stretched out on the floor with her hands and feet tied. She knelt beside the senior director and began to remove her bindings while explaining the status of the situation.

"No time for questions, Khranga. Afron has decreed that should we fail to get these humans into more acceptable quarters with food and water by the end of this shift, you, me, and your entire staff are to be reclaimed. The only way out of this is to work together. Do you understand?"

Khranga grunted a reluctant agreement.

While Teela untied one of the warriors, Khranga untied the other. The group of humans remained in the prayer circle, holding hands as the Korlah warriors retrieved their weapons and body armor. Teela picked up the weapon Beth had set in the corner and handed it to Khranga.

"The food and water is not a problem, Teela, but where else can I contain these beasts? You have spoken with Afron; where does she want me to put them?" Khranga asked, trying to avoid responsibility for another bad decision. Thinking quickly, Teela made the choice for her.

"The last Nursery at the forward end of the Shell section is empty and will not be needed for another cycle. It is only one drop and four levels down from here and has only one way in from the aft end, making it easy to guard and contain. The birthing units can see to the delivery of food and water, and your section will only have to provide guards."

"Afron selected this location?" Khranga asked, shocked that the beasts would be placed in such a sensitive location.

"The choice of the location is not your concern; yours is getting this group there in the next fifteen bits."

"You will assume the responsibility for this location choice; do you agree to this?" Khranga asked.

"Yes, Senior Director, I assume responsibility," Teela answered, bowing and gesturing with respect.

Khranga left one of her warriors to stand guard outside the door and then departed with the other to confer with her lieutenants. Teela stood just inside the door, keeping watch for problems both inside and outside the room.

The prayer ended and the members of the group either stood or sat, except for Beth, who leaned back in the corner. As Teela moved through the group she felt everyone watching her, and she didn't need to look at their dry, chapped lips, thirst-glazed eyes, and angry, bitter expressions to know they hated her. She was keenly aware that they believed she and all the other Korlah were responsible for their suffering. To a large degree, she agreed with them. What she didn't know was how she was going to repair the damage that had been done. How would she be able to build trust and understanding between species so different, and yet so much alike in their stubborn inflexibility?

She approached Beth and explained what she believed was needed to safely execute the move to their new quarters. "Beth, this move will not be without risk. Many, if not all, who are monitoring our movements will be looking for an excuse, any excuse, to hurt us, and especially you. They desperately want revenge for the embarrassment we have caused them and their leader. For this reason, I'm asking you not to take any provocative actions, regardless of what happens along the way. You must do this for the sake of the others, if not for yourself."

Beth studied Teela's features closely while she spoke. Her face remained expressionless, and when she spoke, her voice was steady and calm.

"Yeah, I get it. We're gonna have to eat crow or they're gonna thrash us. That right?"

"Yes, precisely," Teela replied.

"Okay, I can deal with that. But … this is all weird enough as it is, and now you understand slang and are sure using a lot of big words for someone who could barely speak the language five minutes ago. How is that possible?"

"We don't have the time for this," Teela said, blanching and avoiding Beth's eyes. "Now pay attention. I want you to escort Bill, not in the front of the group or the back, but somewhere in the middle. Be sure to tell everyone else what I said about not reacting to any instigation; I am certain we will be baited, and we must not take the bait."

"Sure, we'll play it according to your calls. But you didn't answer my question, and that makes me even more curious," Beth said, holding out Dade's wallet.

Teela reached for the wallet, but Beth held firmly onto it. Teela's expression hardened as an unfamiliar emotion flared deep within her, causing her crown tendrils to redden and her claws to fold out and into the leather of the wallet.

"We don't have the time," she replied, fighting the urge to challenge Beth's icy stare.

"We're gonna make the time. You see, I figure Bill's a pretty easy guy to describe and recognize when you put him with a group of women, but how is it you know who I am? How is it you know my name?"

Teela felt her crown tendrils losing color again as she tried to conceal the truth. Korlah required exceptional emotional control to be able to lie effectively, a trait Teela had never been able to master. This was not the question she had anticipated, and she struggled to come up with a convincing lie, certain that Beth could see right through her. After a moment's hesitation, Teela responded.

"Your delays are going to cost these people their lives. Is that what you want?" Teela shouted.

"You're gonna answer my questions. Maybe not now, but you will tell me what you've done with Dade. You got that, Squirt!" Beth shouted back. "Until then, you won't mind if I hang onto this until I can give it back to him, personally." Beth twisted the wallet and tried to pull it out of Teela's grasp.

"No, of course not," Teela said. She retracted her claws and released the wallet.

Hearing activity in the hall, she looked to the door and then back to Beth. "You need to get your group briefed and ready to move. Remember what I said: these next few minutes will be very dangerous for all of us." Teela turned and walked to the door.

"Oh, and by the way, Shorty," Beth called after her, "Dade give you that gold necklace you're wearing? It sure looks pretty with that cute little blue dress."

Blue. My tah is blue, not light gray, Teela thought, realizing the error of her perception in the way her combined memories had defined it. Rebecca's crimson hair appeared as slate gray now. She wished she could see colors with her Korlah eyes, like the colors now clear and vivid in her memories.

Khranga's lieutenant, the one that had been so hostile to Teela earlier, approached the door with ten warriors. Behind them a line of other warriors each pushed one of the traylike gurneys. Teela panicked at the thought of trying to get the group to voluntarily climb into the gurneys; she didn't want to consider trying to do it forcibly. She placed herself in the middle of the doorway as the lieutenant arrived.

"It will take too much time to put them in restraints. I will lead, and they will follow," Teela said to the lieutenant.

"If they resist being put into restraints, they will be damaged." The lieutenant grinned viciously.

Teela smiled in the most patronizing manner she could summon and bowed her head. With palms up, she responded with saccharin sweetness. "They will not resist, Lieutenant; however, you will use up the last few bits loading them, and then you will have insufficient time to deliver them to Shell section before the end of this shift. Soon after, Afron will have you and all your brave warriors reclaimed, as she has promised. And I am certain you are aware that she's very good about keeping her promises."

Teela bowed deeply and stepped out of the way, holding her breath and hoping that if her bluff didn't work, Beth and the others wouldn't resist being put into the gurneys.

The lieutenant stood in the doorway and looked at the group of humans. They had formed a line, two by two with their heads down, looking very submissive. Turning, the lieutenant screamed orders on the change in plans to her troops. She turned and hissed orders to Teela.

"You will lead the beasts to the Shell section, and if one so much as raises a hand in defiance, I will exterminate the lot."

Moving close to the lieutenant to ensure tight eye contact and speaking with calculated certainty, Teela emulated the intimidation she had seen Afron utilize so effectively.

"Do not assume that you can silence all who would tell of dishonorable actions. You know that the beasts have terminated Kahshinki. Your orders are to preserve them. To terminate their existence without just cause would be suicide. Or are you too dense to realize that's why Khranga sent you, and didn't choose to handle this herself?"

The lieutenant's eyes burned with rage and her crown tendrils rose up and darkened as she fought to restrain her fury.

"Get them moving, now!" she screamed, her crown tendrils fully engorged and claws extended. Teela shrank back involuntarily. Turning away, she signaled for the group to follow.

"Come, stay close, and do nothing to provoke them," Teela advised.

Carefully skirting the angry lieutenant, the group moved down the narrow corridor toward the transit spoke where they would drop to the inner levels. At each intersection, alcove, and doorway stood armed warriors. The group shuffled slowly down the corridor, bumping into each other in their efforts to move as a tight column. Behind Teela were Crystal and Catherine, then Beth and Bill, Margaret and Rebecca, and Ann and Tiffany, with Ruth and Marsha bringing up the rear. As they approached the transit spoke, Teela realized that the humans had never dropped or risen in a transit spoke before. Quickly providing instructions as she would for a group of young shells, she described the process of transiting the low-gravity tubes that ran from the inner to the outer levels of the immense vessel.

"Do not be afraid to travel down the spoke. When you step into the opening, you drop slowly and directly down to the Shell section. That will take us two hundred levels into the ship, or about a half mile. Once in the Shell section, we will go down four more levels, only ten feet each, one at a time. Step out of the spoke as soon as you land at the bottom. We have no time to waste. Follow me."

With that brief explanation, Teela stepped in backward, motioning for the next two to follow. Gliding down through the dimly lit spoke, Teela looked up and watched as the group entered in pairs, a few seconds apart. The descent took about three minutes, falling at a maximum controlled terminal velocity of three feet per second. The transit spoke echoed the sounds of the group traveling down. There were a few gasps and moans and Rebecca was praying, but to Teela's relief, no one screamed.

Teela stepped out of the spoke when she landed and waited for Crystal and Catherine to land a few seconds later, giggling as they stepped out. Teela had seen the same reaction from many of the young shells on their first encounter with a transit spoke. Waiting until Bill and Beth arrived safely, Teela stepped into the next spoke down.

Three more times, three more levels, and Teela finally stepped off into level 36 of the forward Shell section corridor. Crystal and Catherine stepped off next. After a pause, much too long of a pause, Teela looked up the spoke in time to see Rebecca and Margaret forcibly shoved into the spoke at the level above. She shouted for Crystal and Catherine to gather the group together and wait for her.

Teela jumped into an adjacent out-spoke and used the ridges lining the spoke as rungs to accelerate her ascent. Leaping out at the level above, she found Bill and Beth surrounded by three warriors. Bill was crouching protectively over Beth, who cowered on the floor. Two warriors were striking at Beth with the butts of their pulse rifles, while the third tried to drag her out from under Bill.

"Kahshinki slime!" Teela screamed, hurling the insult at the warriors with all the volume her small frame could produce. Teela knew that if she attacked them, a physical or armed reprisal would likely result, one that she couldn't hope to win. Setting her priorities, she stood by the transit spoke and directed the others onto the next spoke down as they arrived, all the while hurling insults and threats in an effort to shame the warriors into stopping their assault.

"Cowards, scrum beetles, refuse worms! You Kahshinki slaves do not deserve the title of warrior. You are nothing, less than the vacuum we travel through. Attacking these two fearless Kahshinki killers, you shame Korlah! You shame our Mission! All will hear of this deed. I will see to it. Real Korlah warriors will curse your names for eternity."

The warriors stopped their attack and turned to face the birther that dared to threaten them. The rage in their eyes was vivid. Teela fought to suppress the fear welling up within her. Focusing the anger she had repressed for years as the lowest of lowly birthing units, she could feel her crown tendrils engorge and darken; the erubescence stimulated her olfactory nerves and heightened her sense of smell.

"You speak boldly for a food whore," the nearest warrior said. "I know of you; you are Teela, the stunted one, the littlest of mothers who will pleasure anyone in exchange for a day's ration. You dare to challenge not only one but three warriors?" The warrior sneered, slinging her pulse rifle as she approached.

Teela looked around the area with mock concern. "I see no warriors. I see only Kahshinki duplicates attacking damaged and defenseless beings that deserve our honor."

She didn't see the warrior's backhand coming. Catching her on the side of the head, the force spun her around and sent her tumbling backward onto the floor.

The anger she had been struggling to access finally exploded within her. Before she was aware of her actions, she was on her feet. She did a hop and a skip, and then placed a well-aimed kick into the warrior's upper abdomen, sending the warrior flying backward off her feet. She landed in a seated position and slammed into the wall of the corridor. The look of surprise on the warrior's face quickly transformed to one of murderous intent. She clambered to her feet with claws extended and crown tendrils fully engorged. Her eyes locked on Teela with predatory intent as she began a cautious stalking approach.

Someone stepped between them; a warrior about three heads larger than Teela and more than a head taller than most warriors. With its back to Teela, the giant was a mountainous barrier between her and the warriors.

"Get out of my way, Shawaugh! This birther has insulted me, and I will take my honor by beating her," the angry warrior cried, her tone more of a request than a demand.

"I am this unit's Spectacle adjutant. We are disciplined and obedient to the rules set by our leaders. We do not brawl in the corridors. If you wish to take honor, I will arrange an event. Do you have an adjutant?" the giant rumbled.

"This is none of your concern, Shawaugh!" the warrior shrieked.

"You are in violation, instigating an unauthorized contest. If you and your accomplices leave immediately, I will see fit to forget this incident; otherwise, I will log this and the other events I have been witness to this shift."

Teela heard a muttered conversation between the warriors and then the sound of their steps as they beat a hasty retreat.

"You should not have interfered, Shawaugh. I swear this error will cost you!" the warrior shouted as she and the two others departed.

The enormous warrior turned around. Teela felt as though her heart had stopped and that she was suddenly living her recurring nightmare. She recognized the face. She had seen it many times in her dreams: a ragged scar ran from deep within the crown tendrils, across the empty eye socket to the bottom of the opposite side of its face. She shrank back, her crown tendrils fading in horror.

"You … I know you," she whispered, wanting to flee but frozen with terror. She was certain that this was the warrior who had pulled her from the wreckage of the Nursery and thrown her injured body in with the dead for reclamation.

"Yes, we are old acquaintances, little mother," Shawaugh said, "but no time to reminisce. You must get your Kahshinki killers to safety. Beware Afron's plans. She means to take control of this Campaign Vessel, to seize power from Shyron and terminate the Mission. You and your new friends somehow fit into her plans. Keeping them safe may prove to be very difficult."

"Yes, thank you," Teela said meekly, her deep bow serving as much to honor Shawaugh for her assistance as to relieve her from seeing the scarred face. Fear and gratitude seized her heart. The cold, crushing grip of the first would not let the warm embrace of the other permit her to ask the question that had tormented her sleep since the last time she looked at this face. She cautiously stepped around Shawaugh with lowered eyes.

Bill was helping Beth to her feet. The hand she held to her mouth was covered with blood that ran down her arm and dripped off her elbow.

"How bad are your injuries?" Teela asked.

"Didn't never touch me. The bastards was trying to get Beth, but I wouldn't let go of her. Nope, I wouldn't let go."

"Thanks, Bill. I'm okay," Beth said weakly. "They sucker punched me, a few loose teeth and split lip is all. I'll be all right. Let's get back to the others. Thanks for coming back, Squirt, and thank your buddy for me."

Teela looked around, but the giant, like the phantom of her nightmares, had vanished.

They found the rest of the group waiting for them on the Shell section level. Within a few minutes, Teela had led the group through the Nursery's isolation hatch. Leaving the armed warriors outside the entrance, she closed and sealed the massive door, locking it from the inside with a seal pin. This emergency isolation method would be apparent in the master control room and entered on the log at two bits, twenty non before the end of the shift, proof that Afron's orders had been followed. The large transparent wall with the integrally mounted access door belied the strength of this chamber. This chamber, like all of the new nurseries, was self-contained, armored, and designed to withstand a full and sustained assault. They were safe. At least, for now.

Khranga was true to her word. Water and protein cakes that looked like oat and currant granola bars were supplied in the dining chamber. Upon discovery of the bounty, the humans surrounded the carts like a pack of hungry dogs. Even Beth with her bloodied mouth drank thirstily from a large flask of water. Margaret made sure Bill got his share while she eagerly consumed her own.

Teela sat down at a large semicircular desk facing the transparent wall adjacent the door. The desk, intended for the senior mother of the Nursery, was equipped with a very comfortable seat that felt heavenly to Teela's aching back. Feeling exceptionally tired and sleepy, she leaned back and closed her eyes to rest them—just for a minute.

10 - Repair

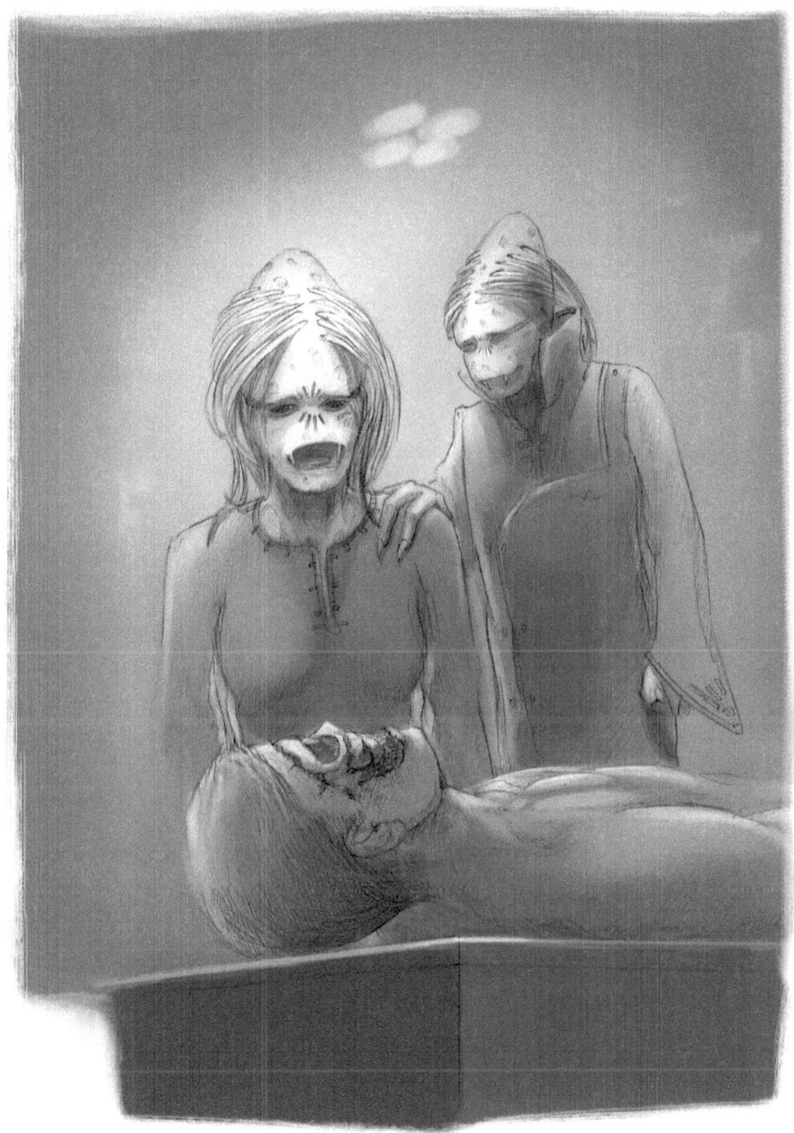

Her slippers made a soft slapping sound that was absorbed by the vastness of the dimly lit corridor. Her head was down and shoulders slumped to make her look small and inconspicuous. She plodded along mechanically, not really thinking of where she was going, relying on instinct. Suddenly she stopped and looked back from where she had come and then forward to where she was going. The corridor was unfamiliar, lacking any marking as to level or location. There were no alcoves, doors, or communication consoles for as far as she could see. A feeling started at the base of her spine and traveled up through her abdomen—the icy flood of terror. For the first time in her life, she didn't know where she was.

Waking with a start, Teela sat up. The details of the dream quickly faded, leaving only the anxious discomfort that follows a frightening experience. The communication panel was flashing and a warrior on the other side of the transparent wall was banging on it with the butt of her pulse rifle, making a muted tapping sound. Once she saw that Teela was awake, the warrior returned to her guard post across from the Nursery door.

Teela pressed the display pad on the communications panel and read the message:

> TEELA20.10127, REPORT IMMEDIATELY TO LEADERSHIP SECTION THREE, TACTICAL AFFAIRS. AFRON 35.7

Only two shifts earlier, such a message would have sent her into a panic. Yawning deeply and stretching, she stopped once again to marvel at the way her claws retracted into the tips of her four digits. She tried unsuccessfully to remember what five fingers without claws had been like.

The group was sprawled out around the sleep chamber in a chaotic array. Bill sat in a corner with his hands crossed over his lap, swaying back and forth. Teela saw his jaw muscles working in response to the pain he was suffering. The others were all over the place. Most had pushed several of the little beds together, but a few had just draped themselves over one and gone to sleep. Beth and Margaret were snoring loudly.

Teela quietly approached Bill and told him it was important that he get to the medical facility as soon as possible, and then woke Ruth to instruct her to close and lock the door after she and Bill left. Arm in arm, the large black man and the little birthing unit made an unlikely couple. As soon as they exited the Nursery, the senior warrior challenged them.

"The beasts are to be contained within the Nursery by order of Senior Director Khranga."

"This human is to be taken to the Biotech section for repairs by order of Director Gremensh and Leader Afron. Please feel free to confirm the order, and while doing so, arrange for a protective escort for us. We are already very late, so be quick," Teela demanded, imitating Afron.

The warrior stared at her, daring Teela to meet her gaze. Her challenge ignored, the warrior punched her message into the communication panel and then resumed her contemptuous glare. Avoiding her eyes and feeling suddenly conspicuous, Teela looked down at her filthy tah and dirt-streaked arms. She certainly did not present a very intimidating appearance. The message screen flashed, and the warrior read the reply. Turning back to Teela, the warrior bowed respectfully.

"The director expresses honor for your successful Mission and is anxiously awaiting the arrival of the … beast. Your escort is on its way and should arrive shortly." The warrior relayed the message, unaware that Teela, unlike most birthing units, could read.

Both warriors were studying her closely, making Teela feel exposed and uncomfortable until a four-warrior escort showed up and rescued her from their relentless stares. They proceeded to the outer levels, two warriors leading, two following.

"What's your name, mistah?" Bill asked as they walked.

"Teela, and I guess you could say I'm a miss. My official name, translated literally, is T series, E Group, Ela Clan, Twentieth Generation, Shell 10127."

"I'm sorry. I thought 'cause your voice was so raspy, an' I can't see an' all," Bill said.

"No offense taken, Bill. I'm the one who should be sorry for taking so long to get you some help. It won't be much longer now. We're almost to the medical facility."

When they arrived at the Biotech section, they were directed into one of the large repair chambers where Gremensh waited with a team of six biotechs.

"Teela!" Gremensh ran up and looked her over with genuine concern. "Are you damaged? You look terrible, and your eye is badly swollen!"

"The result of insulting angry warriors. But let me tell you about it later. This human—his name is Bill—has suffered a serious lacing of his face and hands. Will you be able to repair him?"

"Him? It is a male, as I suspected. How many of the beasts … ah … humans are male?"

"He's the only other one. Does it matter?" she asked, seeing Gremensh's disappointment.

"No, not at all. Come, come, this will be interesting, most interesting!"

The director was obviously excited about the proposed repair and directed Teela's attention to one of the platforms in the room, where the attending biotechs waited. As the techs stepped away, she saw Dade, or, more aptly put, the eviscerated remains of what had once been Dade spread out in pieces across the table. Teela stood transfixed, unable to pull her eyes away. A thick, heavy weight formed in the center of her chest, a nausea that seized her ability to breathe. Something like a voice started as a whisper in the depth of her mind, finally screaming that this was not, could not be real. Unaware of Teela's distress, the director described her discoveries with the eagerness and excitement of a child with a new toy.

"We have been doing cellular examinations and regeneration studies with tissues from this terminated unit. The results of analysis performed using Korlah tissue-grafting processes and chemical compatibility testing have been exceptionally promising. Although there are considerable biological differences between Korlah and human physiology, the genetic similarities are incredible. Standard cellular acceptance treatments have allowed me to graft Korlah and human tissue!

"I believe I could affect tissue repairs on this human with Korlah spares. Unfortunately, the eye sockets are too large and would require extensive reconstruction, and since the human optic nerves are abnormally complex, I doubt that I would be able to make an effective nerve splice. Fortunately, interspecies grafting will be unnecessary because the human tissue and viable eyes needed are available. The salvaged eyes, however, appear to be defective; not from damage sustained, but defective at a genetic level. Vision will be approximately sixty to seventy percent. Will that be acceptable?"

Teela didn't respond. Gremensh's words had gone unheard, muted by the screaming in her mind. She stood silently, staring at the dismembered remains. Gremensh looked at the table and then at Teela's blanched complexion. Suddenly realizing the emotional implications, she ordered the cadaver covered and then inserted herself between Teela and the grisly remains.

"Teela? What is wrong?" Gremensh inquired softly, looking into glazed eyes that were open, yet unseeing. Teela's eyes snapped shut, and she shook her head violently. When she opened them, she focused on the director, whose face was now pursed with concern.

"I apologize, Director. I was thinking … um …. Oh yes. Bill is hurting. Is there something you can do to ease the pain from the damage, at least until you are able to perform the repairs?" Teela asked mechanically, scrunching her eyes shut and rubbing her temples with the heels of her palms as she tried to expunge the frightening image and voice that lingered in her mind. The mannerism was quite unusual for a Korlah, and Gremensh eyed her warily as she answered.

"Temporary nerve paralysis will be utilized for sensory attenuation. This is part of the repair process that we are prepared to commence now. Direct the human onto the adjacent repair platform, and my team will begin."

Teela paused, finding it difficult to consciously switch to English. Closing her eyes, she clenched her fists and concentrated to initiate the process needed to speak to Bill. A few seconds later, she straightened from her slumped posture, and her eyes snapped open.

"Good news, partner. We've got a bunch of doctors and nurses here who think they can fix your hands, rebuild your face, and maybe even give you a set of working eyes. Best of all, they're standing by and ready to stop the pain."

"I like that idea… no pain, I mean, but I'm kinda scared bout the rebuilding. Where's Dade? Thought he was spose to be here."

"Dade's nearby," Teela said, glancing at the covered remains. "He's sleeping. Listen, Bill, I got you and the others out of that hole you were in and got you food and water, too. You said earlier that your gut feeling was that I could be trusted. What's your gut telling you now?"

"I'm sorry … I'm just real tired, an' … Beth was saying how maybe they kilt Dade, an' that you … well, when you talk, it's like I can see his face. Ahm jus' scared, ya know?"

"Yeah, I know. I'm scared too. Listen to me, Bill. Trust me. They're gonna fix you. The doctor sounds real confident, but I won't bullshit you. There are no guarantees, at least none that I've found. For what it's worth, you have my personal guarantee that these folks are going to do everything in their considerable power to heal you. I've seen them repair the face of one of the workers. I know they can do it. No one is forcing you into this. This is your decision, Bill. I'll take you back to the others right now if that's what you want. You tell me what you want to do."

There was a long silence while Bill chewed his bottom lip, moving his head around like he was looking for an answer—something, anything other than the choices he had to select from.

"I hurt so bad I cain't take it no more," Bill said, his deep voice beginning to crack.

"They say they can stop the pain right now. If it doesn't work, I won't let them continue, okay?"

"They gonna tie me down?"

Teela looked at the table. The restraints were laid open and ready. Teela began speaking to Gremensh in English, but stopped midsentence to switch to Korlah.

"Can … you do this … repair … without restraints?" Teela asked, finding it difficult to separate the English from the Korlah words.

"Considering its violent nature, I think it would be prudent to keep it restrained. I insist on it," Gremensh answered, unnerved by the suggestion.

Switching back to English, Teela spoke to Bill, "The Doc has seen a video of you beating that toad to death and is worried about being included in an instant replay. They are more afraid of you then you are of them. I'll stay right here the whole time. If I don't like how things are going, I'll stop it, like I did when they attacked Beth."

After another long pause, Bill responded, his attempt at sounding casual unable to mask the fear in his voice.

"Okay, if we're gonna do it, let's giterdone."

Gremensh had prepared the operating table specifically for this scenario. The main table was equipped with two smaller platforms on each side for Bill's injured hands. The arrangement had the disquieting appearance of a crucifix. The director had apparently done her homework and was prepared to treat all of Bill's injuries simultaneously. There was a workstation set up at each hand and one at Bill's head. Tools and instruments Teela had never fathomed floated in neat rows, suspended as if by magic above each station.

As soon as Teela eased Bill onto the table, six anxious biotechs went to work affixing the restraints, removing his filthy bandages, attaching sensory attenuation leads, and moving additional equipment into position. Teela suddenly felt she was in the way and moved out of the busy work area to a nearby wall.

It wasn't long before the activities stopped and the biotechs stepped back to permit Gremensh to inspect the preparations. Gremensh walked from Bill's right hand to his head to his left hand, closely examining each of the damaged areas.

"The human's tactile and sensory pain perception of the affected areas should be completely attenuated. Confirm this."

"Bill, the doctor says you should not be able to feel any pain."

Bill mumbled something, the effort sending a thick rivulet of saliva running from the corner of his mouth.

"Is your mouth numb?" Teela asked.

Bill nodded affirmation.

"Can you feel your hands or face?"

Bill shook his head no.

"Is it okay for the doctor to begin?"

Bill took a deep breath that he shakily exhaled, and then slowly nodded yes.

"He is ready for you to begin, Director," Teela announced. Before Gremensh could turn away to begin, Teela added, "Director Gremensh, I've given my blood oath that this human warrior of demonstrated honor will not be harmed."

Giving Teela an unconcerned sidelong glance, she turned to the table and responded without looking back.

"I, unlike many of my sisters, do not cause harm. I repair it."

Somehow the statement didn't give Teela the warm fuzzy feeling she would have liked. Agitated and anxious, she clenched her fists and flinched from the stinging pain of her claws piercing her callused palms, reopening wounds that had only just begun to heal.

The three teams began to work simultaneously. Teela stopped watching when they began cutting raw festered tissues away from the open wounds. A visual recording was being displayed at each station depicting the removal of Dade's hand and facial tissues. Teela suspected the techs would use the recordings later as a reference for reattachment to Bill. Gremensh moved about the table like a conductor on stage, stopping at each station to examine the progress and provide guidance whether it was needed or not. Confident that Bill was being properly cared for, Teela looked for a place to wait. She spied a gurney by the door and climbed up onto it. Within moments, she was fast asleep.

11 - Hope

Since the resumption of birthing, the entire surviving population of birthing units had been placed into service. In a recent directive to maximize production before the onset of campaign, the current birthing cycle required each unit to carry six embryos. Now, as the end of their cycle approached, the mothers found their abilities significantly curtailed by the physical demands of this directive. Teela and the much younger eight-to-ten-cycle shells were assigned to assist the mothers with all of the Shell section duties. Since Teela was the only mature birthing unit who was not pregnant, she was now expected to fill in for the senior mothers who more and more frequently demanded her assistance.

She knew that unless she found a good hiding place on her off-shifts, she would be located and directed to cleaning duty or some hectic administrative tasks. A young shell would be sent to find and wake her whenever her services were needed. To avoid these search parties, she had taken to napping in the deep recesses of the archives, curled up on the cases of log bars.

She imagined herself in her hiding spot, trying to get some much-needed sleep before the next shift of cleaning up after the fives. The five-cycle shells were the worst to care for: they could spread more filth in one shift than all the younger shells put together. The idea that her group was scheduled to move to the training section in just a few more on-shifts made Teela smile in her sleep. But someone had found her. They were shaking her and telling her to wake up.

"It's my off-shift. Find another, and leave me alone!" she demanded, refusing to open her eyes.

Grabbed by the shoulders and pulled roughly to her feet, Teela was rudely awakened as she was half-carried and half-dragged out of the biotech chamber by four Leadership section security guards. Her warrior escorts stood outside the door. They looked embarrassed and avoided eye contact as she was dragged away. Struggling to keep pace, Teela tried to pry one of their hands from her arm. Both guards drove the claws of their thumbs deep into the soft flesh of her armpits. Teela screamed.

"Worm spoor! You have no honor. What have I done? Why are you treating me this way?" Teela shrieked with wounded pride. The guards remained mute as they took her deeper into the bowels of the ship to an area where only the leaders and their specially-trained security guards resided.

The Mission Potentate and her ten section leaders were housed in the most remote and heavily-shielded area of the ship with a contingent of elite security guards that acted as the eyes, ears, and arms of the leadership. Since the Kahshinki attack, it was rare to see a leader outside of the Security section, and no one other than the leaders and their security force were ever allowed in. It was rumored that those unfortunate enough to be taken there would not return.

The single spoke that dropped into the Leadership section was guarded at both the top and bottom. Once past the first checkpoint, the group threaded their way through a maze of heavily armored guard stations before arriving at an enormous door that looked like the entrance to a bank vault. One of Teela's guards tapped a communication into an adjacent command console and waited. With a low hissing sound and the groan of heavy machinery, the door moved toward them and then slid to one side, revealing a brightly illuminated archway the size of a normal door. Her two guards guided her through it by the shoulders. The opening was filled with a bright light that caused Teela to cup a hand over her eyes.

"Walk in eleven paces and kneel," one of the guards commanded, pushing her into the archway with a jab in the middle of her back.

The guards stepped back and Teela turned to see the vault door closing. Walking forward, she strained to see beyond the bright light shining down from overhead. She had entered a very large semicircular room from a door in the center of the flat wall. The curved wall was about three times as tall as she was. Approximately halfway up the wall and spaced at equal distances were the decorative insignias of the ten sections, with the large emblem of the Mission in the center. Her eyes slowly adjusted and she began to make out the outlines of figures seated above each insignia.

"Oh Christ!" Teela whispered aloud in English, realizing that she was standing in the center of the Council Chamber.

She fell immediately to her knees and assumed the posture of respect, realizing that she hadn't counted her steps and hoping she wouldn't be punished for failing to recognize the ten section leaders and the Mission Potentate. She thought she could hear murmurs from the leaders, undoubtedly criticizing her pitiful entrance. As she knelt and waited, she realized that the chamber was silent; what she had heard was the murmuring of their thoughts.

It seemed like an eternity that she knelt there, her hands and arms shaking from fatigue and fear. She held the position long enough for the wounds beneath her arms to stop bleeding and the rivulets they had formed on her tah to dry and blacken. The murmuring stopped and the chamber grew menacingly quiet.

"Rise, birthing unit," she was commanded in a soft but demanding tone. Even without introduction, she knew it came from the Leader Potentate.

Teela rose stiffly to her feet, keeping her head bowed. Her tah had stuck in the places where blood had dried. Pulling nervously at the soiled and torn fabric, she tried to make it hang smoothly.

"You do not appear to be the frightening menace my Council has described."

There was a long pause. Teela did not know how to respond to such a comment.

"If you can't speak with your mind, you can speak with your mouth, can't you?" The words stabbed into her thoughts as both question and demand.

"Yes, Your Eminence. I apologize. I didn't realize you were expecting a response."

"Who are you?" the Leader Potentate asked in a tone edged with hostility, expecting an honest answer.

"Birthing Unit T-E-Ela, 20.10127. I … I have not yet been classed or ranked, Your Eminence," she answered, her voice wavering.

We did not ask who you were! We asked who you are! the telepathic voice boomed. Any softness that may have been in the leader's communication was gone, its volume amplified to a skull-splitting command.

Teela clapped her hands to the sides of her head and stood mute. She did not understand the question that made her head ache painfully. She struggled through her tormented thoughts to provide an answer. Finally, after a painfully long silence, she looked up at the Leader Potentate and sobbed.

"I don't know!"

Slowly standing, the aged leader looked around the room until she focused on Afron. "We believe that is the first truthful answer we have been given since this situation came to our attention."

Afron leapt to her feet. "Shyron, it is my responsibility to develop the strategies for dealing with this threat. I have presented no untruths and have done nothing beyond my authority. I have broken no laws!"

"What of your responsibilities to this Council? You have conspired with section directors outside your jurisdiction to bring enemy forces onto our vessel, and you arranged and coordinated an unauthorized transference. Both of these actions violate Council protocol."

"It has not been proven that these are enemy forces, and had I waited for the Council to make a decision before bringing them aboard, they would have ceased. The transference was a tactical decision to facilitate communication. The birthing unit I selected is without utility and was designated for reclamation, so no viable shells would have been wasted in the experiment," Afron responded, defiantly meeting Shyron's glare.

"Yes, the birthing unit was designated for reclamation by you ten cycles ago; however, the order had been delayed because you received threats of retaliation from an individual or individuals you have since told us do not exist. It is unusual, though, how these nonexistent entities seem to have significant influence where our security officers feel comfortable traveling. But that's another matter. We will be dealing with it and your other activities soon enough.

"On the present subject, while you were dabbling in these dangerous political adventures outside the Security section, the Council met and agreed that the only sure way to prevent the Kahshinki from utilizing this violent species for additional attacks would be to institute a long-range preemptive strike to sterilize the planet before the Kahshinki can commence harvest."

"What?" Teela screamed. "You can't do that! I … we … they didn't know you were trying to help them. You can't destroy their planet because of a misunderstanding. It's … it's against the Laws of Korlah!"

A look of indulgent surprise creased the deeply wrinkled face of the Potentate. Slowly sitting back down, she folded her hands in her lap and smiled broadly.

"We believe we have discovered another truth," she said, looking down at Teela. "Afron has played down the success of this bestial transfer. You have received more than just the memories, as we were told. You feel as though this beast is a part of you and that you are a part of it—that you share its fate. We further believe that you really are unaware that the leaders of this … human planet are allied with the Kahshinki and have already engaged Korlah forces twice, the first time without provocation. Therefore, by the Laws of Korlah, we are required to order retribution to the full extent of our capabilities.

"You, Teela, or whoever you are, are very quick to quote our laws. But with your composite memories and the fact that by your own omission you do not know who you are, and therefore what alliances you will choose, how can we expect you to follow the Laws of Korlah?"

The Potentate made the painful effort to stand and hobble to the edge of her dais. Placing her bony, withered hands on the rail, she leaned out and looked down at Teela with an air of expectation. Teela looked away, trying desperately to get control of her thoughts. A thought, a voice like a whisper coming from behind or from within, told her that an unprovoked attack from the humans was not possible. She looked around for the source of the whisper, and finally engaged the Potentate's waiting eyes. Recalling the logs she had read of trials and tribunals held in this very chamber, she formulated a plausible response.

"I have neither seen nor heard of any evidence of human involvement with the Kahshinki. For retribution to be honorable, substantiation of complicity is required, and the condemned should be provided the opportunity to present a defense for their actions." Teela fought the urge to smile. Her recollection of a winning argument in Council proceedings regarding matters of cowardice and desertion seemed a reasonable foundation for a defense.

"Are we to assume that you are willing to speak in defense of these human leaders, and that you would be willing to accept our decisions? And, of course, share the consequences as their defender?"

The trap Shyron had set was clear. Teela had known coming in that she would not likely live to see the next shift, and had decided in that instant to make ordering her reclamation as difficult and painful for the leaders as she could.

"Not without first seeing the evidence, Your Eminence." Teela bowed respectfully, straining to anticipate the leader's next twist.

Shyron stood and pointed a gnarled finger at the education leader. "Display the logs depicting human involvement and complicity with the Kahshinki."

The aged leader moved slowly to her seat, and as the logs began to display on the flat wall behind Teela, she provided narration. The room dimmed and the wall seemed to disappear. It was replaced by giant three-dimensional images, four angles of a single docking bay split into segregated areas. Teela moved away from the wall to bring the images into proper perspective.

"Eighteen cycles, sixty-four shifts ago, a time in our lives that we who were fortunate enough to survive recall with bitter clarity. A long-range patrol returned shortly after having departed. Claiming a fault with their hyperlight drive, they requested docking for repairs. The arriving ship met the description of one that had departed recently. It also presented the correct sortie designation and was, therefore, directed without further investigation to the aft accoutrements bay to facilitate repairs. Once shuttled from the docking bay to the repair facility airlock, the occupants departed their vessel."

The images shifted from the docking bay to the airlock. The midsection of the vessel dropped open and a group of twelve individuals, wearing outfits that Teela's combined memories recognized as chemical weapon suits, exited at a trot. From their shape and stance, Teela could see they were neither Kahshinki nor Korlah, and could, in fact, be human. They immediately split into three groups of four. Two carried large automatic carbines, and the other two worked together to move a very heavy package of seven cylinders, each approximately three feet long and strapped together in bundles on rollers.

The screens shifted as the teams moved out of the airlock and into the corridors. There was an armed soldier in the lead and another following the two carrying the cylinders. The armed intruders shot all Korlah they encountered, the weapons' flashes giving the dim images a stroboscopic appearance. One group proceeded into the Energy section, one continued to the Supplies section, and the third headed to the Shell section. Along the way, each group stopped at key ventilation and access junctions, released a cylinder from the bundle, and activated what appeared to be a timing device on the end. In each section, groups of Korlah dropped to the ground in spasmodic convulsions. Explosions in the areas where canisters had been left began blanking out the monitoring screens one at a time.

What followed were visual logs of the aftermath taken with handheld recorders. Entire community sleeping chambers were filled with lifeless bodies contorted in death, their mouths agape in evidence of their final agony. Thousands and thousands of bodies, some riddled with bullet holes, were stacked on top of each other. Scenes from the Shell section showed stacks and stacks of tiny bodies, some twisted from the convulsions, others burned and dismembered by explosions. Teela covered her face and began to weep. She recognized the area she had been recovered from. The dead were most certainly birth sisters and mothers she had known.

"Over two point five million died! The main propulsion drive coils, agricultural production gardens, food processing, atmospheric regulation, and other critical components were severely damaged in what was an exceptionally well-orchestrated attack. This was a tactic the Kahshinki had never attempted in all of the campaigns we have ever fought. Since leaving our home system, we have always been on the offensive, and the Kahshinki have fled before us. We therefore conclude this cowardly attack was of human origin, perpetrated in complicity with the Kahshinki."

Teela uncovered her face and looked up to see battered and burned human soldiers, their rubber-edged dog tags and uniform patches and paraphernalia on display. The visual record of examinations performed on weapons, shoes, helmets, uniforms, and other manufactured items played as the leader continued.

"We had never seen this species before, and the manufacturing techniques and weapons technology are primitive and not of Kahshinki origin. The murderers were delivered in a short-range Kahshinki fighter disguised as a long-range Korlah scout ship. This disguise enabled them to use the engine section as a cargo bay. The fighter and its Kahshinki pilot did not escape, but the long-range freighter that had ferried it here jumped to hyperlight before we could destroy it. The freighter had to be at the end of its range and vanished in black space. This was a suicidal act, wholly unlike the Kahshinki. At first, we thought these were new hybrid duplicates from the current Kahshinki harvest; however, genetic examinations verified that each and every human warrior was a genetic original.

"Since that attack, we have lived in constant fear of this new and unpredictable species. We have been forced to concentrate all our regenerative powers on rebuilding our defenses and restoring propulsion. The entire complement of this vessel has been suffering the consequences of this attack ever since."

Pausing for effect until the silence became uncomfortable, the Leader Potentate finally spoke.

"We are sorry that you have been forced to share your mind with one of these beasts, knowing as I do that you yourself bear the scars of their cowardly deceit."

On the wall in giant proportions appeared the image of Teela's naked body being examined on a bio section implantation table. Beneath the image, excerpts from the technician's examination were displayed. The entry read: 'Severe damage verified to be cause of lost reproductive function. Repairs not practical or recommended.' Teela looked away from the images, shamed by the enormous display of the most emotionally damaging moment of her existence.

Numbed by the onslaught, Teela stood silent, staring at the floor. After what seemed like eternity, the picture wall finally went blank and Shyron continued speaking.

"The attacks we expected never came. We have been able to restore propulsion and repair most of our systems. Unfortunately, we lost eighty percent efficiency of our botanical gardens from toxic contamination. The cleanup and repair activities cost us the lives of an additional twenty-seven thousand units from residual toxins. Our limited organic reserves and food generation capacity have required severe rationing to meet our needed population-generation requirements. The recent decision to increase production to six embryos is causing premature deliveries and unacceptably high losses of both new shells and birthing units.

"With the next campaign less than two cycles away, our population of pilots consists of a few hundred trained units, most of which are past reclamation age. The fifteen hundred new pilots we have are barely seventeen-cycle shells that have just now begun flight training. Our assault fleet is one-tenth what it should be and is completely inexperienced. We are gravely concerned about our ability to achieve victory. In our extensive memory, we have never been so unprepared to pursue our Mission objective. Since the attack, we have not encountered these humans again. Until now.

"At first, we believed these humans were staging this apparent escape as a ploy to perpetrate another assault; however, after analysis of the vessel's records and logs, the escape was determined to be genuine."

The wall illuminated again with views from inside the Kahshinki freighter. Images of Bill and Dade killing the Kahshinki crew filled the wall, followed by views of the battle between Kahshinki and Korlah fighters around the disabled freighter.

"Further analysis of the vessel's records verified that the collection was sanctioned by the humans operating the planetary defenses and that the pursuing Kahshinki vessels were piloted by human originals."

"What!" Teela shouted. "Wha … what … do you mean 'sanctioned'? And how do you know the pilots were human?"

The wall filled with excerpts from the freighter's navigational records, depicting its approach to Earth, atmospheric penetration, and a descent toward the west coast of the North American continent. The display was provided in an accelerated mode, slowing to real time only when a message scrolled across the bottom of the screen. The messages were in the random blinking lights used by the Kahshinki and made no sense to Teela. Shyron interpreted the translations during her narration.

"Although we have never been able to completely break the Kahshinki communication codes, we have been able to translate the basic intent of their meanings. On approach, they sent a communication requesting permission to obtain samples. A planetary station acknowledged the approach and granted permission to sample within the confines of designated areas. Coordinates fed from the ground installation were received by the Kahshinki navigational systems and identified as a corridor that the freighter had to remain within. The freighter acknowledged the requirements and continued its approach, until it stopped and obtained its first sample."

The views that followed were rapid vignettes of the abductions, including that of Dade, which Teela recognized with startling clarity.

"Once completed, the Kahshinki signaled that twelve samples had been taken and requested departure coordinates. A different ground station than the first provided a departure trajectory, at which point the freighter left the atmosphere, departed the solar system, and subsequently jumped to hyperlight."

The next images were of charred human remains, the only recognizable portions being an occasional five-fingered glove or a boot. Remnants of instrumentation with English labels and Arabic numerals were spread out for examination.

"This evidence was collected from the debris of the ships destroyed by the escaping freighter and the liberating Korlah fighters. Fortunately, a collision between the freighter and a Kahshinki fighter disabled the fighter and permitted a live capture."

The wall filled with images of the human pilot being extracted from the damaged fighter. The last image, the pilot pacing within a small cell, faded as the lights came back up. Teela wiped the tears that streaked the dirt on her face as she shuffled back to the center of the chamber. Taking a deep breath and concentrating to calm the rage and disappointment that were causing her hands to shake, she turned and faced the Korlah Leader Potentate.

"As I awoke following transference, I felt that I had achieved a state of agreement within. Although I still feel great sorrow at the loss of my human receptacle and a great responsibility to ensure the safety of the humans that escaped from the Kahshinki, I have accepted my role in the Korlah Mission. The agreement I feel is based on the belief that the Laws of Korlah are good and just, and I will continue to follow and support them in the future as I have in the past. However, I do not believe that the wholesale slaughter of an entire planet for the crimes committed by a few leaders of a single species is the retribution our laws imply. Not when, by your own words, you have indicated that there are other options."

A rumble of murmuring rippled around the chamber, rising in intensity as the Council began to debate Teela's statement. The Potentate rose to her feet and extended her arms, causing the chamber to fall silent. Walking back to the edge of her platform, she again leaned on the rail and looked down at Teela. When she spoke, her voice sounded tired and frail.

"We have remained within this aging receptacle long after its utility began to fade. Whereas some of our sister leaders tend to change their shells as some would change their garments, we intend to keep this shell until cessation is imminent. We do this because it helps to remind us of the value of our existence. Having seen and ordered more death and destruction in our many combined memories than any other in this room, we have come to loathe the onset of a campaign. We do not relish the responsibility for ordering the slaughter of millions of a unique species, as it would seem that we are being accused, and we would welcome any options that you may have for the Council's consideration."

"The decision has already been made!" the warrior leader Tooron stood and shouted. Shyron stared with open hostility at the presumptuous protest.

"Decisions made using incomplete or erroneous information are fraught with dangerous consequences. As Mission Potentate and Council Leader, we have authority to either revoke such decisions or invoke consequences, should the decisions be determined to be faulty. Based on the new information that has only recently been revealed to us, we therefore revoke the decision for sterilization, pending review of the new information and any other options that are presented. Are there any who would challenge our authority on this?" Shyron asked.

Looking around the chamber for support and seeing none, Tooron sat down with an angry grunt. The Potentate looked back and forth across the chamber, sifting their thoughts for additional comments. Finding none, she turned back to Teela.

"The Council believes that if it does not eliminate the human threat now, it will be fighting a dual campaign. In our current weakened state, it is doubtful that we will survive even one. If we sterilize the human planet now, before they have a chance to build their forces and before the Kahshinki begin to harvest it, we deny the Kahshinki access to resources they will need to quickly recover from any damages we may inflict. In anticipation of our failure, we have already dispatched long-range couriers to our last outpost to warn of the human threat and have requested a replacement battle vessel be sent to this sector. If we are able to provide enough of a delay, the replacement vessel may arrive before the Kahshinki forces have a chance to depart to the next target system.

"During campaign, whenever an attack group is sent out into battle, every pilot and warrior is prepared to sacrifice their existence in the effort to achieve the Korlah Mission goals. Since our current campaign plan will likely result in the destruction of this vessel and the loss of all on board, we who have enjoyed its relative safety must be no less prepared for this sacrifice than our field counterparts.

"We have memories from before the arrival of the Kahshinki parasites, and we would like to have the memory of their final extermination. So please, tell us, Teela, what option is it that 'by our own words' can save this campaign?"

Teela scanned the faces of the section leaders. Only the Leader Potentate and a few of the others seemed interested. The Potentate told Teela she had to choose an alliance between the Korlah and the essence that now shared her mind. Whispers and visions flashed through her mind like a sudden memory; she began organizing the fragmented thoughts into a logical proposal. She must have stood there too long because Tooron stood in a fit of impatience and exclaimed, "Either you have options, or you don't!"

"Sit down, Tooron, and be patient. Our young guest has much on her mind and deserves time to confer with these thoughts," the Potentate said calmly as she returned to her dais. She sat down and assumed a relaxed posture.

Teela felt the bite of her claws as she unconsciously tensed her fists. Forcing herself to relax, her chaotic thoughts focused and a plan came to her with startling clarity.

"Your Eminence, you told me that I must choose an alliance. I have made that choice, and if you do the same, we can win this campaign and destroy the Kahshinki expansion here, without another campaign vessel!"

Teela paused to look around the Chamber for the effect she had hoped to achieve. All the leaders were now looking at her, their disinterest replaced with skeptical anticipation as they waited to hear how such an impossible goal could be achieved under the circumstances.

Satisfied that her opening statement had obtained the desired effect, she continued. "Like our campaign vessel, the human planet, Earth, has very few leaders. The remaining millions … no, billions, of humans on the planet have no knowledge of the Kahshinki or Korlah. If they were to learn that their leaders were allied with the Kahshinki and that as part of that alliance they have been allowing the Kahshinki to abduct their people for use as slaves and for consumption, the leaders would be deposed, and new leaders would take their place. The new leaders, once aware of their options, will be willing to enter an alliance with the Korlah to defeat the Kahshinki."

Security Leader Krron stood to be recognized. Teela paused to allow her to speak.

"My section controls and monitors communication on this vessel. Do the human leaders not control and monitor the communication on their planet?"

"Yes and no," Teela answered. "There are many forms of communication. So many, in fact, that no leadership organization, theirs or ours, can control them all, at least not very effectively. Once it is known that the leaders have lied to or misinformed their subordinates, the truth spreads uncontrollably throughout the masses. The leaders may be able to slow its dispersal, and they may try to discredit it as a lie or exaggeration, but ultimately the truth will be known. The leaders will lose the credibility they need to remain in power."

The Council Leaders looked around, nodding at the correlation between the current unrest aboard their vessel and that on Earth. Afron stood and for the first time waited respectfully to be recognized by the Potentate before speaking.

"Why would the humans of … Earth believe you and not their leaders?" Afron asked.

"I wouldn't expect them to. However, we have in our possession ten witnesses and ample evidence of their leaders' treachery that I am confident the citizens of Earth will believe."

"And what if they choose not to believe? Or if the leaders are successful in preventing the communications?"

"Option two. We exterminate the leadership, crush their military defenses, and then use the planet's population and resources to wage our campaign against the Kahshinki from the Earth's system."

A roar of protest surged through the chamber. The entire Council was standing, each attempting to exert her thoughts above the others'. Shyron once again extended her arms, directing them to be silent. Pointing to Population Leader Gilron on her far right, Shyron indicated that she would be the first permitted to speak.

"We are not Kahshinki! We do not subjugate sentient species!" Gilron shouted. Murmurs of affirmation followed from the other leaders, who began to sit back down, their anger having been voiced.

In a gesture of hostility, Teela jabbed her finger toward the Population Leader. She began to draw a slow arc around the chamber with her extended claw as she spoke.

"There are three choices, three possible options. First, we can sterilize the planet under the premise of strategic action, murdering billions of innocents to exact revenge on a few. Such an act would make us worse than the Kahshinki and bring shame on the name of Korlah for eternity."

The rumble of protests rose again.

"Silence!" Shyron shouted with a punitive mental blow. Once the chamber had quieted, she directed Teela to continue.

"Second, we could attempt to defeat the humans, subjugate their population, and plunder the planet's resources without their permission to achieve our Mission goals. Although this would be a vile act of aggression untypical of Korlah protocol, the human species would at least be intact when we left.

"Or third, we could negotiate an alliance, multiplying our military might many thousands of times and gaining technological and strategic advantages over the Kahshinki. And very possibly gain a long-term ally in our mission to eradicate the

Kahshinki infestation in this galaxy. Although this option will be the most difficult and dangerous to coordinate, it more closely resembles the Korlah law that speaks of restoring and defending sentient species damaged by Kahshinki domination."

Teela faced the Leader Potentate. Bowing her head, she indicated that she was finished speaking. The rumble of ten leaders speaking simultaneously filled the chamber. Again, the Potentate silenced the group.

"This negotiation with the humans that you speak of; am I to assume that you will be the one to perform this amazing task?"

"Yes, Your Eminence," Teela bowed respectfully.

"The Council will now discuss this matter in detail. Until determined otherwise, we are reassigning you to the Strategy section. Your title will be Assistant, Third Rank. Afron will see to your accommodations and ration allocation."

The security guards that had brought Teela to the Council Chamber appeared at her sides, summoned silently by the Leader Potentate.

"We will call for you soon. I anticipate the Council will have many questions about how this is to be implemented.

"Guards! You are to escort Mission Assistant Teela and see to her protection. If we come to find that she receives any further injury at your hands or any others, our honor will be insulted and yours will be forfeited."

The guards bowed. Turning simultaneously away, they waited for Teela to lead them. With one final bow, Teela turned and left the Council Chamber with the guards following closely.

Teela's mind raced with the burden of all the combined events. Her chest and shoulders felt constricted, as though she was about to have an attack of stress or panic. Walking in a subconscious daze, she was barely aware of the guards following her.

Security guards were the police force of the leaders, inspecting and investigating the activities of other sections. With the enactment of rationing, food and water had become currency that could be used to buy products and services previously purchased with influence and favors. Seeing this as a threat to their authority, the leaders had imposed sanctions against this very popular market. As a result, the guards became associated with the enforcement of these sanctions and were generally considered an unwelcome sight. More and more frequently, unnamed forces were attacking the guards. There were places on the ship where it was rumored the security forces could not go, even in large numbers, without fear of attack.

Teela and her escorts were stopped at the last outpost near the heavily-fortified access to the Security section. The guards there ordered her guards to stand by while they escorted Teela into a small chamber off the main corridor and directed her to wait. Too tired to argue, she considered lying on the floor, but instead sat in one of the two chairs, bending over to rest her head on her knees.

How long has it been since you slept? a voice asked. The words in her mind startled Teela, causing her to sit up abruptly and aggravate her many bruises. Shyron was sitting in the chair across from her, wearing a long robe with a deep hood that nearly obscured her features.

"Don't get up, please!" Shyron said, seeing Teela strain to stand. Teela bowed her head and held her palms up to show respect to the Leader Potentate.

"I can't remember," Teela said.

"What?" Shyron exclaimed.

"I have been trying, but I can't remember the last time I really slept, Your Eminence. I … I'm sorry."

Shyron put her head back and laughed.

"No, it is we who should be sorry." Shyron said, gently taking Teela's hands. "We are the last of the true elders. We don't really know how many lives we have lived. Before the Kahshinki, before our world was destroyed, there was a time of peace and harmony between the many Korlah clans. Only elder males of the faith would transfer their memories to child males as a means to sustain the memories of our laws, religion, and culture. It was sacred and involved a very intricate and secret ceremony. But our world was being destroyed. They were taking the males and killing those who fought. The females hid them for as long as they could, but capture was inevitable. Rather than letting the memories cease, the memories of a mature male were transferred to a mature female. That was our first transfer. Although transference between adult minds was expected to result in insanity, at least in our own feeble way, we resisted the

Kahshinki." Shyron took a deep breath and shook Teela's hands gently.

"That was a long, long time ago, and our minds are still together in this aging shell." With a bony finger, she poked Teela painfully in the forehead.

"Now, *both of you* listen closely. I don't know how your two minds joined as well as they apparently have, but from all accounts you have managed the extraordinary. Utilize each other's strengths, recognize each other's weaknesses, and listen to each other's advice. Make your decisions together, and do not argue, as conflict between you will be disastrous. Do you understand me?"

"Yes," Teela heard herself say weakly. "Yes," she said again more confidently, articulating the agreement whispered by the voice within her.

"I want to speak to the essence of the beast," Shyron stated bluntly, taking Teela firmly by the wrists and staring intently into her face.

"What?" Teela asked, knowing what Shyron wanted but unsure of her ability to comply. "It doesn't talk, not like a voice. More like an emotion or a thought that I normally wouldn't have." The half-lie made her feel exposed and suddenly ill at ease under Shyron's piercing glare.

Your name. What do you call yourself, human? Shyron demanded mentally, her claws digging deeply into Teela's wrists as her thoughts dug into her mind.

"Daedalus! I am Daedalus Rimes. Now … let … go … of … me," Teela heard herself growl as menacing thoughts of overpowering the aged leader filled her mind.

"There you are," Shyron hissed, holding tight onto Teela's wrists.

Do you really believe that an alliance between the Korlah and human leaders can be negotiated? Shyron pressed her thoughts into the hostile wall of incoherent, alien thoughts that she could now perceive behind Teela's scowl.

"Not without your complete support," Teela answered calmly, relaxing even though Shyron's grip had not slackened.

If I give my support, I want your loyalty, human, your complete loyalty in return. Do humans have honor? Do you know what loyalty and honor are? Shyron asked, loosening her grip on Teela's wrist and easing the intensity of her probe.

"You give me the support I need, and you will have my complete loyalty. However, although I know and respect honor and loyalty, most humans you will be dealing with do not." Teela responded mechanically, her face now blank.

Releasing Teela's wrists, Shyron withdrew from her mind and exhaled as she composed herself.

"We must talk like this again … later. Now, we must get ourselves back to the Council and obtain consensus for action, and you must get some sleep.

"We will communicate with you through messages handled by our personal guards. Afron has spies everywhere. If she thinks you are helping us, and not her, she will very likely find some means to end your existence," Shyron said as she rose from her chair and pulled the deep hood down to obscure her face.

Turning away from the door, she disappeared into a narrow slit in the wall that vanished seamlessly behind her. The door opened, and the outpost guard led Teela to her waiting escorts.

12 - Gift

Seeing a bruised, bloodied and filthy birthing unit exiting the security section flanked by four guards must have presented a sufficiently titillating image. A hush followed them wherever they traveled, and personnel of all ranks and titles stopped to gawk at the unusual procession.

Physically and emotionally exhausted, Teela decided to follow Shyron's advice and get some rest before checking up on

Bill and the other humans. Traveling over a mile through the maze of corridors and spokes, she arrived in the familiar surroundings of the Shell section sleep chamber and stood before the platform and storage cubicles that had been hers for the last twelve cycles. Energizing the glowlamp, she found the platform had been stripped of its pad and bedding and all her meager possessions, her extra tahs and slippers, were now gone. She stared at the empty station, slowly realizing that her section mates had not expected her to return. Embarrassment and a sense of deep isolation washed over her, threatening to drown her in suffocating depths of despair. She stumbled from the sleep chamber choking back sobs and ran down the corridor to her old friend's compartment.

"Nerhala!" Teela shouted as she entered the small private quarters for the sections ranking birthing unit. But the cubicle was as empty as Teela's. She stood dumbfounded. The one person she had always been able to confide in was gone.

"They took her away," a soft voice whispered. Unsure if this was the voice in her mind, Teela didn't turn at first.

"Your existence was dropped off the birthing roster. We assumed you were … gone."

Teela turned to find Manalla standing in the shadows across the narrow corridor.

"Where is Nerhala?" Teela squeaked, her voice cracking, realizing the obvious.

"Reclamation," Manalla answered somberly, looking down at her distended abdomen to avoid Teela's piercing eyes. "She was too old to be carrying six. It was too much for her. After you were taken, she was very upset, and the next shift she delivered the shells too soon, lifeless. And then … like you, they took her." Manalla continued to stare at her own abdomen as though she were watching the six embryos swelling within her.

Pushing roughly past the guards, Teela closed the distance between her and Manalla in two strides. Manalla fell to her knees and covered her face.

"I will give back what I took!" Manalla cried, expecting to be struck. When no attack came, she removed her hands to find Teela kneeling to face her, eyes wide and tears streaming down her cheeks. "But I traded it for food. I'm sorry. I thought …," Manalla finished weakly, her voice trailing off to a whisper.

"It's all right, little sister," Teela said softly, taking Manalla's hands in hers. "I hope you and the others ate well. I know Nerhala would feel the same way." Teela cocked her head and narrowed her eyes in a more relaxed composure.

"Feel no guilt for what you must do to continue your existence. I don't know how long I have before my end, but I will remember my sisters and do what I can to change these terrible things." Patting Manalla affectionately on her abdomen, Teela pressed her face to Manalla's. Teela rose to her feet and ran down the corridor to the nearest up-spoke. Her escorts ran after her, giving the appearance of a chase to a few who had witnessed the strange event.

Moving outward through the Health, Supplies, and Accoutrements sections, Teela bolted forward into the Arms section, three miles away. Many of the areas she traveled were unused and unoccupied, most of them dark, littered with debris and dust. Teela knew these areas well and jogged deftly through the maze of corridors and tubes. Breathing heavily, she stopped in the midranking housing section and faced a door that she hoped held refuge within. She looked around and noticed for the first time since leaving the Shell section that her escorts were nowhere in sight. A feeling of complete isolation and abandonment swept over her, weighing her small frame down with despair. She leaned her shoulder heavily against the door and pressed her face against the cold metal.

The apartment was assigned to one of the more affluent members of the crew's upper ranks. Teela cleaned and provided services for her in exchange for additional rations. She knew this individual cared for her, and although the affection was not mutual, she could think of no one else that might help her.

She stood there and leaned on the door, wanting to knock but afraid that if she did, she would find yet another piece of her life was missing or somehow irreversibly damaged. Before Teela could make up her mind, the door suddenly opened and she fell through the doorway. Challmara screamed with surprise as Teela tumbled onto the floor at her feet.

"I'm sorry!" Teela sobbed. "I … I didn't mean to frighten you." She painfully picked herself up off the floor and bowed.

"I need somewhere I can rest and clean myself," Teela said. "I'm sorry. I didn't know where else to go."

Challmara stood silent, her eyes wide with surprise, unsure of what to do.

"Please … can I rest here, just for a little while?" Teela sobbed.

Drawing Teela into the compartment by the elbow, Challmara looked suspiciously up and down the empty corridor and then closed and locked the door. She pulled Teela through the chamber to the farthest corner, pushed her down onto the floor and crouched next to her.

"What did you do, Teela? Why is the leadership so interested in you? I tried to find out why they were taking you. I had some of my director friends inquire. They were seized by Security section guards and questioned. I have been expecting them to come get me any time now. What … have … you … done?" Challmara whispered, fear and panic rattling the voice Teela had always admired for its strength and confidence.

"It's nothing I've done; it's what I may do that concerns them. You don't have to be afraid. I think they were just surprised to find that I actually had friends, that someone was concerned about what had happened to me. Thank you. Thank you, Challmara, and your friends for trying to help me." Teela said, wiping a tear from the corner of her eye with a dirty knuckle, drawing a muddy streak across her face.

Taking a cleansing pad from a storage compartment by the room's wall basin, Challmara began to wipe Teela's face and crown tendrils with the care and tenderness a birth mother shows her newborn. Gently guiding Teela onto the sleep platform, she pulled off Teela's soiled tah and continued the nurturing bath. Teela fell fast asleep.

The concept of an alarm clock would be lost on a Korlah. They have exceptionally accurate biological rhythms that, once established, require no adjustment. Teela had been working double shifts for as long as she could recall, and if her birth sisters had their way, she would work two and a half shifts when they were heavy with the next generation of Korlah duplicates.

She had not been able to get a complete rest period for as many off-shifts as she could recall; but regardless of how sleep-deprived she was, she would wake instinctively before her on-shift.

The soft bedding caressed her bruised and tender skin. Teela reveled in the deep cushioning of Challmara's sleep pad. Unlike the papery bedding and thin pads of the Shell section, this was truly luxurious and beckoned her to drift off into sleep again. Sitting up suddenly, she shook her head in an effort to clear the sleep from her mind, knowing that her on-shift periods were about to begin.

Ten sets to a shift, and she had slept only a little over two. In the blackness of the chamber, there were no objects of sufficient warmth to register a thermal image. Scanning the small chamber, Teela confirmed that she was alone. She switched on the glowlamp by the sleep platform and surveyed her surroundings. The com screen established that her on-shift would begin in a little over thirty bits, but since she was no longer assigned to the Shell section, who would she report to?

Her concerns were temporarily interrupted when she noticed an intricately embroidered garment draped over a seat, a message board sitting on it. Something about the patterning of the fabric drew Teela from the warmth and comfort of her sleep pad. The sensitive pads of her clawed toes lifted to avoid the cold floor. As she walked over to the intriguing garment, she shook off a shiver. When she opened the message board, a flat triangular access key fell to the floor. Teela picked it up as she read the illuminated message.

> "Gentle Teela,
>
> I apologize for acting like such a coward, but so many unusual and disruptive events have happened lately. I have heard rumors of things you cannot imagine. I have an appointment I can't miss and regret that I won't be there when you awaken. My on-shift follows yours, so I only hope we can see each other after that.
>
> "I had these garments fabricated for you a while ago. I had planned to give them to you to wear at the next story

gathering, but it would seem appropriate that you wear them now, at least until you can obtain a replacement tah. You may stay in my compartment whenever you wish, as long as you wish. The key will provide you access.

Your affectionate sister, Challmara."

Lifting the garment from the bench, Teela marveled at the light silky material. Made from the same fabric as the uniforms of high-ranking section leaders and directors, it was a floor-length sleeveless tah, hemmed with a metallic soutache. Ancient Korlah hieroglyphs were embroidered in the same metallic material in a neat maze over its entire surface. It was an exquisitely-crafted interpretation of the garment worn by the ancient warrior of her favorite sculpture.

Teela's throat tightened as she remembered Challmara's apparent disinterest when she had expressed how much she loved the sculpture and the costume, and how she wished she could have been a warrior during such a time. She now realized that Challmara must have been paying very close attention; she had to have accessed the log record of the sculpture to have this outfit made with such extraordinary detail.

Beneath the tah was a high-collared vest of tough armor. Patterns similar to those embroidered on the tah were embossed on the tough padding. Its waist had long overlapping strips of a light fabric with the texture of coarse sand that extended to about knee length. Beneath the vest, Teela found a wide belt rolled tightly into a coil, made of the same heavy material as the chest and shoulder plates with the addition of metallic inlays. As she unrolled the belt, she found rings attached to each side, intended to hold the bladed weapons of a warrior. At the center of the coil she found a delicately engraved and heavily inlaid Mission emblem on the buckle. The foot coverings she found on the floor were no less exotic. Molded from the smooth shiny cloth used for warriors' armor, they were padded and lined with the same silky fabric as the tah, trimmed with metallic filigree, and soled in a soft, resilient material that Teela didn't recognize.

The tah slid over her shoulders and glided down the curves of her body, falling into an exquisite fit that fell loosely after it passed snugly over her hips. Teela ran her hands along the smooth fabric on her chest and abdomen, enjoying its silky texture and the sensations it created. She could easily imagine the motivation Challmara had for obtaining such an obviously costly gift. Imagining how Challmara would certainly run her hands over the fabric and her body, the thought failed to produce the uncomfortable feeling she usually experienced when Challmara was physically affectionate. This time, as she considered the possibilities, she felt something new, a longing to both give and receive those pleasures.

This was a gift of incredible worth, and Teela was keenly aware that whatever Challmara had traded for this exquisite garment could have paid for the companionship of a dozen birthing units for an entire cycle or more. Challmara was more than a client and more than a friend. As much as Teela desired her companionship, she feared the events now unfolding would jeopardize whatever hope she had for maintaining their relationship.

Coarse and heavy in comparison to the light silky tah beneath it, the vest was obviously fabricated for utility rather than sensory enjoyment. Its eleven highly-polished horizontal metal clasps compressed Teela's breasts uncomfortably when fastened, so she left them open above the waist. The belt fit comfortably, cinching the loose fabric snugly around her waist. Teela looked around the room for the swords that would have hung in its rings, but much to her disappointment found none.

Standing before the polished panel over Challmara's washbasin, Teela admired her reflection from various angles, feeling as though she were seeing herself for the first time. In this garment, she felt she could be the warrior of her fantasies.

Teela sat down at Challmara's communication panel and placed her hands on the link pads. Manalla had said that according to the birthing unit roster she no longer existed, but she wanted to see for herself. Entering her identification code, the one matching the sabat tattooed on the skin of her left cheek, TEELA20.10127, she found that her code was no longer recognized.

What rank and title was it that Shyron assigned me? Teela could not recall for a moment.

Mission Assistant. I'm assigned to the Mission section! Teela remembered as the events of the last shift returned vaguely. Entering the glyph for the Mission section, Teela expected to be searching a list. Only two identification codes were displayed: Shyron, Mission Director, Campaign Potentate; and Teela, Mission Assistant, Campaign Adjutant.

This can't be right. Teela thought, entering the code to list the current shift duties of the Mission Assistant.

49.1: REPORT TO HEALTH/BIO SECTION, LEVEL 40, CHAMBER 6701. ASSIST WITH ANALYSIS OF OBJECTS RECOVERED BY PATROL CRAFT.

49.5: REPORT TO BIRTHING SECTION, LEVEL 04, CHAMBER 1071. VERIFY ADEQUATE SERVICES AND CONDITIONS ARE MAINTAINED FOR DESIGNATED OCCUPANTS.

49.9: PROVIDE SHIFT REPORT AS REQUIRED.

Shyron has assigned me to report directly to her. How could Afron not think I will be helping Shyron? Does she want Afron to terminate my existence? What game is Shyron playing? Teela wondered as she cleared the information from the communications panel.

She picked up the message board and wrote a note to Challmara, thanking her for her kindness and generosity and promising to meet with her as soon as she could. Reading the message, Teela knew that it lacked the gratitude she wished to convey but was unable to put into words. She slipped the key bar to Challmara's compartment into the pocket of her new tah and left.

13 - Blades

Throughout the city-sized campaign vessel, various forms of transport were available. Transit tubes ran in and out from the inner depths, some sized for a single individual and others the size of rooms, with controls for regulating speed. From the outer skin to the inner core, there were two hundred and forty levels of varying height, depending on function. Every forty levels, a dividing layer was dedicated to power distribution, ventilation, reclamation, and other components that fed the life functions of the forty levels above it. Transit forward and aft on these dividing levels was accomplished with room-sized cubes that, without sensation of movement, whisked their occupants three tenths of a mile between intersections.

Teela walked through an empty corridor. Those reporting for duties had already left, and those going off-shift had not yet returned. Shyron had given Teela an entire set, one tenth of the shift, for travel time; an incredibly generous allotment. Even Nerhala had expected her to travel off-shift. Driven by habit, she was unable to resist the compulsion to hurry down the corridor, but she soon realized that if she continued at her current pace, she would arrive at Gremensh's conference chamber long before her required report time. She turned away from a transport cube and forced herself to walk slowly through the Accoutrements section. She planned to drop down through the Supplies section and into the Health and Bio sections to the conference chamber.

Approaching a transit hub crowded with technicians, laborers, and warriors, Teela had to slow her pace even further. As she moved through the crowd, she was repeatedly stopped and asked about her new attire. Where did she get it? How could they get one? What value of exchange did it require? Unable to answer the questions satisfactorily and having drawn the attention of an approaching security patrol, she pressed her way through the small crowd that had formed and stepped into a down-tube to escape the growing attention. Once considered an act of rebellion, wearing garments other than one's uniform was becoming a more common sight, especially to the off-shift gatherings that were becoming popular among those of higher rank.

With the exception of being approached for services, Teela, like most birthing units, was treated as if she were invisible. But now she was being noticed, and although she enjoyed the attention, the crowds had made her feel vulnerable. She left the transit tube in the upper levels of the Supplies section, knowing this to be one of the many uninhabited areas of the ship. It had been severely damaged during the assault and was completely deserted. As she walked alone through the corridor, the thick dust muffled her footsteps and provided the quiet solace she preferred.

The glowlamps on the ceiling and walls were few and far between. Most were missing and some lay broken in the dust and debris, forcing her to walk carefully. Teela had traveled these corridors many times and knew her way instinctively, barely needing light to see where to turn or how far it was to the next spoke. Plodding along slowly, she scanned the ground immediately before her and traveled the familiar corridors. The silence created few distractions, allowing her to reflect on recent events. Soon, she was deep in thought and trying to understand the many new memories and troubling emotions that bombarded her. She became so engrossed that she was unaware of the dark-cloaked individuals moving up behind her.

Unsure if it was something she heard or smelled, Teela suddenly felt very uneasy. The feeling turned to fear when cloaked figures stepped out of the shadows to block her path. Turning quickly, she found her retreat blocked by more figures that emerged from the shadows behind her. The dim light of the glowlamps glinted off their long bladed weapons.

Darting to the side of the large corridor, Teela stood with her back to the wall as the two groups merged before her. Her claws extended instinctively and she held her arms in a defensive posture, aware that her claws would be ineffective against their blades.

"I have no food or water for you to steal!" Teela shouted, spitting out the last word. They were fighting words, but only if her attackers had honor to lose. The group's leader pointed its long blade at Teela and began a cautious approach, closing the distance between them. Unable to discern the face hidden in the shadows of the deep hood, Teela could only see the sparkle of the glowlamps reflected in her eyes.

"Birthing unit?" the leader asked, posing the question more to herself than to Teela.

"It's a birther!" she called out, returning Teela's insult. There was a momentary murmur amongst the group.

"Why are you wearing the tah of an arbitrator?" she asked, moving the blade closer to Teela's chest.

The question caught Teela by surprise. Until the thief asked, she hadn't even thought about what she was wearing. When she didn't respond, the leader shouted at her.

"Who has sent you dressed like this, birther? Where are your blades? What peace do you hope to negotiate without blades?" Her voice rose in volume and hostility with each question, the point of her blade a fraction of an inch from Teela's bare chest, just above her armored breastplate.

"What's an arbitrator?" one of the others asked.

"You ignorant fool!" the leader cried, turning her head to shout. "If you listened to the Oracle's teachings instead of—"

Before the thief could finish speaking, the voice in Teela's mind shouted for action and her body reacted. The events unfolded before her as though she were a spectator of her own actions.

Her right hand made a deft, circular sweep, knocking her enemy's blade to one side. She leaned forward and it slid past her. She grabbed the hilt with her other hand and threw herself back against the wall, jerking the thief off balance. The wall stopped Teela's backward motion, but the thief fell forward until Teela's right foot was planted in the center of her chest. With more strength than she could ever imagine she possessed, Teela twisted the blade from the thief's hand and kicked, sending her flying backward into her companions.

Transferring the blade to her right hand, Teela launched herself forward, using the wall for leverage. Her first target was completely unprepared, its blade only partially raised. Teela adroitly tapped the weapon aside with her own and stepped in so close that she could feel the thief's breath on her face. She took the blade with her free hand and knocked her opponent senseless with the pommel of the sword. The crudely fabricated yet razor-sharp blades had a comfortable familiarity to them. Moving quickly to one side, Teela positioned herself in front of all of the thieves.

I've fought with blades before! Teela realized as memories of Daedalus' participation in Renaissance reenactments came to her.

The group of thieves was in disarray, shouting at each other and brandishing their weapons in a feeble attempt to look threatening. Gaining confidence, Teela began pinwheeling the long blades on each side, sweeping them in front of her in wide arcs. The blades whistled through the air with increasing speed. She began to take menacing lunges forward with each sweep of her blades. The group bolted into the darkness, leaving only the two she had knocked down, one of them unconscious and the other cowering on the floor. Only one fighter remained.

The thief threw off her long cloak and cautiously eyed Teela's approach. She neither advanced nor retreated, her defensive stance showing that she knew how to handle a blade and was merely waiting, gauging the skills of her opponent.

The thief was old by Korlah standards, gaunt and emaciated by the hard existence she had been forced into. Teela saw from the rags that hung loosely on her skeletal frame that she must have been a warrior, and knew from her age that she would be particularly skilled. But this one was also undernourished, and this was the weakness that Teela decided to exploit.

Teela feigned an attack. The thief ducked the blow and slashed upwards, aiming for Teela's neck but missing. Now in close, Teela pressed an offensive attack. Her two blades met the thief's single defending blade in rapid succession.

Teela gave her opponent no opportunity to do anything except deflect the blows that were now increasing in speed and ferocity. Their blades clashed, sending sparks flying, and the din of their impacts echoed down the dark corridor. Exhausted from the onslaught, the aged warrior was forced to back up, no longer able to ward off the blows that Teela was meting out with an efficiency and endurance developed by a lifetime of hard labor. The warrior-thief suddenly tripped and fell backward onto the debris-littered floor, her weapon clattering just out of reach. Gasping for air and coughing from the dust they had kicked up, she held her forearm across her face in anticipation of the fatal blow to come.

After what seemed an interminable length of time, the warrior-thief peered over her arm to find Teela standing over her, arms crossed and hands ready to pull the blades from their belt rings.

"You are fortunate I am old and weak," the warrior-thief croaked. She cleared her throat and spat the dusty phlegm onto Teela's boot. "You have little skill, birther. Your style is all show and no substance. You got lucky, and then you overpowered me. There was a time when I would have beaten you with ease."

"Still, warrior, you were beaten by a birther," Teela said, delivering honor and insult with fluid precision.

"Why have you not ended the Spectacle?" the warrior-thief rasped, breaking her defiant glare in acknowledgment of her defeat. "You must realize I would not have hesitated to take your existence. I won't serve you, and I have no honor to lose. I have nothing left. Why don't you finish me?"

Teela offered her hand. The warrior-thief took it, allowing Teela to help her up. Looking up into the face of the much taller warrior, Teela smiled warmly and held her palms up in respect and honor.

"Each of us does what we must to survive. You may have lost your ration allocation, but honor is something that cannot be taken. You are what you choose to be. Like honor, who you are cannot be taken away. Campaign is about to begin, if in fact it has not already started. As a warrior, do you believe this vessel is prepared to battle a Kahshinki harvest force?"

The warrior's gaunt face wrinkled in anguish. She shut her eyes tightly and bowed her head in a profoundly negative response.

"With some help, I intend to change that!" Teela said proudly.

With a turn of her head and a nod of dismissal, Teela hurried down the corridor with a pace more typical of her usual gait.

God help me end this misery, she prayed silently, empathizing with the plight of the warrior-thief and her companions and unaware that she was projecting her thoughts telepathically. The thieves heard and felt the sincerity of her prayer and watched in stunned silence as she disappeared into the darkness. Wisps of dust swirled after her rapid departure and slowly settled back to the floor.

"Roche Hah Shawlmon," the grizzled warrior-thief whispered as Teela disappeared into the shadows.

Thieves were nothing new to Teela. She had been robbed returning from a cleaning arrangement. The encounter was settled for a generous payment of four biscuits and two rations of water, a two-shift ration that cost her half a shift of much needed rest. She risked the bite of their blades when she cursed the thieves and called them names for taking her hard-won food and water, but they were shamed by her comments. They returned half the rations and begged her forgiveness, explaining that they were starving and had been forced to hide in the abandoned areas to keep from being forcibly reclaimed. Although she felt pity and empathy for them, Teela had sworn an oath to herself that she would not lose what little honor she had by fleeing her final duty when she was called for reclamation.

Since that first encounter, she had been careful to avoid these areas when carrying food or water, and although she had been confronted several times, she'd had nothing for them to take and was always allowed to continue on her way without incident.

The thieves were referred to as Nons. An English pronunciation of the word would sound like someone spitting, but in Korlah, it was an abbreviated version of "without existence"—dead. Slated for reclamation and removed from rations rosters, these were Korlah from all trades, rank, and status that had fled the grinders, trading their honor for a limited and pathetic existence. They stole and scrounged to survive from one shift to the next, hiding in the mazelike bowels of the massive ship.

Two tube jumps and a shuttle ride later, Teela arrived at the repair facility where she had left Bill over two shifts ago. Thick layers of nutrient gel covered the repaired areas of his face and hands, which were still strapped securely to the tables. He was snoring loudly, apparently comfortable enough to catch up on some sleep. Four biotechs monitored his condition, and warriors were stationed in pairs at every access point. Seeing that Bill's repairs had been performed and that he was apparently in good health, she headed for Gremensh's conference chamber. Without stopping at the desk of Gremensh's assistant, Teela headed for the large ornate door of the conference chamber.

"Stop!" the assistant cried in panic. Unable to ascertain the rank and status of the new arrival, the young technician spoke quickly and carefully in an effort to avoid offending Teela. "Afron, Gremensh, and other directors are having a meeting. They gave explicit instructions not to be disturbed."

Teela stopped when she realized her breach in protocol.

"Please inform Leader Afron that Mission Assistant Teela is here, as ordered by the Leader Potentate." Teela smiled pleasantly.

Staring incredulously, the assistant noted Teela's sabat and the claw punctures on her palms, and recognized her as the birthing unit from a few shifts previous. She gave Teela's new garments a quick study, and decided that the risk of challenging Teela's request was greater than the risk of disturbing the leader and directors. She entered a message into her communication panel and received a reply within a few moments.

"Please go in," the assistant said, bowing in respect and apology.

Teela entered the large chamber and closed the ornate door behind her. The room was dominated by an enormous table that was molded as a continuous piece with the floor and surrounded by raised cylindrical seats fabricated in the same way. The objects on the table were the only loose items in the room. Standing in a cluster at the end of the table were directors from Arms, Accoutrements, Energy, Health, and Education. Afron turned as she entered and called out.

"Teela, where have you been? I have half the security force out looking for you. Your guards reported that they were attacked by Nons and—" Afron paused in surprise to look Teela up and down, then sauntered slowly around her as she examined her garments and the swords at her sides with a critical gaze.

"You are out of uniform. These garments you are wearing … this is Shawlmon's tah, and without exception the most impressive recreation I have ever seen. Your form suits it well; however, leaders and directors do not wear tahs, even when they are this … inspiring. And as for the blades, I was under the impression you knew our laws."

Teela bowed deeply with an apologetic gesture. She was embarrassed by Afron's comments and solicitous manner.

"I apologize for my inappropriate clothing, Your Eminence," she said softly. "The garments are a gift from a friend. I only intended to wear them until I was issued my section uniform. As for the blades, I took them from the Nons that attacked me. I thought it wise to keep them since I no longer had escorts to protect me. If you wish, I will go and procure more acceptable attire immediately."

"No! Your friend has excellent taste. I may choose to make this the uniform for all my personal assistants from now on. As for the story about *you* taking blades from nons…,"

Afron slid her hand suggestively down Teela's back to rest on the silken fabric at the curve of her hips. Teela felt Afron's mind probing her thoughts, so she concentrated on the table and the objects spread across it.

"Please join us at the table. We have questions we hope you can answer," Afron said, walking with her arm around Teela. The position of her hand and the unusual closeness made Teela uncomfortable.

At the table, the directors had stopped talking. They stared as Afron introduced each of the section directors. It was apparent that it wasn't just her tah that they found impressive, but rather the way it displayed her body. Although her breasts were not any larger than the other birthing units', they appeared larger on her stunted frame. The uniform of a birthing unit was a loose-fitting, floor-length sack dress designed for utility. The design did little to accentuate the body or breasts, unlike her new tah. The shining garment clung to her breasts and the vest lifted them together, making them appear even larger. She had never really thought about it until now, but the birthing units were the only genotype with fully developed breasts. Units from the other sections came from four originals, none of which developed breasts comparable in size. Many of her clients had taken unusual interest in her breasts, which she found rather irritating.

On the table were items of human manufacture. A portable radio, CD, and tape player; a walkie-talkie; several flashlights; two guitars and an amplifier; books; backpacks; the pistol Daedalus had used; suitcases; a military flight helmet; clothing; and various other personal belongings. Teela recognized Daedalus' pocketknife and picked it up, turning it over in her hand. She was amazed at how much smaller it seemed now.

"That is the weapon that was used to kill one of the Kahshinki pilots," Afron said to the directors, pointing. "And Teela was the recipient of that human's memories."

The directors nodded with grave understanding and renewed respect, eyeing her long, roughly hewn blades with concern.

"We have formed some opinions on the function and operation of these items, and would like you to confirm our analysis," Afron said, motioning.

"Your Eminence, Honorable Directors," Teela said, bowing in respect and slipping the knife into her pocket. Picking up a portable CD player, she began.

"This device is for listening to recorded sounds, or …" She hesitated, trying to think of an explanation. There were no Korlah words for radio broadcasts that she knew of, so with her limited knowledge of how radios functioned she attempted to explain. "Sounds that are changed into pulses … of … electrically generated waves that are broadcast through space. This broadcast is then collected and reproduced as sound by devices like this."

"A communication device?" the Arms director asked.

"Yes, but this unit can only receive. It cannot send communications. It is used for entertainment," Teela explained.

"How is sound used to entertain?" Gremensh asked.

Teela examined the player. There wasn't a CD in the player, but there was a tape. She popped it out and examined it. "MM #5" was scrawled in felt marker on the otherwise blank label. Slipping it back in, she pushed the power button and was rewarded with a glowing light. Pushing the play button with the point of a claw resulted in a soft hissing sound from the speakers. The directors and Afron cautiously backed away. Teela turned the volume down to about three on a dial that went to ten—just in time, as a blast of electric guitar and feedback shot from the small speakers. It was a Metal Maiden rock song, and the lyrics, sung in English, could not be understood by the group. Although Teela tried to explain their meaning and that there were many other types of entertainment sounds besides this, the group seemed doubtful as to its value.

When it came to the walkie-talkie and the pilot's helmet with a microphone and headset, the group listened with rapt interest. The questions quickly changed from function and use to electrical and electronic theory, to which neither portion of Teela's combined memories could provide satisfactory responses. The directors began arguing about how they could possibly develop and exploit this new technology in time for the impending campaign, and the session threatened to turn into a shouting match. Although it was still too early for her to present her plan, Teela felt that she could use this opportunity to reveal one of its key concepts.

"Directors, honorable directors," Teela said, trying to get their attention through the din. *Shut up, damn it!* she thought, wishing she could scream the command.

The shouting stopped and all eyes turned to Afron.

"What did you say?" Afron asked with an indignant glare.

"Nothing, Your Eminence. I … I said nothing," Teela said, suddenly worried that she had spoken the demand.

Yes, yes you did! We all received your communication. It was most *effective,* Afron's sarcasm was silently projected. She was both surprised and perturbed by Teela's ability, which had not surfaced in Afron until well after her fourth transfer.

"So now that you have our attention, what new item of eminent importance do you have for us?"

"We have no time to waste studying and attempting to develop technology from this junk. Everything we need to win this campaign is on a planet that is now within reach. We are wasting time. We just need to make the decision to go there and ask for it."

An uncomfortable silence filled the room as all of the directors looked nervously to Afron for her response to such obtrusive disrespect.

"I couldn't agree more with the urgency of this situation, but studying this new technology while concurrently preparing our long-range expedition is a critical tactic necessary to prepare the strategies formulated by the leader of the Strategy section—and that would be me!" Afron said.

"Forgive me, Your Eminence," Teela responded, struggling to sound sincere. "I am not well-versed in the protocol of speaking with my superiors. I mean no disrespect." She finished with a deep bow and an apologetic display of palms.

"Of course you didn't," Afron said for all to hear, grinning with great satisfaction at her ability to keep this presumptuous soubrette in line. And then, for only Teela, she telepathically added, *You wouldn't dare.*

With the exception of the guitars, the remaining objects on the table solicited little interest. The directors had believed the guitars to be some crude form of pulse weapon and were greatly relieved to discover otherwise. Among the smaller objects on the table, Teela spotted the wire-rim glasses that Daedalus had been wearing. Twisted and bent out of shape, the glasses barely resembled their original condition. Teela began to meticulously clean and straighten them while listening to the discussion of Afron's plans.

The craft used for the expedition would be an assault pod. Like scaled-down versions of the campaign vessel, assault pods were cylindrically shaped. The large throat of the gravitational amplifier, compression shaft, and flux accelerators comprised the bulk of the relatively large vessel; however, instead of multiple levels, a single level wrapped around the compression shaft. Snugly situated in recessed docking bays were auxiliary vessels, each with access to the mother craft. These were comprised of five heavy fighters that ringed the forward end, five troop carriers that ringed the center, and ten light fighters that filled the back. When joined together, the crafts appeared to be one vessel. The mother ship could travel the vast distance to the target so that the attached fighters could be built without the large, bulky plasma-conversion components they would otherwise need for long-range travel.

The captured Kahshinki fighter that the human had piloted was being disassembled and examined in detail. The Arms director briefed the group on how the weapons system, propulsion, and shielding were considerably inferior versions of those the Kahshinki would have normally sent against them. With such a significant disadvantage, the director estimated it would require at least ten-to-one odds for an enemy to achieve victory against even their most inexperienced pilots. Control modifications that appeared to streamline the piloting and communication requirements were particularly relevant to the warrior director.

No longer hearing anything of interest and approaching the time of her next task, Teela made a courteous, brief good-bye to each of the directors. Teela slipped out the door, but Gremensh stopped her just outside. Gremensh pressed something into her palm and held it with hers.

"The human, Bill, is doing well. I will follow his recovery closely to ensure that nothing goes wrong with the repairs. The first one, your transfer donor, and this one are males," Gremensh whispered. She continued to hold Teela's hand expectantly.

"Yes, I know," Teela answered, confused.

"All the others are females, aren't they?" Gremensh asked. Knowing the answer, she continued. "Afron is planning something. She has been holding secret meetings and making modifications to the storage rooms across from the transfer chamber. She's interviewing for ten positions to—"

"What are you two conspiring about?" Afron hissed as she came out of the chamber.

Gremensh's face and crown paled. "I had almost forgotten to give her the metal band, as you had requested, Your Eminence." She pulled her hands away from Teela's, leaving a gold wedding band in Teela's palm. Teela closed her hand quickly, as though the ring might jump out.

"Where are the escorts I ordered? Where is she going without escorts?" Afron demanded.

"Your Eminence," Teela said, bowing deeply to Afron. "From what happened with the Nons, I believe, at least for now, that I am safer without escorts. Thank you, Gremensh. Thank you both for your assistance, support, and concern." Teela pulled first Gremensh and then Afron into a tight hug, pressing the side of her face against theirs in an affectionate gesture common only in the Shell sections. Without giving them a chance to respond, Teela turned and hurried out of the chamber, leaving them in stunned silence.

14 - Opposition

Teela hurried down the corridor with her hands on the hilts of her blades to keep them from swinging wildly. The absence of warrior guards at the entry to the biorepair chamber was the first indication that something was wrong. Through the glass wall, she could see that the tables were empty and the biotechs that had been tending Bill a few sets before were now cleaning and rearranging the chamber. She stormed through the open door.

"Where is the human?" she demanded, cornering a technician between two tables. The technician looked around franticly for the warrior guards that had been there a short time ago. Pulling her blades halfway out of their rings, Teela slammed them back down and shouted into the biotech's face.

"Where?"

Teela didn't realize her command was both verbally and mentally projected, which gave it much deeper impact. Falling to her knees, the biotech grabbed her head from the pain coursing through her frontal lobes.

"Transfer chamber! I heard them say they were taking it to the transfer chamber," she moaned and trembled.

Teela had severely frightened this unit. She was trying to find the words to apologize when she heard a voice, so loud and close behind her that she jumped.

We have no time! Go now!

Turning quickly, she found the area behind her empty, but two technicians moved stealthily toward the door.

"What did you say?" she shouted at them, her concern for Bill turning to anger and confusion. The technicians bolted out the door without answering. Disorientation swept over her. She looked at her hands, thinking about how foreign they looked.

"I must find Bill," Teela said in English to no one in particular, and then she rushed out the door.

Moving with purposeful strides, she knew where she was going and why, but she felt disconnected from her movements, as though she were dreaming. Scanning the corridor, her senses burned with an acuity and awareness she had never experienced before. Perceiving eye contact as a threat, Teela would lock eyes with anyone she caught staring at her. Her clothing, weapons, and very likely, the highly engorged state of her crown tendrils now spread around her head like a lion's mane, were enough to convince all she encountered to avoid meeting her eyes. Throwing herself into a transit tube, she clawed her way up, accelerating to such a degree that she nearly hit the ceiling before landing like a cat in the center of the corridor. Her blades clattered loudly as they struck the polished metallic floor.

Two warriors outside the transfer chamber energized their pulse rifles. Knowing that within a few seconds they would be charged and ready to fire, Teela drew her blades and charged one of the warriors. There was no turning back.

Anticipating the weapon's debilitating blast, she feigned a frontal attack and dodged to the side at the last second, bringing the edge of her blade down on the center of the rifle, intending to knock it from the warrior's grip as she passed. Swinging and missing the second guard, she dove to the floor and was sliding for the cover of a narrow entryway when a tremendous explosion rocked the corridor. A fireball blew past the doorway where she lay.

Although she wouldn't understand what had happened until later, her blade had severed the conduit that carried the high-energy charge from the rifle's pulse chamber to its discharge port. With no conduit to carry the charge, the energy was released in an uncontrolled blast, killing both warriors with the resulting fireball.

Believing the explosion to be the weapons' discharge, Teela rolled out into the corridor, jumped to her feet, and charged forward, hoping to surprise the warriors before they could discharge their weapons a second time. She had to jump and do a double step to avoid tripping over their smoking bodies. Across the ceiling, patches of burning gases danced and chased each other, slowly going out and leaving the smoke-filled corridor in near darkness. The glowlamps were shattered. In the darkness, only thermal traces of the door and the sprawling bodies provided a means for Teela to see.

Placing her blades back on her belt, she picked up the undamaged pulse rifle and cautiously approached the doorway. Blown inward by the blast, the bent and distorted door lay on top of something just inside the chamber.

"Bill!" Teela cried, grabbing the edge of the hot door and flipping it over.

"I'm over here," Bill answered.

"We gotta go, right now!" Teela cried, stepping over the unconscious warriors trapped under the twisted door.

"Cain't move. They got me tied down again," Bill answered from the gurney. Moving with haste, Teela released the wraps and guided Bill out of the room.

"Wait a second," she said at the doorway. As she darted back into the total darkness of the room, Bill stood nervously, feeling weak and exposed in the smoky corridor. He could hear rustling, and within a few moments Teela emerged with a long object wrapped in the gurney's sheet beneath one arm.

"Come on!" she said, grabbing Bill by the elbow and nearly dragging him into a transit tube. They exited at the bio section's lowest level and barely managed to catch a cube headed forward. Teela had Bill face the corner with his head down to minimize the attention his presence would draw. It was little solace that within a few minutes they would reach the Nursery, where the others were being held. It seemed so far away. Teela wished for the invisibility of a birthing unit; with her outfit and Bill's alien appearance, they may as well have had flashing lights on their heads.

Teela deliberated with her confused thoughts. She knew she would be held responsible for the deaths of the warriors in the Bio section, and she believed that Afron was planning more transfers. She groaned as a sick feeling of dread rose and she contemplated her few options.

"Did ya get hurt?" Bill looked down at Teela, who stood with her back against the wall.

"No, I'm not injured, just worried. Things aren't going as planned. There's a bad person here that is planning to … well, I'm not sure what exactly she means to do, but I'm pretty certain that whatever it is, you wouldn't have liked it." Teela looked up at Bill's face for the first time since leaving the dark room. She glanced away quickly. The familiarity of his features only increased her anxiety.

"You're in big trouble for busting me out, huh?" Bill asked.

"Yeah, I think. I don't know what I'm doing, and most of the time I'm not sure why I'm doing it," Teela answered, her voice weary.

"You talk like him, you know," Bill said. He squinted his new eyes and tried to focus his vision, hoping to see some kind of response. Teela kept her head turned away and ignored the comment.

Dealing with Afron was only a fraction of Teela's concerns. When she returned Bill to the others, she intended to inform them of the treachery that had resulted in their abductions and now the treachery that threatened to prevent their return home. In attempting to anticipate the humans' responses and figure out how to avoid revealing the secret transfer, her loyalties and obligations intermingled with agonizing results.

Riding the transit cube the length of the vessel, they left the Bio section and entered the Education section. Teela nervously fingered the objects in her pocket. She pulled the wedding band out and tried furtively to shove it onto one of her fingers, but discovered that the tips of her clawed fingers were too large. Removing the chain from around her neck, she slipped the ring onto it with the Christopher medal and refastened it. Julie once told Daedalus that Saint Christopher was the patron saint of sailors, and would watch over him as he would the souls of wayward seamen, seeing to his safe return. Rubbing the small medallion between the two thumbs of her hand, she wondered if Rebecca knew a prayer that would help the medallion work the magic it would take to guide all of them home.

Exiting the cube and taking a short jump down a transit spoke without incident, the unusual pair approached the entrance to the Nursery chamber where the humans were being held. The area was crowded with birthing units and adolescent shells from the adjacent housing section. They pushed their way slowly through the assemblage toward a familiar sound. Crystal, Catherine, and Marsha were harmonizing to a thumping and chiming rhythm.

One of the older birth mothers in the crowd wore a pair of seriously stretched-out stretch jeans and a silk-screened T-shirt that Teela was certain Marsha had been wearing earlier. The image of a clenched fist with the middle finger pointing up was stretched out of proportion over a grossly distended abdomen. On the back, in bold capitals beneath the female glyph symbol, were the words “Maidens Rule.” *They must be having a good laugh about this*, Teela thought angrily as she pushed her way through the crowd.

Crystal was tapping out a melody on a row of metal drinking flasks lined up across the front desk. Marsha, now wearing the tah of a birthing unit, was beating out a rhythm on the other end of the counter with a pair of slippers while Catherine danced and sang. Ruth and Margaret were sitting by the door clapping their hands to the beat, and Beth sat alone in the far corner. The remainder of the group was back in the sleeping area.

“I thought I told you to keep the door shut and locked!” Teela shouted at Ruth over the music.

Ruth looked surprised.

“Bill!” squealed Ruth and Margaret in unison, jumping to their feet.

Ignoring Teela, they took Bill by the arms and led him into the Nursery amidst shouting and cheers from the others emerging from the sleeping area, roused by her noisy entrance.

The chamber filled with laughter and greetings as Bill made his rounds and the group examined his face and hands, questioning him about his experiences, condition, and treatment.

The atmosphere seemed festive and happy. Unable to participate, though longing to do so, Teela moved to the edge of the gathering, feeling isolated yet satisfied to see these people happy, if only for this brief moment. Surveying the growing crowd of Korlah, she saw warrior guards moving toward the open door of the Nursery. She pushed the heavy door closed and locked it from within. Finding the door bolted, the warriors moved to the large viewing window and stood there glaring at her.

Each of the women greeted Bill in turn, giving his face and hands a close inspection. The newly grafted skin was bright pink with red blotches on the nose and cheekbones, where the previous owner had suffered burns and blisters. The square Roman nose looked plainly out of place by Bill's heavy brow and thick lips. It was apparent that he could see, although not very well, by the way he moved his face close to those greeting him, blinking his new bloodshot green eyes in an effort to bring them into focus.

Teela was thoroughly enjoying watching everyone swarm around Bill and failed to see Beth storm up from the side. Beth grabbed her by the throat and threw her backward. Teela dropped her package as she struggled to keep from falling. She resisted the urge to dig her claws into Beth's hand while trying in vain to pull it free. Beth had her pinned to the wall, one hand on her throat, the other gripping her by the crown tendrils, her right knee was pressed painfully into Teela's groin.

"You killed him! You killed Dade. You killed him and stole what he knew. Did you think giving his face to Bill would make it all right? Huh, did you asshole?!" Beth screamed into Teela's face. Releasing her throat, Beth grabbed the ring and Christopher medal and pulled the chain tight.

"Let go! Don't!" Teela screamed, digging her claws into the flesh of Beth's wrist.

"What? This little thing?" Beth taunted, ignoring the rivulets of blood that began to flow from the puncture wounds. She gave the fragile chain malicious little tugs.

"Why would these alien objects mean anything to you?" Beth demanded, pressing her nose against Teela's cheek. Her eye less than an inch from Teela's.

"How much of Dade is there?" she whispered.

Terrified by Beth's accusation, Teela remembered Afron's threat. *If they learn the secret, none of them will go home!*

Beth's expression changed instantly. She released the chain and her mouth moved as if she were going to speak. Releasing Teela's crown tendrils and throat, Beth stepped back and looked around at the others.

"Did … did you hear that?" Beth asked. "Did anybody else hear that?" She looked to the others, who were now silent and watching the confrontation.

Ignoring Beth's question, Ruth pushed between them.

"Are you the one that was here earlier?" Ruth asked.

"Yes. Why was the door open?" Teela asked hoarsely, rubbing her throat.

"Because I told her it didn't matter," Beth said. "If you noodleheads decide you want to take one of us, or all of us, you just do it, right? Like you took Dade and then Bill. Whose turn is it to disappear next, huh?" Beth cried, recovered from the shock of Teela's mental projection. "Your boss must be pretty happy with your performance, giving you that pretty new dress."

Beth moved around Ruth and assumed an aggressive stance. Teela turned to face her, moving into a defensive martial arts position.

"These people need a leader," Teela said. "One that's smart enough to know how to play the part. You never confront the enemy unless you know their strength and numbers. You never attack without a plan or purpose. You use diplomacy and subterfuge until you are left with absolutely no other options. I believe that you may have been an excellent soldier at one time, but from everything I have seen, you are one piss-poor leader."

A tapping sound interrupted Teela, directing her attention to the door.

A runner from the Security section stood at the viewing window, holding a small case. After verifying that the warriors were a safe distance from the door, Teela opened it just enough for the runner to pass the case through the door. Bowing respectfully, she accepted it and locked the door again. Teela opened the case. Inside were military dog tags and several log bars, one of which was intimately familiar.

"The commander of this vessel has sent something for you to see, a little show-and-tell session that I believe you will find most … illuminating," Teela said.

Teela removed the chain from around her neck and withdrew the knife from her pocket. Holding her hand out to Beth, Teela waited for her to take the items. Beth, puzzled, finally held out an open hand, and Teela dropped the keepsakes into her palm. Beth looked at the objects and then at Teela, waiting for an explanation.

"I had promised to return these to Dade's … next of kin, personally. But I can see now what a foolish notion that was. I apologize". Raising her voice and turning as she spoke, Teela addressed the others in the room.

"I apologize to all of you for not telling you sooner. Dade did not survive his injuries." There were some muffled gasps around the room, but mostly there was an uncomfortable silence.

Walking slowly across the large chamber toward a com panel at the far side, Teela continued to speak, subconsciously rattling the box she held in her hand.

"I know you don't trust me. I know you probably won't believe me. But I truly do wish to see you all get home safely. Unfortunately, there are events and politics currently outside my control that threaten to prevent that. As unpleasant as you may find the facts, you need to know what I now know so that you will better understand the obstacles ahead." Teela set the box down when she reached the communications console and turned to the group of ten humans.

"First, I will tell you why we, the Korlah, have come to your area of the galaxy. Second, I will tell you of the treachery that tore you from your homes and brought you here. And finally, I will tell you why it is imperative for us to work together."

Opening the box, Teela sorted through the contents, placing the logs in the order she planned to display them. There was an educational log on Korlah history, the Kahshinki-backed human attack, Teela's medical log, and the log from the Kahshinki sample-gathering vessel. Teela placed the medical log back into the box.

Bill moved to the front and leaned forward, squinting his eyes. The others formed a loose semicircle around the com panel.

Teela pushed in the first log bar, dimmed the chamber's glowlamps, and moved behind the group to narrate. The screen filled with images of a barren wasteland, the ruins of roads and buildings barely discernible in the gaunt, lifeless landscape.

Nervously fiddling with the contents of her pocket, Teela withdrew the wire-rim glasses and handed them silently to Bill, who studied them for a moment before putting them on. Seeing clearly for the first time since his injury, Bill smiled broadly and nodded at Teela. She smiled, but her smile quickly faded when she turned her attention to the projection displayed on the wall.

"This was our home planet," Teela began. "It didn't always look like this. It was once covered with forests, trees, vast savannas, and great freshwater lakes. The Korlah were a tribal race. Many clans, large and small, lived on the edge of the forests. When the Kahshinki first arrived, we believed they were powerful spirits and gave them great honor and respect. We were rewarded with weapons and technology.

"This soon disrupted the peaceful balance that had existed on our planet for centuries. The dominant tribe waged a great war using the Kahshinki technology, until all other opposing clans had been conquered. The medicine and technology the Kahshinki had provided us allowed our numbers to grow rapidly. While this was happening, our leaders looked the other way as the Kahshinki began taking many Korlah from the planet. When the theft of our people and resources became too much for even the leaders to accept, we resisted. Our forces were crushed within hours, and the Kahshinki proceeded to process our planet in a way that we have come to call the harvest.

"With our defenses destroyed, Korlah duplicates that had been born and raised on the Kahshinki ships stormed our cities with powerful weapons against which we had no defense. Our people were shipped off-world onto vessels like this one, processed, and stored as food. All the males of our species were hunted down and harvested. Procreation was automated using selected genotypes. The utility of the female gender, being much more useful for this purpose, was all that remained. The Kahshinki control their slave population through a strictly regulated cloning process, where only females of selected genetic types are duplicated.

"Within one generation, our genetic diversity was reduced to four originals. Within three generations, knowledge of our previous culture would have been completely eliminated if it weren't for a small group of our leaders who had gone into hiding during the invasion.

"Our planet was being used as a base for the construction and stocking of new ships that were intended to expand the Kahshinki infestation in our galaxy. Two new ships were built and launched into deep space while our leaders struggled to organize a slave revolt. Working from hidden enclaves, they were able to capture and reeducate some of the duplicates, returning them to work for the Kahshinki while recruiting more of the slaves to join their liberation movement. Since the Kahshinki preferred to stay in the low gravity of space, they seldom came to the planet's surface and were unaware that the leaders had seized control of the slave production and training centers.

"Once we had control of our planet, it was easy for us to move into space, filling the positions of pilots and technicians with loyal duplicates. With the exception of the sabat, this marking on the face that is used to differentiate the duplicates, there was no way anyone could tell one duplicate from another. The infiltration took several generations, and the Korlah leadership waited patiently, suffering horrible treatment and conditions. When the third ship was completed and stocked, the fourth was already under construction. As soon as the third ship departed, the Korlah took advantage of the reduced forces of Kahshinki, achieving a quick victory with few losses.

"The Kahshinki must have sent out a distress signal, because the third ship returned. The two giant vessels and thousands of smaller fighters fought a running battle through the system that lasted for three solar cycles. When the Kahshinki realized they were not going to win, they triggered a weapon they had hidden on the surface of our planet that enveloped the entire globe in an energy field that excited the molecules of our atmosphere to the point of spontaneous combustion. The atmosphere burned for less than a single rotation, but before it had finished, the lakes had boiled dry and the atmosphere was poisoned. All life to a microbial level had been extinguished.

"Having destroyed the viability of our planet, the Kahshinki attempted to flee. We pursued, eventually boarding and capturing the Kahshinki vessel. From the records on board, we were able to determine the destinations of the other two Kahshinki invasion vessels. Without the foundation of the base planet to work from, it took many cycles for us to repair and restock the ships to pursue and punish the Kahshinki invaders. A small contingent of Korlah was left at the dead planet with the mission of restoring it using the few plants and animals that the Kahshinki had selected for use in their shipboard farms and gardens. It is the dream of every Korlah to one day return to our home world, but we realize it is a dream that will not be fulfilled during our existence.

"This vessel you are on is the original vessel the Kahshinki used to invade our planet, over one thousand twenty-three cycles, or approximately nine hundred seventy-three Earth years ago. Since then, over twenty generations of Korlah duplicates have operated this ship, fighting twelve successful campaigns against the Kahshinki, destroying five vessels and capturing seven. We have never been so close yet so far from stopping the Kahshinki in this area of their expansion. We have faced armies of Korlah duplicates in other planetary systems. Unable to find any other species in any of the other systems as capable of adaptation to their needs, the Kahshinki have always relied heavily on their Korlah slaves.

"The use of Korlah duplicates by the Kahshinki has always been their weakness. Our most successful strategy has been to capture their pilots and warriors and substitute our own, who then return to the Kahshinki campaign vessel to sabotage their defenses and reveal their attack plans. Unfortunately, the Kahshinki have now found a more suitable species for their armies and pilots."

Removing the first log bar from the console, she snapped in the one of the human attack. She took the identification tags from the box and tossed them into Beth's lap.

"A little over seventeen years ago, with assistance from the Kahshinki, armed forces who were not only from your planet, but from your country, initiated an unprovoked attack on this vessel. Using what appears to have been a deadly nerve gas and explosives, they were able to kill more Korlah and cause more damage than the Kahshinki had ever been able to in all the battles we have fought."

Teela narrated the images as Shyron had, describing the activities of the attackers, the resulting fatalities, and the long-term effects on the vessel and its crew. By the end of the scenes of adolescent bodies piled up in the Shell section, Teela could hear several of the women weeping.

"The Warrior section, where you were previously housed, suffered the most severe casualties. Over 1,880,000 died from toxic gas or decompression when the explosions breached the hull. They were blamed for the failure of our defensives and have been castigated ever since. I was amazed that they were disciplined enough to follow their orders to keep you alive rather than killing you when they had the chance."

Teela removed the attack log bar and snapped in the one from the Kahshinki freighter.

"This log served to prove to us that you were not invaders like the soldiers before you. That you had in fact been offered up to the Kahshinki as tokens of appreciation by the same government and military that assisted the Kahshinki attack our vessel." She paused briefly as several in the group exclaimed their disbelief, then continued. She explained the significance of the communications between the vessel and Earth, noting the locations of the Air Force installations that had provided both the permission and flight path for the Kahshinki kidnappers. The group was deathly quiet as the log played the expedited versions of their abductions. Teela needed to say nothing at this point. What had happened was perfectly clear to each of them.

"This remaining log bar shows our pilot warriors battling the Kahshinki vessels that were attempting to destroy your fleeing vessel. The pilots of the Kahshinki vessels were extremely skilled, much more so than any we had ever fought previously. Even with vessels that were poorly armed and that possessed little shielding and were outnumbered ten to four, they managed to damage seven of our craft with their low-power pulse blasts before we finally destroyed them. The freighter you were in disabled one of the Kahshinki fighters when you collided with it, allowing us to capture the pilot alive. The pilot is human, from your very own government's military."

The image of the human pilot pacing his cell filled the screen.

"Son of a bitch!" Beth said. "I'd like to have a talk with that cocksucker."

The screen went blank, and Teela removed the log bar from the reader.

"What about the last tape, the one you put back in the box. That's another recording, isn't it? What's on that one?" Beth asked, pointing.

Teela's face and crown tendrils flushed with anger.

"Nothing of any interest."

"I'm interested. I got nothing else to do. Why don't you show us what's on that one? Unless, of course, you got something to hide."

Turning away, Teela removed the log bar from the box and rolled it around in the palm of her hand for a few seconds before throwing it spitefully at Beth's face. Beth caught it without flinching.

"Motivation. The motivation that was needed to coerce me into this … this effort. That's what's recorded. See if you can make any sense of it. Feel free," Teela said.

Teela sat down on the desk, her back to the screen. She glared at the guards through the viewing window until they looked away.

"Jeez, I think that's her," she heard Bill whisper.

"You don't have to be embarrassed," Marsha offered. "There was a whole room of your people's kids here, and none of um were wearing a damn thing. Besides, a big pregnant one traded me her dress for my clothes, and she changed clothes right here in front of everyone."

The comments did little to comfort Teela.

"So are you going to tell us what this is supposed to mean or are we supposed to guess?" Beth asked.

The visual portion of the display was over, and the screen was filled with the technicians' summary of the examination.

Teela approached the screen, her crown tendrils blanched to a pale gray as shame and embarrassment replaced the flush of anger she had felt. Withdrawing the log bar, she dropped it into the box with the others and snapped the lid shut.

"This vessel is governed under strict utilitarian guidelines. There is no disability program, no welfare, no social security, and no elder care. When a member of this crew can no longer perform her intended function to a predefined optimum, she is recycled like a used tire. Terminated painlessly, or so I've been told, and ground up as organic feed for a host of worms, insects, rodents, and eels that make up our staple diet. The examination you have had the pleasure of observing revealed that I am incapable of performing my primary function as a birthing unit. An order for my termination was subsequently initiated.

"Since I was considered expendable, I was the perfect candidate for use as an experimental communicator with a dangerous and hostile species. You see, they were pretty sure you would kill me the first chance you got. In which case, it would be no great loss.

"The good news is, since you didn't kill me, I'm being given a chance to develop a strategy that, if it can be proven to be in the best interest of the Korlah campaign, will result in returning all of you home."

Margaret started clapping, and the rest followed suit. A few of them whistled and hooted.

"When … how long … until we can go … home?" Ann asked.

"There are problems," Teela said, pausing as the group grew quiet and pensive.

"I think she killed a couple of them soldier types to git me back here," Bill whispered to Ann, his deep voice carrying quite effectively in the silent room.

"The Korlah leaders have no intention of fighting a battle on two fronts, and if the Kahshinki invasion force were to win this campaign, as it is feared they will, our leaders will not permit them to use Earth to bolster their defenses and continue their expansion. If we, meaning me and this group, are unable to negotiate a military alliance between the Korlah and Earth's leaders, the Korlah leaders intend to sterilize Earth, using the same type of weapon the Kahshinki used to sterilize our home world."

Teela's statement was greeted with stunned silence from everyone but Rebecca, who stood and launched into a prayer for the condemned.

"Shut up! Shut up damn it!" Beth shouted at Rebecca, who cowered and silenced.

"They would destroy the planet? Are you saying they're planning to destroy the whole damn planet? You bastards are that cold-blooded?" Beth exclaimed.

Nodding gravely, Teela calmly responded. "What you call 'cold-blooded,' they consider merciful. They would do it to spare the inhabitants the horrors of harvest and to stop the Kahshinki before they can expand to another system."

"Mighty fucking white of them," Beth mumbled, moving toward Teela. Ruth stepped between them.

"Knock off the profanity, Beth. I'm sick of your foul mouth," Ruth said. Turning to Teela, she softened her voice and expression. "Although I obviously can't speak for everyone here, I'd like to apologize for the way you've been treated by … some of us. I wish now that I had spoken up or done something to stop it. I'm sorry. I don't know what else I can say. What can I do to help?"

The girls, Bill, Margaret, and Ann nodded agreement with Ruth's apology, offering their support as well. Teela put her hand out to Ruth, who recoiled at first, and then paused and confidently accepted it. Teela turned her around to face Beth and extended her other hand to the scowling woman.

"If this is going to work, we're going to have to do it together, as a team. I have committed to this endeavor, and I need each and every one of you to do the same," Teela said as sincerely as her rough Korlah voice permitted.

Taking Teela's hand, Beth gave it a firm, slightly painful squeeze.

"Save the planet Earth? Why not? Ought to be a walk in the park after the bullshit we've been through so far."

Nervous laughter from the others helped break the remaining tension. The group began to talk about the information they had just been inundated with, and the buzz of conversation filled the room.

Beth squeezed Teela's hand harder, the challenge subtle and unnoticed by Ruth. Teela squeezed back, grinding the bones in Beth's hand together. If Beth was in pain, she gave no indication of it. She winked at Teela and released her grip, and Teela followed suit.

Teela sat down at the communications console and entered her end-of-shift report to Shyron. Her experience and training on the use of the console being as limited as it was, the action was both tedious and time-consuming. Teela described the meeting with Afron and the directors. She told of how the area by the transfer station was being prepared for the human captives, and how Bill had already been bound to a gurney and taken there. She told of the explosion and the dead warriors, going to great length to apologize for the accidental fireball. She related her fears that there were plans to experiment with the remaining humans and of her determination to prevent that. She did not mention that Gremensh was her source of information on Afron's plans or that the actions she suspected were of Afron's design, nor did she give mention the three pulse weapons and two blades lying in a bundle on the floor of the Nursery. After sending the message, Teela cleared the screen and looked at the bundle, wondering if what she was about to do was the right thing. She clenched her fists nervously and grimaced at the burning pain as her claws opened the wounds on her palms. Then she clenched them again; the pain helped to clarify her thoughts. She left the console and moved deliberately to the bundle. She picked it up and took it into the sleeping chamber.

"Beth, Bill, Ruth! In here, now!" Teela shouted as she passed out of sight of the warriors behind the viewing window. She unwrapped the weapons, wiping the blood from her hands with the fabric.

"You're bleeding! What happened?" Bill asked, concerned.

"It's nothing. A nervous tic. I accidentally did it to myself." Teela showed him the punctures.

"Oh yes!" exclaimed Beth, seeing the weapons on the floor as she entered the room, but when she bent to pick one up, Teela put her foot on it.

"Not yet! I have some things I want to say before I let you take them."

"Let me take them? What makes you think you can stop me, stumpy?" Beth said.

"Shut up! Shut the hell up!" Ruth shouted angrily at Beth. "If you want to die here, I don't care, but don't take the rest of us with you. If you are so stupid that you cannot recognize friend from foe, just … just … damn it, Beth. Please … stop it."

Beth retreated, her hands up in surrender. "For the record, I don't trust this noodlehead any more than the rest, and I honestly don't think we stand a snowball's chance in hell of ever getting back home. I do think they're gonna jack our brains and cut us up like frogs in an eighth grade biology class. I have no desire to die any sooner than anyone else, but when I do, I don't want to be tied down screaming my lungs out like Jimmy. I'd rather die fighting."

"We gotta trust her. We have to keep hoping there's a chance out of this. Don't we?" Bill pleaded.

"Never give up hope. Never!" Teela said. *Reject despair,* she thought using the Korlah equivalent of hope.

The rest of the group had taken seats on sleep platforms.

"Trust in each other," Teela implored. "Trust your combined strengths. There are politics afoot that are threatening to destroy the plan I have for getting us home. I can guarantee that you will not be consumed; yet, Beth's fears of experimentation are probably not far from the truth. I brought these weapons because I don't know which way the political struggle will go. If my plan fails, they will come to take you. If you resist, they will use physical force. If you use weapons, they will use weapons. Since they will want to take you alive, their weapons will be set low, nonlethal. Since you have already demonstrated that you will not honor that battle convention and because they don't want to risk losing trained and experienced warriors in a firefight with lethal consequence, they will sacrifice their youngest, least-experienced warriors to deplete your weapons. If you use the high lethal setting on these weapons and kill any of these child warriors, you will prove that humans are brutal, cowardly, and unworthy of honor. Although they may not kill you, at least not immediately, your actions will certainly convince the Korlah leadership that sterilization of Earth is justified."

"Jeez Louise! So why did you bring us weapons?" Bill asked, dismayed.

"I have been trying to convince my leadership that the humans who perpetrated the attack on this vessel do not represent the inhabitants of Earth. I have been trying to convince them that you, a random sampling, best serve as an example of your planet's honorable residents. If I can—"

"Why bother resisting at all?" Beth interrupted. "It hurts like hell to get shot by one of these goddamn guns. You say they're probably gonna nuke Earth anyway, so why shouldn't I heat one of these babies up and kill as many of you ugly bastards as I can?"

"Korlah, especially the warriors, love a good fight. The longer the fight, the more difficult the battle, the greater the requirements for honor gained and honor lost. If you can hurt them and bloody them, without killing, you will gain honor and earn their respect. Having done so, it will be extremely difficult for any of the Korlah leaders to do anything that is in any way less than forthright and honorable without losing their own honor by doing so.

"You must understand, if you kill even one without observing protocol, every one of its birthmates will be bound by honor to see your existence ended. It is this blood honor that has driven us to pursue the Kahshinki halfway across this galaxy with the sole purpose of effecting their complete and utter extermination. Right now, there is a debate as to whether or not Earth belongs on that agenda. If you kill a single Korlah in a dishonorable manner, for any reason, the debate will be over."

"What about the ones we killed when they found us?" Ruth asked with somber reckoning.

"None have died!" Teela exclaimed, realizing they didn't know. "Badly damaged, yes. They are embarrassed and ashamed, but none have ceased their existence. You have taken honor from our warriors twice now. Bill is a legend for having gained victory over a Kahshinki in unarmed combat, and Beth is notorious as the 'brutal one' for her fearless, aggressive battle tactics. Every one of our warriors wants to defeat you and regain our honor." Teela removed her foot from the weapon and stepped back.

"You make it sound like losing is inevitable. What if we win?" Beth asked.

Teela considered the question as she watched Beth sling the rifle over her shoulder, energize it, raise the setting to high and back to low, and finally de-energize it with agile confidence.

"I don't know," Teela said. "I would expect the warrior in charge to be punished for failing and another to be sent in her place. This would continue until victory was achieved."

"They shot me point blank. I wasn't armed, and your brave fucking warriors shot me! What's all this honor crap about? They're gonna do whatever they're gonna do, and I don't think it has a damn thing to do with honor," Beth said.

"I cannot guarantee that every warrior will behave honorably. In fact, I can guarantee that some will not. Much of the tradition and history of Korlah culture has been lost or forgotten. While our leaders and their loyal supporters get fat, those who oppose them or are too weak to resist are starving. With the damaged condition of our vessel, many have traded their honor for greed and power or food. But still, despite the corruption and decay, honor remains a powerful bargaining tool, and likely the only one we have. Already, stories abound of how the beasts, as they refer to you, are fierce and fearless. That even though you have no fangs or claws and are unarmed, you have defeated armed warriors."

"You're talking about public opinion," Ruth said. "You think that if we behave honorably and they don't, it will make a difference in their decision?"

"That is my hope," Teela answered somberly.

"Bullshit!" Beth coughed. "Okay, let's talk about bang for the buck. With regard to this Korlah honor mumbo-jumbo bull, if this is going to be some kind of glorified prize fight, how do we negotiate the biggest purse for the match?" Beth asked, intending to be anything but constructive. Teela stared blankly at her for a few seconds before grabbing her and giving her a quick hug. Jumping back to dodge Beth's right hook, Teela laughed.

"Yes! Yes! A prize fight. A Spectacle!" she cried. "I will teach you how to pick a fight, Korlah style. Win or lose, you will demonstrate honor in its most recognized and accepted form. Winning, of course, would be very, very helpful."

Winking at Beth, who was still recovering from the surprise hug, Teela moved in close. “Ms. Porter, are you half as tough as you pretend to be?” she asked, her voice mimicking Beth’s sneering sarcasm.

“I never pretend. I am who I am. I am what I am. No excuses and never any apologies. Who do I have to fight?” Beth asked.

“Who you fight is unimportant. How you negotiate the fight is critical. I will teach you the protocol and the words. The showmanship, I think, will come naturally.” Teela moved to a corner of the chamber and proceeded to clear an area of sleep platforms. When she finished, she motioned for Beth to join her.

For the next several hours, Beth and Teela discussed and rehearsed the actions and words needed to challenge a would-be Korlah aggressor into unarmed combat. Refusal would be tantamount to cowardice and would be the best thing for their cause. Winning the contest would be the next best thing, although Beth would likely find herself facing another and then another challenger until she were exhausted or defeated. But a defeat would not be without benefit; the victor would be bound by honor to treat Beth and her section mates with the respect due a warrior.

Feeling that she had taught Beth as much as she could, Teela left her practicing the guttural grunts that comprised the necessary Korlah words, and she moved to the outer chamber to see if she could contact Shyron for instructions. The communications console was flashing, indicating a message had been sent to this terminal specifically. Standing at an angle to block the inquisitive eyes on the other side of the viewing glass, Teela fanned the control. The first message appeared, but the light continued to flash, indicating that there were more.

The first message was from Afron, directing her to report to a chamber near the one where she had found Bill. Although expected, the message gave Teela a sick, sinking feeling. She fought the tremors in her hands as she thought of how angry Afron would be and of the certainty of punishment she would face upon arrival. She slammed her fists against the table, exchanging the fear for anger and pain. The next two messages repeated the first with increasing urgency. She gripped the sides of the console with her bloodied hands as though she would rip it from the wall.

When she read the final message, she exhaled a long breath of relief and relaxed her grip.

> T MISSION ADJUTANT, ASSISTANT TO THE POTENTATE. MESSAGE RECEIVED. AFRON HAS REPORTED DAMAGED HUMAN REPAIRED AND RETURNED TO THE SHELL SECTION. TWO WARRIORS REMOVED FROM SECTION ROSTER DUE TO THE ACCIDENTAL EXPLOSION OF A FAULTY PULSE RIFLE. SEND NO MORE MESSAGES; WE MUST MEET TO DISCUSS YOUR PLAN. I AM DISPATCHING SECURITY SECTION GUARDS TO RELIEVE WARRIOR SECTION OF HUMAN CONFINEMENT DUTIES. YOU BRING GREAT HONOR TO OUR SECTION WITH YOUR DEFEAT OF THE NONS, BUT YOU HAVE GREATER RESPONSIBILITY TO THE SUCCESS OF THE MISSION, AND SUCH RISKS ARE UNACCEPTABLE. A PERSONAL CONTINGENT WITH INTIMATE KNOWLEDGE OF OUR DISCUSSION WILL ESCORT YOU TO MY CURRENT LOCATION. SEND NO MESSAGES; WE MUST MEET TO DISCUSS OUR PLANS. BY FANG OR BY CLAW, MISSION, HONOR, GLORY.
>
> SHYRON 32.7.

Teela wanted to shout with joy. She was relieved that Afron was taking responsibility for the return of Bill and that no blame was sought for the deaths of the warriors. By the time she finished reading the message, she beamed with pride that the Mission Potentate was assigning her honor and giving her personal recognition as a section mate. Teela turned to the viewing window, wanting someone, anyone, to see the recognition she was being afforded. But the prying eyes were gone, replaced by the backs of ten Security section guards in full battle armor. Clearing the screen, Teela peered between the guards at the situation unfolding outside the Nursery.

A warrior and security guard gesticulated intensely in the middle of the main chamber in what looked like a heated argument. Across the chamber, the remaining five warriors stood with energized pulse rifles pointed at the security guards, who stood behind their shields, pulse rifles energized but not aimed.

"Oh shit!" Teela said out loud. She ran into the sleeping chamber, slid through the doorway and almost fell as she turned the corner on the highly polished floor.

"Things are heating up outside. I need to go try and defuse the situation. When I go out, they may try to force their way in. You will need to cover the door," Teela stammered, trying to conceal her desperate concern. "I have to leave for a while. Don't let them in."

"What about the prize fight?" Beth asked with surprise.

"If I fail, if something happens to me, the spectacle event will be a last resort. If they force their way in, you submit your challenge, but not until. I told you that," Teela said.

"Crystal, Marsha, Catherine, you three handle the door!" shouted Ruth. "Bill, Beth, grab your guns and heat 'em up. Stay out of sight and don't shoot unless I say."

"Sir! Yes, sir!" Beth shouted. She grabbed a pulse rifle, energized it and moved to one side of the door with the fluid movement of an experienced soldier. Bill, slower but with precision and skill, energized his rifle. Using his body to conceal the weapon, he crossed the threshold and assumed a position opposite Beth, nodding to Ruth.

"Whenever you're ready," Ruth said. Crystal opened the door just wide enough for Teela to slip through.

"Hey, Dade!" Beth called out, not quite shouting. Turning her head in response, Teela caught herself halfway. Without looking back, she slipped out the door. Crystal and Marsha pushed it shut, and Catherine latched and locked it.

"Good luck, Squirt," Beth said softly.

15 - Shyron

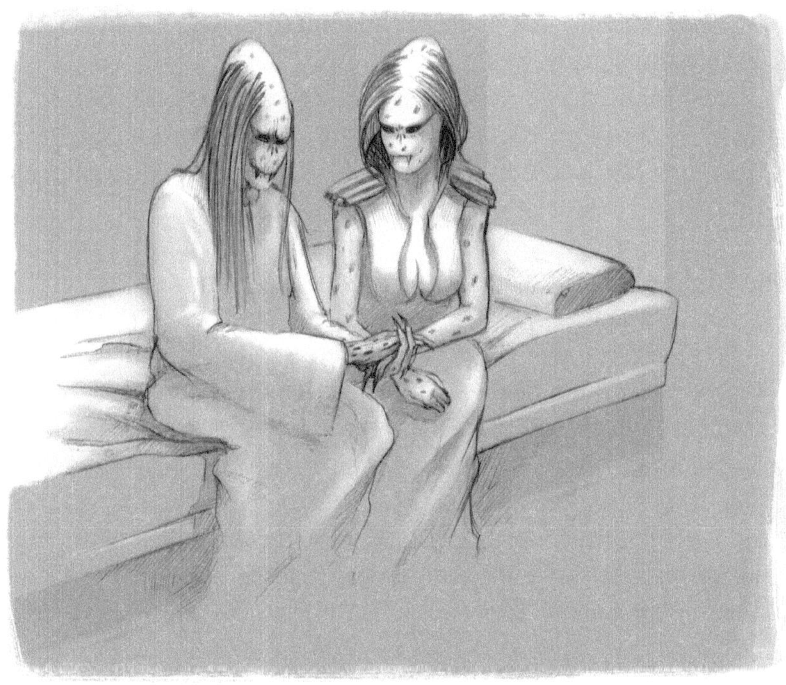

The Security section guards gave no indication that they were aware Teela had slipped out of the Nursery. In the center of the chamber, a heavyset warrior and a lean, muscular Security section guard were arguing.

"Strategy does not make decisions without Council authorization. Until I can verify that you are here on Council business, you and your warriors must leave," the security guard demanded calmly.

"Both the Warrior and Strategy sections are undertaking actions critical to the Mission objective. Security has no business here. Return to your duties protecting our esteemed leaders before I am forced to remove you," the warrior shouted, brandishing her pulse rifle.

"As Mission Adjutant," Teela interjected, "Assistant to the Potentate, it is my responsibility in this section to ensure actions critical to the Mission are undertaken as directed by Shyron and the Council leaders."

The Security section guard, a senior tenth-level, glanced down at Teela. Stepping back and bowing deeply, the guard crossed her hands at the chest, palms out, and extended her claws in a respectful soldier's salute.

"Your Eminence, I apologize for ignoring your arrival. I was distracted. I am Senior Guard Plefauna. As directed by Shyron, I am here to allay the concerns you have regarding the safety of our guests and to escort you to your next appointment."

"I am aware of your assignment, Senior Guard Plefauna," Teela responded politely. She approached the senior warrior, fifth level, closely and locked eyes with her. The warrior's eye slits narrowed in disrespect.

"I understand the desire of the Warrior section to redeem their honor following the embarrassing handling of our guests earlier," Teela began. "I have expressed my belief that you have since handled the situation adequately, restoring any honor lost, and should now return to your assignments to prepare for campaign. The Security section will assume the responsibility for guarding and protecting this Mission asset, for that is what they are trained to do.

"I am surprised to see energized pulse weapons in the Shell section. I see no enemies present to warrant such a serious violation of section protocol." Teela cocked her head and narrowed her eyes, indicating that the challenge would escalate if continued.

With a loud growl the warrior broke eye contact.

"Secure weapons!" she barked. The other warriors immediately de-energized and slung their rifles. The security guards complied without being ordered.

"My assignment comes from the Strategy section and Warrior section leaders. My orders are explicit. I have been given no alternatives," the senior warrior barked.

"If every time the assignments of one section overlapped or conflicted with the assignments of another and weapons were utilized to resolve the conflict, we would likely destroy ourselves long before the Kahshinki could. What exactly is your assignment, Senior Warrior RIAUGH19.01057?" Teela asked, reading the sabat on the warrior's face.

The warrior's crown tendrils blanched slightly. Teela knew she had struck a nerve. Believing that Teela could access her shift duty assignments for confirmation, the warrior was forced to answer truthfully.

"I have been specifically directed to undertake actions critical to the Mission."

"What actions!" Teela cried, stomping to the com console. The young warriors sidestepped out of Teela's path and snapped rigidly to attention, unsure of her rank or status in this situation.

"To guard and contain. My posted assignment is to guard and contain," the senior warrior called out to Teela. "But I have explicit instructions—"

"Until your explicit instructions appear as a duty assignment, they have no official basis outside your own section. This is not your section; it is mine. These guards are here at my request, and their assignment is posted. I am instructing you that your services are no longer needed in my section. You may stay if you wish, but it has been my personal experience that warriors detest the odors of the Shell section and loathe the company of birthers." Teela stomped back to the agitated warrior. Once again, she attempted to make eye contact. The warrior stared straight ahead, avoiding Teela's gaze. Her crown tendrils had shrunk from their earlier enraged state.

"I have my instructions," the warrior repeated evenly, her aggressive demeanor gone.

"Senior Warrior Riaugh, exercise great caution when following undocumented instructions, regardless of how explicit they seem. I have reviewed many records in the archives of those who followed undocumented instructions and broke laws, or by circumstance, failed to meet their assignments and were consequently punished, often quite severely. Very few who admitted to providing these undocumented instructions were punished, usually claiming their instructions were misunderstood. Without a record, it was the word of the superior over that of the subordinate. Be certain, absolutely certain, that the instructions you follow are clearly understood. It would be a shame, so close to campaign, to lose such a clearly valuable asset due to a simple misunderstanding." With that, Teela turned her back to the warrior.

"I apologize for the delay; I am now ready to leave," Teela said, bowing to the senior security guard.

Plefauna issued instructions to her subordinates in the sign language used for communicating with Kahshinki that had become a private language within the Security section. In response, the guards lifted their chest-high shields and drove them down with a resounding boom that echoed throughout the Shell section.

Three security soldiers marched forward to take up positions around Teela. Once Plefauna had taken the lead, Teela was encased in a protective envelope of shields, weapons, and soldiers.

"Your Eminence, for your safety, we will be moving at an urgent pace. Please follow my steps and stay close. You may find it helpful to hold onto my belt," Plefauna instructed, her face disappearing with a hiss and click behind the thick reflective lens of her helmet's shield. With a thump of her shield, the group moved forward as one. After stumbling several times, Teela finally fell when they turned from one corridor into another. The procession ground to a stop and patiently waited for her to stand up. Taking a grip on the back of Plefauna's thick belt, Teela found it much easier to follow her movements, falling into a rhythmic pace as they progressed rapidly through the ship.

With the population now at less than half capacity, it was not unusual to walk for a mile or more down the long dim maze of corridors without seeing any other crew members. On this shift, however, the corridors were completely devoid of activity, causing Plefauna great concern. As the procession approached an intersection, three warriors stepped out and blocked their path. Teela's guards energized their weapons. She recognized the center warrior as the one she had fought outside the transit spoke near the Nursery.

"I have a message for the damaged birther you are escorting," the warrior growled.

"Deliver your message quickly and then clear the corridor. You are obstructing Mission business at great personal risk," Plefauna growled back, leveling her weapon at the warrior's head. Even on its nonlethal setting, a blast would likely result in terminal injuries at such close proximity.

"I have my adjutant, birther, and I have authorization for a dispute spectacle," the warrior sneered, holding out a log bar. Plefauna snatched it and examined it to verify it was not a threat, then passed it back to Teela.

"Tell that milk-sucking Shawaugh that Ruwaugh is looking forward to another opportunity to take her honor. Ruwaugh and I will bring her down slowly so we can take satisfaction from her pain, and you, well, with you we may just take satisfaction," the warrior taunted, gesturing lewdly.

"Just as before," Teela called from within the circle of guards, "when you attacked without provocation, you hid behind anonymity. Am I to know who challenges me, or must I wait until I face you during spectacle?"

"I am Apoulauh, little mother. I will mark it on you with my riz, so you will always remember it," the warrior said, strutting back down the corridor, her two companions falling in behind her.

"You have taken Shawaugh as your adjutant and challenged these assassins?" Plefauna asked incredulously.

"Yes, Shawaugh was kind enough to offer. Apoulauh is a weak fool who is angry because I knocked her down. As for Shawaugh, she chased away three armed warriors. If I am to participate in a spectacle event, who would be better to have as an adjutant?" Teela asked, concerned over the shocked faces of these stoic guards.

"Shawaugh is the living shame of the Warrior section. She was aft section director at the time of the Kahshinki attack. If she had any honor, she would have volunteered for reclamation long ago," Plefauna said with unconcealed contempt.

"She's a genetic freak!" a guard from behind Teela exclaimed. "An experiment to make stronger warriors discontinued because it also made them irrationally hostile. Shawaugh is proof enough of that. She will challenge anyone to spectacle that makes a comment about her ugly face. That's why the leaders changed the rules to require teams. Until now, no one would agree to fight with one who is said to have no honor to lose."

"You should submit an appeal to the section leader," Plefauna offered. "She will certainly dismiss the challenge since

Shawaugh has obviously tricked you into taking her as an adjutant."

Teela acknowledged their comments with gracious nods but did not reply. She was experiencing an emotional moment, one that was new to her Korlah persona. The flush she felt wasn't fear or embarrassment; those emotions she knew well. She wanted to fight, to hit someone, to hurt them. Anyone would do. It didn't matter who.

These thoughts flooded her mind, engorging her crown tendrils and turning them dark. Spectacle would give her an opportunity to unload some of the hostility she had accumulated throughout her entire life, and she had no intention of requesting a dismissal. Shawaugh was the perfect adjutant for her; they were both freaks with a score to settle. To be able to strike out without apology—the thought was intoxicating. Teela unconsciously growled. The guards edged away, exchanging expressions of surprise and concern.

"Let's get moving!" Teela demanded, giving Plefauna's belt a push.

Marching along briskly, the group traveled farther and farther toward the back of the ship on their way to the Security section. The Shell section corridor they were following was abandoned, and unusually littered and poorly maintained. Traffic in these areas was usually thin, but now no one could be seen in any direction. Many of the overhead glowbars were broken or missing, and all of the com stations they passed had been damaged or disabled. As they approached a transit section, the lights ahead of them went out.

"This is the work of Nons. We must go back; it is not safe for us here," Plefauna whispered.

"You will go back, security scum, as worm cake for your masters," a voice shouted from the darkness. The corridor behind them winked into darkness, leaving Teela and her escorts in a small island of light. The deadly silence was broken by the crackle of energizing pulse rifles. Teela was thrown to the floor by her guards, who formed a ring around her. She pushed her way to her knees and strained her vision, trying to make out the thermal signature of the voice she had heard.

"Get down, Teela! They mean to kill us," Plefauna shouted.

"Hold!" another voice from the darkness behind them shouted. "Who is it you escort? What name did you say?"

"Teela 10127," Teela answered, standing to her full height, her head above the protection of the shields.

"Teela 10127 has ceased. Afron seeks to divide us with more tricks," an angry voice shouted.

"Come this way, Teela 10127. Come alone," the voice ahead of them called.

"My escorts are not to be harmed," Teela demanded.

"If you are Teela 10127, you have no reason to protect these Loyalist scrum. I would think you would enjoy seeing them fed into a grinder," the voice responded.

"They are Korlah!" Teela shouted. "Preserving the existence of one is reason enough. On this vessel I have a million reasons, and out there," she said looking up, "billions of reasons why I am willing to work with Shyron and the Leadership Council to win this campaign." The significance of her statement registered with clarity for the first time and she held her upward gaze.

"If you are who you claim to be, on my honor, your guards will not be harmed. Come this way, now!" the voice demanded.

Teela slipped slowly from the protection of the crouching security officers. The guards glanced down shamefully as she left, knowing they were now under her protection. Stopping next to the senior officer, Teela spoke just loud enough for their assailants to hear.

"These are Korlah, warriors by their own right with a worthy cause. I am confident that they have honor, and if you do not provoke them, they will not harm us. Secure your rifles and stand without fear. If they wish to end our existence, it will be so." Then, lifting her head high, she strode down the corridor into the darkness. Behind her, the security officers de-energized and slung their rifles, watching nervously.

"Stop!" a voice called from a darkened alcove. Teela stopped and squinted into the darkness. She could hear the faint hum of an energized pulse rifle, but there was no thermal signature of it or its owner.

"Show me the scar," a voice asked politely, right in front of her. Teela jumped with surprise. She could feel the speaker only inches from her face, but her thermal signature exactly matched that of the wall, making her invisible in the darkness.

Looking around and feeling more vulnerable than ever, Teela pulled up her tah to expose both scars and wondered how many were watching.

Directly ahead of her, she heard a scrape and a hand appeared, or more appropriately, the thermal signature of a hand. There was a snap, a sliding sound, and then a face appeared, her sabat obscured. The camouflaged warrior knelt before Teela and ran her ungloved fingertips over the scars. She stood and put her glove back on and then moved her face uncomfortably close. Dropping the hem of her tah, Teela smoothed the fabric and stared defiantly into the warrior's face.

"I am going to ask you some questions," the warrior stated. "I have great skill at seeing deception by even the most skilled liars. Do not attempt to deceive me." There was an uncomfortable silence before the warrior continued. When she did speak, it was barely audible.

"You have received the essence of an alien warrior?"

"Yes," Teela answered. Honesty would likely be her best hope for gaining the confidence of these Resistance warriors.

"An alien like those of the 1006 Kahshinki attack?"

"Yes," Teela replied.

Her inquisitor took a startled breath and blanched to a cooler signature.

She may be a master of reading others, but she is no master of her own emotions, Teela thought.

"You intend to negotiate an alliance with these aliens to defeat the Kahshinki?"

"Yes, and I'm looking for help from those seeking an honorable battle," Teela responded calmly, filling her mind with violent thoughts and forcing a thermal flush that she hoped would read as confidence and determination.

"Ahh!" the soldier cried fearfully, stepping back. "You mind-talk! You … your thoughts, you … you showed me the death of a Kahshinki."

With a click and a snap, the face disappeared into the darkness.

Teela stood in stunned silence. The violent thought she had used was of the death struggle with the Kahshinki, specifically of when she beat its head with hers—no, Daedalus's. She had somehow projected the thought to the warrior.

In the distance, she could hear a whispered conversation. After an interminable period of time, there was silence.

"You may leave," a voice stated flatly from the darkness, which was followed by rustling and the muffled sounds of many feet retreating.

Teela turned and walked back into the light where the security guards waited. First the lights behind them switched on, one area at a time, and then the lights ahead, until the entire corridor was illuminated. During the balance of the journey, Plefauna and the other guards remained silent.

Traveling two levels out by tube, the band of guards and the small birthing unit emerged into the spacious chamber outside the Security section. The large hatch was shut, and the normally heavy guard contingent stationed there had been augmented threefold. Every guard wore battle armor and helmets like her escorts. Four powerful pulse cannons had been set up behind shields and barricades, covering the main corridor and the smaller passages on each side. No longer a checkpoint, the area now resembled a fortress under siege.

The guards wordlessly opened the barricade and allowed Teela's group to move through without slowing their harried pace. Plefauna saluted with crossed arms and claws and signed with the senior guard, who looked away when Teela met her gaze. Teela noted that most of the soldiers were staring at her, yet when she looked at them, they averted their eyes.

With a rumble of heavy machinery and the dull drag of metal on metal, the heavy door opened slightly. Much to Teela's surprise, Plefauna and her escorts continued the march with shields and weapons at the ready, Teela securely centered between them. They passed several armored and barricaded checkpoints as they followed a labyrinthine path deep into the heart of the Security section. Teela was aware that without her escorts, she would be helpless to find her way out.

They emerged from a small passageway into a large, elongated chamber with a high vaulted ceiling that resembled a medieval banquet hall. Large, columnar conduits were spaced evenly down each side of the chamber. Instead of a throne, at the far end behind another heavily fortified and manned barricade was another circular door, about one-quarter the size of the door at the main entrance, but with the same stout appearance. The bands that girded its length and breadth reminded Teela of a bank vault.

Plefauna saluted and signed with the senior guard, and Teela passed alone through the vaultlike door, which closed and locked behind her. Shyron lay on a large sleep platform in the relatively small chamber. Her personal biotech stood nearby and two guards were posted on either side of the door. Pushing herself up into a seated position with the biotech's help, Shyron slid her feet over the side of the bed, smoothed her robe, and faced Teela.

"Come sit with us," Shyron said, her voice weak and frail, lacking the command Teela remembered. The Potentate's sallow, waxen complexion and limp crown tendrils made it clear that Shyron was seriously ill. With no place else to sit, Teela sat down next to Shyron.

She's sick, maybe dying, Teela thought. She avoided eye contact to show respect as much as to avoid the urge to study the leader's diminished condition. She clasped her hands together nervously and stared at the embroidery on her tah, searching for words to express her concern.

Our health need not concern you. The thoughts of Shyron entered her mind, along with feelings of warmth and sincerity that embraced and soothed the loneliness that had plagued Teela since the first moments following transfer. Teela gasped and choked back a sob of relief. The perception of light chasing away a dark cloud swept through her mind. She turned to face Shyron. The aged leader's head drooped forward, her eyes barely open. As Teela was about to speak, Shyron raised her pallid, bony hand to Teela's mouth.

Speak with your mind, Shyron imparted telepathically, lowering her hand and placing it over Teela's clasped hands.

"I … don't know how," Teela said.

"Try," Shyron said, giving Teela's hands a reassuring squeeze.

Teela closed her eyes and concentrated. She tried to imagine placing words into her thoughts, rather than images, as she had with the invisible soldier. Her thoughts were interrupted when Shyron's claws pricked her hands; her strength belied her emaciated body. Teela opened her eyes to find Shyron staring at her, her mouth agape.

"You will need to concentrate on how *not* to throw your thoughts!" Shyron said. Teela blanched, sensing the shock and discomfort her thoughts had brought Shyron. Teela quickly formed her apology, but the bite of Shyron's grasp stopped her midway.

"Yes, like that. Only, you need to contain them. Compartmentalize your thoughts. Hold them within and release them—specifically or randomly, as the situation requires. You are projecting your thoughts like inarticulate shouts heard throughout the ship. When we first experienced it, we did not believe that what we heard was real until others with these abilities spoke of it. Waves of anguish, commands, apologies, and unimaginable images have been flowing through us without a logical purpose or origin. We believe that only we have been able to pinpoint their origin. It was your written reports that brought the unusual projections into perspective."

Shyron released Teela's hands and touched the center of Teela's forehead with the claw of a thumb. With eyes no longer as bright as Teela remembered them, Shyron's gaze seemed to bore a hole into the very essence of her being.

"You are only a first, and as such should not yet have even a glimmer of this ability. I know of thirds and fourths who are showing signs, but only signs, no abilities. The abilities that are achievable with intense concentration appear around the fifth or sixth transfer, and mastery only after many cycles of practice. Yet here you are, with intensity, ability, and unbridled and unimaginable potential less than six shifts after transfer. We understand now the basis for Afron's ruthless actions toward gaining control of this ship and our human guests."

She plans to transfer the memories of the humans into Korlah shells, Teela blurted out the thought.

"That was good. Your thoughts are clear, yet still too intense. Yes, Afron is planning on more transfers, but it is the humans she wishes to use as shells."

"Why? I have agreed to help!" Teela cried. "I have done everything asked of me. Why would she jeopardize our plans for an alliance with the humans?"

"She considers you a failure, an uncontrollable liability to plans that do not include an alliance or even campaign. After the successful repair of the darkly pigmented human, Afron called an emergency session of the Council to present startling information on the biological similarities of humans and Korlah. The director of the Health section claims to have successfully developed and implanted birthing units with human duplicates using genetic material obtained from the subjects examined. She also claims to have successfully generated viable Korlah-human hybrid embryos, using Korlah eggs and human male reproductive cells. Based on these developments, Afron has proposed a controlled breeding program using the five Korlah genotypes and twelve human genotypes. This program would eventually breed out human characteristics and leave a predominantly Korlah biological identity capable of natural procreation within the twenty generations that it would take for this vessel to return to Korlah."

The conflict in Teela's mind exploded long before Shyron finished speaking. The human part screamed outrage at the thought of being duplicated for experimentation, breeding, and use as a receptacle for Korlah minds. But her Korlah half rejoiced at the news that the prospect for biological normalcy of the Korlah culture was no longer a dream. Now it was a technological possibility.

The essences of two distinct and wildly differing views clashed violently, deep in the folds and synapses of Teela's brain. Arguments for and against the proposals were brought to bear, withdrawn, and modified with dizzying speed. Teela found herself engaged in a cerebral shouting match with the essence of Daedalus Rimes.

Silence! Shyron screamed with her mind. Teela opened her eyes, suddenly realizing she had clenched them shut. The sensation of spinning coalesced into a dull nausea, and the throbbing of her wrists informed her that, once again, she had lacerated her own palms.

At Shyron's bidding, the biotech in the room ran to Teela and pried her hands open to repair the damage.

"Your consternation is unnecessary. The Council declined the proposition and demanded the destruction of the hybrid and duplicate embryos. It was determined that the Health section director was acting on Afron's behalf; therefore, Afron was chastised before the Council for perpetuating the argument against engaging the Kahshinki in campaign. Additionally, she has been formally charged with circumventing the authority of the leaders by coercing the directors and supervisors of sections outside her authority to participate and support actions contrary to Council directives. Individually, none of her actions constitute a serious breach of law, but when combined and examined for their purpose and intent, they demonstrate a serious effort to overthrow the authority of Council law."

The glazed look in Teela's eyes began to clear. The biotech had finished sealing the punctures on one hand and was starting on the other. Seeing that Teela was returning from her introspective journey, Shyron reached up and jabbed her painfully in the forehead with a thumb claw.

"Damn it!" Teela cried out in English.

We told you two to get along! Shyron chastised mentally. "Human! Without a Korlah shell, your existence would be over. What chance do you think your sisters or planet would have without her cooperation? And, Teela, without your human essence, you would be nothing more than a damaged birthing unit capable only of marginal duties and limited utility. Together you are ... much more than Afron or we ever could have imagined. But, if you are unable to successfully merge your thoughts, your difficulties will escalate and neither the humans nor the Korlah will benefit from your efforts."

Teela took a moment to gather her disarrayed thoughts. "What must I do?"

"First, you will need to stay out of Afron's reach. While you were still moving the humans to the Shell section, she reinstituted your order for reclamation; however, by assigning you to our section as our assistant, she could no longer execute such an order legally. The challenge you have received to settle a dispute with a spectacle event is a ruse devised by Afron to end your existence within the limits of the law. We have issued a delay order, if we cancel the spectacle, you will lose the impressive reputation you have gained among the warriors, who by virtue of the grossly exaggerated 'blade battle with the Nons' and the rumors of your transfer with a warrior beast, have elevated you to an unprecedented status. This notoriety will serve to protect you far more than any amount of armor or guards we could provide for you. Once you and the humans are on your way, we can cancel the spectacle, and your honor will remain unblemished."

"When can I take them home?"

"Loyal Security section guards control the hangar where the preparations of the assault pod continue. They also control the Shell section where the humans are contained. The challenge lies in moving them across the ship. We expect Afron to employ all of her assets to seize the humans during transit. Expect the worst from Afron; she has surrounded herself with others who have abandoned honor and replaced it with the hunger for power. After being charged by the Council, she fled the Security section and is now operating from somewhere in the Warrior section. Shipments of water and food are being intercepted, and warriors have been massing in the aft end of the Shell section and lower levels of the Bio and Health sections. The only conceivable purpose for this is a siege on the security section." Shyron said.

"I don't understand why the warriors would follow Afron," Teela said. "They long for commencement of campaign and the opportunity to redeem their honor in battle. Why would they turn away when the fight lies within reach?"

"Afron's grip on the warriors below the rank of area supervisor is exceptionally weak. All the comlinks from here to the Warrior, Strategy, and Health sections have been severed. For the last four shifts, only information beneficial to Afron's cause has been released in these areas. If she can keep us isolated long enough, we will cease, and she will challenge you for control of the ship."

"Why would she challenge me? How could I prevent her from taking control?"

"You are Mission Adjutant, Assistant to the Potentate, and as such, successor to the Potentate."

"I cannot … I … I wouldn't know how to lead the Council. You must transfer!" Teela exclaimed out loud as she backed away from Shyron's bed.

"Look at me!" Teela cried. "I am a birthing unit, not a leader. This robe and armor are nothing more than a costume, copied from a sculpture I saw in a picture, be … because …" Teela paused, realizing the irony of her confession.

"Because," Shyron continued, "when you envisioned yourself wearing it, you became a warrior for the brief periods that you escaped into your mind. You became someone else. Someone capable of all that you found lacking in yourself and your existence."

"Yes!" Teela cried. "But that was fantasy. This is not. Beyond the operations within the Shell section and what I have learned in the archives, I am ignorant. I am told that I wear the tah of Shawlmon, yet I don't even know who she was."

Shyron laughed loudly, her first vocalization since Teela's arrival, but her laughter ended with racking coughs, drawing the ministrations of the biotech, who insisted that she lie down.

"You are uninformed, Teela. That much is true, but you are far from ignorant. What you don't know can be learned, and what you possess in raw leadership potential and charisma can neither be learned nor taught. Every report we receive indicates that your popularity—or notoriety, depending on the source—is soaring to epic proportions throughout every section. Entire quadrants of birthing units have abandoned their duties to join the Nons or the Resistance because it is rumored that 'Teela, the reincarnation of Shawlmon' has pledged her support of their cause. In little more than two shifts, you have brought to existence the legend of Shawlmon and utilized it to draw three feuding factions into a debate over which faction Shawlmon will support and defend."

"I told you! I don't know who Shawlmon was," Teela cried.

"Then listen, and I will tell you," Shyron said extending her hand to Teela.

Teela resumed her place next to the leader. Shyron pulled Teela's hand close and held it with both of hers. She closed her eyes and took a deep breath.

"The priests and Gods of Korlah were long ago abandoned and replaced by Council law and Kahshinki technology. Yet, every now and then, something happens that we do not understand, something that technology and logic cannot explain. Take for example the process of transfer; our technology has never been able to explain it, just as there is no explanation for you or the fact that you have assumed the role, and now the tah, of Shawlmon."

Shyron opened her eyes and moved her gaze across Teela, studying her face and the intricacies of her vest and tah, as though the visage fueled her thoughts.

"Shawlmon was the most famous of all Korlah warriors. He was an arbitrator and bladesman with no ties to the parties in conflict, who attempted through skillful debate to settle disputes. And if debate and discussion failed, he would battle with blades of metal to vanquish unreasonable or dishonorable foes.

"And now, we find ourselves without options and without hope. We have lost our appreciation of existence and embraced despair. For the first time in over one thousand cycles, I called to the Gods of Korlah and begged them for guidance, and then you appeared. It cannot be explained, and we will not try.

"My existence will soon end, Teela. You are the answer to my prayers. It shall be you who arbitrates this dispute as only Shawlmon could. It will be you who guides both the humans and Korlah to victory."

"How, Shyron? How? I cannot do this by myself. I need help—your help. You must not cease. You must transfer."

"It is no longer a choice. You have noticed, yet said nothing. Within this shell there are the essences of many. Unlike my sisters, I have, as you have, allowed the essence of those with whom I have merged to remain. We are a council of one. Unfortunately, this choice severely complicates transfer. For us, transfer is difficult and takes time. Without sufficient time and access to the transfer chamber, the many essences of who we are cannot be moved to a new shell. If we leave the protection of this section, Afron will have us murdered. If we stay, we will eventually cease.

"It would be difficult for her to kill us here, so she must wait for us to cease. Do not despair. Our technician tells us Afron will have to wait many shifts. Do not concern yourself with our health. We have no intention of ceasing our existence until you have secured an alliance with the humans."

Teela withdrew her hand from Shyron's and stood without speaking. Carefully guarding her thoughts, packaging them as Shyron had described, and staring blankly at the floor, Teela made a respectful bow and palm display to signal her goodbye.

"You need to visit the unit called Challmara," Shyron said, pushing herself up onto an elbow and turning stiffly to face Teela. "I learned of Afron's plans when she came to the Security section with a petition for your continued existence. It was an impressive document validated by six directors, each swearing a blood oath to your utility and value as a functional asset toward the Mission objectives. We don't recall the exact words; however, they were sufficiently demanding to force our subordinates to bring it to our attention. We were so impressed by her devotion to you that we found ourselves envious. Envy is an emotion we have not felt in many cycles. We gave a blood oath that we would do everything in our power to ensure your safety and have requested her assistance to that end. A most talented and capable technician, this unit Challmara. We have therefore elevated her to director in charge of your assault pod preparations."

Teela did not look up. She was embarrassed by the tears that dripped from her chin. She switched her thoughts from Challmara to her primary consideration of moving the humans safely from the Shell section to the assault pod.

"The humans are well protected," Shyron said, reading Teela's intentions. "We were able to divert food and water deliveries in ample quantities to ensure they will not go hungry until we are ready to move them. Go see Challmara; she holds a gift for you. We would like to have given it ourselves, but since she coordinated the fabrication, it was easier to have her give it to you.

"Now, go! We are tired and need to rest." Shyron lay down and closed her eyes.

Teela waited as the guards unbolted and opened the door. She paused, cocking her head to one side. Shyron's parting thoughts came to her as a whisper, inaudible unless the listener was willing to hear. *Teela, both you and Daedalus have a chance to find something of this existence beyond that of the Mission, something that fills the void you feel within. You don't want to be like us, longing for something no longer within reach, envious of the innocence we lost along the journey of our combined existences.*

16 - Affection

Not wanting a repeat of the incident with the invisible soldiers, Plefauna tripled the number of guards protecting Teela. With five guards to the front, one on each side, and five to the rear, Teela exited the security section with authority. Warriors scrambled to clear the passageways as they approached. However, when they emerged from a transit cube outside the arms section, they were confronted by a barricade of warriors. Teela's guards raised their shields and energized their high-power pulse cannons, and the five warriors grudgingly relented.

Ill at ease with her destination, Teela struggled to identify the source of the emotion troubling her. *What is it? Why are you making me feel this way?* Teela asked the essence within her, an entity Shyron had told her she must blend with. Images of Julie and the love, loyalty, and devotion that Daedalus felt for her emerged from Teela's subconscious mind. She abruptly stopped walking, which forced her escorts to stop as well.

"Why have we stopped?" Plefauna called back from the lead.

"*Wait*!" Teela shouted with her mind. Each of the ten guards flinched.

Holding her hands up and turning them over, Teela examined them with slow intent and directed her thoughts within.

Daedalus has ceased. This is what you are now. This is what we *are. Whatever responsibilities and commitments you had to Julie ceased with your shell. We cannot change that. We are a different person, a new person. Our existence will be what we make of it.*

"We must be one!" Teela finished her thought, mumbling the demand aloud in English.

"What's wrong? Why have you stopped?" Plefauna asked.

"Who are you?" Teela asked the senior officer, echoing the question Shyron had asked her several shifts earlier.

"What? You know who I am," Plefauna answered, confused.

"Imagine yourself standing in the center of the Council Chamber," Teela said, waving her arm in an arc around her. "All the leaders are looking down at you, and the Leader Potentate asks, 'Who are you?' How would you answer? What would you say?" Teela placed her hand on Plefauna's shoulder and studied her confused expression.

"I . . . would answer, 'Security Unit 9205, Plefauna, Tenth Level, Senior Guard.'"

"That's not who you are. That's what you are. Who you are is what makes you different from her, or her, or her," Teela said, pointing at the other genetically identical guards. "It's what makes you different from me."

"It's a foolish question. There could be no answer. *What* we are is *who* we are! The Leader Potentate would never ask a question like that," Plefauna responded defensively.

"She asked me," Teela countered. "And, like you, I had no answer."

Without further comment, the procession continued down the dimly lit corridor toward Challmara's quarters.

They stopped in front of the door and Teela removed from her pocket the access card Challmara had given her. Running her hand over the sabat stenciled on the door, she pondered the meaning of the occupant's name and designation. Teela hesitated for a moment, listening for the nagging whisper, expecting pangs of guilt. She heard only the rustling of her guards taking up positions in the corridor and felt only the cold metal of the door. She finally pressed the card against the access pad. The door popped open with a soft click, and without looking back Teela slipped in and quietly pulled the door shut behind her.

The glowlamps were turned off and the compartment was dark. Teela could see the glow of Challmara's heat signature curled up on the sleeping platform. Her scent was thick in the air. She was snoring softly like the purring of a cat. Teela stood next to her. In the inky blackness, Teela could see the heat rising off Challmara's body. The gently waving strands of warmth looked like mist rising off a lake on a cold morning. Teela's eyes had never seen a lake, but she knew what one looked like and she remembered the smells. The smell of pine trees and crisp mountain air, damp canvas, and the way Julie's hair smelled in the morning, a musty combination of her natural scent, the campfire, and perfume.

Teela shook her crown tendrils in the rising mist of warmth, saturating her olfactory nerves. It wasn't the need for sleep that drew her here, nor was it desire for the gratification of feeling wanted or needed. The whispering feelings grew stronger, not of guilt, but rather of a growing primal need, something driven by memories from another life and fueled by an exigency she had only partially felt in her prior experiences with Challmara. Teela stripped off her garments and dropped them to the floor where she stood. After a momentary hesitation, she climbed onto the sleeping platform.

Pressing her body against Challmara's, Teela swept her crown tendrils back and forth across her face and chest, thrilling in the sensations of touch and smell.

"Teela!" Challmara said, taking in a surprised breath. She recognized her scent as she woke.

Teela pressed her open mouth against Challmara's, an act not unheard of, but rare even in the most passionate Korlah pleasuring sessions. Surprised more than offended by Teela's aggressive behavior, Challmara tried to pull away from the suffocating embrace, but the many cycles of arduous physical labor had developed strength and stamina in Teela's smaller frame so that she easily overpowered the larger female. Realizing that Teela was finally physically dominating her, something she'd asked for but never really received during their previous encounters, Challmara relaxed and accepted Teela's control.

Challmara tended to Teela's needs with the tender, eager attention and sincerity she had always hoped to receive from her hired partners. As she immersed herself in the sensations, all other thoughts, memories, and concerns disappeared from Teela's conscious mind, allowing her to completely enjoy the pleasuring experiences for the first time. Crying out in ecstasy as her partners had done, and as she had imitated, Teela achieved orgasm for the first time, her cry one of genuine release. Falling limp onto the sleeping pad, Teela reveled in the swirling sensations, wanting them to last and regretting their dissipation.

Before she could regain her composure, Challmara threw herself on top and pressed her open mouth against Teela's. Without resisting, Teela assumed the submissive role, pleasuring Challmara in the same ways and in ways Challmara had not considered. The earnest intensity with which she wrought Challmara's pleasure far surpassed anything she had ever before offered or Challmara had ever received.

Alternating between giving and receiving and experimenting with the newly discovered pleasures, they eventually collapsed into each other's arms, exhausted. Embraced in the thick warm folds of deep sleep of the thoroughly satisfied and secure, they slept without moving for the remainder of the shift.

Teela woke first, her inner clock in sync with the Korlah timetable. The communicator on the wall displayed the date, shift, sets, bits, and nons. She didn't need to hurry. Absently stroking Challmara's arm and shoulder, Teela pondered the difficulties she was sure to face and whether she would be able to live up to Shyron's grandiose expectations. Waking to Teela's touch, Challmara languidly rolled over and rested her head on Teela's breasts.

"That was really special," Challmara drawled sleepily. "I hope I can afford it," she added.

An icy feeling gripped Teela in the center of her chest, sending numbness through her arms and legs. Rolling out from under Challmara's head, she sat up on the edge of the sleep pad and slid onto the cold floor.

"Where are you going?" Challmara asked, surprised by her abrupt departure.

"I've been reassigned. I'm working doubles," Teela answered, dressing with stiff mechanical movements.

"We have more than fifty bits until we have to report. Let's get something to eat. I know where we can get some fresh braddle," Challmara offered, sitting up and switching on the glowlamps.

"Do you like the new tah? I had it made special for you," Challmara said, admiring Teela.

"Yes, it's exquisite. Everyone who saw it was quite impressed," Teela answered coldly. "I apologize if I have been insufficiently grateful. If you wish, I will leave it for you to give to your next servant."

Challmara bounded off the sleeping platform and grabbed Teela by the shoulders.

"That's not the arrangement I wanted. You know that!" Challmara cried. "When we first met, you were just a cleaning servant, a child from the birthing section who would work an entire shift for a few protein cakes and a ration of water. I never wanted you as a servant, but you rebuffed all my attempts at friendship. I wanted you. I wanted you so much I hired you to clean for me. You're the only one I've ever wanted, the only one I have ever hired for pleasure. But I could tell you didn't enjoy it, and I always felt guilty afterward. But I hoped . . . I just kept hoping . . . that maybe things would change.

"And then you woke me. It was as if you yourself had just woken up and somehow realized how much I needed you to need me in the same way. I don't care what the arrangement is. It doesn't matter to me. Whatever you want. Just don't leave, not like this."

Teela put her arms around Challmara and pulled her into a long, tight embrace. Even when Teela relaxed, she continued to hold her close.

"I'm sorry I said that," Teela said softly. "That's not the arrangement I want either."

Challmara returned the hug, pressing her open mouth against Teela's. The two held the embrace until they had to break apart to take air. As she backed away, Teela wiped tears from Challmara's cheeks.

"Your hopes for me to change have been answered," Teela said cautiously. "Who or what I have become may not be what you had hoped for. I am very different from the last time we were together. Only recently have I begun to understand how much I have changed, how I am still changing, and I don't know what I will ultimately be like."

Challmara backed away and sat down on the edge of the sleeping platform. "Rumors abound. The technicians spend their time at the communication panels tracking the latest stories. It is sometimes difficult for me to keep them engaged in the project. Some of the rumors about you are so outlandish that they couldn't possibly be true. But they are true, aren't they?" she asked.

"There is often more truth in rumors than in official reports. Tell me of these rumors," Teela replied.

"Since there are no official reports, they vary in degree and detail. My official sources are refusing to confirm them, so I have been forced to decide their validity."

Challmara described in detail the encounter with the Kahshinki and the hostile aliens like those that had attacked the Korlah campaign vessel. She went on to describe the capture of these new aliens, the transfer of an alien's memories, the escape and subsequent surrender of the aliens, and, of course, the many strange activities taking place down in the lowest, most remote area of the birthing section that were drawing more and more interest as word spread.

She described her petition to the Council of Leaders and how she was assured Teela would be kept safe, but wasn't given any explanation of where she was or what she was doing. She described threats issued by the Resistance claiming retribution against anyone responsible for Teela's reclamation or damage. Teela was amazed at the accuracy and detail of the information that Challmara had collected through the rumor circuit.

"Do you believe these rumors to be accurate?" Teela asked incredulously.

"Yes, I believe them, but there are many others that I don't believe."

"And what are some rumors that you don't believe?"

"Well, to start, that unarmed you fought twenty Nons and pulled the blades away from them with your bare hands, besting them with blade skills and yet drawing no blood and claiming no honor; that you are the leader of the Resistance; that it was you who killed the birthing section director; that you are working for Afron and are helping her with her plot to seize control; or that you are a mindtalker sent by the Gods of Korlah to lead us to a victorious and final campaign."

After a short pause, Challmara laughed nervously and whispered, "That you and the living shame of the warriors, Shawaugh, are friends, good friends."

"It was only eight Nons. I fought only one with blades and was lucky to win. I am responsible for the deaths of two warriors, but it was not intentional. I did not kill the birthing section director, and until last shift, I didn't even know there was a Resistance. I work for Shyron, not Afron, and if the Gods of Korlah have sent me, it was without my knowledge. As for Shawaugh, like me, she is an outcast, a survivor who sees to her own existence without depending on others. Without my asking, she has volunteered to be my adjutant during a dispute spectacle."

"What! You . . . can't fight . . . not in a spectacle," Challmara stammered.

"Apparently, I can," Teela said, handing her the log bar and trying to maintain an air of confidence despite her growing anxiety.

Challmara moved quickly to her log reader, a much more sophisticated model than most, snapped in the bar and called up the challenge details onto the large screen. She leaned back slowly, putting her hands together under her chin.

"Oh, Teela, no. Oh no! You are to fight Ruwaugh and Apoulauh. Do you know who these two scrum filth are?

"Assassins, or so I've been told. Afron plots to end my existence, but what she fails to realize is that I have every expectation that if and when the event occurs, Shawaugh and I will be victorious."

Challmara frowned at Teela's boast. Taking Teela by the shoulders, she shook her gently. "Transfer notwithstanding, you are still just a birthing unit, and a small one at that. I go to the events whenever I can. I know who wins and who doesn't, and I seldom lose a wager. If I were to hear that Shawaugh was going up against Ruwaugh or Apoulauh alone, I would wager in her favor. But against both of them, with you as her bloodmate, her existence is as good as over. No one in her right mind would wager even a single water ration on such a ridiculous match."

Challmara's expression was one of grave concern as she slid her hands down Teela's arms and took her by the hands. "This is a contest that cannot be won, not with you at Shawaugh's side. I am certain that Shyron will support your petition for cancellation."

Slipping her hands out of Challmara's, Teela took Challmara by her wrists and began to squeeze, gently at first and then ratcheting the pressure up in degrees.

"You're hurting me!" Challmara cried out, attempting to pull her hands free. But Teela was nowhere near the maximum potential of her grip. Giving Challmara a blank stare, Teela continued to increase the pressure.

Challmara screamed, more from her injured dignity than anything physical, as Teela applied downward pressure, forcing Challmara to her knees. Then releasing the pressure, she maintained her grip on Challmara's aching wrists.

"I may be just a birthing unit, and a small one at that," she hissed with a caustic vehemence that Challmara had never witnessed in Teela or anyone else of her caste, "but for the last seventeen cycles, I have worked two of three shifts, most of it physical labor. Amazing how strong these skinny arms really are, isn't it?" Teela asked, pulling Challmara to her feet, spinning her around and forcing her to sit on the sleep platform using careful pressure on Challmara's arms and wrists. Challmara stared at the thin but muscular arms that held her so securely and realized how much she had underestimated their strength.

"For cycle after cycle, I have been scrubbing the dung of young shells from the floors of the birthing section, cleaning the filth from the quarters and clothes of the privileged, and carrying the loads that others are too lazy to carry themselves. I have strength beyond that of the physical, strength forged in anger and frustration that I am just beginning to realize. My new memories tell me that there is nothing I cannot accomplish. I have fought and won many fights in my other life, and I swear to you now that you will see degrees of skill and effort that will surprise many who perceive me as just a birthing unit . . . and a small one at that."

Teela released Challmara and assumed an unimposing pose to exaggerate her transformation from dominance to submission. "I am neither the leader of the Resistance, nor am I one of Afron's puppets. I need help, and I believe the Council leaders have directed you to provide it, rewarding you with both rank and status."

Challmara rubbed her wrists as she eyed Teela's sinewy arms. Her expression was one of injured pride. "I am working on preparing the assault pod you will take on your mission. Every improvement, all the new technology we have developed, is being incorporated. The Council is taking great risks using these innovations so early in campaign."

Challmara reached beneath the sleep platform into a concealed compartment and withdrew an eighteen-inch cylindrical container. She held it up for Teela to see, tapping the container with an extended claw as she spoke.

"This is a gift for you that Shyron commissioned me to fabricate. They have very special capabilities." She cradled the container in her lap, her hands cupping each end. "Shyron has issued an authorization for you to bear weapons."

One end of the container opened with a soft hiss and Challmara withdrew two beautiful, half-meter bladed weapons with intricately detailed scabbards. They were splendid reproductions of the swords depicted in the ancient Korlah sculpture that Teela had admired for so long. They were the weapons of war and battle that she had often dreamt of wielding.

Teela drew one of the blades partly from its scabbard. It immediately began to crackle as arcs of electrical energy flashed to and from the blade and scabbard. She looked at Challmara for an explanation.

"They are not mere blades, as they appear to be. They have other capabilities!" Challmara exclaimed excitedly, lifting the other weapon.

"Balanced and razor-sharp, as any edged weapon should be, it is more, much, much more than any edged weapon has ever been. Many cycles ago when I worked as a fabricator, I designed an edged pulse weapon, but the proposal was dismissed by the Council as impractical and unnecessary for the type of campaign battles we fight; however, I kept the plans and specifications. Shyron remembered my proposal and commissioned them to match the same sculpture I modeled your new tah after. The hilt, although made of polished bone, contains a modified power cell. The pommel has an amplification chamber, the guard functions as particle accelerator, and the blade is actually a conductive array. It's a pulse weapon!" Challmara said with great pride.

"The firing node is located beneath the shield. You can trigger a pulse with the claw of either thumb. Each sword will produce five moderate pulses with a nominal charge and should never be charged above nominal. The conductive array is designed to function as a pulse collector. I've added a dampening filter, a charge suppressor, and the latest high-capacity power cell so that, theoretically, it will not explode if charged beyond capacity."

"What do you mean, 'theoretically'? Haven't you tested them?"

"Yes, of course they were tested. The testing involved firing pulse weapons at the blades in a test chamber. The blades attracted the pulse charges as designed and channeled them into the storage cells, demonstrating their utility as shields while also charging the storage cells. The capacity of the cells proved to be much greater than anticipated, which is good. Automatic discharge will occur if an overload condition occurs; but that is not recommended."

"Why not?"

"If discharged in an overload condition, the dampening filter will prevent disintegration of the power cell and any excess charge will either dissipate around the weapon or trigger the release of the overcharge. In case that were to happen, I have designed insulating boots and gloves to protect you from the natural grounding effect your body would otherwise provide. I will send them to you the moment they are ready."

"Superb!" Teela whispered as she withdrew one of the fluted, double-edged Korlah rapiers from its highly polished sheath. "They're perfect." She returned the weapons to the cylinder and gave Challmara a customary face-pressing embrace.

"There is something else I need that I'm hoping you can obtain," Teela said, bowing respectfully, acknowledging that she was already greatly in debt to Challmara.

"I have been instructed to provide you with whatever you need, although I hope you realize it is something I want to do."

"I need thirteen of the suits that mask thermal signatures," Teela said.

"What kind of suits?" Challmara asked.

"Thermal camouflage suits, the kind that mimic the temperature of the objects around them, masking the thermal signature of the person wearing it and rendering her invisible when there is no light," Teela explained.

Challmara looked at Teela without saying anything for a moment. She had a confused expression that finally turned into a grin. "That's a wonderful idea!" she laughed. Then she grew serious. "I don't believe a suit of this type is even possible, but if it were, it would be a very dangerous weapon our enemies could use against us."

"These humans have no quarrel with the Korlah; they only want to go home. I am trying to help them achieve that goal while serving the Mission."

Teela was certain of what she had seen during her meeting with the invisible warrior, but she was uncertain why Challmara was unaware, or claiming to be unaware, of their existence.

"It was just an idea," Teela said, dismissing the request with a wave of her hand.

Taking the cylinder from Challmara's lap, she stood and bowed respectfully. "Thank you. Thank you for everything you are doing."

Without further comment or discussion, Teela left. As she proceeded down the corridor, she wondered if she would be able to see Challmara again in two shifts, realizing that she wanted to.

17 - Shawaugh

The twelve security section guards who were patiently waiting to escort Teela filled the narrow corridor outside Challmara's quarters. As Teela emerged, they snapped to attention and moved into position. Unable to see over the living wall that the guards formed, Teela had to crouch to look through their forest of legs to see the activity she could hear beyond.

"They are curious, Your Eminence. Nothing more," a guard commented.

On the other side of the guards, a young supply technician was crouched in the same fashion. Upon seeing Teela, she pushed forward against the nearest guard and shoved a clenched fist through the legs toward Teela. She was rewarded with a punishing blow from a guard, knocking her to the ground; another guard placed a boot on the shoulder of the offending arm. The technician screamed in pain. She opened her hand and a log bar tumbled to the ground at Teela's feet.

"I deliver a message! I told you—it's just a message!" the technician squealed, her eyes wide with fear and pain.

"Release her!" Teela demanded. The guard immediately complied, allowing the captive to scramble away and disappear into the crowd. After examining the log bar and determining that it presented no threat, Teela had her escorts take her to the next com panel where she displayed its message.

> TEELA 20.10127. SERVICES AND RESOURCES FOR YOUR EVERY NEED ARE AVAILABLE UPON REQUEST. I AWAIT THE OPPORTUNITY TO SERVE YOU. PLEASE MEET WITH ME. ACCOUTREMENTS, LEVEL 27, COMPARTMENT 11072. MEEZRA.

"Your Eminence, this is not an official message. The courier would not reveal its source, so I refused to accept it," Plefauna explained, sounding apologetic.

"Accept all messages, regardless of their sources. And please, just call me Teela."

"Yes Your Emi— Teela. As you command."

"I'm not commanding. I'm asking. Now please escort me to accoutrements, level twenty-seven."

Level twenty-seven of the accoutrements section was one of the large levels with ceilings forty or more feet high. The area was a central distribution hub, a warehouse that stretched out into the distance, vanishing with the curve of the ship and the clutter of objects and machinery. As Teela and her escorts traversed the chamber and searched for the specified compartment, the workers paused and stared from their positions near loading bays and distribution tubes. Teela approached someone she assumed was in charge of the area's activities.

"Where is compartment 11072?" she asked politely.

The worker studied Teela's sabat for a moment and then straightened, skeptically scanning her twelve guards. The lead worker looked around and motioned to one of the tube loaders.

"This is Teela, the one you have all been jabbering about. Meezra's favorite—Teela," she said derisively, shoving the young laborer between them. "Take them to Meezra." Then she rushed off to spur the idle workers back to their tasks. Work in the area resumed as Teela was led toward the loading tubes.

The worker motioned for them to wait and disappeared through a small, dirty door just beyond the machinery that fed refrigerator-sized shipping cylinders into the transit tubes overhead, which would move the containers to the outer levels. Emerging from the doorway, the young laborer bowed awkwardly at Teela and moved to rejoin the other laborers. A thin, unkempt laborer with a uniform as dirty and smudged as the door emerged and scanned Teela's face with eyes glinting with mischief and guile. Her eyes widened as she focused on Teela's sabat.

"You're *the* Teela 10127!" the filthy worker exclaimed, looking around to see if anyone could have heard her. "I am Meezra! The one and only. Come with me. I can get you anything you need. And if I can't, I know who can," she said with pride. Taking Teela by the arm with her dirty hands, she directed her through the narrow doorway.

She let Teela enter first, then Meezra stopped in the doorway and turned to face the guards. "Small room. Insufficient space for everyone," she said before shutting and locking the door, leaving the surprised guards standing outside.

The room was truthfully quite small. All available wall space was covered with shelves filled with small boxes. There were several log readers and recorders and an elaborate communication panel that was even more sophisticated than Challmara's. Meezra pulled a large box out from under a table and wiped off a layer of grime with her already soiled sleeve.

"Here, sit down, Teela. Teela 10127. I can't believe you came. After what I have heard—here with me!" Meezra beamed with excitement.

"I don't understand," Teela said. "Your message said you wanted to help me."

"You help me. I help you. Everyone is happy. Everyone profits," Meezra said, pointing to the dusty box as though it contained all the answers. "Even before everything that has happened, your logs have always been among those most commonly requested. Some just want the boring stuff. I don't know why. I don't ask. Others just want the rebellion activities and the threats. And some want the really old stuff. But I have them all, the whole collection. And now! The new logs! I'm expanding my activities to meet the demands. And the rumors . . . if I get the logs that can substantiate them . . . Well, I won't be in this dung pit much longer." Meezra unlocked a cubicle under the communication panel and pulled out another box. This one was smaller, with a complex locking mechanism.

"I have a first generation copy of the visual log of the murder that resulted in the postponement of your reclamation," she said, lifting a log bar from the box as if it were as fragile as a newborn.

Feeling suddenly ill, Teela sat down on one of the many piles of boxes in the room. Realizing that her presumably anonymous life had in fact been a subject observed as entertainment came as a shock to her. She could feel the color draining from her face and crown tendrils.

"You didn't know? No one ever told you why you were allowed to continue your existence, did they? I knew it. I just knew it!" Meezra said, smiling broadly at her discovery as she placed the log bar into the display unit.

The display filled with a standard message screen. The Korlah language glyphs read:

> IF BIRTHING UNIT TEELA20.10127 IS RECLAIMED, INITIATOR, AUTHORIZOR, COLLECTOR AND IMPLEMENTOR WILL BE EXECUTED FOR CRIMES AGAINST KORLAH.

"That message was sent to every section supervisor, director, and leader," Meezra narrated as the screen changed from the message to a coarse video image of a bound and gagged Korlah wearing the uniform of birthing section director. The unconscious individual was lying in the idle jaws of one of the many reclamation unit macerators. Painted on the director's chest was the glyph for "initiator." As the director woke up, the jaws of the macerator began rolling, dragging the struggling individual into the grinding teeth. Teela looked away from the gruesome scene.

"This is why my reclamation was never executed?" Teela asked weakly.

"That, and the fact that the original log bar turned up in the personal chambers of the authorizing leader, Afron, who immediately put the reclamation order on hold. For the last ten cycles, she has tried but been unable to track down the murderer. Fearing a conspiracy within the security section, she left the reclamation order on hold, hoping to eventually catch the guilty parties and execute the order. Since you were taken from the birthing section six shifts ago, Afron has had large, heavily armed contingents continuously stationed at all reclamation units. It is rumored that the Resistance has initiated multiple attacks on security section guards and collaborating warriors for that reason. Word is, your time was up. If it weren't for the rumors, I would have believed your existence over." Meezra removed the log bar and carefully placed it back into the box.

"Why would someone, the Resistance, care . . . about me?" Teela asked.

"It wasn't the Resistance. They didn't even exist then. No one seems to know. That's what makes it all so interesting. I don't believe it's about you at all. You were just lucky enough to be designated as a nonpunitive reclamation at a time when the overzealous use of reclamation had created a rift between the leaders and the newly unprivileged. You were, or I should say, *are* the living symbol of the resistance against the leaders. The last of the damaged that hasn't gone into hiding and become one of the insignificant—a Non.

"Look! I have thousands of security section surveillance logs," Meezra said, jumping up and tapping several of the boxes. "You have been monitored continuously since the murder. I believe Afron hoped you would lead her to your protectors, or that they would come to you. Or perhaps she just hoped you would do something she could use against you. But you never broke any laws. Well, you did, but the leaders and security section are the worst violators of the laws prohibiting services in exchange for favors. Anyway, I never saw a single log where you solicited an exchange for favors; they were always requested."

Suddenly angered by the invasion of what minimal privacy she'd believed she had, Teela rose and crossed over to the boxes Meezra had tapped. Pulling a box out of its cubicle, she snatched one of the bars that filled the box to overflowing and shoved it at Meezra.

"Show me!" she said angrily.

"It's not a bad thing, collecting logs," Meezra said sheepishly, turning the bar over in her hand and examining the label before placing it in the reader. "You are very popular, uniquely attractive. Others find your situation . . . interesting. I follow the existence of others. Yours is just . . . well . . . my favorite."

The log was from a typical area monitor of the birthing section's adolescent feeding area. Teela could see a considerably younger version of herself on the floor, scraping up food and other foul things that accumulated between shifts until she was available to clean them up.

"Some have said they would voluntarily climb into the reclamation unit rather than do the things you have had to do. You have handled your burden with great honor!" Meezra said, trying to sound encouraging. Removing the log bar from the reader, Meezra gingerly placed it back into the box Teela was still holding.

"And what pieces of my life do you keep in that box!" Teela demanded, glaring at the box Meezra had removed from the locked cubicle.

Meezra deftly locked the box and slipped it back into the cubicle. "The pieces I find interesting. The pieces I believe others will want to view. You are both important and insignificant; this makes your life unique and fascinating. It's not a bad thing to collect and trade logs. There are no laws against it. The logs on your life are boring compared to some of the logs I have been asked for," Meezra replied, trying to downplay Teela's question.

"How many *customers* have asked for my logs?" Teela asked.

"There are many copies available, but mine are the best, first generation copies, all of them. I'm the contact when people want clarity and quality. I have the best selection, and if I don't have what someone wants, I can always get it. With everything that's happening, and with your help, I could multiply my trade ten times, maybe one hundred times more, and, of course, from now on I would share with you whatever favors I gain," Meezra answered with a smile, hoping to negotiate a collaboration.

"How many!" Teela screamed, throwing the box of log bars at Meezra. The small bars tumbled across the floor.

"I don't know," Meezra whined, cowering behind the display screen. "I've used the favors for this room, for my equipment. I have little left from past trades that I could share with you."

"I don't care about your dirty little trades or favors," Teela hissed. "The only thing I want from you— Wait. Did you say you can get anything? What exactly do you mean by that?"

"Anything you want: garments, food, water, personal servants, promotions, even invitations to private spectacles and social gatherings. When someone wants something, they come to me. If I don't have it, I know how to get it."

"Find me thirteen suits that block thermal signals and make those that wear them invisible in the dark."

Meezra stared blankly at her for a few moments. "Some things have a value beyond reach," Meezra whispered.

"I need thirteen. Either you can get them, or you have no utility toward the Mission objectives," Teela said ominously, quoting the words commonly contained in reclamation orders.

Dropping onto a stool by the message console, Meezra entered and sent a coded message. Teela watched closely but was unable to read what Meezra had entered or to whom she had sent it. When she had finished, Meezra leaned back casually and tried to mask her concern.

"Is there anything you think you might want to view while we wait?" Meezra offered, trying to sound hospitable while fiddling with the log bar in her hand.

"I have many special logs. Very stimulating logs that you might enjoy viewing with your clients. I just obtained this one of the captured aliens. It is of the dark beast and will certainly be highly sought. No one has ever seen a male engaged in . . . pleasuring acts," Meezra added with a suggestive grin and nod. Teela snatched the log bar from Meezra's palm, and when Meezra tried to grab it back, Teela punched her hard in the center of her chest, just below the chin.

"That's mine!" Meezra squealed indignantly. "That was a costly trade, demanding a premium. A premium, I tell you. It's mine!"

Quiet! Teela commanded with her mind, soliciting a shocked look on Meezra's face.

Snapping the log bar into the viewer, Teela fanned the power on. The view was from a monitor on the wall of the Nursery's sleep chamber. Teela accelerated the log and watched the women come and go until Bill entered, led by a biotech carrying a small case. Bill sat on the end of one of the small sleep platforms while the technician commenced to examine the repairs of his hands and face.

When the tech reached into his lap, Bill looked nervously around but made no movement to stop the action. The technician took his fully erect penis and pointed it into a container, as though expecting him to ejaculate. After a few moments of clumsy poking and prodding, Bill pushed her hand away and, using his, stroked himself repeatedly. Then he stopped and took her hand and placed it back on his penis. Taking the cue, the technician stroked as Bill had demonstrated. Within less than a minute of her attentions, Bill grabbed the sides of the bed and grimaced as he ejaculated onto the front of the technician's uniform. The technician then collected the semen by scraping it off her uniform and hands using the small container that was intended for that purpose. Teela reached to remove the log bar from the reader.

"No, wait! Meezra whispered. "There is much more."

When the technician had finished collecting the semen, she bent over an adjacent sleep platform and busily organized the equipment within the case, Bill stood up, his erection in no way diminished, and approached the technician from behind. Reaching around her, he placed one hand on her breasts and the other between her legs. Aside from the initial surprise, it was apparent that she did not resist his advances. By her own action, she released her uniform, allowing it to fall to the floor. Bill entered her from behind, his movements slow and rhythmic. Within a few minutes, the tempo had accelerated, with both the technician and Bill throwing their bodies together with mutual impassioned thrusts. There was no doubt that both parties were completely engrossed in the activity and ignoring the spectators Teela could see in the distance. Teela jerked the bar from the reader and the screen flashed bright, then faded.

"There's more," Meezra whispered, placing a trembling hand on Teela's upper thigh. Teela struck at Meezra's hand, hitting her own leg as Meezra quickly withdrew. With a hand that was also trembling, Teela placed the log in her pocket, ashamed by the feelings the log had stimulated.

"That's mine!" Meezra whined.

"If those recorded agree, you have my oath that I will return it."

It suddenly dawned on Teela that for the last ten cycles of her life she had spent much of her free time viewing logs in the archives. Not as blatantly or invasively as Meezra, but Teela nonetheless felt guilty of the voyeurism that Meezra was marketing for gain. Removing the log bar that contained the dispute spectacle challenge on it from her pocket, she placed it into the reader.

"Do you have any logs on dispute spectacles?" Teela asked as she read the details of the scheduled event.

"I have all the latest team spectacles, a few vintage one-on-one events and some superb Kahshinki execution spectacles," Meezra answered excitedly, believing she had finally stirred Teela's interest in her main trade.

"Team dispute spectacles only. And if you have any recent ones with the warriors called Ruwaugh or Apoulauh, I would like to see those," Teela said, smiling as pleasantly as she could at the dirty little smut dealer.

"What message log is this?" Meezra asked, moving around from behind the screen where she had taken refuge. Upon reading the challenge and the named participants, she sucked in air with a surprised gasp. Meezra had a look of sincere dismay on her face. "I knew Afron wouldn't have you used for spares or ground you into worm food. This is how she intends to end your existence without instigating a reprisal. She intends to eliminate you both at the same time," Meezra said.

"The events are nonlethal. We will be wearing riz," Teela replied, trying to mask her concern that yet another individual had voiced her belief that the spectacle would result in her death.

"The battles are *supposed* to be nonlethal. The riz deliver temporary, although painful, paralysis, but they do not kill. You will be fighting two of Afron's well-known assassins. Even with gloved hands and feet, they can deliver blows that kill," Meezra said as she pulled down another box of logs. "These are very popular logs, authorized dispute spectacles that resulted in deaths. In reality, they were sanctioned executions. All appeals for dismissal of the challenges were refused, and the challenged died accidentally as a result of injuries received during the event. All of which is lawful and honorable under Korlah law.

"Afron has been trying to kill Shawaugh without success since her demotion. Shawaugh has accepted every challenge made to her and has defeated all in single spectacle combat, killing several opponents. Not all of her battles were fought in the spectacle chamber. Shawaugh has spent several cycles doing punitive labor for engaging in unauthorized battles, all of which she won. I do not believe the myth of her invincibility. She can't win a match like this; she's getting too old. They will team up and kill her, and then they will kill you, and it will all be legal and authorized."

Teela noticed Meezra was working the controls of the log reader, making a copy of the challenge log Teela had placed in it. When Meezra went to extract the copy from the machine, Teela grabbed her hand roughly.

"Argh! I was going to offer a trade!" Meezra squealed at Teela's painful grip.

"You can have the copy for five logs of my choice, or you can have the original for ten."

"Message logs are not like visual logs. They are unaffected by what generation of copy they are. It makes no difference in the quality whether or not it's the original," Meezra replied.

"Yes, I know. But it would be the original given to me and held by me. It is rare. Maybe I should ask for twenty," Teela countered.

"Ten for the original. I accept your offer," Meezra quickly replied to lock the trade. She smiled and opened her hand to give Teela the copy. Taking the original, Meezra stood admiring the latest addition to her collection while Teela went through the spectacle event logs.

Selecting several recent spectacles, Teela placed one into the reader. Much more sophisticated than the recordings of area monitors, this recording divided the screen into four sections. Each section displayed a different view of a transparent spherical room that was approximately thirty feet across and suspended within another larger circular room with seats that lined the entire inner surface of the outer sphere. Positioned ninety degrees apart, the four views provided adequate coverage from all directions.

The contestants entered from opposite sides of the sphere via two narrow transit tubes, first one team and then the other. The flush opening closed behind them and blended into the transparent sphere as the transit tubes retracted. With the exception of the riz gloves on their hands and feet and across their mouths, the contestants were naked.

Moving in unison, the first team proceeded around the inner surface of the sphere toward the opposing team. As they approached, one member from the second team took a defensive stance while the other ran across the sphere at an angle, turning and then proceeding away in a move to approach the first team from behind. Before they were able to close the gap and force the first team to respond, the two members of the first team attacked the member in the defensive posture. With a combined flurry of blows and kicks, they left her motionless on the floor as they continued past, turning to face the one that was approaching them from behind.

The two members of the first team charged the single member of the second team. One of them feigned an attack, only to turn away at the last second. Trapped between the two aggressors, the single fighter moved sideways and attempted to fend off their combined attacks. It wasn't long before they had knocked her down and kicked her unconscious. The victors exited in the same manner they had entered while workers entered through the other door to remove the lifeless bodies.

A knock at the compartment door broke their attention away from the viewer. Meezra unlocked the door and peered out cautiously. One of Teela's guards shoved the door open against Meezra's protests and pinned her behind it while she looked in. When the guard stepped away, Shawaugh entered the doorway, the bulk of her massive frame filling it completely.

"A request was made on your behalf from this location! Who made it?" Shawaugh demanded, glaring at Teela.

"You have been misinformed; no requests have been made from here," Meezra said weakly. Shawaugh looked behind the door, turning awkwardly so that her one good eye could see who had spoken.

"Meezra!" Shawaugh shouted. She stepped into the center of the room and slammed the door shut, nearly hitting one of the security guards that had moved in to see what Shawaugh's intentions were.

"You sneaky little pile of braddle dung. I should have fed your filthy carcass to the scrum beetles cycles ago," Shawaugh growled at Meezra. Cornered, Meezra screamed, dropped to the floor, and covered her face with her hands. Shawaugh grabbed her by the crown tendrils, pulled her up on her feet, and pinned her against the wall.

"What mischief or treachery are you peddling today, you little spy?" Shawaugh asked, forcing Meezra's hands from her face.

"Aiiyya! I've done nothing to deserve this attack, Shawaugh! Why do you always hurt me?" Meezra whined as she tried to pull her hands from Shawaugh's crushing grip.

"Let her go, Shawaugh! Teela cried. "I came here looking for equipment I need. She is helping me."

"Meezra helps no one except herself," Shawaugh said, relaxing her grip but not releasing Meezra's arm.

"Where is it? Tell me where it is or I'll crush your hand," Shawaugh threatened, encasing one of Meezra's hands within her massive fist.

"There!" Meezra whined, pointing to the corner of the room.

Pulling Meezra with her, Shawaugh went to the corner and looked where she had pointed. She pulled down a box with a hole carefully cut in the side, took out a portable visual recording unit, and removed the log bar from it.

"She is a spy. There are others like her who trade their spy logs for favors and privileges. They don't care who they endanger or ruin; it is all about profit," Shawaugh said, tossing the log bar to Teela and raising her hand as though to strike Meezra.

"Don't . . . don't hit her, please," Teela pleaded.

Released with a rough shove, Meezra stumbled to the door and stood there rubbing her arm with an injured expression on her face.

"Meezra wants to be my friend. Don't you, Meezra?" Teela said soothingly, walking over and putting her arm around Meezra. "A spy could be helpful, don't you think?"

"She cannot be trusted," Shawaugh growled.

"I have many friends now. If someone were to betray me, my friends would see to ending their existence, slowly and painfully—or so I've been promised. You wouldn't betray me, would you, Meezra?"

"No, I wouldn't. I wouldn't Shawaugh!" Meezra cried to Shawaugh's skeptical one-eyed glare.

"Have you ever watched a dispute spectacle?" Teela asked Shawaugh.

"Why would I want to?"

Teela placed her copy of the challenge into the log reader and called up its contents.

"I am aware of this. Don't be afraid. I will beat them both, and you will never have to feel the sting of the riz," Shawaugh said, dismissing the challenge with a wave of her hand.

"Meezra has logs of Apoulauh and Ruwaugh's spectacles. Wouldn't it be wise to review these logs and study the techniques, skills, and, most importantly, the weaknesses of these two? We can learn from them and plan our strategy to ensure their defeat and humiliation. I trust your confidence, but much more than my honor and existence is at risk."

"The battle will likely never occur. Shyron has already issued a delay. And once you and the beasts have left, campaign will begin and the significance of this challenge will be quickly forgotten."

"You asked about a message being sent from here?"

"No message was sent!" Meezra cried out.

"Meezra is right. No message was sent. The equipment you look for does not exist, and those you send looking for it may cease to exist as well," Shawaugh said, directing her last comment at Meezra.

"Don't threaten me! I could just as easily arrange for your disappearance," Meezra hissed spitefully, then immediately regretted her words as she narrowly dodged Shawaugh's fist and rolled onto the floor. She scrambled on all fours to get to the other side of Teela.

"She's going to damage me again!" Meezra screamed. "I've never touched her. I've never done anything to her, and I've had to go for repairs twice from her beatings," she screeched, crouching behind Teela.

"Done nothing?" Shawaugh roared. "Your spy logs cost me three cycles of punitive labor, you worthless mouthful of rouk slime! If you would fight me, instead of cowering like braddle, I would end your pain!" Shawaugh growled, stalking her slowly around Teela.

Stepping forward to intercept Shawaugh's advance, Teela took hold of Shawaugh's wrists. Her tiny hands were barely able to encircle their sinewy girth. She looked up and tried to make eye contact with the giant.

Why didn't you end my pain, Teela whispered with her mind, *instead of throwing me with the dead to die slowly?* With thoughts bitter from years of nightmares, she released Shawaugh's wrists and slugged her in the chest with both fists. Shawaugh stepped back, not in response to the blows, but in response to the projected thoughts. Glancing down briefly at Teela's accusing glare, Shawaugh dropped her gaze to the floor, her shame evident.

"I am sorry," Shawaugh offered without emotion.

"Sorry about what?" Meezra asked, having heard only Shawaugh's side of the exchange.

Silence! Teela ordered, the command striking Meezra's mind like a hard slap in the face. Stunned, Meezra stumbled backward and fell into a seated position on a box.

"You knew I was alive!" Teela screamed with both her voice and mind, no longer afraid to face her nightmare. "You left me with the dead. Left me to bleed to death, alone among the rotting, empty shells. I still wake up screaming at the memory of your face. How could you do something like that? Why? Why would you? I was so glad when you finally came . . . and you . . . you . . ." Teela began to sob. She stood quaking, her head down, arms at her sides and hands tightly clenched. Blood dripped from the fresh punctures she had made through the wrappings on her palms.

"I see you, and hundreds of thousands of others like you, every time I close my eyes," Shawaugh said listlessly. "Clearing the bodies from the birthing section was the first punishment of many that I have endured. It took nearly one hundred shifts before I finished. Near the end, I had to roll the bodies onto bed pads and drag them because they would fall apart when I tried to pick them up. I saw that you had crawled off the pile, and I followed your blood trail. I didn't know what I would do if I found you. All the injured I had found, all that I thought I had saved, were sent for reclamation. I was relieved when I saw that Nerhala had found you because the burden of turning you in for reclamation would be hers and not mine. You don't realize . . . how connected we are, you and I."

Raising her head to face Teela, Shawaugh pointed to the scar on her face. "We both bear scars from the same attack," she said. Moving her finger from her face, she pointed to Teela's lower abdomen. "And we both have refused to conveniently cease our existence. I didn't know what to do then, but I have learned. All of us must resist and defy our Kahshinki-trained leaders until all unnecessary reclamations and this suicidal pursuit of the Kahshinki is stopped.

"We must resist, fight if necessary, to gain control of this vessel, replenish our resources, and rebuild before we engage in another campaign. I am not alone. Between the Resistance, those sympathetic to the Resistance, and the Nons, we control most of what happens on this ship. And once Afron and Shyron are through destroying each other, we will seize control," Shawaugh exclaimed fervently, finishing with a violent flourish of her arm and hand, her claws extended.

"Are you insane?" Meezra whispered, running over to the door and pressing her ear to it to listen for activity outside. "They'll end my existence just for being in the same room when something like that is said."

"And if someone were to tell them I said something like that, they would burn off my crown tendrils to find out who my accomplices were, and I would be sure to name you as one of them," Shawaugh hissed.

Moaning as if she had been kicked, Meezra slid down the door and sat on the floor, covering her face with her hands.

"Enough of this!" Teela barked. "Whether you like it or not, Meezra, you are now involved, so you would be well advised to use your resources to help us. Shawaugh, you should be careful of what you say and where you say it. There are more important issues that both of you are unaware of. Things that could affect the survival of everyone aboard this vessel."

Teela glanced at her bloodied palms and looked around for something to wipe them on.

"Clawing oneself is an indication of damaged reason," Shawaugh growled softly.

"It is an indication of overwhelming anger and frustration," Teela shot back, wiping the blood off her palms with the remnants of her bandages to examine the freshly opened wounds. Teela moved close, holding Shawaugh's gaze. Shawaugh's one eye narrowed.

Looking up into Shawaugh's scarred and scowling face, Teela spoke with her mind. *There is no honor when one Korlah ends the existence of another or allows another to cease by failing to prevent harm. Shyron's plans . . . my plans to forge an alliance with the humans could make victory over the Kahshinki here and now possible, but only if the loyal Council leaders, dissident leaders, Resistance, and Nons can put their differences aside and join together. The odds of success are slim, and the difficulty overwhelming. I understand why you fear failure.*

With a deep growl, out of place coming from one so small, Teela broke eye contact with Shawaugh and opened the door to leave.

"I do not fear failure. Do not bait me with such challenges," Shawaugh growled.

"What failure? What challenge? It is disrespectful to mindtalk like that," Meezra whined.

Teela exited the compartment and slammed the door shut behind her.

The security guards waiting outside snapped to attention. Heading quickly across the chamber, Teela marched toward the transit tubes. The guards scrambled to fall into step with Teela's rapid pace.

Birthing section! she ordered telepathically, sensing their confusion.

18 - Attack

Teela and her escorts made their way through a street-sized corridor and around the vessel's circumference by way of smaller, alley-sized passages to a transit area that would take them to the birthing section. The normal activities and traffic of these fully occupied sections were conspicuously absent, replaced by heavily armed contingents of warriors, ten or more strong, stationed at nearly every intersection. The warriors made no effort to inhibit their progress and moved out of the path of the column of armed guards. Taking a freight cube rather than a transit tube, Teela and her escorts proceeded inward to the birthing section.

In sharp contrast to the empty halls they had just traveled, the area immediately outside the Nursery was crowded. The unusual mix of Korlah who filled the narrow corridor included education section instructors, apprentices, birthing units, adolescents, biotechs, security section workers, and warriors.

With her escorts trapped in the gridlock, Teela aggressively wormed her way through the densely packed crowd. The area's ventilation and climate control were unable to adequately support the size of the crowd; the air was thick with moisture, warmth, and the musty odor of many Korlah. The entrance to the Nursery's antechamber was blocked by three security guards and their large shields. Squeezing past two biotechs, Teela ended up trapped between the surging crowd and the guards' shields.

"Let me pass!" she cried out. When she received no response, she pushed hard against the shield that blocked her path. It pushed back with unexpected force and speed, smacking her painfully on the forehead and knocking her back against the crowd.

"You jerk!" Teela shouted in English, reflexively and randomly projecting the thought. The noisy, surging crowd grew quiet and still. The offending guard looked down at her from over the shield and spoke to her, saying something that Teela could not understand.

"What?" she asked in English. The guard cocked her head in confusion. Her face suddenly looked foreign and frightening to Teela, who stumbled backward into the crowd and nearly dropped the cylinder she cradled in her arms. She was again pushed forward, but this time the guards moved their shields aside and she stumbled into the antechamber. The security guards around the Nursery's entrance stared, marveling at the sounds she made and her dazed, disoriented behavior.

Although it was Teela standing before them, it was Daedalus who looked back at their strange alien faces. His legs were weak and unwilling to respond to his desire to run. He dropped the object in his arms and gaped in horror at hands that he knew were not his, with eyes and perceptions he had never experienced without the moderation of his host. It was as though he had awakened into a reality that could not possibly be. The unintelligible sounds of the guards became muted and muffled. He stumbled as the room began to spin and he tumbled forward onto the ground. Rolling onto his back, he tried to raise arms that refused to obey his commands. Faces far in the distance looked down on him; he tried to talk, but could not. He closed his eyes and darkness calmed the fear and panic as he listened to the unfamiliar beat of Teela's heart. He felt as though he was drifting in a dream state between consciousness and oblivion, and he longed for the embrace of deep sleep. He let the feeling carry him away, back to the nothingness of his borrowed existence.

Teela bolted upright. The strong odor of humans flooded her crown tendrils. It was a locker room smell, heavy with sweat, dirty feet, and unwashed clothing. It was all too familiar and yet incredibly strange, and it was all around her. She shook her head to chase it away and clear the cobwebs of sleep that clouded her vision. She was in the dimly lit sleeping section of a Nursery. The location was both familiar and comforting, but she couldn't remember how she got there. Sounds from the outer chamber attracted her attention—rhythmic, musical sounds.

Teela rubbed her temples to soothe the dull ache in her head and noted that her hands had been freshly bandaged with a coarse fabric, like that of a birthing unit's tah. On the floor near the sleep platform lay her intricately embroidered slippers, belt, and vest, and a long metal cylinder. The cylinder triggered a flash of memory; she recalled receiving the gift from Challmara. Then slowly, vaguely at first but growing in clarity as she fought the urge to go back to sleep, she remembered meeting with Meezra and Shawaugh. She could remember heading to the Nursery but not arriving.

As she stood up, she felt weak and thirsty. Hunger cramps reminded her that it had been many shifts since she had taken any nourishment. She moved to the doorway and stood in the shadows as she peered into the outer chamber, leaning against the wall for support. Crystal, Catherine, and Marsha were performing with makeshift instruments. Security guards and birthing units stood at the viewing window, watching the humans like spectators at a zoo.

The girls wore modified tahs shortened nearly into miniskirts, the sleeves removed at the shoulders and made into belts they tied around their waists. Each girl had twisted the first few inches of hair around her face into tight braids and pulled the remainder into a bun at the back of her head to look more like the Korlah. Tiffany danced on top of the desk in a light-colored leotard and appeared at first glance to be naked. Combining aspects of gymnastics and modern dance, she moved with mesmerizing grace. Teela was transfixed until Bill walked through the doorway and stopped. He was startled when he spotted her in the shadows.

"You feeling better?" Bill asked.

"Yeah, I guess so. What happened?"

"Passed out an' hit the floor purdy hard. Maybe got a concussion, least that's what Margaret said."

Teela studied Bill's face, noting how the thin, narrow nose looked peculiarly stretched across his broad face. With the exception of a few residual blotchy red patches, particularly across the bridge of the nose, Bill's face was smooth and clear. Teela leaned closer to examine the way the two distinctly different skins had been joined. It didn't look as though they were stitched or even butted together; more like they had been blended. The coloration at the junction went from deep black to pale white within an eighth-inch, as if mixed together at a cellular level. Bill's face blushed a deep red and he looked away, nervously pushing the wire-rim glasses up on his nose and shifting his weight uneasily.

"I apologize. I just . . . couldn't help noticing how well you have healed," Teela stammered, realizing she had been staring.

"It's not that; everybody wants to look at my face. An' I don't mind. You can look all ya want. It's jus' that I probably shouldn't get too close to y'all."

Bill turned away and adjusted his trousers, failing to conceal the object of his embarrassment. He eventually relented by covering the erection stretching the front of his pleated pants into a tent with his hands.

"Oh! That reminds me. Do you know what that is?" Teela asked, pointing to the nearest monitoring camera located high on the wall. Bill squinted in the direction she pointed.

"What? That bump?"

"Yep. Smile. You're on *Candid Camera*."

Bill blushed an even deeper shade of red. His head turned to look at an area in the back of the sleep chamber and then to the bump on the wall near it.

"Oh man! Everybody seen me. Oh no!" Bill moaned, pulling his glasses off and rubbing the prickly heat from his face and eyes.

"Since ah got this dang nose, the smell, when any of y'all get near, well . . . it makes my Henry get all wound up. I'm not like this. I never used to get this wound up. Least not so much and not so fast. And no offense, but y'all ain't so good-looking. Just cain't understand why I'm getting so wound up."

Teela pulled the log bar of Bill's escapade from the pocket of her tah and held it in her hand, making sure Bill saw it. "I think this is probably the original copy. It was about to become the most highly sought-after pornography on this vessel. I took it from a dealer who buys and sells recordings, and you, my man, were about to become a porn star."

"What you gonna do with that?"

"That's up to you. I figured you wouldn't want a bunch of unattractive alien women getting off watching you do the wild thing."

"Don't matter much; everybody here already seen. They was all watching, ya know. They got real mad, calling me names and such. The one I done it with, I think all she wanted was more of my spooge. Like the times before, real interested in my Henry and my boys, and 'specially interested in my spooge."

"Jesus, Bill, how many times?"

"Bunch a times, right after ah woke up. The smell of 'em standing round me got me all wound up, like now. They seemed to think that was purdy neat. Soon as they touched my Henry, I let go. Couldn't seem to help it. After that, they just kept pulling it and poking it, trying to get more an' more. But after a while, my Henry got so sore it quit working.

"I was real glad when you came an' got me outta there, 'cause I was afraid they was gonna do some damage."

"I'm sorry they did that to you, Bill. And I'm not trying to make excuses for them, but I believe they were just trying to learn as much as they could about how your gear works before you leave."

Bill shrugged his shoulders and scratched the thick beard developing on his face.

"Ain't no thing. I jus' wish the smell didn't get me so wound up an' all. Cain't seem to think 'bout nothing else."

"You say it's the way we smell that gets you aroused? Could be pheromones, or maybe something caused by the repairs to your nose. Since this only happens when you smell us, why don't you try plugging your nose and see if that helps?"

Bill nodded thoughtfully, experimentally pinching his nose shut.

"Better watch out, Teela," Beth said, pushing Bill out of the way so she could get through the narrow door. "Don't turn your back on Black Bone the Pirate here, 'cause he jus' cain't control hissef," Beth taunted.

"Screw you, Beth!" Bill retorted.

"In your dreams, you fucking rapist!"

Bill blushed deeply, acted as though he was going to reply for an instant, then stormed into the darkness of the sleeping area.

"I'm not kidding! Don't turn your back on him. He jumped one of your buddies, grabbed her from behind and popped her right in front of everyone."

"You shouldn't be so hard on him. He actually may not be able to control himself. There could be something about our smell that arouses males. Does the way I smell affect you at all?" Teela asked, moving closer to Beth.

"Yeah, you make me wanna puke!" Beth growled, backing away.

"I'm serious. What do I smell like to you?"

"Hell, I don't know. Like beeswax, only too sweet. A sickening sweet, kinda like jasmine. I keep my distance, cuz it seriously makes me want to puke. Listen, I'd love to stand here and sniff armpits with you all day, but we've had some unusual deliveries since your last visit. Do you know what we're supposed to do with these?" Beth asked, pointing at two large covered containers. "They're full of things that look like rats and snakes."

Opening first one container and then the other, Teela examined the contents. In one there were hairless creatures akin to small rats, with long pointed snouts, short ears, and long prehensile tails. In the other there were eel-like creatures like water snakes, about thirty centimeters long with fins and scales near their flat-faced heads that blended into smooth, thin bodies.

"These are braddle and rouk. You are being honored with food now reserved for the privileged and powerful."

"Food? We're supposed to eat these?" Margaret said with disgust as she approached them.

"These are very good quality, young and undamaged. The braddle are worth at least ten biscuits each, and the rouk more than twenty. This is the closest thing to fresh food you will see on board this vessel. But if you decide your palates are too delicate, there are about fifty thousand starving birthing units on this level alone that would be happy to take these off your hands, although not at those prices."

"And what would we do with a stockpile of your nauseating biscuits?" Beth said.

"Biscuits are one of several rates of exchange on board this vessel that you can trade for anything, from food and cleaning services to sex and garments. In fact, you can even wager them to multiply their value," Teela answered quietly. She was embarrassed by her intimate knowledge of the economic subculture, where she had learned her bartering lessons by trial and error.

Beth's expression shifted from her usual bitter-taste frown to an almost pleasant smile.

"I think I can speak for all of us when I say we will pass on the sex, but a few more pulse rifles, I believe, would make interesting keepsakes."

Teela stood and looked at the contents of the containers. She had received many braddle the last few cycles as the quality of her patrons had improved. But only twice had she ever received rouk, and never this fine a quality.

"How do you prepare them?" asked Beth.

"These are prepared," Teela answered, pointing to the ratlike creatures. "Their fur has been induced to fall off, and their digestive systems were purged before they were brought here. You may notice, there are no droppings in the containers."

"You eat them alive!" Margaret said with disgust.

"No. If you tried that, you would likely choke or get bitten when they struggled. You kill them and then eat them. The rouk, however, you must be very careful with. They exude a slime that has a paralyzing agent in it. You must clean most of it off, or you could find yourself incapacitated."

"Oh . . . my . . . God! That is sooo disgusting!" Margaret exclaimed.

"What's disgusting?" Ruth asked, catching the tail end of the conversation. Ann and Rebecca also joined the growing assemblage.

"We're supposed to eat these raw," Margaret said, "a Korlah delicacy for the rich and famous, or so we're being told."

"If they're so good, why don't you eat one?" Margaret said, directing her comment to Teela.

"Thank you. I would love to. I normally can't afford braddle, and rouk are way out of my league. I am hungry. Thank you. This is great!" Teela bared her teeth in a ridiculous grin and bent over the container to select her prize.

The group watched in expectant silence, waiting to see if she would really eat it. Teela surveyed the contents for a few moments, then reached in and snatched up one of the plumper occupants. Holding the squirming rodent in her hand with its head over one of her thumbs, she punctured the back of its head with her thumb claw. Tilting her head back, she dropped the limp braddle into her mouth. After the first swallow, a large lump appeared in her throat, and the tip of a tail still wiggled in the corner of her mouth. After the second swallow, both the lump and tail had disappeared.

"Oh! That was gross!" Ann exclaimed amid a chorus of agreement from the other women.

Beth reached into the container and scooped up a braddle, holding it as Teela had done.

"Don't, Beth!" Margaret cried. "You don't know what kind of diseases that thing is carrying."

"When in Rome," Beth said, her pale blue eyes locked on Teela's. She crushed the head of the braddle with her molars and dropped it into her mouth as Teela had done. Gagging, she choked it down with four swallows.

"Umm, that was good," she said weakly, wiping tears from the corners of her eyes.

Teela laughed loudly, a coughing sound that Korlah make when greatly amused. The others just stood in shocked silence, disgusted and awed.

"You will find the rouk much easier to swallow," Teela said. She reached into the container and carefully caught one of the snakelike creatures just behind its head. Squirming and writhing, the creature wrapped itself around her wrist and its dark body turned milky white as it exuded a slippery slime. The rouk opened its mouth to display two rows of needlelike teeth and it began to click like a rattlesnake. Ann and Rebecca took two steps back. Beth, however, was motionless, maintaining her deadpan expression.

"The bites are not poisonous, but they are painful, so do be careful," Teela instructed. "The slime makes them very slippery, so you need to get a good grip and hang on tightly." As before, she punctured the head with a claw. Then using her other hand like a squeegee, she ran it down the length of the rouk and removed the milky ooze, which she threw back into the container. She repeated the process several times. She dipped her hand and the dead rouk into the tank and removed the majority of the remaining gunk from the flaccid creature.

"You need to get the slime off; that's what's poisonous."

Sucking its head into her mouth, she tilted her head back and lowered the rouk into her throat. The long body slid slowly into her mouth and disappeared.

"Makes your throat numb and takes your voice away," she whispered, reeling from the intoxicating residual slime.

Beth reached into the rouk container and jerked her hand back when one struck at her.

"Come on, Beth! Don't do it. These things could be lethal to humans," Margaret pleaded. "You don't have to prove anything to us or Teela."

Beth ignored Margaret and reached back in to pull out a rouk. She bit the head, removed the gunk, and swallowed the rouk in an expedited version of Teela's.

"Not bad. Really! Not bad at all. Easier than the fuckn' rat," Beth whispered with a slur, leaning against the wall as though she might fall down. Ann and Margaret dashed over to provide support.

Beth put her head on Margaret's shoulder, burped loudly, and laughed.

"How long is this going to last?" Ruth demanded.

Teela had closed her eyes and was swaying to the beat of the music, enjoying the numb and tingly sensations that coursed through her body.

"Mmmm . . . only a few bits or so . . . if I remember right," Teela slurred in a mixture of Korlah and English. Then she abruptly sat down and leaned back in the niche between the wall and rouk container.

"They're stoned. They are completely zonked out of their minds," Margaret said with disgust. "What should we do?"

"I wouldn't worry about Teela," Ruth said, "but we better keep a close watch on Beth's vitals."

"I am perfectly fine!" Beth slurred loudly, straightening up and pulling her arms away from Ann and Margaret's grip. She stumbled away from the wall and approached Ruth, stopping in front of her and swaying slightly off balance.

"Mind seems clear," Beth mumbled. "Body . . . kind of numb. Tingles all over and inside . . . not a bad feeling. Real good feeling, actually. Better than booze or pot. This would be some hot shit at a sushi bar."

The sound of someone banging at the door diverted the group's attention. Ruth orchestrated the preparations, and when everyone was in position she unpinned and cracked open the large access door.

Standing a head taller than Bill and outweighing him by at least sixty pounds was the largest Korlah Ruth had ever seen. Shawaugh stood there impassively and stared down at Ruth, not making a move.

A much smaller Korlah carrying a bundle peered around Shawaugh and spoke. "We're here to see Teela," Meezra said in Korlah.

Recognizing Teela's name and noting that Shawaugh's scarred face fit Beth's grudging description of the Korlah who had assisted with her rescue, Ruth let them enter.

"You are the biggest, ugliest, son of a—" Ruth whispered under her breath as Shawaugh walked in, but she stopped when the massive warrior turned her head and glared with her one good eye. Ruth looked away and gave a quick bow as she had noticed Teela doing, and closed the heavy door.

Shawaugh and Meezra stood inside the door and looked around. The band, which had been silent during their entry, began to play again and Tiffany resumed her dance routine. Bill and Margaret restashed their pulse rifles and all eyes followed the visitors closely. They carefully avoided eye contact as Teela had instructed.

When she spotted Teela, Meezra walked over and dropped her bundle at Teela's feet. She crouched down next to her and glanced nervously at the strange aliens.

"What is this sound they are making? And what is that one doing?" Meezra asked, pointing to Tiffany.

"Music and dance," Teela answered, using the English words since she knew of no Korlah equivalents. "Meezra, how would you like to be able to make logs of this music and dance and be able to make them with sound? Do you think they would have value?"

"Your thoughts are impaired from eating rouk. The odor is strong, as must be the effects."

"I'm serious, my dirty little friend. These creatures make logs that contain the visual record as well as the sounds that go with it."

Meezra's eyes sparkled at the lucrative prospect, and she moved closer to Teela. "If what you say is true," she whispered, "and I were able to combine sound with the visual displays, the profit would be limitless." Moving her mouth to Teela's ear, she whispered so quietly that Teela could barely hear.

"We could easily accumulate enough wealth within the next two cycles to guarantee a memory transfer. It is possible that I could even negotiate directorships."

"If you help me with my plans to return these humans to their home world, you can keep all the favors and profits for yourself; however, if you betray me, I give you my blood oath that you will find yourself feeding the scrum beetles and dung worms in the reclamation vats! This is the only offer I will make."

Meezra's eyes narrowed as she considered both the offer and the threat. Greed overruled any concern she may have had.

"Accepted, on the condition that I see the successful implementation of this sound log system before I am required to provide any services involving risk. Do you accept my condition?"

"No conditions! This requires the return of the humans and all the risks that go with it in order to obtain the technology. If you don't accept, I'm certain there is someone with greater influence and vision than you."

"Offer accepted," Meezra countered immediately, annoyed by Teela's reckless bargaining but fearing the offer would be retracted.

"Done!" they said in unison, finalizing the arrangement as an honor contract, an agreement more sacred and binding to the Korlah than any written human equivalent could ever be.

"Meezra has already committed her assistance. She seeks advantage during your intoxicated state!" Shawaugh shouted, reaching down to grab Meezra, who dodged her grasp and scurried out of reach on all fours. Teela stood and faced Shawaugh, who was considering pursuing Meezra. "Profit will secure her loyalty more than threats will. Are you here to offer your help as well?"

Shawaugh surveyed the area. She moved so that her back was facing the area monitor and then leaned down close to Teela. Her deep voice was uncharacteristically soft, imparting gravity and danger. "The Resistance Leadership will support Shyron if she agrees to their demands. They await a meeting on the first level of the energy section, below where we are now."

"Shyron is sick," Teela replied. "She can't leave the security section. If she did, Afron would attack. They must know that."

"They don't expect Shyron. They expect Shawlmon to arbitrate the dispute." Shawaugh glanced at Teela's garments.

"Shawaugh, I only just learned who Shawlmon was. These are just clothes, a costume—nothing more. I don't know what Shyron will agree to, so how can I speak for both sides? I'm not really Shawlmon, and I wouldn't know what to say," Teela replied.

"These garments you wear and the rumors that you are a warrior and bladesman who walks freely without fear of Afron, the Resistance, or the Nons has brought Shyron back into favor among the sections because of her affiliation with you. The belief is that you, with Shyron's backing, will lead us to a final victory over the Kahshinki. But even more important than victory is the belief that there will be a return to traditional Korlah beliefs and that you will eliminate the great inequities that have developed.

"You have changed, Teela. No one knows that better than I, not even Afron with all her spies. You are no longer the timid, weak birthing unit you once were. When the time comes, I am certain you will know what to say."

"I feel like I'm in way over my head. I wish I shared your confidence," Teela replied.

Shawaugh cocked her head and pursed her lips in confusion. "I don't understand. What is it that is over your head?"

Teela laughed a non-Korlah laugh and poked herself in the forehead when she realized she had used a human analogy. "I'm sorry. I meant that I don't feel adequately skilled for the task."

"I will go with you. I give my blood oath that no harm will come to you. You will find those of the Resistance to be . . ." Shawaugh paused, sensing someone's approach. Meezra peered around Shawaugh's bulk at Teela, exercising caution to remain out of Shawaugh's reach.

"At Shawaugh's request, I have made contact with the many gangs of Nons. They are a most unusual group, very disorganized, and they often rob each other. They have never agreed on anything until now. They have a leader they call the Oracle who claims you have promised to have their existence restored. They are now massing in the lower levels of the accoutrements section awaiting your return. If you truly made this claim, it was a very dangerous thing to do," Meezra finished with her trademark whine.

"I don't remember making this claim, but it doesn't matter. Calling someone dead and withholding food and water is wrong. No guts, no glory. I'm expected to know what to do? All right then, let's do it! Accoutrements you say? So they'll have no problem getting supplies if authorized.

"Okay, Meezra, you claim to have influence and contacts? It's time you prove it. Get a message through to Shyron. Tell her I want to restore the existence of every Non, feed them, and equip them to support our efforts. Allocate the resources you need, and don't even think about skimming."

"Shyron would never . . . you must be . . . damaged," Meezra stammered, her eyes wide in disbelief.

Teela put her hand on Meezra's shoulder, and when Meezra tried to pull away, her firm grip and the threat of her extended claws drew the worker's slight body close to her. Meezra's eyes opened even wider in terror. Teela directed her thoughts specifically to Meezra, her request a powerful and unquestionable demand. *Contact Shyron. Tell her Daedalus requests this. Now go!*

Meezra fell backward. The mental impact caused her to wince, and she winced again when she hit the floor. Rolling over and jumping to her feet, she ran to the door of the Nursery, unlocked it, and bolted away without looking back. Ruth hastily closed and repinned the door, shooting Teela and Shawaugh questioning glances.

"Mindtalking, even for the experienced, is a physical drain that should be used with great care," Shawaugh said. "This ordeal is wearing you in ways you do not understand. I see it in your eyes, the texture of your skin, and the way you damage your hands. You must eat and rest before we go." She placed her massive hand on Teela's shoulder.

Beth walked over and held out her hand. Without looking at Beth, Shawaugh addressed Teela. "I have nothing for this one. What does it want from me?"

Teela barked a quick Korlah laugh, amused at Shawaugh's discomfort. "Humans have many different customs. The meeting of eyes is rarely intended as a challenge. This is the unit that was being beaten by Apoulauh. She wishes to thank you for stopping the beating. If you wish to accept the offer of gratitude, take hold of her hand and shake it up and down. Use a firm grip, though, or she will think you are spiritually weak."

"I didn't stop its beating; I stopped yours."

"By stopping mine, you stopped hers. Shake her hand; it is a gesture of respect."

Reluctantly reaching out, Shawaugh wrapped Beth's much smaller hand with hers. Seeing Beth's shoulder drop and her eyes widen, Teela realized she probably shouldn't have suggested a firm grip. When Shawaugh began to shake Beth's hand, Teela feared that she would break Beth's arm. She lunged forward and grabbed their joined hands.

"Gently! I didn't say to crush her hand," Teela advised. Shawaugh relaxed her grip and continued to shake Beth's hand much more gently.

"Beth, this is my good friend, Shawaugh . . . Shawaugh, this is . . . Beth," she said. She hoped the introduction would help bridge the cultural abyss between these strikingly different, and yet similar, individuals.

"Rouche Hah!" Shawaugh grunted the Korlah greeting for a fellow warrior. It roughly translated to English as "My honor" or "Honored to meet you."

"Rouche Hah!" Beth grunted back the way Teela had taught her. "Now, can I have my hand back?" Beth said, attempting to withdraw her hand from Shawaugh's crushing grip. Sensing the meaning, Shawaugh released her hand. Beth looked at her white-knuckled hand for a second and experimentally bent her fingers.

"That's one hell of a grip, Tiny! I can see why those stooges backed off when you showed up," Beth said, rubbing her hand and admiring Shawaugh's massive physique.

"Is this the other one?" Bill asked. "The one you was telling us about?"

"Yep, a little bigger than I remembered, though," Beth said.

"All right!" Bill shouted, causing Shawaugh to turn and face him defensively. "Hey, everyone, this here's the one Beth told us about," Bill said excitedly, taking Shawaugh's hand and shaking it vigorously.

Ruth came up next and cautiously offered her hand. Shawaugh took it and shook it gently, bowing her head in a less formal greeting of respect. Each of the others, with the exception of Rebecca, filed by, shaking hands and offering greetings and gratitude. When they had finished, Rebecca stood before Shawaugh. She put her hand up on the massive Korlah's arm, tilted her head back, and began a prayer.

"Lord, oh Lord, we thank you for sending this archangel during our hour of need. We pray, Lord, that you will forgive us our past sins and deliver us from this evil pit into which we have fallen. Please, Lord, dear merciful Lord, protect our angel and guide us so that we may find our way back home. Amen."

"Amen!" the group responded in unison.

"That was great, Becca. Now beat it!" Beth ordered, sending Rebecca scurrying away. Teela noted that Rebecca's eyes were wide open and wild-looking, with dark rings under them. Her cheeks were sunken and her normally pallid complexion was waxen and corpselike. Dropping to her knees in the distant corner, Rebecca clasped her hands together and continued praying in silence.

"What's the matter with you?" Teela said to Beth. "Do you always have to be such a bully? I thought I asked you to look after her, not bully and berate her."

"Nah, I don't think so. *You* never asked me to look after her. Dade did, but not you. Maybe you're just confused again, you know? Mixing up things Dade told you, that he told me. You think it might be something like that?"

Teela looked down and shook her head slowly from side to side as she replied, her voice quiet and sincere. "Yeah, something like that. Beth . . . now, I'm asking. Have some compassion for the woman. Make sure she eats something. I didn't like Rebecca when I first met her, thought she was a real nutcase. There was a time, long ago, when I used to pray. Not a lot and only for real important things. But you know what? Not one of my prayers has ever been answered. I always thought it was because I lacked faith, but faith is something Becca has in abundance, and under the circumstances I admire that. Don't be so mean. It isn't necessary. Is it really too much to ask?"

Without looking up, Teela stood patiently and waited for Beth's reply. She clasped her hands together to control the urge to clench them into fists.

Beth studied Teela for a moment, and Teela tensed in anticipation of another adversarial remark. Instead, Beth's perpetual scowl seemed to soften slightly.

"Yeah, sure thing. I'm here for the team," she said, her voice emulating Teela's quiet sincerity.

Teela paused for a moment, unsure whether the response was true sincerity or just more sarcasm. She finally gave a bow and palm display to demonstrate her gratitude and respect.

Teela turned to Ruth and Margaret who had been watching and waiting for a confrontation. Teela said, "Get everyone together in the sleep chamber, including Tiffany and the band. I would like to address the group about events that have transpired and the plans to take you home."

Margaret and Ruth smiled broadly and broke away to gather the group together.

The dormitory-style sleeping chamber was designed to house one hundred adolescent shells during the four-cycle training period prior to dispersal into their designated sections. One hundred sleep platforms were arranged in ten neat rows of ten, unused except for those now claimed by the humans. The group had taken up residence at a cluster of beds in the corner nearest the door, with the exception of Bill and Beth, who had moved bunks away from the group and away from each other.

Teela followed the joking, laughing humans into their corner of the chamber, where they made themselves comfortable on the beds. The upbeat mood contrasted with the fear and depression that had been the norm since their arrival. Shawaugh stood near the door, looking and feeling out of place. Teela moved into the corner and turned to face the excited and anxious group.

"A transport vessel is being prepared to take you home, and provisions to escort you to it are being made as I speak."

The group began to applaud, but Teela held up her hands until they stopped. "I don't want to dampen your hopes, but . . . there are complications and forces working against my efforts. I told you about the attack on this ship and the damage that was done. Now I need to tell you about the effects the attacks had so you will understand why this is going to be so difficult and dangerous.

"Before the Kahshinki conquered my home world, our culture had not progressed beyond that of your preindustrial Iron Age. All of our current technology is based on that which the Kahshinki imposed on us. Although we have modified and improved upon it, we have never really researched new technology during the one thousand years and twelve campaigns that we have been at war with them.

"I believe the key to our victory against the Kahshinki, and Earth's ability to resist the impending Kahshinki invasion, lies in my ability to negotiate an alliance with Earth and to arrange for an exchange of technology. The difficulty will lie in convincing Earth's leadership that the Korlah are not invaders, but allies that would help ensure the sovereignty of Earth rather than undermine it.

"Unfortunately, there is a division in the unity of this vessel. One group would like to break off the pursuit of the Kahshinki rather than engage in a battle we cannot possibly win in our damaged condition. Another group feels that the risk of attempting an alliance is too great, and that because Earth represents the next strategic goal in the Kahshinki plans for expansion, it should be sterilized to ensure their plans are impeded long enough for another Korlah support force to arrive.

"The group I represent wants to forge an alliance with Earth's military forces to jointly engage the Kahshinki before they are ready to invade Earth. We want to stop them here and now so that the Korlah on this vessel can begin their long journey home.

"I would like to say that your journey home is guaranteed, but the fragile condition of the politics on this vessel are such that I think we should make preparations for multiple possibilities. We have become complacent, accepting our roles as prisoners and victims. This is not acceptable and must change if we expect to survive this situation. If the current leadership changes or turns against us, we will need to exercise options that require a unified and disciplined effort to ensure our ability to take matters into our own hands."

Beth raised her hand and waited patiently.

“Yes? What now, Beth?” Teela asked, anticipating harassment.

“I’m sorry, but you are not one of us, and yet you keep referring to yourself as though you are. Are you planning to escape to Earth with us, or is there some other reason you repeatedly talk like this? Something perhaps that you would like to share with us?”

Teela flushed white and her fists clenched with the realization that she had been completely in the role of Daedalus and had been actually thinking of Earth as home. The stinging pain in her palms brought her back.

“No, of course not,” Teela said, putting her hands behind her back, self-conscious of the blood beginning to trickle down her knuckles.

“I am still learning your language. Please forgive any errors I make in referring to myself. I am your designated representative and have taken the role of ensuring your safe return home. I know . . . I . . . I realize it’s not my home,” Teela’s voice tapered off to a whisper as she spoke. Her eyes dropped to the floor, no longer able to meet the eyes of the group that seemed to be burning a hole into her soul. Her hands fell limply to her sides and blood dripped from her fingertips.

A long silence followed. Some shifted uncomfortably and a few coughed nervously, but no one spoke. Finally, Shawaugh moved between Teela and the others, making herself a physical barrier to their stares. She pulled something from the pocket of her uniform and held it out to Teela. “Put these on,” Shawaugh said softly, holding out a pair of fingerless gloves made from thick, coarse fabric.

Teela’s hands trembled violently as she accepted the gloves. She dropped one while fumbling to put on the other and then nearly fell over when she bent down to pick it up. Shawaugh gripped her by the shoulders to steady her.

“Teela, you must listen to me,” Shawaugh whispered. “The essence of this human you allow to remain within you has no regard for this shell. It is driving you to self-destruction. If you do not rest soon, you will lose control of it, and it will destroy you. You must expel it, while you still can.”

"I'm in control. I can handle it. Really, I am all right," Teela said, first in English and then again in Korlah when she realized her error. Shawaugh released her shoulders, gave her an admonishing glance, and rejoined the others. As Teela straightened her uniform, she noticed that Shawaugh was wearing an identical pair of gloves.

"Be prepared to leave at a moment's notice. Everyone needs to learn how the weapons work. Learn as much of our language as you can. The birthing units will be glad to teach you in exchange for food."

"Or clothes!" said Crystal, who then added in Korlah, "I am Crystal. You Teela. My tah for your tah. Good deal. You accept?"

Teela smiled with effort. Crystal's exuberance helped to ease the pressure of the icy fist she felt gripping her heart.

"That was very good. But if it's just the same to you, I think I'll hang onto this outfit for now. Honestly though, that was really good, Crystal. Try to learn more. I will help when I can."

A loud pounding on the chamber's access door interrupted Teela.

"Something is happening!" Shawaugh said loudly, peering through the window into the outer chamber.

There appeared to be another confrontation between the warriors and the four security officers guarding the Nursery. While they watched, the security officers and warriors energized their pulse rifles. Teela ran to the communication console to notify Shyron that her guards would need backup, only to find the console was dead.

"I will find out what's going on," Shawaugh said sternly. She opened the main door just enough to slip out.

As Shawaugh walked toward the armed standoff, Teela followed to determine the cause of the confrontation. The security officers and warriors had spread out within the main chamber. Their energized weapons were pointed at each other, but there was no conversation that Teela could hear.

"Get back! Get back inside!" Plefauna, the senior security officer, shouted when she saw Teela.

The warriors directed their weapons at Teela. In an instant, the room was thrown into pandemonium. The officers and warriors screamed and pulse weapons fired. Realizing that Teela was the warriors' target, Shawaugh grabbed her with an agility that defied her mass. Shawaugh enveloped her within her arms and spun around, presenting her back to the discharge of the warriors' pulse weapons. Teela felt the heat of a lethal pulse as it struck the doorframe where she had just been standing. The force of multiple blasts drove them both back into the narrow opening of the door with Shawaugh on top and Teela buried beneath. Hands seized their shoulders, and Teela and Shawaugh were dragged as one the rest of the way through the door as Bill rammed it shut with a resounding thump that shook its thick frame. Just as it closed, two more pulse blasts struck the lower portion of the door, scorching it a darker shade.

"What the hell has happened?" Beth shouted as she struggled to roll Shawaugh's motionless body off of Teela. With Ruth's help, Teela wormed herself out from under the heavy warrior and bent to check the extent of Shawaugh's injuries. Inundated with the overwhelming smell of burnt flesh and plastic, Teela shook her head in an effort to clear her crown tendrils and fought the urge to vomit.

"Pin the door!" Teela screamed at Bill, who immediately began to fumble with the small pin that pivoted into the operating fulcrum, locking the door from the inside.

"She's still alive. Please, somebody help me," Teela pleaded, choking from the stench and trying to avoid looking at the dinner plate–sized crater in the middle of Shawaugh's back that emanated thin ribbons of blue smoke from its edges. Ruth, Margaret, and Bill worked together to roll Shawaugh over. They sat her up and began to strip off her smoldering uniform.

"Look! She's wearing body armor," Beth said with a hopeful glance to Teela.

"Get it off, quickly! Margaret, please . . . please do what you can to help her," Teela cried as she glanced at the smoking metal of the door and then at Shawaugh's back. She jumped to her feet and ran to the sleeping chamber.

"Would somebody please tell me what the hell is happening?" Beth cried out to no one in particular.

Teela stripped off her embroidered tah and ripped open the package Meezra had brought her. Inside she found a pair of soft suedelike thigh-high boots and a pair of gloves with thick gauntlets. She rolled up the boots, gloves, and her vest in the embroidered tah to form a large ball that she tied around her waist using her thick ornate belt. She removed the two swords from the cylindrical box and considered leaving them behind.

A voice without claws will not be heard, she thought as she tied the weapons to her shins with fabric torn from bedding. From a pile of clothes on the floor, Teela extracted a birthing unit's soiled tah and began to put it on.

"Hey! That's mine," whined Catherine, who decided to say nothing more when Teela shot her an intimidating glare and fanged snarl. Pulling the tah down over the bundle and smoothing the fabric over its bulge, Teela addressed the five remaining humans, who until then had been observing the unfolding events in stunned silence.

"Be prepared for an armed entry. Do not display the weapons, but have them ready in case they force their way in. I'm going for help." Teela turned and waddled to the main door, looking very much like a pregnant birthing unit.

"If *who* gets in?" whispered Ann a few seconds after Teela had left the room.

The shooting had stopped; Teela moved to the viewing window and surveyed the carnage beyond with shocked disbelief. Warriors and security officers were strewn in crumpled heaps across the floor of the main chamber. The walls were scorched with pulse blasts and weapons lay scattered about. Several lifeless bodies were still smoking.

"Let me out and lock the door after me," Teela commanded Bill, who stood by the door.

Bill stared at her for a moment and then glanced at Beth, who was looking at her with a puzzled expression.

"Teela? Is that you?" Beth asked, staring at the bulge at her waist.

"Yes, communications are being blocked. I'm going for help. I need to go now, before more warriors arrive," Teela explained hastily, straining to remain calm and suppress her impatience.

"Open the door," Beth said to Bill. "So much for Korlah honor," She nodded her head at Shawaugh, who was being bandaged by Ruth and Margaret.

“I’m going for help, and then I’ll be back,” Teela repeated defensively.

Beth put her hand on Teela’s shoulder. “I know you will. Don’t worry ’bout us,” she said. “We’re going to take good care of your big friend, and we’ll hold down the fort until you get back. Now get going.” Beth nudged Teela gently toward the door.

Teela squeezed out the access door, which Bill shut and locked behind her. The smell of charred flesh hung heavy in the air. Teela gathered up pulse rifles as other birthing units checked the fallen warriors and security officers for survivors. Dropping the rifles by the Nursery door, Teela headed for the transit spokes.

“Teela! Come here!” called a birthing unit who crouched over one of the security officers. As Teela approached, she could see it was Plefauna. Her arm was nearly burned off at the shoulder. The young birthing unit held her ear to Plefauna’s mouth. Plefauna’s face contorted into a tight grimace and relaxed, her eyes glazed and expressionless. The birthing unit rose up and faced Teela with a grave expression.

“She said Shyron is dead, and Afron has claimed command. The warriors were here to take the humans to the bio section and to process a reclamation order for . . . you,” she whispered, her voice shaking with fear and shock. The rumble of many heavily booted feet coming down the corridor interrupted their conversation.

Warriors with weapons energized and ready to fire began to pour into the main chamber. Teela and her sister birthing units froze where they stood. The warriors rushed past them to take up positions in the room and around the Nursery’s door. Teela put her head down and shook her crown tendrils forward to cover the identification sabat on her face. She slowly moved along the wall toward the opening to the corridor as the senior warrior pounded on the door and demanded that it be opened.

Frustrated, the warrior fired her pulse rifle at the door until its charge was spent. Although it glowed red-hot, the door gave no indication of weakening. She stormed around the room from one fallen security officer to the next, kicking them with a hope of finding one alive. Finding none, she grabbed the young birthing unit who had heard Plefauna's dying words and dug her claws into her shoulder, causing her to shriek loudly and drop to her knees.

"Do you know Teela?" the warrior shouted at her.

"Yes!" the young mother cried in pain.

"Where is she?" the warrior shouted without releasing her grip.

"In there," she whimpered, pointing to the Nursery. "She's been shot. The beasts pulled her inside. I think she has ceased."

The senior warrior released her and directed her subordinates to set up a perimeter around the Nursery door and all the access corridors. They didn't give a second look to the birthing units scurrying away.

The last census showed that the population and education sections represented the majority of Korlah on the massive campaign vessel. Shells, warriors, and birthing units made up most of those groups, outnumbering the remainder of the population ten to one. As Teela hurried through the crowded corridors of the population section, this was readily apparent. More warriors were arriving every bit.

Teela worked her way to the transit tubes through compartments and maintenance tunnels to avoid the checkpoints the warriors were setting up at all the access and egress areas. Passing the access spokes for the energy section, one level below the population section, Teela noted that the pressure shields over the tubes had been closed and sealed. The corridor beyond was blocked by a heavily armed contingent of warriors who were setting up an armored and fortified checkpoint. The perimeter they were establishing was apparently intended to lay siege to the security section's access point. The transit spokes to the upper levels were blocked by guarded checkpoints. The spoke down to the energy section had also been sealed; however, warriors had forced it open and were arguing nearby. Teela crept closer. Trying to stay out of the warriors' lines of sight, she listened to the argument.

"I sent down the entire squad and none have returned. I can hold this access, but I cannot progress without shields and pulse orbs to clear the lower chambers first."

"You won't be getting shields or pulse orbs any time soon. The accoutrements and supplies sections have also sealed their bulkheads. Life support in the warrior, arms and strategy sections has been secured. We need access to the energy section to restore life support immediately."

"Birther! Where are you going?" shouted a warrior at the checkpoint by the transit up-tubes. Teela looked over to see the warrior pointing at her. Not wanting to chance being questioned or searched, Teela looked around for an escape route. A column of warriors was approaching from the direction she had just come, and the area ahead was blocked by the checkpoint. The only way out was down.

Darting between the wall and the warriors, she leapt into the tube that led to the energy section. "Stop!" was the last thing Teela heard as she plunged down the tube at a high-gravity descent.

Someone had altered the tube so that instead of dropping her slowly, it grabbed her and pulled her down. The effect multiplied rather than reduced, and Teela desperately grabbed for the ridges and rungs she knew should line the tube, but she found only slick walls. She kicked off her slippers, pressed her back against one side, and clawed at the opposite wall with her hands and feet. Her tah was pulled up behind her shoulders and the bare flesh of her lower back and hips absorbed the friction that slowed her descent. She still struck the bottom of the 360-foot tube with sufficient force to knock the wind out of her and send her tumbling into the corridor. She lay on her side in the blackness gasping for air. Her hips and feet were numb from the impact, and the abraded flesh on her back burned ferociously.

19 - Rescue

"Hold! It's just a birthing unit," came a whisper from the darkened corridor. Teela stifled her labored breathing and searched the darkness. She could see bodies on the floor around her, warm bodies, but from their dull thermal signatures, she realized they were deceased and had begun to cool. Groaning, she struggled to stand. Someone gently lifted her to her feet. Looking into the blackness, Teela could not discern the signatures of those assisting her. She touched her hisnah to check the function of her thermal vision. Her fingers gave off varied, glowing hues, traces of the radiant heat they emitted, confirming that the organ was undamaged. Someone in the darkness, someone who radiated no body heat, gently took her by the hand and arm.

"You are not badly damaged. Come with me, mother," a voice said, guiding her.

Teela could hear several more invisible soldiers behind them, dragging the bodies she had seen. Although unable to see any details, she could tell from the subtle thermals, acoustics, and air movement that she was being led further aft, down the main corridor past several junctions, turning right down one and then left down smaller corridors, until they arrived at an illuminated chamber somewhere in the tenth level of the energy section.

In the dim light of the chamber's glowbars, Teela was finally able to see her escorts. They were wearing full-body suits covered with fine fishnet webbing over the entire body, gloves, boots, a helmet, and even the face shield. A single lens, looking very much like a standard military-issue night vision scope, was mounted like a visor, which the soldiers lifted as they entered the illuminated room.

"The cowardly scrum threw this birth mother down a disabled transit tube. Treat her injuries and then transfer her to our birthing section," the soldier leading Teela said to the pair of armed energy section workers guarding the door.

"We have many ceased warriors for spares. Let us know if you need more," one of the other soldiers said, dragging a deceased warrior into the room. Without another word, the three soldiers snapped their visors down with a click and disappeared into the darkness of the corridor.

The room was a makeshift biotech repair facility. Several repair stations had been set up and were currently occupied by energy section workers being treated by biotechs for injuries and burns from pulse blasts. There were rows of beds throughout the remainder of the large chamber, half of which were filled with standard workers and laborers recovering from battle injuries. Six seriously injured workers were being tended by other laborers waiting for treatment at the repair stations. These were not warriors or security officers; these were the mythical Resistance soldiers Teela had only heard rumors of, until now.

"I am here to see the leader of the Resistance," Teela demanded.

Although the room had been relatively quiet, what little conversation there was stopped, and with the exception of the moans and groans of the injured, a strained silence filled the room. The two guards glanced at each other and then stared at Teela.

"Nobody sees the leader!" one of the guards said.

"What business do you have with the Resistance?" the other asked.

"I wasn't thrown down that transit tube. I jumped. I came to both offer assistance and ask for help," Teela said, trying to maintain her confident and stern demeanor.

"Hah!" the nearest guard jeered. "We have more volunteers than we know what to do with. Go to our birthing section and deliver your shells. Then if you survive, maybe we will make you a soldier."

"I don't like the looks of this unit!" the other guard growled. "Jumped it says. Wants to see the leader. It doesn't sound or behave like a birthing unit. It is more likely a spy for Afron and her army of dishonorable scrum." The guard pointed her weapon at Teela.

"I have been appointed by the Mission Potentate. I represent the Korlah Mission and the interests of the human inhabitants of the planet Earth. I have been requested to speak to the Resistance leader. It is critical to the Mission!" Teela said, opening her hands and moving them slightly forward to emphasize that this was not a request but rather a demand—behavior totally inconsistent with the rank and status of a birthing unit.

The guards stared at her in disbelief. The nearest armed worker bent over to look closely at the sabat on her face, noting that it didn't match the one on her tah.

The guard moved back and cleared her throat nervously. "This unit is Teela 10127!" she exclaimed. The room began to buzz with a dozen whispered conversations.

Pleased that these guards knew of her, Teela wanted to take advantage of the moment and drive home the importance of her visit. The tah of a birthing unit was no longer her designated uniform, so before all those who were carefully scrutinizing her, she began to remove her tah. Her muscles and joints ached and the coarse fabric scraped painfully against her raw back. Despite all the bruises, cuts, and scrapes that covered her ravaged body, she made certain to give no indication of her intense discomfort.

After removing her tah, Teela released the bundle and belt from around her waist. As she removed the swords, the nearest guard energized her pulse rifle and leveled it at her head. Teela turned her back to the warrior, demonstrating a nonaggressive posture, and continued her task. Now completely naked, she unrolled her long robe and removed the vest, boots, and gloves. She put the boots on first, then the robe, vest, belt, and finally the gloves. With slow, deliberate moves, she lifted first one sword, sliding it into the loop on one side of her belt, and then the other.

The robe, gloves, and swords had a mesmerizing effect on Teela, transforming her into an ancient warrior. Her many dreams of participation in battle, rather than being a victim of it, engorged her crown tendrils and mottled her complexion with a dark flush as she received the Korlah equivalent of an adrenaline rush. She stretched to alleviate the stiffness from her fall and rose to her full height rather than her usual hunched stance. Tilting her head forward, she assumed an aggressive posture and faced the armed guards defiantly.

"I have been requested to come here for a meeting. It required a journey that was not taken without risk. If I cannot meet with your leader, can you at least help me contact her?" Teela asked, her politeness only a formality.

The costume, her name, or the rumors preceding her arrival had had a marked effect on the guards. The warriors stared until their gazes were returned. Their behavior and body language had changed in the last few moments. When Teela made eye contact with the nearest guard, the guard looked down and de-energized her rifle, embarrassed.

"Your suspicions are justified," Teela said. "You should treat me, and any others that you don't know, as an enemy of the Resistance until we are proven otherwise."

When the guard looked up, Teela smiled and gave a respectful warrior's salute. The armed guard saluted in return and straightened up.

An energy section worker came forward and escorted Teela to a communications console nearly buried behind a pile of empty medical supply containers, soiled rags, and bandages.

"Enter your message, and I will transmit it to the leader's coordinates," the worker said.

Teela sat down at the console. It had been her intention to contact Shyron for assistance; however, events had led her to the Resistance, and now she had to gather her thoughts and compose a communication to an entity she had every reason to believe would be unwilling to assist the humans on board, let alone the humans of Earth. Teela pulled the thick gloves from her hands and nervously massaged her injured palms. She struggled to find the words that would gain her the assistance she needed, but could doom everything she had struggled to accomplish since the arrival of the humans. She looked up at the blank screen and reached for the controls when a message began to scroll onto the screen.

> TEELA 10127, ROUCHE HAH!
>
> I AM PLEASED TO SEE THAT YOU HAVE MADE YOUR WAY SAFELY TO THE PROTECTION OF OUR RESISTANCE FIGHTERS. YOUR ROBE IS MOST IMPRESSIVE. I SUSPECT THAT ITS SIGNIFICANCE IS LOST ON THOSE NOT EDUCATED ON OUR PAST. THE BLADES, ALTHOUGH EXQUISITE, I FEAR WILL NOT BE MUCH USE AGAINST PULSE WEAPONS.

Teela stared with her mouth agape, then noticed the video monitor above the console and in other strategic spots throughout the room. Before she could respond, the message continued.

> HELP ME CONVINCE SHYRON TO SUPPORT OUR DEMANDS IN THE COUNCIL, AND THE RESISTANCE WILL RETRIEVE AND PROTECT YOUR HUMAN FRIENDS.

Everything Teela was preparing to say crumbled, leaving her with a hopelessness that threatened to overwhelm her. She did not want to reveal that Shyron was dead for fear that this

Resistance leader would not help her, yet she also did not want to delay the news of her death and delay the possibility of a rescue. Groaning under the weight of her decision, Teela followed the instincts that had brought her success so far and quickly typed her response.

> I HAVE RECEIVED WORD THAT SHYRON IS DEAD. I CANNOT MAKE ANY GUARANTEES, BUT I GIVE YOU MY BLOOD-OATH THAT I WILL DO EVERYTHING I CAN TO CONVINCE THE COUNCIL TO SUPPORT YOUR DEMANDS.

She sent the response and removed her hands from the cold metal console with loathing. The screen went blank, then the video image of a small, smoky compartment appeared. The compartment was crowded with armed security officers. Shyron lay weakly in her chamber with a biotech at her side. The guards stood focused on the smoking and sparking door. The screen went blank and a message appeared.

> SHYRON AND HER PERSONAL GUARDS ARE UNDER SIEGE IN THE SECURITY SECTION. I EXPECT THEY WILL BE TAKEN SOON, AND THEN AFRON WILL ENSURE SHYRON'S LONG EXISTENCE WILL COME TO A RAPID END. SINCE YOU HAVE BEEN SO SUCCESSFUL IN OBTAINING SHYRON'S SUPPORT OF YOUR INTERESTS, I WOULD LIKE YOU TO ASSIST IN HER RESCUE AND CONVINCE HER TO ACCEPT THE PROTECTION OF THE RESISTANCE UNTIL THE COUNCIL CAN BE RESTORED. IN EXCHANGE, SHE MUST AGREE TO SUPPORT THE DEMANDS OF THE RESISTANCE DURING THE COUNCIL DELIBERATIONS. IF YOU ARE SUCCESSFUL, IN EXCHANGE FOR YOUR ASSISTANCE, THE RESISTANCE WILL ALSO PROTECT THESE HUMANS YOU HAVE BONDED WITH. DO YOU ACCEPT MY OFFER?

Teela knew there was no time for the debate this contract required. Those granting a favor in exchange for one always claimed the advantage. If the individual she was dealing with felt strongly about maintaining that advantage, there would most certainly be a counter offer. She typed her response, praying it would be accepted without further delay.

AGREED UNDER THE FOLLOWING CONDITIONS: THE DEMANDS OF THE RESISTANCE MUST NOT VIOLATE KORLAH LAW, AND THE ACTIONS TO RETRIEVE THE HUMANS AND PLACE THEM UNDER THE PROTECTION OF RESISTANCE FORCES MUST BE TAKEN IMMEDIATELY AFTERWARDS WITHOUT FURTHER DELAY.

Teela held her breath and waited for the answer.

"AGREED," came the response.

"DONE," Teela quickly typed, securing the agreement.

Teela watched the screen, waiting for her instructions. The screen remained blank. A hand on her shoulder startled her.

"Please come with me. The rescue team is waiting for you," said a young birthing unit dressed in a mesh jump suit, carrying what appeared to be a carbine projectile rifle over her shoulder.

"You're a birthing unit?" Teela said, regretting the statement as soon as she had uttered it.

"I am a soldier of the Resistance," the child of no more than fifteen cycles responded defiantly.

"We are all what we choose to be," Teela responded, smiling at the child's bravado. "I have finally realized how insignificant these markings really are." She ran her top thumb under the genotype sabat on her cheek. "Just as you have, Eemela, soldier of the Resistance," she said, using the young soldier's birth name.

"Yes, Teela," Eemela giggled, then resumed her serious demeanor and outfitted Teela with a mesh suit and night-vision helmet of her own.

Dressed for invisibility in the darkness, the two emerged into the unlit corridor. Through the night-vision scope, it appeared brighter than it did with its glowbars illuminated. Eemela took Teela through a maze of access shafts that grew smaller and smaller until they were crawling through a small ventilation shaft. Teela was keenly aware that the time spent in transit was taking her further away from the humans and she was beginning to regret her arrangement. She heard the dull thud of pulse blasts as the small shaft opened into a larger yet cramped plenum. In the closet-sized chamber, six Resistance soldiers crowded together waiting for them.

"They must be through the door. We need to move now," a soldier at the far side of the chamber hissed.

"She's here now, so go!" Eemela hissed back.

"Get ready," the lead soldier said. The other soldiers scrambled into position.

"Now!" the lead soldier cried. With a blinding flash the far side of the chamber fell away and the light in the next room went out. The soldiers' carbines crackled off semiautomatic fire as they charged in. Pulse blasts illuminated the room with flashes of light as the surprised warriors fired into the darkness, unable to see the camouflaged soldiers. Teela watched the massacre from the cover of the chamber opening as the soldiers moved quietly from one position to another: taking aim, firing, and then moving away before the warriors could fire in the direction of the carbine flash.

For Teela and the Resistance soldiers, it was like daylight. For the warriors it was pitch black, and the only thermal signatures were theirs and the heated spots on the walls where their pulse blasts had missed their targets. When more warriors charged into the room from a chamber to Teela's right, the warriors began shooting in panic at the thermal outlines of their own compatriots. The Resistance fighters scored a head shot nearly every time they fired. More than twenty warriors died, having injured only two of the Resistance soldiers. Once the last warrior fell, the remaining four soldiers took up defensive positions around the now silent room. One of them motioned for Teela to come out.

"Shyron is in there," the warrior whispered, pointing to a door on the left side of the chamber. Teela could see the heated tips of pulse rifles inside the room as well as the security officers holding them. The way they were blindly scanning the darkness, she knew they could not see her or the soldiers with her. Moving as quietly as she could, she approached the shattered doorway.

"Don't shoot. I'm a friend," she called from behind a heavy column, watching where the officers were aiming their rifles. One of the officers pointed and fired at Teela's voice. The lethal blast struck the column and dissipated in a shower of sparks. Without exposing herself, Teela called out to the officers.

"I am Teela 10127. The Resistance is offering to protect Shyron and help restore the Council in exchange for an opportunity to voice their demands."

She quietly moved from one column to another while the officers at the door whispered together urgently. The sound of carbines being fired behind her caused Teela to drop to the floor. On the opposite side of the room, warriors with glowlamps tumbled to the ground; the lamps eventually were shot and extinguished by Resistance soldiers, plunging the room back into darkness. Pulling a glowbar from its mount on the column, Teela twisted the manual switch on its base, energizing the bar and illuminating the area behind the column where she stood.

Raising the visor of her helmet, she stepped out and approached the door. To her relief, they did not fire their weapons. The soldiers stared in disbelief as the thermal signature of her face was carried toward them by a shadowy figure holding a glowbar.

"There are only a few of us, and the warriors will eventually gather more forces and charge. If you wish to escape this death trap, you must come with us now," Teela implored.

"Teela, come to me," Shyron's weak voice called from within the room. Teela pushed past the officers and rushed to the leader's side. Shyron looked up into her face and smiled.

"Teela, my existence will soon end. Do not waste time trying to save me; take my officers to safety. I command it!" she said, closing her eyes against further discussion.

Snapping her night-vision visor down, Teela bent and scooped Shyron up in her arms with ease. The aged and emaciated leader weighed no more than a six-cycle shell.

"Move!" Teela shouted, sending the security officers bumping into each other as she pushed her way out the door.

The security officers followed closely, and the Resistance soldiers in turn followed them. Teela carried Shyron as far as she could, then pulled and pushed her through the narrow ducts. When the passage finally opened up enough, she took Shyron up again and ran the rest of the way back to the Resistance's biotech repair chamber. There she found biotechs waiting with a complete set of tables and all of the equipment necessary for conducting a transfer. Placing Shyron on the table indicated by the technicians, Teela leaned against the nearest wall, her lungs and muscles burning painfully. Exhausted, she slid down to the floor with her back against the wall and watched the flurry of activity.

A young shell of no more than twelve cycles sat waiting on the adjacent table. Teela noted the shell's sabat was that of a leader genotype. Rare and very closely guarded, leader shells were created for the sole purpose of perpetuating the existence of the leadership elite. This would be Shyron's new body, her millennium of knowledge, experiences, and memories obliterating the insignificant memories of an innocent child. Teela winced at her guilt and regret of having participated in many such events.

The biotechs moved in immediately, checking Shyron's vitals and inspecting the blood-soaked wrapping on her shoulder. Shyron opened her eyes and searched the room. Focusing on Teela, she frowned gravely.

"You disobeyed me."

"No, your Eminence, you directed me to get your personal guards to safety. I knew they would not leave you. I only brought you so that they would follow me. I was sure you would cease long before we arrived."

Shyron chuckled softly and then coughed and grimaced in pain.

The young shell on the adjacent table began to cry hysterically. The attending biotech was unable to calm her. The child jumped from the table and tried to run but was gruffly intercepted by a soldier.

"Nooo, I don't want to. Nooo, please."

"I refuse this shell," Shyron stated flatly.

"But, Your Eminence, we will not be able to obtain another, not before—" the attending biotech stammered before Shyron interrupted her.

"Look at her eyes," Shyron said. "Look!" The strength in the frail leader's voice caused the biotech to cringe. The biotech examined the struggling child, trying to determine what the Leader saw that she did not.

"Your Eminence, I can find nothing wrong with its eyes."

Motioning for the tech to bring the child closer, Shyron reached out and gently stroked the terrified, sobbing child with her gnarled hand.

"The eyes reveal the true essence of an individual," Shyron said as she tried unsuccessfully to calm the child. Exhausted by the movement, she dropped her withered hand down on the side of the platform. The biotech quickly lifted her arm and set it gently back on the table.

"Windows to the soul," Teela muttered in English. The Korlah word for essence did not seem to fit. Giving Teela an acknowledging glance, Shyron continued.

"I see innocence and purity in this child's eyes. She fears what resides in this shattered body of mine. She fears what she doesn't know. She should be afraid, for I would bring things to her mind that no one, especially a child, should have to bear. I will not, I cannot permit another transfer. Not for me. It is time for my end." She closed her eyes and a single tear coursed down the deeply creased parchment of her cheek.

"It is you, Shyron, who is frightened!" a defiant voice declared from behind the soldiers and technicians that surrounded the dying leader. All eyes turned toward Eemela. The birthing unit and soldier who had led Teela on the raid to rescue Shyron stood defiantly, her carbine across her chest.

"Two of my birth sisters ceased so we could save the great and mighty Shyron!" Eemela hissed. Her crown tendrils were fully engorged and her complexion mottled darkly—she was in a blood rage.

"And now our great leader would rather cease than invade this pampered shell's vacant mind?" Eemela shouted as she stomped toward Shyron, using her carbine to menace her way through the crowd.

"Don't, Eemela, don't do it!" one of the other soldiers cried.

"Don't do what? She wants to cease, and I just want to help!" Eemela hissed as she saw at least a dozen weapons pointed at her. She shouldered her weapon, leaned over, and placed her face directly over Shyron's. "I'm not afraid of your memories. And I'm not afraid of you! Tell me, have you seen the eyes of a mother who has watched the six shells she fought to carry to term delivered without existence? Eyes that have seen her sisters starved to the point where they would rather end their own existence than face hunger any longer? Open your eyes, and tell me if you see fear in these eyes, you withered rouk! Do you see anything resembling the self-serving existence you and your sisters have enjoyed?"

Slowly opening her eyes, Shyron looked into Eemela's. A nervous hush settled over the room. "I see anger and frustration," Shyron said. "But that is just a mask, a barrier you have constructed to hide that which you truly fear."

"I fear nothing and no one!" Eemela screamed into Shyron's face as she moved even closer and bared her fangs.

"Fearless?" Shyron chuckled. "I believe you aren't afraid of losing your existence. You are, however, deeply terrified of how your existence will end. Your fear runs deeper than any concern over your physical pain or discomfort. You feel this fear every time you look at one of your birth sisters. More than anything, you fear spending your life as that for which you were created. That is why you are with the Resistance. You would rather die fighting than birthing." Shyron smiled into Eemela's face, which was now twisted in anger.

Eemela swallowed, opened her mouth to speak, then closed it tightly and retreated a bit. "If your anger and passion are as impermeable as they seem," Shyron continued, "they would counter the apathy and depression I have suffered since learning of Afron's many betrayals. I would be greatly honored to join minds with you, Eemela," Shyron murmured as she closed her eyes and broke the intense staring match, submitting to Eemela.

"Your Eminence, this is a birthing unit. You can't join with a birthing unit!" Shyron's biotech exclaimed.

"Teela," Shyron asked, "does a birthing unit possess the qualities needed to be Potentate?"

Teela considered Shyron's question. It was related to another question that Shyron had asked her earlier, a question that had been nagging her subconscious mind. She modified the key elements of the answer she had been working on.

When she had arranged her thoughts she responded, "A great leader of Earth once said that a person often becomes what they believe themselves to be. If you keep on saying to yourself that you cannot do a certain thing, it is possible that you will really become incapable of doing it. If you have the belief that you can do something, then you will surely acquire the capacity to do it, even if you may not have been able to do it in the beginning."

Without opening her eyes, Shyron smiled, satisfied. Eemela tossed her rifle to one of the other soldiers, stripped off the armor on her torso, and climbed up onto the opposing table. Nothing more was said. They had made an agreement of voluntary transfer.

Technically, all transfers were voluntary; however, many young shells were frightened when faced with the event, and a birth mother was usually assigned to calm the shell so that the process could be performed. All shells were trained at an early age to accept the mind of another, but most shells were not needed for transfers and went on to apprenticeships at thirteen cycles, having developed personalities that could cause conflict during transfer. Eemela had been so trained and knew what was required to successfully accept Shyron's mind.

Shyron and Eemela lay head to head on two tables and the biotechs directed the crowd to move away from the tables during the transfer. When the biotech attempted to put the gas box over Shyron's head, she pushed it away.

"I won't . . . need that," Shyron wheezed. The biotech nodded respectfully and then joined the others around the perimeter of the room. Everyone became deathly silent.

Teela watched Shyron's chest rise and fall slower and slower, and then finally Shyron opened her mouth wide, letting out her last breath with a long shrill moan that sent a chill up Teela's spine. Shyron lay there motionless while Eemela continued to breathe normally.

Teela could hear the muted whispering of a dozen conversations around the room. Speculation and discussion on this event would certainly run rampant throughout the vessel for some time to come. She glanced up at an area monitor, wondering if a recording of this would join Meezra's collection. A hand on her shoulder brought her out of her deep thoughts. It was Lahsoon, the senior Resistance soldier that had led the assault that rescued Shyron. She was of a labor or soldier genotype, but had not yet been apprenticed; her sabat had not been changed to indicate one or the other, yet she was many cycles beyond apprenticeship age. *Another runaway*, Teela reasoned. Lahsoon led her out of the chamber and into the darkened corridor.

"The leader has coordinated a group of volunteers to help you take the humans from Afron's warriors. Our enemies control access to power conduits in the forward sections, so we will not enjoy the safety of darkness. Many of my sisters will give their existence for this. I hope these humans are worth the cost this favor demands," Lahsoon said while briskly walking down the corridor, forcing Teela to trot to keep up.

"Did you volunteer for this, this fight to save the humans?" Teela asked.

The soldier slowed her pace and turned her face toward Teela. "My leader says that you have accepted a human transfer, a great warrior and leader, and because of that, you will be able to forge an alliance with this fierce species, an alliance that will enable us to win this campaign and obtain the necessary materials to restore our vessel." Looking away, she added, "Afron says this campaign cannot be won, with or without a human alliance. I believe that when Afron opens her mouth, lies emerge."

"What your leader says is true, and although I can't guarantee the humans will agree to an alliance, I swear on my honor that I will do everything I can to accomplish those goals," Teela said. She tried to sound confident, but she suddenly felt burdened with the knowledge that young Korlah were sacrificing their lives in the belief that she would provide something she was not certain she could deliver.

The darkness of the corridor swallowed Lahsoon, the thermal camouflage obscuring Teela's ability to discern her presence. The natural thermals of the corridors were normally enough for any Korlah to walk with confidence in total darkness. The dim glowlamps found in most areas were installed to light the corridor and chamber identification numbers, and over time had become standard in all on-shift areas.

She followed Lahsoon by sound, noting how the edge of thermal signatures would blur as Lahsoon passed over them. After a while, Teela noticed her hisnah, or dark eye, became more sensitive to the thermal variances in the pitch black corridor. She could make out a thermal shadow that was subtly cooler or warmer than the background, and on the cold floor, Lahsoon was leaving a trail made by the warmth of her feet, a trail that disappeared after five or six paces. Noting the echoes in the corridor made by their progress, Teela concentrated on walking silently, holding the scabbards against her thighs in an attempt to stop their incessant rattling. Her efforts at silence must have been effective because Lahsoon stopped and turned to verify she was still there.

"Lower your visor!" Lahsoon snapped. "Your face will be a target if we encounter a warrior patrol," she added, adjusting her tone respectfully. Teela followed her instructions without comment and they proceeded into the darkness.

20 - Surrender

Pulse blasts pounded the main window of the Nursery. The warriors initially set up perimeters, eventually they began a concerted effort to use multiple weapons to breach the compartment by blasting their way through the thick viewing window. The sporadic shots at first merely turned the tough material milky, absorbing and diffusing the energy as light and heat. But more recently, to the growing concern of the humans within, the Korlah had begun to pummel the window continually with multiple blasts. The humans spread themselves between the three rooms and armed themselves with the pulse rifles Teela had obtained for them. As the onslaught progressed, the air within the large chamber grew oppressively hot. Ruth was the first to notice the smoldering window as it began to sag.

"Get ready people, the window's gonna blow!" Ruth shouted over the rumble of pulse blasts. Within seconds, the window bulged with a blast, and before it could sag, another blast blew it inward, spattering blobs of molten window throughout the room. Crystal shrieked when an errant globule landed on her shoulder.

"Hold your fire! Wait for a target!" Beth screamed as blasts struck the opposite wall.

The shooting stopped. A ragged hole in the window six-feet in diameter smoldered and dripped onto the pulse-scorched floor beneath.

"Wait . . . wait for targets," Beth advised with professional calm.

They didn't have to wait long. A line of warriors charged through the window, the first firing as she came through. Three blasts struck her simultaneously, sending her flying back into the warriors charging behind. Tumbling to the ground, they screamed as they fell onto the molten remains of the window. Before they could recover, the humans pounded them with additional blasts, leaving a smoking pile of four unconscious warriors just inside the ruptured window. The warriors behind them took cover to either side of the opening in the now nearly opaque window.

"Now they know we have weapons, so this is where it's gonna get ugly. If they're as fanatical as Teela said, they'll keep throwing themselves at us, and we'll have to keep shooting 'em down. If you don't have the stomach for it, give your weapon to someone who does," Beth said from behind the bedding pads she had piled in the doorway of the sleeping area.

No one spoke, and no further pulse blasts were directed at the ruptured window. The oppressive lack of sound was overshadowed only by the stench of burnt flesh that now filled the chamber.

"What are they waiting for?" Crystal squeaked.

"They probably have gear for this type of situation," Beth answered. "Grenades, tear gas, you know, shit like that. But they didn't bring it because they didn't expect us to be armed, and now they have to go get it. So if they toss something in, take cover. If they use gas or smoke, cover your mouth with something to filter it. They didn't know we were prepared to fight; they weren't ready, and right now they're trying to regroup and plan what to do next."

A sound like a whining dog broke the silence, causing the humans to shift into their defensive positions. There were Korlah shouts outside. A robustly pregnant birthing unit stumbled awkwardly through the ruptured window and tripped over the pile of warriors. She fell to the floor just inside the window.

"Hold your fire!" Beth screamed.

The shouting outside the window continued.

"I think they're ordering her to open the door," Crystal said.

The birthing unit stood up and began shouting back through the window.

"She's calling them names," Crystal said.

The birthing unit's shouts changed to an ear-splitting shriek as a pulse blast came through the window and vaporized a portion of her right leg just below the knee. Falling back to the floor, she clutched the smoking stump screaming. Seconds later, another blast caught her between her shoulder blades, spun her body across the polished floor of the chamber, and sent it crashing into the far wall. Her head, nearly severed from her torso, lay facing the door where Crystal was hiding, a wisp of blue smoke rose from her open mouth.

"Eepalla!" Crystal screamed, recognizing the sabat of her friend on the scorched and lifeless face.

Crystal screamed incoherent profanities, charged from the doorway, and fired her pulse rifle as she ran. Ruth, Beth, and Bill shouted a simultaneous "NO!" The window illuminated with pulse blasts as she leapt through, her silhouette disappearing into the room beyond. There were a few more blasts, then silence.

"Jesus! Oh Jesus!" Ruth sobbed.

"She's dead; we aren't," Beth growled. "They mean to kill us. All we can hope to do is take as many of the ugly bastards with us as we can. Switch your weapons to high power." She adjusted her weapon, which crackled with its own angry growl.

"Eepalla was our friend! What about her you heartless bitch? What about her!" Ruth screamed.

Before Beth could respond, another pregnant birthing unit was thrown through the opening in the window. Falling to the floor, she lay curled in the fetal position and whimpered with terror. Again, the warriors shouted at the birthing unit to open the door. Ruth stood, tossed her pulse rifle out onto the floor, and walked into the chamber with her arms over her head.

"No Ruth! They'll kill us all!" Beth shouted.

Ignoring Beth, Ruth walked slowly toward the heavy chamber door.

"Stop! I mean it, Ruth. If you don't stop, I'll shoot you," Beth said, pointing her rifle.

Bill threw his weapon out onto the floor and stood up in the doorway.

"We done voted, Beth. Ruth's the boss. We're all supposed to do what she says, and that means you too," Bill rumbled ominously, walking to the doorway where Beth was lying.

Beth looked at Bill and the others who were now emerging from the rooms. Giving the pulse rifle cradled in her arms a kiss, she hesitated for a moment and then tossed it into the center of the chamber with the others.

"I'd rather die fighting. Can you understand that?" Beth said to Bill, who was now extending a hand to help her up.

"Yeah, but maybe now ain't the right time, just maybe," Bill said as he pulled Beth to her feet.

Ruth opened the door. Once the warriors were sure the humans were surrendering, they poured in through the door and window.

21 - Counterattack

Lahsoon led Teela through the lower levels of the energy section, areas only the technicians who serviced them dared traverse. Warned of the dangers, Teela moved carefully around and through the ducting and corridors. There was little room for transit; the passages were laced with high energy lines, tubes, and fibers that routed power from the light-wave compressor to the flux accelerator of the campaign vessel's massive hyperlight drive coils. Contact with one of the energized conduits, Teela imagined, was similar to being electrocuted—with the exception that she would be completely vaporized, according to her escort.

Electrocuted? Teela questioned the human word that popped into her conscious mind. In that instant, she realized that many of the technological concepts that were previously above her level of education now made sense to her. She looked around with renewed interest at things she'd always considered incomprehensible.

At the end of a corridor, in the back corner of a storage chamber, Lahsoon stopped at a communications console and snapped what looked like a walkie-talkie into the log bar indentation. Pressing a button on the side of the object, she bent over and quietly said, "By fang or by claw, resist despair," and released the button before placing it back in the pocket of her black uniform. A soft clicking sound came from behind the console, and with a slight hiss, it receded into the wall. Lahsoon crouched over and followed it. Teela followed her into a darkened room where six armed soldiers wearing thermal mesh suits and night-vision equipment waited for them. Once they were both inside, the console slid back into position, and the glowlamps in the compartment energized.

Teela looked around in amazement as she passed through compartments dedicated to birthing, weapons fabrication, food processing, and training, all of which were being performed without the knowledge of the Council Leaders. Teela noted that one of the fabrication facilities was assembling the radio-like devices Lahsoon had used to obtain access to this area.

"These are radios?" Teela asked, picking up one of the partially assembled objects and using the English word.

"Radios?" Lahsoon questioned.

When Teela could not think of another word, Lahsoon continued. "They are called talkers; a new communication device based on human technology. With these, we just talk, and our message is heard. The leader has us use codes because the Loyalists are also developing this technology. With all of the illiterate birthing units that have been joining the Resistance, this form of communication is critical."

Having finally reached the forward area of the energy section below the humans' temporary quarters, they passed through another hidden access panel and began their ascent through the transit spokes. At the last energy section, one level below the birthing section, they met a group of approximately thirty Resistance soldiers armed with pulse rifles, carbines, pulse orbs, and thick, portable shields. Lahsoon briefed them on the plan to seize control of the access corridors that led to the Nursery. Teela scanned the faces of these would-be Resistance fighters, noting that two-thirds of them were birthing units, several of whom were less than eleven cycles. Their uniforms hung on their small undernourished frames like sacks. Their eyes were bright with youth, yet tinged with hollow fear.

One of the soldiers, a shell Teela once had under her care, gave her a discreet wave. Teela fought the urge to learn the young soldier's name and origin; knowing it would only make leading these children into battle more difficult. Instead, she stripped off her mesh suit and helmet and checked the fasteners of the body armor beneath her robe.

Having finished the briefing, Lahsoon directed the soldiers to form three groups of ten. Lahsoon would lead one group up through the forward corridor's transit tubes, Teela would lead another up through the aft transit tubes, and the remaining group would be led by a young technician named Ohmensh, who would enter through the center tubes.

Maintaining communication with handheld radios, the groups coordinated their efforts to open the transit tubes and insert sections of segmented ladders so they could climb up the de-energized shafts. When they reached the level of the Nursery, the soldiers opened a side access panel within the transit tubes and the groups slipped between the walls. They had to climb and crawl through conduits and ducting, passing their weapons and shields to each other through especially tight areas. Each of the teams eventually reached its position behind access panels in the walls at three strategic locations within the Nursery.

The small radio Teela carried crackled softly. "Forward is ready."

She pushed the button and said, "Aft is ready."

After what seemed like an eternity, the radio crackled again. "Center is ready."

After a brief pause, she heard, "Stand by." On that cue, the soldiers carrying pulse rifles energized their weapons and the ones carrying carbines chambered a round.

"Now!" Lahsoon commanded over the radio.

Four small charges blew the fasteners that held panel to the wall. Teela and the Resistance soldiers charged through it and scrambled into defensive positions. The corridor was empty.

"Aft corridor is secure," Teela said into the radio, her pulse racing. Communications that both forward and center were secure quickly followed. Teela heard no indication of any fighting; no pulse discharges or carbine reports. They stationed soldiers to cover their retreat and secure the corridor, and she entered the main chamber of the Nursery.

The sight made her ill. The room stank of burnt flesh. The warriors and security officers killed earlier lay where they had fallen. Added to that body count were three warriors positioned against the wall opposite the window, which was blackened and charred, a gaping hole in the center. The heavily pockmarked door lay open.

Teela walked stiffly toward the door, knowing what she would likely find beyond. Inside, crumpled against the wall by the access to the sleep chamber, lay a badly pulse-damaged birthing unit. Teela gingerly stepped past the corpse and into the sleep chamber. Much to her relief, there were no human bodies visible, but blood was spattered on the floors, walls, and ceiling. Bloody smears on the floor indicated that a desperate hand-to-hand fight had been fought here. She moved quickly through the sleep section and looked between the blood-spattered sleeping platforms and pads, checking the corners and searching for bodies.

Sensing movement from the corner of her eye, she spun around and pulled a sword from its sheath; the blade crackled with static electricity as the pulse weapon automatically energized. Behind one of the sleep platforms, she saw a warrior's boot, toe up, extend from under a pile of mattresses. While she watched, the boot slid back, the knee raised slightly, and the boot slid forward again.

Cautiously walking over, Teela used the tip of her sword to lift the pad from the prone warrior's face. When she saw who lay beneath, she dropped the sword and frantically pulled the pads off the fallen warrior.

"Shawaugh! Oh no! No!" Teela cried, able to recognize her friend only by her bulk and blood-soaked sabat on the chest of her shredded uniform. Deep lacerations creased her face, arms, and torso. Shawaugh coughed and a blood-tinged froth coursed down the side of her face. Her jaw moved and she made a croaking sound before she was able to form words.

"They took turns . . . beating us . . . The brutal one . . . fought with honor. My sisters . . . fought without honor . . . no honor," she said hoarsely, struggling to stand.

"Help! Help me!" Teela shrieked frantically. Her companions charged through the door with weapons poised to fire.

"We need to take this warrior to our biotechs. You four, and two more of you, you two there," Teela shouted, identifying the youngest of the soldiers, including the two in baggy uniforms just outside the door.

"Four will carry and two will cover. Now get moving! Hurry! Hurry!"

The four soldiers slung their weapons and quickly fashioned a gurney from a bed platform. They slid Shawaugh's considerable bulk onto it and lifted, two soldiers in the front and two in the rear.

"Bio section," Shawaugh groaned.

"We're taking you to the biotechs in the energy section instead. It's closer and safer," Teela said.

"Not me!" Shawaugh moaned, "Them, the hu-mons . . . they took them . . . to bio section. For transfer," Shawaugh gasped.

"We will find them and get them back; you must rest and repair. You will have the chance to take back the honor stolen from you; now go and repair," Teela said as Shawaugh was carried out of the chamber.

Teela wiped Shawaugh's blood from her gloves while she finished her search of the chamber. Lahsoon entered and reported that there were no other bodies or survivors in the other areas of the Nursery. Teela picked up her sword and slid it back into its sheath with a resounding metallic clack as she turned to face Lahsoon.

"I'm going to the biotech section," Teela growled, anger and frustration causing her complexion to mottle darkly.

"If you go in a rage, you will lead us to our deaths," Lahsoon advised. Moving close and lowering her voice so that only Teela could hear, Lahsoon continued, "The fools have given us access to the power hub that controls lighting to all the lower sections, including the biotech section. They will never see us coming," Lahsoon paused and frowned before continuing, "except you. I will send someone to get your thermal cloak," she added, noting that Teela had left hers behind.

"I won't need one. I intend to tell them I'm coming, and I want to be seen."

"What? Is your mind damaged? Afron does not observe Council Law or the conventions of honor. She will take your existence without hesitation."

"Perhaps, but I have a plan." Teela said with a smile, realizing that the theatrics she intended to employ were not part of the customary Korlah strategies. She knew she should be frightened, but she was excited at the prospect of a fight.

I will fight with honor, Teela thought.

Honor is for fools and heroes. We will fight to win. The words came into her mind as clearly as if spoken. With them came odd feelings of shared perceptions and experiences. Her instincts told her to block the intrusion, but she resisted, and instead embraced the thoughts of physical conflict that thrilled her longing for emotional release and caused her heart to race.

As with most of the compartmentalized sections, the long access corridors of the education section's lower levels ended at the main bulkhead of the biotech section. Certain that Afron would establish a defensive barrier at that juncture and that she and her forces would be nearby, Teela sent her message to that general area. Although it was addressed specifically to Afron, Teela made certain it would appear on the thousands of screens within the biotech section, and that it would be accessible to anyone who wished to read it.

The message read as follows:

AFRON AL35.20,

GREETINGS. I AM EN ROUTE TO BIO SECTION FORWARD ACCESS HATCH B-74. ACTING ON BEHALF OF THE LAWFUL MISSION POTENTATE, SHYRON, I BRING THE FOLLOWING OFFER TO YOUR FOLLOWERS:

SURRENDER NOW, AND YOU WILL RECEIVE A FAIR HEARING BEFORE THE COUNCIL OF ELDERS.

DELIVER THE HUMANS SAFE AND UNDAMAGED, AND YOU WILL BE ABSOLVED OF ANY CRIMES AND RESTORED TO YOUR ORIGINAL RANK AND STATUS.

DELIVER AFRON ALIVE INTO OUR CUSTODY, AND YOU WILL BE REWARDED WITH IMPROVED RANK AND STATUS.THIS OFFER OF ARBITRATION IS ONLY VALID UNTIL THE END OF THIS SHIFT.

TEELA20.10127

Shortly after the message was sent, a heavily armed contingent of Afron's personal guard set up a ring of blast-resistant shielding just outside the biotech section's bulkhead access door B-74. The reinforced opening was then closed and locked behind them.

The contingent was comprised of Afron's handpicked elite. Trained since apprenticeship to be loyal bodyguards, there was little chance that they would surrender.

Teela expected Afron to use warriors to take the initial assault, preserving her bodyguards for her personal protection. On the way there, she was certain that she would be able to appeal to their honor and negotiate without violence.

When the lights outside access hatch B-74 went out, the security officers took cover. They periodically fired random shots into the dark corridor. The glowing fireballs briefly illuminated the areas and dissipated in the distance. Between shots the corridor faded once again into visual and thermal darkness.

After a few minutes, the security officers saw lights in the distance. The main corridor was larger than most and ran the length of the education section. In the far distance, a figure appeared under a glowlamp; it was walking toward them with long, purposeful strides. The corridor ahead and behind it was dark, but sections of glowbars came on as the lone figure approached them, then blinked out as soon as the figure had passed.

Partially hidden behind a low barricade, Teela could see the thermal outlines of the energized pulse rifles and the figures holding them. She watched for the flash that would signal a discharge, hoping they wouldn't fire on a single individual. Her arms were crossed, her hands tightly grasping the handles of her swords. Realizing that they were fully charged, she hoped circumstance wouldn't force her to test their shielding capability. That thought came at the same instant that a group of pre-ignition flashes from the pulse rifles at the barricade blinked in unison.

In the fraction of a second it took for the pulse rifles to discharge their concentrated fireballs of highly charged particles, Teela crouched and pulled her swords from their sheaths. The static danced on the blades as she crossed them before her.

The rifles had been fired chest-high and their pulses should have passed over Teela, but her blades acted like lightning rods and made them arc down at the last second and strike the precise spot where her swords crossed. The dissipation of the multiple charges' kinetic momentum sent Teela sliding backward on the polished floor and a halo of crackling static jumped from the blades and pommels of the swords to the walls of the corridor around her in a pulsing aura. As she slid on her knees to a stop, Teela saw remnants of static electricity tracing the walls and floor dissipate. Not wanting to wait for another volley, Teela pointed her swords at the center of the large round hatch behind the barricade and triggered both weapons simultaneously. Nothing could have prepared any of them for what happened next.

Arcs of static electricity flashed from the walls, floor, and ceiling to her blades as a single fireball erupted from the joined tips of the two swords. The kickback hurled Teela backward nearly fifteen-feet, leaving her on her back in the center of the corridor, still gripping her swords. The fireball, meanwhile, raced down the corridor, growing larger and faster in the split second it took to travel the three hundred-feet to the door. The kinetic impact ripped the door and its threshold from the bulkhead and sent it tumbling into the corridor through the warriors that were preparing for a counterattack behind it. The security officers outside the door were mostly vaporized—an odd patch of armor, helmets, pulse rifles, and shards of barricade the only things that remained.

Oblivious to the devastation she had just unleashed but aware that there was no longer a visible threat down the corridor, Teela scrambled to her feet and walked toward the open door, pointing her smoldering blades defensively before her. Within the swirling mass of smoke, Teela could hear warriors screaming in anger and pain. The scorched walls and thick smoke masked any thermal images she may otherwise have been able to sense. As she cautiously approached the door, she waited for the smoke to dissipate and reveal the death and destruction before her.

Where the door had been, a jagged hole lay open, the twisted and torn metal bent inward like teeth in a shark's open jaws. Ninety-feet beyond the gaping hole lay the heavy metal door in its shredded threshold, supported by the bodies of dead and dying warriors pinned beneath it. The corridor between the torn bulkhead and the door was strewn with the bodies of more crushed, dismembered, and scorched warriors.

Stepping through the hole and stroking the drifting smoke with her swords, Teela strained to see if any threats remained in spite of the overwhelming carnage. She sensed movement to her left and instinctively brought the points of her weapons to bear on a group of warriors huddled behind the remains of a barricade. Farther down the corridor, Teela could see another group retreating, dragging their injured with them.

She heard movement behind her, but kept her eyes and weapons firmly fixed on the immediate threat before her. A shadow passed silently across the warm outline of a fallen warrior to her right at the same time that another crossed the corridor behind the warriors at the barricade. She knew the Resistance soldiers in thermal camouflage were flanking her in the darkness.

The warriors also sensed the soldiers' movements, their eyes nervously scanning the darkness. One slowly stood, bowed, and held her palms up in surrender. The others followed, some grumbling indignantly. When they had all surrendered, Teela sheathed her swords one at a time with slow deliberation while moving closer to scan their faces. Checking the series numbers of their sabats, Teela ascertained that none was older than seventeen cycles and most were less than fifteen.

"How is it that I find apprenticed shells dressed as warriors and bearing weapons against the Potentate of this campaign vessel?" she asked the group, keeping her voice level and firm.

"Shyron is dead. Afron is—" a warrior began.

Teela interrupted sharply. "Shyron is alive. Afron has dishonored herself and all who follow her with these despicable acts and violations of law. The Council rules this vessel, not Afron." Teela approached until her face was inches from the warrior's bowed head. She looked up into the face of the warrior.

"I have a message for Afron, and you will deliver it," Teela hissed. The warrior nodded, averting her eyes.

"Tell her that Teela is coming on Shyron's behalf to arbitrate a resolution to this conflict. Tell her that if any harm comes to our human guests, by fang or by claw, by the blood of my existence, I will rip her to pieces."

"Now go!" she shouted, making the young warrior stumble backward into the wall before turning to pick her way through the dark corridor over bodies and debris.

"Leave your weapons where they lay. Get the injured to repair facilities, and then return to your quarters to await further orders," Teela said to the remaining warriors, her voice soft with an underlying sadness.

She followed the retreating warriors down the dark corridor, listening to the soft rustle of her invisible escorts. The corridor ahead was illuminated by what seemed at first a glowing orb that grew larger and larger as she approached. A section of the corridor had been lit with portable glowbars on either side of the walkway several feet apart. Just beyond the lighted area was another barricade with movement behind it. Teela strained her senses to perceive any energized pulse weapons. Her hands gripped the hilts of her swords.

Her escorts dropped back to take up positions behind the limited cover that the wide corridor had to offer. Taking confident strides down the center of the corridor, she stepped into the bright light and rapidly closed the distance to the barricade. The instant she heard the unmistakable sound of an energizing pulse rifle, she yanked the swords from their sheaths. The blades arced through the air, crackling as electricity danced along their glimmering length. Crossing them in front of her, Teela stopped and braced herself, expecting to be fired upon at any moment. The barricade was only a dozen feet away.

When she had been fired upon at the access door, Teela had been thirty times this distance from the source. Now she tried to imagine how the close proximity would affect the swords' shielding reaction. Suddenly, without the usual pre-flash warning, a pulse weapon fired from behind the barricade, blasting the ceiling immediately above it. The dissipating halo of the pulse charge moved through the air toward Teela like smoke toward a fan. The blades of her swords crackled loudly as ribbons of free electrons were absorbed at the junction of her crossed blades. She pulled the blades apart. Charges of static electricity jumped from the blades and pommels to the floor, walls, and ceiling, their lacework patterns brightening the corridor for a few moments.

Muted grunts and growls came from behind the barrier. One of the portable shield segments that formed the barrier was pulled inward and a young warrior emerged, her arms loaded with a bundle of pulse rifles. Gently placing the weapons at Teela's feet, the warrior bowed her head respectfully, and holding out her hands with palms up, she addressed Teela.

"Khranga would like to discuss your offer."

Teela sheathed her swords but kept her hands on their grips. Khranga emerged from behind the barrier. One of her legs was wrapped in bandages and her uniform was burned and torn. She leaned her considerable bulk on another warrior, but stood as straight as she could manage, eyeing Teela.

"Why is the Resistance helping Shyron?" she growled, looking past Teela into the darkness.

"This shift ends in five bits, at which time my offer will be significantly altered. Do you think it wise to waste time discussing matters beyond your control?" Teela responded curtly.

Khranga shifted her weight, grimacing with discomfort. "The humans are now in my care. I did not order them brought here, and I was not with the forces that captured them," she hedged.

"They have been damaged?" Teela asked.

"Only two of them . . . have serious damage. Since Afron and her personal guards fled, Gremensh has been attempting to repair the one that is most damaged."

"Take me to them now!" Teela demanded. Khranga didn't flinch or move.

"I offer the humans and the immediate loyalty of both the warrior and health sections in exchange for the absolution of any perceived guilt, along with the retention of rank and status for myself and my subordinates," Khranga countered, meeting Teela's challenging glare with one of practiced ferocity.

"Give me your blood oath that you will personally take responsibility for the safety of our human guests as long as they remain on this vessel, and I will accept your offer."

Khranga shifted uncomfortably on her injured leg, considering the dangerous ramifications of Teela's offer.

Teela's inner clock, which all Korlah possessed, told her the shift had ended. She glanced around for a communication console that would confirm the time. Khranga answered quickly.

"I accept your offer."

"Blood oath!" Teela snapped.

"As you have offered, by fang and by claw, by the blood of my existence, I accept," Khranga recited grudgingly. If she broke her pledge, she would lose her existence and her honor for all time.

"Done," Teela answered, locking the arrangement. She removed the radio from the pocket of her robe, held it to her mouth and pressed the button. "The warrior and health sections have surrendered, swearing loyalty to Shyron. Cease hostilities unless fired upon." Khranga looked on with amazement.

Lahsoon's voice crackled from the small speaker on the device. "I understand. Should I have power restored?"

"If you can do so without compromising your safety."

"Restoring power now."

Within a few moments, the glow orbs came on, driving the darkness away. Teela's escorts formed two groups. One group headed down the corridor the way they had come and the remaining six approached Teela and Khranga.

"How is it they can hide body heat?" Khranga asked.

"Take me to the humans," Teela demanded with growing impatience.

Khranga responded with a slight bow of her head, watching the Resistance soldiers approach. She shifted her gaze back to Teela. "You wear the robe and weapons of a bladesman. If you intend to resurrect ancient tradition, I would have expected you to wear the plain robe of a negotiator?" Khranga intoned the statement as a question while she hobbled her way through the barricade.

Realizing that it would be unwise to reveal how little she knew about ancient tradition, Teela dodged the comment. "An inappropriate event would be unworthy of appropriate attire," she stated with as unfeeling a voice as she could manage. Khranga shook her head as though Teela had made a statement of deep significance.

Behind the barricade, two of Afron's guards were being bound by a group of young warriors.

"When Afron received your message, she instructed these two to finish what their sisters failed to accomplish at the access door," Khranga offered. "However, regardless of the promised political benefits, I do not share her affinity for taking the existence of my sisters, so I intervened."

Hah!" Lahsoon cried. She spat on the ground at Khranga's feet. "Your sisters are starving to death while you stuff your bloated stomach with their stolen rations."

Khranga looked away.

"If we can keep from killing each other long enough to get these humans back to their home planet, I should be able to negotiate for enough provisions to restore our food production facilities to complete self-sufficiency," Teela said, placing herself between Khranga and Lahsoon.

It was a short distance to the transfer chamber where the humans were being held. Teela shuddered at the threshold, recalling the transfer she had experienced there with sobering clarity. The room seemed much smaller than she remembered, but there hadn't been ten gurneys in it then. With the exception of one, each gurney held a human. A table surrounded by Gremensh and several biotechs held one more. Teela couldn't see who it was.

Lahsoon and the soldiers took up positions at the compartment's access doors while Teela hurried into the room.

"What are you doing?" she demanded, skirting around Khranga and heading straight for the table.

Gremensh moved between Teela and the table, countering Teela's efforts to get around her as she spoke. "Your Eminence, ah . . . Teela," she stammered, unsure how to address Teela now. "This unit is now stable, and I . . . um, with everything my previous . . . ah . . . exercises in human physiology have taught me, I believe it can be completely repaired without any loss of function." Avoiding Teela's eyes, she glanced back and forth between the swords that Teela unconsciously gripped with tense arms.

"Thank you, Gremensh," Teela managed to say, her voice strained by fear that rose up in her throat and choked her speech. She released the hilt of one sword and moved Gremensh out of her way.

Crystal lay naked on one end of the wide gray table. From the hurried way the biotechs were moving to clean the drying blood from her head and face, it was apparent that they had just begun to tend her injuries. Her face was barely recognizable; a swollen bloody mask with features swallowed in folds of grossly burned and distended tissue. The large, dark bruises and mild burns on her chest and abdomen indicated that she had been pummeled with pulse blasts. A charred burn deeply creased her upper left thigh and lower abdomen, evidence that she had been nicked by at least one lethal blast. Looking for signs of life and seeing none, Teela lifted Crystal's hand and cradled it in hers. Although Crystal's thermal signature was weak, like those of most humans, her hand was warm. When she checked for a pulse, Teela found a faint but steady beat.

"Hang in there, Crystal. You're going to be all right," Teela said softly in English, patting Crystal's hand gently as she placed it back on the table.

A muffled but audible scream made Teela look to a nearby gurney. Marsha was bound in the gurney's wrapping. As soon as Teela released the binding, Marsha pulled a gag from her mouth and pushed herself up to sit.

"Teela! I knew it was you! When the lights went out and the bomb went off, I knew you were coming," Marsha cried, her voice cracking. Struggling out of the gurney, she saw her friend lying on the table only a few feet away. Marsha sucked in a deep breath of air and turned her head away from the gruesome sight, stumbling. Teela caught her arm to comfort and steady her.

"She's going to be okay," Teela stated with false confidence. "The doctor said that they're going to fix her up as good as new. Don't worry, our medical technology is really good."

Marsha began to sob with relief.

The disdain on one of the warrior's faces told Teela that their behavior was a pitiful display of weakness. She took Marsha firmly by the shoulders and locked her dark ebony eyes on Marsha's emerald green, red-rimmed eyes—eyes that were at once familiar and incredibly alien.

"I'm sorry, but I need you to be tough right now," she said, changing her tone from soft to severe, her statement a demand rather than a request.

Marsha swallowed deeply and nodded in agreement, wiping her eyes with the back of her wrist. "What do you want me to do?" she asked, sniffing and wiping her nose.

"Help me get everybody else loose for starters. If you make eye contact with any of these warriors, growl loudly before you look away," Teela instructed, breaking away and moving to the next gurney.

"Growl?" Marsha asked.

"Eye contact or staring is considered a challenge, while looking away signals surrender or acceptance of the other's superiority or higher rank. If you growl before you look away, you are dismissing the challenge without acknowledging the other as a superior. I know it sounds kind of stupid, but it's part of the Korlah culture," Teela explained. "Watch, I'll show you."

She turned to the warrior that was glaring at them with an expression of disgust. Teela met the warrior's eyes, maintaining contact as she moved closer. Looking up at the much taller warrior, she put her arms out at her sides with the backs of her hands facing forward as she continued her defiant stare. The warrior put on her fiercest expression and growled menacingly at Teela before looking away.

Turning to Marsha, Teela explained, “If it goes on too long, it can get physical. This way, no one loses face—no harm, no foul. Both of us were able to maintain a position of strength.”

Marsha nodded her dubious understanding as they both worked to release the remainder of the humans. The warriors, obviously uncomfortable with the activities, moved into a tight group near the chamber’s main access door.

Teela found Beth in the last gurney. From the intense expression on Beth’s pallid face, she dreaded removing the gag; however, to her surprise, Beth said nothing when it was removed and she made no effort to sit up when Teela loosened the bindings. Lifting the bindings away, Teela found the gurney filled with pooled blood and Beth’s arms and torso lacerated by multiple claw strikes. Beth clutched her blood-soaked abdomen with both hands.

“Not too honorable . . . these warriors,” Beth rasped from between clenched teeth.

“I know. I’m sorry. I’m so sorry,” Teela stammered. “Things have happened . . . which I don’t understand.”

“They were gonna do us all, mind-swap, like they did you. They were preparing to do Crystal when the lights went out. They put a kid on the other end of the table there,” Beth said, pointing at the transfer table with a badly swollen hand. “The kid got up on that end and lay down. They put a box over her head, and right after that the lights went out. They brought in a bunch of portable lights and were planning to continue when they got your message. I’m not saying I understand your language, not entirely; but your name was bantered about, and I think I understood enough to get the impression that they weren’t too happy to hear you were coming.

“I learned a little Korlah listening to Eepalla; she is . . . was a good teacher. They killed her. They didn’t just kill her, the rotten bastards murdered her to punish us.” Beth coughed violently, turning her head to spit on the side of the gurney. From the dark color of her spittle, Teela thought she probably had a punctured lung as well. She turned to the table where Gremensh was overseeing the treatment of Crystal.

“This one is also badly damaged,” Teela barked.

Gremensh bowed deeply, avoiding Teela's eyes as she moved to examine Beth.

"The lungs have been damaged and are bleeding. I suspect other injuries as well," Teela snapped, directing Gremensh's attention to Beth's mangled abdomen.

"I'm not hurt that bad; you tell them to fix Crystal first," Beth said weakly, her usual conviction absent.

"They will. I want you to stay with Crystal. They're going to move you both to a medical facility designed to treat . . . complicated injuries. Beth, I want you to take care of her, and make sure they do what they have promised," Teela explained, eliminating any chance that Beth would argue further.

"And how am I supposed to make sure of anything?" Beth asked, nodding her head in the direction of the armed warriors clustered around Khranga.

Without answering, Teela strode to the nearest warrior, reached out, and took hold of the warrior's pulse rifle with her gloved hand. Not surprisingly, the warrior grasped her weapon tightly.

"Give me your weapon!" Teela demanded.

When the warrior did not relinquish it immediately, she pulled one of her swords halfway out of its scabbard with her other hand. She then leaned into the warrior so that when the blade began arcing as it was withdrawn, it touched the warrior's weapon. The electrical energy passed through the pulse rifle and into the warrior's bare hands. Screaming as the electricity grounded to her body, the warrior jumped back and released her grip. Turning quickly, Teela placed the pulse rifle in the gurney with Beth and then turned back to face the warriors. Several of them energized their pulse rifles, and in the same instant Teela pulled her swords from their scabbards. When a warrior close to her raised her rifle, Teela brought the tip of her sword up just behind the pulse chamber of the rifle before it could be brought to bear. A fireball erupted from the rifle as her sword effortlessly cleaved the weapon in two. The static pulse followed the path of the sword like a flashing comet, grounding to the blade. In the same instant, bolts of electricity arced from her sword and armor to the floor, walls, ceiling, and several nearby warriors. She swung her other sword as the first completed its arc and crossed the blades before her. They produced a loud crackle as they touched. Unsure of Teela's intentions, the warriors stumbled backward, knocking Khranga to the ground.

"You dare defy a blood oath!" Teela shrieked, stepping toward the surprised warriors.

"Hold! Hold! Hold!" Khranga shouted from where she lay on the floor. With reluctance, the warriors de-energized their weapons and two of them helped Khranga to her feet.

"They killed three of my warriors. You said nothing of giving them weapons!" Khranga shouted, her face contorted with rage.

"If you continue to violate Council directives and attack them, more of your warriors will cease. How many ceased when I was forced to defend myself? How many do you think will cease if we attack their planet? You have given your blood oath to abide by Council rule, and I speak for the Council!" Teela shouted back, matching Khranga's ferocity as she sheathed her swords.

Khranga and Teela squared off in a fierce challenge-stare. Their unmasked hostility made the room deathly silent. After an uncomfortably long pause, when neither ended the challenge nor took physical action, Teela spoke, her voice low and controlled. "Your warriors died because they were following orders that were contrary to the laws that govern this Mission. Orders without authority. Orders that lack honor. Murdering an unarmed birthing unit bearing the embryos of future Korlah warriors deserves the most severe punishment Korlah law can mete out. If it were not for the greater good of our Mission, I would seek all of those who were present during these dishonorable acts and feed them to starving Kahshinki.

"You gave me your blood oath that you would protect these humans. If you have chosen to recant your oath, I am prepared to do spectacle here and now. It will be my pleasure to end your existence and spare you any additional loss of honor." Teela finished with a sustained and threatening growl.

Khranga didn't break the stare, but her crown tendrils blanched. "No warrior would ever recant a blood oath, and no warrior would ever lose honor to a birthing unit," Khranga hissed back.

"I have proven that I am something more than a birthing unit. And now you are going to have to prove to me that you are, at the very least, a warrior with honor."

Khranga growled viciously and broke eye contact. She turned to her second-in-command and barked instructions to establish and maintain a protective perimeter around the humans. Emphasizing their role as protectors, Khranga dispersed the remaining warriors, directing them to keep their distance from the humans while ensuring their safety at all times. Then she limped over to the communications console and began to compose a shipwide directive outlining the role she had sworn to support.

With the exception of Khranga, the warriors departed the transfer chamber. Lahsoon and the Resistance soldiers watched with apprehension as Teela armed the remaining humans with abandoned pulse rifles.

"Is it wise to give the beasts weapons?" Lahsoon asked.

"These humans are only a threat if they are attacked. I don't want you to leave, but I understand you only agreed to help me liberate them. If you wish to leave now, I understand, and you leave with honor," Teela responded, bowing deeply.

"I agreed to get them to safety," Lahsoon shot back defensively. Moving close so Khranga would not hear, Lahsoon whispered, "I do not trust that overstuffed sack of braddle spoor. We need to move. We have already proven that this is not a good defensive location."

"I agree," Teela said. "We have no choice but to leave the severely injured for now. I would like two of your soldiers to stay with them. We will take the rest to a secret location that I will designate while we are en route. For this to work, we will all need to be invisible." She whispered her last sentence.

Lahsoon nodded enthusiastically and turned to quietly brief each Resistance soldier in turn. Two of them stripped off their thermal camouflage and brought it to Teela, then took up positions near where Crystal and Beth were being treated. Teela gathered the humans together and quietly instructed them on what was planned.

While Teela was busy talking to the humans, Gremensh directed two of the biotechs to discreetly remove a body hidden beneath Crystal's gurney. The body was that of a young, otherwise undamaged, Korlah, her eyes open and staring blankly forward. Without a sabat to distinguish its identity, her face and eyes were like any other Korlah, but she had a tiny scar, a thin white line just above the right eye. Gremensh's assistants carried the body to the back of the room and spirited it out through an access panel.

22 - Memories

Gremensh wiped her hands repeatedly as though unable to get them clean. With quick nervous gestures, she spoke with her assistants, her voice barely audible. When her specific instructions were complete, Gremensh spoke so that Teela could hear. She emphasized the urgency of completing the repairs on the two humans as she admonished her assistants for being too slow as they moved the gurneys containing Crystal and Beth into the corridor. Much to Gremensh's ire, Beth refused to release the pulse rifle Teela had given her, cradling it in her arms. Two Resistance soldiers walked on either side of the procession as it moved toward the bio section's severe damage and trauma repair area. Khranga, with the assistance of one of her warriors, limped along behind.

The moment Khranga left the chamber, Teela had Bill and Ruth put on the thermal camouflage. The mesh suit was a snug fit for Bill and baggy on Ruth. Teela helped her tuck in the excess folds of fabric. The helmets were another story. The much longer, conical shape of the Korlah cranium made them uncomfortably loose. They slid around when Bill and Ruth turned their heads and nearly fell off if they looked down.

"We need to find something to stuff the back of these helmets with," Teela explained to Lahsoon, who was observing impatiently.

"We will find something, and then we must go. We have a rendezvous we must make," Lahsoon said and directed the waiting soldiers to find some towels. Within a few minutes, one of the soldiers returned with a bundle of washcloth-sized towels. Teela stuffed a couple of handfuls into Bill's helmet and was helping him strap it on when a soldier burst into the room.

"Across the corridor there is another beast and a ceased unit, tortured, and the designation and genotype have been destroyed," she reported to Lahsoon. Teela threw the rags to Ruth and rushed to the soldier.

"Show me where," she demanded.

"Teela, we must leave now!" Lahsoon pleaded.

"I have instructed the humans to follow you. Take them to the designated location now, and I will join you shortly," Teela replied, making a sweeping gesture with a closed fist to indicate that it was not a request.

Lahsoon struck the wall with the butt of her rifle. "Two bits, no more. And then you must proceed to the rendezvous," she growled.

"Agreed." Teela bowed deeply. "Go with them, Ruth. I will meet up with you shortly!" she shouted over her shoulder in English as she rushed to keep up with the soldier who had already taken off on Lahsoon's cue.

The soldier led Teela two doors down and across the corridor from the transfer chamber. As soon as Teela entered the open door, her crown tendrils were assailed with the stench of filth and burned and decomposing flesh. The main chamber contained washbasins, gurneys, large aprons, and gloves, which gave the impression of a hospital scrub room. Teela continued into an adjacent chamber where the stench was nearly overwhelming. In the center of the room, the naked corpse of a Korlah was strapped to a table. The crown tendrils were shriveled and black from being systematically burned to the scalp, and portions of her body lay ravaged by the apparent application of the many frightening torture implements spread on a tray near the table. The body showed evidence of previous torture. It was deeply scarred and the claws and fangs had been removed, but those wounds had healed long ago. Teela shook her head, unwilling to believe that one Korlah would do this to another.

"The beast is in there," the soldier whispered, pointing to one of four cell doors.

"And the other cells?" Teela asked.

"Empty," the soldier answered, glancing around uneasily.

Teela approached the cell the soldier had designated and opened the door. A human male in his mid- to late thirties in a pilot's jumpsuit was sitting on the floor. He had short-cropped black hair and stubble that was well on its way to becoming a beard. His back was against the far wall, and he faced the door. Shielding his eyes from the light streaming into his unlit cell, he looked up at the figures silhouetted there.

"On your feet! I don't have time to explain. We need to leave, stat. I'm going to take you to join some other humans for the purpose of returning to Earth. Do you understand?"

"Yeah, sure. Whatever you say. Just get me out of this shit hole," he answered. He scrambled to his feet and used his hand like a visor to see who was speaking.

"You follow her, and I will follow you. We need to move fast," Teela said.

"Yeah, okay, okay. I'm ready when you are."

Moving at a trot, the soldier led them off the main corridor and into a labyrinth of dimly lit support tunnels that contained cables, conduits, and contraptions that serviced the adjacent compartments. The layers of dust that covered everything stirred into a spiraling cloud behind them as they worked their way through the densely packed equipment.

Before they crossed or entered one of the larger corridors, the soldier would cautiously check for activity. Shortly after they entered a tight ventilation conduit, she stopped and waited, looking up and down the conduit and listening intently. Satisfied that they were not being followed or observed, she slid a large component that appeared to be fastened to the wall to one side, revealing a circular opening behind it. The soldier directed Teela and the human to crawl into the hole. After they were safely inside, the soldier backed in and pulled the component back into place. Although the chamber was unlit, Teela could see the thermal outline of a door and moved toward it.

"Wait!" the soldier exclaimed. "Traps! There are traps set to deter security forces." The soldier removed a plate from behind a stack of containers, set it down, and slid it up to the threshold of the door. Stepping onto it, she tapped a code into the communication console by the door. With barely an audible click, the door unlocked and opened.

The soldier directed the human and Teela through the door and then returned the plate to its place. She then jumped across the area it had covered and joined them in the next room. The door was closed and locked by a Resistance soldier who had been guarding the door. Inside the room, Teela found a group of Korlah from various sections and genotypes helping the humans into thermal camouflage. Lahsoon approached her as soon as she entered the room.

"Rouche Hah." Lahsoon trumpeted. "The corridors are empty. Afron's security officers have fled to the arms, strategy, and security sections and barricaded all access points. We should be able to easily transit to the energy section unobserved."

"Rouche Hah," Teela replied, bowing deeply and with slow precision in gratitude and respect. "You have done well. But we will not be going to the energy section."

"But preparations have been made for a safe location. I have been directed to deliver them three sets from now. Where else would they be safer?" Lahsoon asked.

Teela drew her away from the group and moved close, lowering her voice so that only Lahsoon could hear. "They will be safest if they are not where they are expected to be. We will need eight more soldiers that you can trust to keep a secret, and we will need enough body cloaks with hoods for the rest of the humans and myself. My agreement with your leader is to get the humans to safety. Where they will be safe was not decided. I believe that is my decision."

"If I violate my directive, I could lose my rank and status. What advantage could there be for me to agree to such an action?" Lahsoon's question bluntly indicated that her compliance would require a sizable favor.

"There will be no advantage should we fail to resolve the conflict and reinstate the Council; although, if we succeed, I will need someone to lead the Korlah contingent that will accompany the humans on the journey to their home world. The risks are comparable to the potential advantages to one interested in improving their rank and status. How much would you risk for an opportunity of this magnitude?" Teela responded.

Lahsoon smiled slyly at Teela's offer, unaware of the fragility of its basis. "We are starving and bickering amongst ourselves. Our ability to defend our own vessel, let alone a planetary system, is questionable, so why would the human leaders agree to an alliance with us?" she asked.

"We have much to offer the humans. Even with our current leadership crisis and material conditions, we are a force to be reckoned with. In human terms: I will make them an offer they cannot refuse," Teela replied.

Lahsoon realized that Teela meant what she said, whether or not she could accomplish her lofty goals. "The reason I am with the Resistance is that, like many of my Resistance sisters, I have been terminated and expunged from the Mission records. In the eyes of the Council, we no longer exist. The leader believes you can change this," she said.

"You and your Resistance sisters will be the ones who change this senseless situation and restore equality. All I can do is help to facilitate and expedite the transition back to where it should be—where you want it to be," Teela replied.

“I will have what you asked for in two bits. Rouche Hah!” Lahsoon crossed her hands at the wrists, palms forward and claws extended in a parting battle salute.

Lahsoon had just stepped away when Teela was cornered by Ruth, Marsha, Bill, and the pilot.

Ruth hammered out questions in rapid order, her voice tense and emotional. “What’s happening? Why are you killing each other? This is Captain Jason Ramsey. He’s the pilot of the ship they captured, and he said there was one like you, a Korlah with a human mind, that they tortured to death. Is that what they are planning to do with us?”

“We have been caught up in the middle of a civil war,” Teela replied, trying to sound calm. “There has been an attempted military coup. A group within the Korlah leadership considers an alliance with humanity too risky, and made a move to seize control to eliminate those plans. Fortunately for us, a group of dissidents within the lower ranks of the vessel believe an alliance with humanity is the only way to obtain the materials and provisions needed to prepare us for the impending battle with the Kahshinki.

“I honestly don’t know anything about another Korlah like me. If that’s what was planned for you, it has been stopped, and together we will make sure it is not attempted again.” Teela was worried by the anger, fear, and exhaustion on the faces confronting her.

“It was a marine, a U.S. Marine inside a spaghetti head,” Ramsey said angrily. “I was able to gather that they were asking him about radio technology. Unfortunately for him, he didn’t have the technical knowledge to answer their questions. You look to be in a lot better shape than that poor bastard. What kind of answers have you been giving them?” he asked accusingly.

“Dade ain’t no traitor! He wouldn’t tell um nothing to hurt us,” Bill said.

“This isn’t your buddy Dade, dimwit. It’s some kind of mind-sucking freak,” Ramsey shot back.

Bill reached out with lightning speed. His open hand struck Jason’s chest with a dull thud that drove him hard against the wall. He grasped the pilot’s jumpsuit and apparently, from the way Jason screamed when he was lifted off the floor, a good portion of his chest hair as well. When Jason tried to use a double fist to strike Bill's wrist, Bill swung him like a ragdoll and slammed him into the wall with such force that Teela thought his skull would crack. With a single thrust, Bill drove the two-hundred-pound man up the wall until the side of his head was pressed firmly into the corner of the low ceiling. Bill's other hand was clenched into a formidable block of flesh and bone that was winding back to deliver a blow. Teela grabbed the fist with both hands.

"Let him go. Please, Bill. This won't help," she pleaded, holding on tightly.

Bill turned his head toward Teela. His face was twisted in anger. A face that had once belonged to Daedalus. The green eyes and pale pink skin were framed by the dark hair and skin that covered what remained of Bill's face. Teela could see her distinctly Korlah image reflected in the lenses of Dade's glasses that rested crookedly on the end of Bill's nose. The visage unleashed a flash of memories that the combined personality of Teela and Daedalus had been repressing in order to concentrate on the needs of the present.

Teela exhaled sharply and stepped back, releasing Bill's fist and tripping on Marsha, who had been standing close behind. Marsha and Ruth caught her as she fell backwards. Bill released Captain Ramsey, who crumpled against the wall.

The room spun slowly around Teela as the floor turned soft and spongy, preventing her from regaining her balance. The images of those around her grew smaller and dimmer, blurred, and finally faded away.

Who are you? a voice called softly from the distant blackness. *Who are you?* the voice asked again, this time more demanding. *Who are you?* the voice shrieked with panicked confusion.

I am Teela. Teela 10127. No! No, I . . . I am . . . someone else? I am . . . so tired, so very, very tired. Need to rest a while.

A grunting noise and words she couldn't understand drew her from her daze and the comforting respite that she longed to embrace. Teela opened her eyes to find those of Daedalus staring back.

"She's waking up!" Bill announced. Teela realized she was lying on the floor with Bill, Ruth, and Marsha kneeling over her.

"You had another spell, bin talking nonsense. How you feeling now?" Bill asked with genuine concern.

Reaching up and touching Bill on the cheek, she ran her finger down the scar where the white and black skin joined.

"I know you. Your face, something about your face," Teela said, examining Bill's face for clues. Bill stared for a moment, not understanding the Korlah words.

"You don't look so good. All pale, like when ya hit your head. An' I cain't understand that language of yours. Are you all right?" Bill asked, his forehead creased with concern.

"Please help me up," she said, continuing to speak Korlah while reaching out to Bill.

Understanding the gesture, Bill took her hand and pulled her to her feet. Teela looked around to find everyone in the room, Korlah and human alike, staring at her.

"I'm all right," Teela barked in Korlah. "What's wrong?"

There was an extended pause of silence in the chamber and then Lahsoon stepped up behind Teela and put her hand on her shoulder. Already in a tense and excited state, Teela jumped.

"I'm sorry," Lahsoon said quickly, removing her hand and making an apologetic display. "They wait for you to speak their language. I do not believe that they understood what you have said."

"I . . . I was . . . speaking . . ." Teela said weakly, clasping her hands together to stop the palsied trembling that was causing her whole body to quake. "Thank you, Lahsoon," she whispered before turning away. She clenched her fists tightly, but the heavy gloves she now wore inhibited the pain she had hoped would restore clarity. She removed one glove and pressed the claws of her right hand into the back of her left forearm. The pain eased the tremors and helped her concentrate on forming the words that came with such difficulty now. She closed her eyes as much to concentrate as to shut out the piercing gazes of the aliens before her.

Then Teela spoke. "Ha . . . ard . . . speakn . . . These sih-ha-sters . . . hep . . . take hu sefe place . . . meb-ee . . . home," Teela managed to wring out of her tortured mind.

As soon as she stopped speaking, the aliens began to make grunting sounds. She knew the sounds were their language, questions, but the sounds came too fast from too many of the creatures at once. Speaking the language of humans had exhausted her mentally; the points of her claws touched bone, yet the pain did not help her understand their words, so she turned her back to them to indicate that she had nothing more to say. Lahsoon had been standing close behind her and was concerned with her strange behavior and that of the beasts.

Seeing Lahsoon's shock, Teela made a gesture of apology with trembling hands covered in her own blood. She moved close to whisper her instructions to Lahsoon, who assumed a protective stance between her and the now agitated beasts.

"I am . . . not well . . . Lahsoon. Forgive me," Teela whispered, her voice barely audible. "An assault pod is being prepared to return these creatures to their planet. You will find it in an outer repair berth at ring eighty-four, deca-quad two. Take them there, and your obligation will be complete."

Lahsoon had to strain to hear her words over the noise of the beasts. Looking down at Teela's contorted face, she studied her sunken and dull eyes, dry cracked lips, and crown tendrils that hung limply, no longer glistening as they should. Reaching under Teela's vest, Lahsoon felt Teela's abdomen. It was sunken beneath her ribs and trembling like her hands. Teela jumped at the contact, and Lahsoon withdrew her hand.

"When did you last take rations?" she demanded. Teela's eyes darted about nervously, avoiding Lahsoon's prying eyes and searched for an answer. Her lips trembled as she prepared to speak, and she reached for her left wrist to apply the pain she needed to think. Lahsoon grabbed her hand and pulled it away before Teela could claw herself.

"Look at your arm! You open your flesh, yet you barely bleed," she scolded, twisting Teela's punctured wrist up before her face. "You are drying out, like a rouk out of water. If you haven't taken your water rations, I doubt you have taken any food rations either. I have found Nons ceased from lack of rations that were of better utility than you are now." Pulling a flask from her belt, Lahsoon opened the top and held it up to Teela's mouth. "Drink!" she ordered.

Teela started to turn her head away, but Lahsoon grabbed her from the back of the neck and splashed some water into her partially open mouth. The cool water felt good, and although stale and slightly metallic, to Teela it was ambrosia, delicious and immediately irresistible. She grabbed Lahsoon's hand and the flask with both of hers and frantically gulped faster than was physically possible. When she choked, she still poured the water into her throat as Lahsoon attempted to pull the flask away. Teela ripped it from her grasp and continued to pour the contents into her mouth until they were gone. She dropped the empty flask and fell forward onto all fours and vomited the water onto the floor at Lahsoon's feet. She gagged and coughed until no more of the fluid remained within her, then she grabbed the empty container from where it lay in the pool of her vomit and lapped out the few remaining drops.

The sounds of energizing pulse rifles, carbines chambering rounds, and shouting drew her attention away from the flask. The room had divided, humans on one side and Korlah on the other, their weapons directed at each other. Teela was in the middle. A human bent over her, the one known as Ruth. She was making the grunting sounds that were their language, but Teela could no longer understand her. Teela clenched her fists to concentrate, her claws digging into her open wounds. She struggled to speak to the human, hoping her words were correct.

"I sick . . . No foo-ud, wah-ter . . . too long," Teela croaked, the coarse words barely intelligible. When she attempted to stand, Ruth motioned for her to sit, and then she spoke to the other humans. She got them to lower their weapons, and the Korlah soldiers did the same.

Removing protein biscuits and flasks of water that they had concealed in their garments, the humans handed them to Ruth, who offered them to Teela. Carefully regulating how much and how quickly Teela ate and drank, Ruth doled out the food and water rations until Teela could consume no more.

An intensely overwhelming lethargy engulfed Teela. She leaned back against the wall, closed her eyes, and was snoring loudly within seconds. She twitched and groaned, even in sleep she was haunted by memories that demanded her attention.

With the exception of a few stripped and burned-out cars, the city street was deserted. The long rows of brick tenements towered above, their dark broken-out windows appearing to gaze down with ominous intent. A cold wind blew down the street toward him, kicking up scraps of trash, and the cold and dust from crumbling buildings burned his eyes.

The sun had long dipped below the rooftops and the shadows faded with each passing minute. He held his hands over his ears to relieve the prickly ache of cold that gnawed at them, imagining the sensation to be caused by the hungry rats he could see darting from one shadow to the next. She had told him to wait on the step, that she would be right back. He had waited before, but this was much longer than any other time. The pain in his belly combined with a scathing thirst had driven him to disobey her and to try to find his way home. But now, as night approached, the ache of hunger was forgotten and replaced by a chilling fear.

In the dwindling light, the building looked like his. At least, it was similar to a place he had lived before. He ran up the entry stairs and down the long dark hall to the stairway at the back. Light shone down from above, illuminating the bent and rusted handrails in silhouette. He climbed toward the light, up and up, dodging the debris that cluttered the stairs along the way. The light, he finally realized, was coming from the open hole where the stairs ended on the roof amid the crumbled remains of the cupola.

Paralyzed by the realization that this was not his home, he watched as the last sliver of sun disappeared, and with it, his hope of finding his mother. Streetlights in the distance provided nominal visibility on the roof, and when faced with the prospect of climbing back down the pitch black stairway, he chose to wait where he was. As he waited, something deep within, something like the cold that gnawed at his ears, gnawed at his heart and devoured what hope remained for finding his mother.

Lying down, he curled into the fetal position and pulled his coat over his head. As he lay there shivering, the beating of his heart pounded in his ears and an intense loneliness and longing swept through him.

I'm dreaming, no . . . remembering, he thought. He opened his eyes and found a blackness that enveloped him both physically and spiritually. He tried to move, but he found that his body was no longer attached to his mind. He was conscious, yet detached from physical existence.

I'm dead. Oh my God, I remember. I remember! Teela, where are you? Teela! his panicked mind screamed. His thoughts, he knew without understanding why, were trapped in the stygian nothingness of nonexistence, and the only person who could release him was not answering his cries for help.

23 - Breakdown

Lahsoon and the Resistance soldiers were cautiously herding the armed and thermally cloaked humans out the door when Bill, realizing that they intended to leave Teela behind, broke from the group and pushed his way back toward the room.

"Bill! Where are you going?" Beth called back.

"I'm gonna wait here till Dade is better." Bill said, stopping just outside the chamber where Teela slept.

"If he wants to stay with that fucking thing, let him," Ramsey said. "I hope he's right. I hope his buddy Dade really is inside that thing's mind. But I for one want to get the hell off this fucking tub and go home."

"Bill, Teela told us to go with these soldiers. Please don't fight with them," Ruth pleaded.

"I don't care what y'all say. When I had no eyes, I saw Dade when Teela talked. He don't look the same no more, but Teela is Dade. Saved my life, gave me his face. He wouldn't leave none of us behind and I ain't leaving him behind. Teela is Dade, and if she don't go, I ain't going neither. That's all I got to say."

Bill turned away and entered the room, closing the door behind him. He sat down across from Teela, cradled a pulse rifle in his lap and ignored the soldiers who pointed their carbines at him. Lahsoon surveyed the situation and issued instructions to two soldiers, who took positions by the doors. Then by means of gesticulations, she directed the humans down the outer corridor.

Lahsoon had eight of her soldiers put on long hooded robes like the ones worn by the Nons. The remaining soldiers formed up like guards on all sides of the ones wearing cloaks. The remaining soldiers, except for Lahsoon and one other, marched down the corridor away from the humans.

"What are they doing? Where are they going?" Margaret whispered to Ruth.

"Decoys. They intend to make someone think we are being taken somewhere other than where we are actually going," Ruth whispered back.

"Where are we going?" asked Margaret.

"I don't know. Teela said home . . . maybe," replied Ruth.

"Truth is, lady, you don't have a fucking clue," Ramsey said. "There are only two of them now and eight of us. We have weapons. If you're too gutless to make a move, give me your weapon and I'll do it for you."

"Listen, you arrogant prick!" Ruth said. "Truth is, I don't have a clue why Teela wasted her time pulling you out of that cell. It was you who put us here, you fascist! Teela, I am certain, is trying to get us home. I had my doubts, but no more. So you better understand what I am telling you. I will not put up with any shit from you. Get in my way, interfere with our plans, and I will not hesitate to shove this weapon up your ass and pull the trigger. Am I making myself clear?" Ruth put on her best Beth impersonation and pointed her rifle at Jason's groin.

"Loud and clear. I understand that I can't fix stupid," Ramsey growled, his eyes devoid of fear or concern.

"That's real good, Captain, because I'm going to walk behind you. I would suggest that you don't do anything . . . well . . . stupid, because I just might accidentally charbroil your asshole. Now get back in line. It looks like our escorts are ready to go."

With Lahsoon in the lead, Margaret, Ann, Tiffany, Marsha, Catherine, Rebecca, Jason, and Ruth followed in a tight column. A second Korlah followed behind the group, stopping when they changed directions and watching the areas behind to ensure that they weren't being followed. Their route took them through the many conduits, access tunnels, and storage areas that were not monitored or where the monitors had been purposely broken. Although they wore thermal camouflage, this added precaution ensured that their transit to the outermost level would not be observed.

Entering from the furthermost aft area of the engineering section, they passed through sets of thick vaultlike doors into the darkened hangars where the campaign vessel's armada stood ready for deployment.

Through night-vision scopes, the enormous hangars appeared illuminated in a bluish green spectral light, the detail and clarity intensified. Overhead, connected by access tubes like Tinkertoys, assault pods, light fighters, and heavy fighters filled the outer shell of the campaign vessel and disappeared over the horizon of its three-mile circumference.

"Holy mother of God!" Ramsey exclaimed. "I count ten, no thirty, ten light each, five heavy, five troop carriers each. Shit! That's three hundred light and a hundred and fifty heavy. That's more than three times what we have. And that's only what we can see. Good God! You gotta realize this is an invasion force."

"They aren't interested in Earth," Ruth said. "They're after the ugly little toadlike things that you work for. But you better believe if Earth's leaders or military goons like you get in their way, they won't hesitate to use whatever force it will take to accomplish their goal. Teela thinks she can forge an alliance with Earth, one that will be mutually beneficial."

"Civilians!" Ramsey cried. "You dumb bastards have it all screwed up. The spaghetti heads are the bad guys. The toads told us they were coming and have been helping us prepare for this invasion. They've given us weapons and technology in exchange for raw materials and labor."

"And free access to abduct citizens and eat them alive," Ruth spat, giving Ramsey a shove with her pulse rifle. "Excuse me if I believe Teela. I believe that this vessel is on a mission of revenge, and God help the poor fools that join forces with the toads against them. Teela told us that unless Earth joins them against the toads, they will use a weapon like one the toads used on their home world. Whatever it is, it turned their planet, which was like ours, into a desert wasteland. From what I can see," Ruth said, gesturing toward the many rows of assault pods, "they are well equipped to carry out their threat."

Their progress suddenly halted, and Lahsoon came trotting back to Jason and Ruth, making furtive gestures to indicate that they should keep silent. When she was convinced they understood, she returned to the front of the column and they once again began moving forward. In the distance, over the horizon of the vessel's inner structure, something like a sunrise began to emerge, growing ever brighter as they approached.

Gathering the group into a narrow culvert that ran beneath a thick bundle of piping and conduit, Lahsoon began to strip off her thermal camouflage. Underneath, she wore a crisp uniform. Like the others worn by the Korlah, it was a simple jumpsuit, deep blue, almost black, with silver glyphs embroidered onto the upper left area of the chest. Leaving her camouflage and weapon with the other Korlah, she headed toward the light, walking conspicuously down the center of the walkway with her hands clasped behind her back. She moved at a good pace, meaningful but unhurried, and soon disappeared into the distance.

"I can fly any one of these birds. You can all come along if you want. All I'm asking is that you don't try to stop me," Ramsey whispered, inching closer to Ruth. The tip of Ruth's pulse rifle illuminated, the electronic buzz indicating that she had powered it up. She backed away from Ramsey and pointed the weapon at him, staying just out of his reach.

"Turn around and shut up! If you force me to use this, I will," Ruth hissed from between clenched teeth.

"Margaret, Ann, see if you can find something to tie Mr. Ramsey's hands. I think it would be a good idea to gag him. Yeah, gag him too."

"You're making a mistake. The spaghetti heads are setting you up."

Ann and Margaret took pleasure in securing Captain Ramsey's hands behind his back with strips of fabric torn from their clothing. Margaret chose a foul-smelling rag she been using as a sweatband since her arrival to gag his mouth.

Lahsoon returned after a short while and indicated for the group to follow her. Traveling the circumference brought their assault pod into view. The area around it was illuminated with bright white lights, and teams of workers floated around the pod on platforms that hovered between the floor and ceiling. But in this outer chamber, floor and ceiling no longer seemed relevant; workers were walking on the ceiling inside the outer hull. On the assault pod, the top and bottom workers all moved about without falling off. Gravity, it seemed, was wherever they needed it.

The humans craned their necks as they approached the transit tube that would carry them up to the pod. At the tube Lahsoon motioned for Margaret to enter. Margaret, grinning foolishly, waved to Ruth before jumping in and floated up toward the vessel. The remaining humans followed easily, as Teela had instructed them.

Whereas the campaign vessel was built on a grand scale with high ceilings, wide corridors, and room aplenty, the assault pod was claustrophobic. It was large, at least a football field in length, and maybe sixty feet in diameter. Unfortunately for the crew and passengers, it was almost entirely engine, surrounded by a single level of living space, filled with the ships other machinery and connected with narrow corridors that ran the length of the ship.

It was into one of these corridors that Margaret emerged. As she approached the pod, she could see Korlah waiting for her on what she thought was the ceiling. As she entered the ship's hull, she realized that the gravity lifting her was now the gravity she needed under her feet, not over her head. With the assistance of the Korlah waiting for her, she flipped onto her feet. When she looked up into the opening from which she had emerged, she could see Ann and Tiffany approaching headfirst toward her.

"Up is down. You have to flip onto your feet as you enter," Margaret called to Ann as she came through. Ann landed on her feet with Margaret's help and they assisted the others as they entered. The Korlah stepped back a respectful distance from the armed humans. Soon the narrow corridor was filled. Ruth looked down the tube behind her. Lahsoon was nowhere to be seen. She immediately regretted not being able to thank the Korlah that had brought them here safely.

A slender Korlah in a clean, crisp uniform, dark blue like the one Lahsoon had put on, walked through the group of humans, bowing deeply and making polite hand gestures of respect to each. She finally moved down the passage and gestured for them to follow her. Turning a corner, they moved down another corridor that ran around the circumference and passed two more fore-to-aft corridors before turning left into another one. All around them were instruments, and machinery of function and manufacture that were completely alien to them. The Korlah turned and waited until all the humans were within sight, then she fanned a control on the wall to activate a gravity lift. As she floated up through an opening in the ceiling, she gestured for them to follow.

They soon found themselves in a somewhat roomier space, about twelve-feet wide by fifteen long. One end of the room was semicircular, and three thickly padded chairs were positioned before panels and windows. The wall at the other end had two openings on either side.

"This is a ship like the one we were brought in!" Ruth exclaimed. Moving to the back to confirm her suspicions, she found more padded seats, three rows of four each, replacing the trays. When she opened the rear storage compartment and found it identical to the one that had contained their possessions, she was hit with a wave of icy air that at once condensed the room's moisture into clouds of fog. The large rectangular object on the floor was barely visible, but Ruth knelt before it and fanned the fog that had settled in it. Jimmy Bourke stared up at her, his face twisted into a horrific mask, his eyes dull and lifeless. Ruth threw herself backward with a gasp, scrambled to her feet, and closed the compartment door behind her.

"What's the matter? What's in there, Ruth?" asked Ann. Ruth looked for Tiffany. When she saw her looking out the window at the other end of the craft, she whispered to Ann.

"I . . . I think this is *the* ship we came in! Jimmy is in there, just like we left him . . . in a tray . . . We can't let Tiffany see him. We have to keep her away from here. We need to let the others know, but not Tiffany."

"Why would they put him in here? Why him but not Dade?" Ann asked.

"I don't know. Proof maybe. Proof that the toads ate him. What else?" Ruth replied.

The slender Korlah that met them on their arrival approached Ruth. She gestured to the room that Jimmy was in and then pointed to the nearby wall. She opened the compartment and withdrew a narrow case about the size of a dictionary. Cradling it in one arm, she opened it. It was much like a laptop computer; it had a viewing screen and a keypad with several dozen keys marked with glyphs. On one side was an indentation. The Korlah removed an object from her pocket and set it into the indentation. She demonstrated how to actuate the log bar, and Ruth recognized it immediately as the recording of their abductions. The Korlah handed the case to Ruth along with several other log bars from her pocket. Ruth removed the bar and closed the case before taking the remaining bars. Nodding that she understood, Ruth pocketed the bars and tucked the case under her arm before giving a respectful palm display.

The Korlah showed Ruth where food and water were stored, where the waste reclamation equipment was, and how each of the accommodations and controls operated. Satisfied that she was understood, she made a polite bow and left through the portal in the floor. Moments later the opening closed and the lines of its circumference were almost imperceptible.

"What are we supposed to do now?" Margaret asked.

"We wait for Teela to bring the others, then we go home," Ruth replied.

"Teela looked really sick. What if she doesn't get better? What if she doesn't bring the others?"

"Damn it, Margaret! I don't know!" Ruth shouted. "Maybe we get Rebecca to pray for a miracle. Or maybe we should turn Captain Fantastic loose and have him fly us home. Until we are forced to decide, I suggest everyone eat something and get some sleep!"

She stormed to the back of the ship where she sat on one of the rearmost corner seats. She clenched the log reader with hands that shook from fear and anxiety and the realization that the others would look to her to make those decisions.

24 - Chaos

Shawaugh was aware that she was awake, but she kept her eyes shut and lay motionless. After several lifetimes of warrior training it was instinctive; although she may be injured, she would fight as long as she possessed adequate utility. She maintained her breathing, steady and deep, as if she were asleep. Focusing her senses, she listened and used her olfactory tendrils to gather details of her surroundings. The chemical and biological smells indicated she was in a biorepair facility. The soft rustling and quiet footsteps in the area told her that she was not alone.

Slowly opening her good eye, she discovered that it was partially covered by a wrapping on her head. She was lying face down on a biorepair table and could see the backs of someone's legs. She carefully flexed the muscles of her arms and legs to verify that she was not bound. She had passed out in transit to what was supposed to have been a Resistance repair facility, and until she proved otherwise, she had to assume she was among enemies. She leapt from the table and grabbed the technician from behind, wrapping a thick arm around her chest and arms and using another to cover her mouth. Holding the technician firmly, Shawaugh craned her head to see out beneath her bandage and verified that they were in fact alone. Other than tensing in surprise, the technician neither struggled nor attempted to scream or speak.

"When I remove my hand, you will tell me where I am," Shawaugh growled softly. "Do not attempt to deceive me. I am a third and will know if you lie. If you attempt to call for assistance, I will twist your head off so that it cannot be reattached by even the most skilled biotech."

Before she could remove her hand, the technician responded telepathically, a difficult feat for even the most advanced mindtalker to perform without facing the recipient. *I* am *the most skilled biotech, and despite the rumors, even I cannot reattach heads. I know that you are frightened and confused, Shawaugh. I also know that you do not possess the ability to discern my thoughts, and unless I take physical action against you, I am certain you will not harm me.*

Shawaugh realized that this was no mere technician, and that she did not require her voice to call for help. Feeling dizzy and weak, Shawaugh released her and leaned back against the table. Surveying the room for threats and escape routes, she took a moment to consider her options.

"You have nothing to fear. There are no threats here for you to concern yourself with," the technician said aloud, turning to face Shawaugh. "I have no reason to lie to you. I am Sethron, the health section leader and a highly skilled biological technician. Your damaged condition has provided numerous opportunities for me to exercise my skills. Repairing you has been both interesting and challenging. Other than being a little stiff, you should be quite capable of twisting heads off without any difficulty; however, since you had gone so long with only one eye, you may find your depth perception—"

"My eye? You repaired my eye!" Shawaugh roared, ripping the bandage from her head. Blinking repeatedly in an effort to bring Sethron's image into focus, she prepared to unleash her outrage.

"Yes . . . I know . . . but . . . don't say anything. Don't think, just listen," Sethron scolded, reading Shawaugh's thoughts.

"I, as well as everyone else aboard this vessel, am amply aware of your blood oath to refuse repair of injuries sustained during the Kahshinki attack until your honor has been restored. The Council, save two, has decided to restore your honor. I left you the jagged scar because I know how you rely on it to frighten and intimidate your challengers.

"Yes, you do. Yes, you do! Don't waste your time trying to frighten me, Shawaugh. I can see behind your façade of brutal intimidator, and what I see, I admire and respect, because it is real, genuine and worthy of honor. Don't tell me to remove the eye because I know you don't really want me to. No, you don't. Pulling it out will prove nothing to me other than your disrespect for my efforts. If you insist, I will remove it after you have spoken to Shyron, who happens to be quite anxious to speak with you. So unless you intend to 'twist my head off,' I suggest you let me verify that I have successfully repaired you, and then we will get you dressed and off to meet with Shyron."

Shawaugh fumed in silence. Sethron's ability to anticipate what she intended to say unnerved her. Afraid of what her thoughts might reveal, she concentrated on shielding them from Sethron's prying mind.

Turning to a nearby counter, Sethron pulled out a bundle of garments and tossed them high in the air to Shawaugh, who deftly caught them over her head.

"Depth perception, acceptable. Eye repair, satisfactory. Now get dressed," Sethron concluded. Making a respectful palm display, she turned to exit the chamber.

"Oh, if you are also unhappy with your new uniform, save your objections for Shyron and the Council. I for one voted against your appointment," she added as she left.

Shawaugh slammed the garments down onto the table. Angered by her inability to block Sethron's mind probing and groggy from whatever anesthesia they had given her, she strained to recall the events leading up to her repairs. How she had ended up in Sethron's care and why the Leadership Council would restore her honor, she could not fathom.

Shawaugh lived on the fringe of section politics and avoided the Resistance, leadership, security, and everyone else with an agenda to solicit her involvement. For over seventeen cycles, by circumstance and to some degree by a measure of choice, she had maneuvered around the influences of others, operating as a loner with no political or personal obligations. The concept that her honor and rank would ever be restored was a possibility she had long ago abandoned.

Over the many passing cycles, Shawaugh had maintained the singular goal of living long enough to die with honor in battle. And now she was being faced with the return of the responsibilities that had nearly cost her existence and relegated her to a fate much worse than death: the loss of her honor. She had dreamt of this day many times.

As she paused there, contemplating the situation, the cold floor and residual pain told her this was no dream. She tried to understand the feelings that swept through her. She felt weak and nauseous, but not from the injuries or medication; it was from something deep within her, an awful, debilitating feeling of dread. She suddenly realized that she was terrified. This made her angry and she slammed her fists down on the table, spilling the garments onto the floor.

Her new uniform unfolded as it fell, exposing the emblem on the upper chest. Shawaugh stared at the metallic embroidery in disbelief. The Mission emblem, her name, and the title "Director Campaign Warrior Forces" glistened brightly against the dark, finely woven fabric. If she had not at one time held the position, the concept of being advanced from the lowest-ranking warrior, where she had suffered her demotion in shame and dishonor, to that of the highest, most coveted assignment would have been inconceivable.

Shawaugh dressed slowly, stopping again and again to examine the vest's embroidery as though she expected it to vanish like her dreams. When she was clothed, she looked around the makeshift repair facility for a mirrored surface, and finding none, smoothed the fabric of her new uniform and combed her crown tendrils off her face with thick fingers. Satisfied, she let out a low growl to ward off her uncharacteristic anxiety and headed for the door Sethron used. Behind her on the table lay her new vest, neatly folded with the title and rank precisely centered on the garment, as warriors are taught to do.

The temporary biorepair facility Shawaugh exited was in a small chamber off a larger one nearly filled with energy conduits, power distribution junctions, monitoring stations, tools, parts and equipment. An area had been cleared in the center and a group was gathered in a circle. Some sat in chairs, but most were using the equipment or containers for something to sit on. With the exception of a low rumble of machinery that emanated from all directions, the room was silent. From the gesticulations of the participants, Shawaugh knew that a discussion of minds was in progress.

As she approached the group, she recognized each of the Council Leaders by their robes. Balron of Education, Sethron of Health, Krron of Security, Ohhron of Accoutrements, Mesron of Arms, Fezron of Supplies, Gilron of Population, Molron of Energy, and a birthing unit who was too young to be Teela. Conspicuously absent were Afron of Strategy, Tooron of Warriors, and Shyron, the Council Leader. Shawaugh stopped outside the perimeter and waited to be recognized.

The birthing unit stood, walked to the center of the group, and turned to face Shawaugh. Bowing deeply and making a traditional palm display to demonstrate respect, she spoke.

"Welcome, Shawaugh. It was sixteen and seven-tenths cycles ago that forces of Kahshinki origin penetrated our defenses and brought to us damage and destruction never before experienced aboard this campaign vessel. The effects of that damage have required difficult and regretfully flawed decisions that have brought us to our current situation, where Korlah fights Korlah. A situation where two members of the Council believe that by the use of force and intimidation, law by Council will be circumvented. Their efforts have not been without success. The Council has been forced to flee the very chambers where for over nine hundred cycles, vessel operations have been managed and campaigns have been planned and executed."

Shawaugh realized this birthing unit possessed the living memories of Shyron and was now Potentate of the Council. Her eyes flashed the anger she felt toward the Council and the many cycles of punishment and shame she had suffered. It was Shyron who had delivered the decision that outlined her demotion and punishment, and now here Shawaugh stood again, this time waiting to hear what the Council wanted in return for restoring the rank and status they had taken from her so long ago.

"You have every reason to refuse this appointment," Shyron said, reading Shawaugh's eyes or thoughts, perhaps noting the conspicuous absence of her new vest. "Yet to refuse would eliminate the only chance you will have to prove that you are not the incompetent that you were portrayed to be. It will be your opportunity to restore your honor to a level of significance consistent with the event that took it. At the conclusion of this meeting, I will order the flux accelerators to be taken offline to slow our vessel and mark the commencement of campaign. Yet before we can fight the Kahshinki, we must fight our own sisters first."

"You may keep your appointment. I will not lead a fight against my Korlah sisters to settle a Council dispute," Shawaugh stated abruptly. "And even if I did, who would I lead? Afron controls Khranga, and Khranga controls the warriors. The technicians and birthing units that make up the bulk of the Resistance have great courage and honor, but they are untrained and lack sufficient armor and weapons to confront such a formidable and organized force." She bowed slightly when she finished.

Shyron waited longer than protocol warranted before speaking, letting Shawaugh grow uncomfortable with the potential consequences of her disrespectful interruption.

"Teela, with no more than a handful of Resistance soldiers comprised of engineering technicians and birthing units, destroyed a fortified barricade manned by Afron's personal guards. Alone and armed only with blades, she then negotiated the surrender and support of Khranga and the warriors she controls. Afron, Tooron, a few hundred of their warriors, and security and strategy section supporters are all that is left of those who challenge the Council. Afron knows she has failed and will attempt to negotiate for her existence. If not, the Resistance forces will be more than enough to contain and eliminate the remaining threat.

"We need you for something much more important. We need to ensure that the alliance with the leaders of the humans succeeds. Without an alliance, the Kahshinki will surely defeat us. The success or failure of campaign now rests upon it. Teela has been tasked with this obligation and was making extraordinary progress toward that end until . . . she collapsed, and is unable to continue."

Shyron paused, watching for anxiety to flash into Shawaugh's mind, and smiled when her suspicions were confirmed. It was clear that Shawaugh had a deep concern for Teela's health, but just when she decided to query Shyron on Teela's collapse, Shyron continued.

"You have repeatedly demonstrated a great interest in preserving Teela's existence, going so far as to jeopardize your own. Your assignment will be to accompany Teela to ensure her safety and success. Without success, there will be no campaign. Without a campaign, there will be no need for a director.

"So I, Leader Potentate of the acting campaign vessel Council, ask you, Shawaugh; will you accept this assignment and appointment?" Shyron made an exaggerated bow, extending her arms slightly with palms facing back, indicating that her offer was not subject to negotiation. Shawaugh could only accept or decline.

Shawaugh took nine steps forward, eight for each section leader present and one for the Potentate. With a challenging glare at Shyron, Shawaugh made a clawed salute, not the salute of a subordinate, but that of an equal.

"I accept this appointment for the greater glory of Korlah and for the honor of all who have given their existence to achieve the Mission goal. I accept this assignment for my sisters who were fed into the reclamation macerators before their function and utility were diminished. Let it be recorded that I deny any obligation of favor to the Council for this appointment."

The room roared with the voiced and psychic rage of the leaders. Shyron raised her hands to silence the Council and locked eyes with Shawaugh. Ignoring the leaders, she held her hands up until the room was silent. She slowly lowered her arms before speaking.

"Success is your only obligation. Without success, you, me, and all of our sisters will cease to exist. This is an obligation of such magnitude that no favor within the confines of law will be denied to you. However, should you fail, this Council will ensure that your existence is among the first to be lost, and within the skills of our technicians, will take the longest." Shyron lowered her head and bowed slightly, still holding Shawaugh's gaze to relay her determination and deadly intent to the one who had so brazenly challenged her authority.

Breaking eye contact, Shawaugh cast her eyes down and changed her clawed salute into a respectful palm display while bowing slightly.

"I accept," Shawaugh purred. "By fang or by claw, by the blood of my existence, it shall be so."

Twenty levels up and half a kilometer from where Shyron and Shawaugh were meeting, three Resistance soldiers manned a checkpoint at a transit tube junction, which only a shift earlier had been manned by warriors from Afron's forces.

Following the bio section battle, as Teela's confrontation with Khranga's warriors was being called, the warriors had abandoned their checkpoints, leaving much of their weaponry behind, and either returned to the warrior section as directed by Khranga, or fled to the security section to join up with the remnants of Afron's forces. The three soldiers were collecting abandoned and confiscated weaponry and stockpiling it at their checkpoint. Such weaponry was normally never carried, much less used, aboard ship.

Only until a few shifts earlier, these Resistance soldiers had been engineering section technicians, trained to repair and maintain the systems that provided power and ventilation throughout the massive vessel. They were amateur soldiers at best, with only the most rudimentary military training and a briefing on the operation of pulse rifles. They were assigned to this checkpoint to restrict traffic to and from the population section, to report the activities of any warrior forces, and to collect any weapons they found. Frightened and isolated, they were unprepared for the situation they were about to face.

As they sat on pulse rifle charging units, the three would-be Resistance soldiers talked of the deterioration of basic services and speculated on what the leadership and vessel policies would be like after the conflict. Their heated discussion was interrupted by a rumbling sound coming down the corridor. Shoulder to shoulder, filling the wide corridor, a group of birthing units over a hundred strong was approaching the checkpoint. Since their arrival nearly a shift ago, the soldiers had turned away many small groups of birthing units searching for food and water. They couldn't have known that the birthing section had not received any deliveries since the beginning of the conflict, so they could not comprehend the desperation and determination of the approaching mob.

"Stop! Go back to your stations," the lead soldier shouted, stepping around the barricade.

"The new shells are birthing without existence! We must have water and food now!" screamed a birthing unit holding up a tiny newborn, its head and limbs swinging limply.

"Stop!" she shouted again, stepping backward, not knowing what else to do. The crowd continued to advance. A soldier energized her pulse rifle and the tip grew hot with the lethal charge it was set to expel. When they saw this, the birthing units at the forefront of the crowd, now within a dozen meters of the checkpoint, began to shout insults. The lead soldier turned at the sound of the energizing weapon.

"No!" she shouted, raising her hand. Nervous and jumpy, the soldier accidentally fired, vaporizing her superior's arm between the hand and elbow. The remains of the charge diffused into an arc flash, and intense thermal energy scorched those at the front of the crowd, causing their garments to burst into flames. Screams of terror turned to shrieks of pain and the group broke into a chaotic melee as it surged backward. Within minutes, the crowd had retreated, leaving several mothers and their infants trampled in the corridor, one charred from receiving the main force of the diffused pulse. She sat a few meters from the barricade, her burned arms outstretched and her head thrown back as her shrieks diminished to a pitiful wail.

The lead soldier stared in shock at the smoldering stump of her arm. Her hand lay at her feet with its fingers outstretched; the tendons were cauterized at the wrist.

"I'm . . . sorry. I . . . I . . . didn't mean to fire," the errant soldier stammered. She de-energized her pulse rifle and gingerly set it down.

"Report what happened and get some biotechs here," the lead soldier ordered. Leaning down, she picked up her severed hand by one of its fingers. After a brief pause in which neither of the soldiers had taken action, she screamed, "Do it now!" One immediately turned to a communication station to follow orders.

The wailing of the burned birth mother echoed down the corridor while the soldiers anxiously waited for help. The lead sat with her back against the wall and stared at her severed hand, placed on her knees. The others checked the fallen mothers and infants and tried to tend and comfort those still living.

Nearly a set, or one-tenth of a shift, after making their report, a rumble down the corridor drew their attention to where the birthing units had retreated. The soldiers heard many feet and angry voices.

"We should leave," one of them whispered.

The lead soldier stood. Without responding, she placed the severed hand in her pocket and moved around the barricade to face the approaching mob. When they came into view, the group broke from a trot into a full run. The soldier could see the glow of energized rifles and the glint of blades within the charging mob of birthing units and robed Nons. Holding her remaining arm out with its palm up, she offered a feeble apology.

About one-hundred-feet from the barricade, the throng opened fire. Their wild blasts hit the ceiling, floor, and barricade randomly. Without meeting resistance, they charged into the barricade and their blades and weapons struck down the three soldiers.

After allowing the birthing units to vent their rage on the remains of the soldiers, the Nons that had led the attack organized them into groups and armed them with the confiscated weapons.

The crowd parted as a tall figure wearing the hooded cloak of Non entered the circle of cloaked Nons at the center of the mob. She threw back her hood and pulled a long, crudely fabricated blade from the folds of her robe and swung it in a wide arc. The blade whistled through the air only inches from the others' faces, causing them to jump back. She dropped to her knees, held the blade point down, and placed her bowed head against its hilt. Gaunt features, thin gnarled hands, and creased flesh identified her as one who had eluded reclamation for many cycles.

"I am the Oracle. I exist for a purpose, as you exist for a purpose. Without purpose, there is no reason for existence. Many of us have been denied the knowledge of our past so that we could better serve a purpose intended to ensure our future. That purpose has been twisted into something that our existence was not intended for. I must teach you of our Gods so that you can understand why we have suffered and why we must suffer even more before we can restore the true purpose of our existence.

"The Gods of Korlah are Nas and Toma!" the Oracle shouted as she leapt to her feet. She paused before walking slowly around the circle. Her wild eyes challenged any to meet her glare. Most of the Nons had seen the bloody result of failing to look away quickly enough and dropped their eyes. The Oracle knew that the young birthing units' vacant stares were born of ignorance of challenge protocol; she ignored them and paced the circle as she bellowed her message.

"Our Gods represent the extremes of sentient and corporeal existence. One without the other creates an incomplete or unharmonious condition that results in chaos until balance is restored. Nas embodies charity, kindness, honor, love, bravery, and forgiveness. Toma embodies greed, cruelty, dishonesty, hate, fear, and vengeance. For the Korlah to defeat the Kahshinki, they abandoned balance and embraced vengeance, brutal strength, and fearless bravery with honor. The Laws of Korlah were twisted to meet the demands of campaign. Harsh and unconditional, they were devised to control the imbalance. Over time, Toma seduced our leaders and warriors. They have abandoned honor and become greedy, cruel and dishonest. They have lost sight of our Mission and they are frightened by the possibility that campaign will end, and with it, their privileged existence." The Oracle paused and extended a bony finger towards a young pilot warrior in the distance.

"You!" she shouted. "Come into the Circle of Truth."

The warrior's eyes widened with fear. She looked around for support, but every face turned away. With her eyes downcast, she stepped forward and the crowd parted as she shuffled into the circle to face the Oracle. The Oracle cradled her sword in the same manner that the warrior cradled her pulse rifle, then she turned her back in a show of trust and fearlessness.

"Tell our sisters what you were offered to betray the blood oath of a warrior," the Oracle demanded, her eyes closed in disgust. Recruited from the training facility at age thirteen, nearly two cycles early, the young warrior's uniform hung loosely on her thin frame, and the deep folds trembled in concert with her limbs.

"Private quarters, extra rations, and . . . a helper," the young warrior muttered softly.

The Oracle turned and charged up to the warrior. Her gaunt face less than an inch from the trembling and blanched youngster.

"Slaves!" the Oracle screamed. "They were given slaves to serve them in exchange for turning weapons on their Korlah sisters," the Oracle shrieked as she rotated her head in an anguished arch.

"You were offered your own private room, more food than you can eat, more water than you can drink, and a slave to do your bidding. Why would you refuse such a generous arrangement?" the Oracle shouted down the corridors, again pacing the perimeter of the circle.

"They . . . they were hurting a mother of my birth section. They wanted her to reveal what she knew about Teela 10127."

A low murmur rumbled through the corridors at the mention of Teela.

"Why do they want Teela 10127?" the Oracle asked.

"She has received the transferred essence of an alien beast. They say the beast controls her mind and seeks to destroy us all."

"Lies!" the Oracle shrieked. The young warrior cringed. "They take half-truths and weave them with lies to control us. I have met Teela 10127. She has received the essence of another, but it was no beast, and it does not seek to destroy us."

The Oracle paused. Her aggressive demeanor shifted as she changed her stance. She hunched over slightly and dropped her gaze to the floor in subservience and shame. Her voice was laced with regret. "I did not know who she was when we met. I drew my blade against her and tried to take her existence for the food and water her garments could buy."

Those who had not yet heard the story gasped. With exaggerated gesticulations, the Oracle reenacted the battle.

"The corridor was dimly lit. I knew she was a birther, slight of stature and a head and half shorter than me. It was not possible that she had experience with blades, yet . . . she disarmed two of the thieves who attacked her and drove off four more. I charged her, my blade hungry for her flesh, but she countered my attack with not just one blade, but two. Back and back she drove me. Her blades screamed through the air, forcing me to defend rather than attack. I fell down onto the ground where I waited for the blades to rend my flesh and end my miserable existence."

The Oracle paced the circle's perimeter, gauging the emotion of the crowd. The wide eyes and gaping mouths told her the story was having the desired effect.

"As I lay there with my arm shielding my head from the blades I was certain would strike, my eyes were drawn to the hem of her robe. I expected this image would be the last these aged eyes would see. But the blades did not fall. I was spared."

The Oracle paused again. She knelt and placed her head against the hilt of her blade once again.

"Why were you spared?" someone shouted. During a moment of uncomfortable silence, the young warrior faded back into the crowd.

"To serve a purpose. To serve Korlah!" the Oracle shouted as she stood.

"To serve Korlah!" the crowd shouted with a deafening roar, a response indoctrinated at an early age.

"It was not just a robe this birthing unit wore," the Oracle shouted, again pacing the circle. "The robe was embroidered with something more than just a decoration; it was the history of Korlah conflict and mediation written in the ancient text, beginning at the collar and ending at the hem. It not only documented the meaning of our past, it predicts our future. The robe she wore was that of the bladesman Shawlmon! On it were embroidered the last words he spoke on the day his existence ceased: 'Cherish existence, reject despair, and I shall rise for our final victory.'"

The Oracle stopped suddenly and slumped over, listening for her effect on the crowd before she began to walk again.

"A birthing unit no more, Teela 10127 fights like a warrior, and yet she has spared the existence of thieves, embraced hope where only despair could be found, and asked the Gods for help to attain final victory over the Kahshinki."

The Oracle listened as her words were relayed down the corridors. From the time it took for the distant murmuring to abate, she estimated the crowd had grown from several hundred to several thousand.

"Do you cherish existence?" the Oracle screamed at the top of her voice.

"Yes!" shouted the followers she had carefully seeded throughout the ring around her. Immediately, the others around them responded, and the wave of shouts reverberated down the corridors.

"Do you reject despair?" the Oracle screamed.

"Yes!" the crowd shouted in unison, the fervor and tension growing.

Sheathing her sword with a flourish, she spun on a heel in the center of the circle, extended her sinewy arms, and curled her fingers with claws extended.

"As it was foretold, Shawlmon has risen! For those who cherish existence, for those who reject despair, we will obey the demands of the Gods and follow Shawlmon to VICTORY!"

"Victory!" shouted the Oracle's followers in unison. The crowd no longer needed prompting. Another wave of shouts reverberated down the corridor and excited the crowd's fervor.

The Oracle's body began to tremble, with the exception of her arms and hands, which remained rigid above her head. In a voice deep and ominous, she spoke. She was as loud before, but calmer and more controlled.

"Claws, claws, claws, CLAWS!" she shouted down each of the four corridors, each time louder than the first. The followers raised their arms and extended their claws like the Oracle, shouting in response.

When their shouts abated, the Oracle continued. "You are claws of the Gods! You are the CLAWS OF SHAWLMON!"

"Claws of Shawlmon!" the crowd cried back. The Oracle called again, the crowd responded, back and forth until the entire crowd was chanting in unison.

At the back of the crowd, in the corridor aft of where the Oracle was speaking, two biotechs moved slowly away to avoid drawing the attention of the frenzied birthing units that surrounded them. They slipped into an alcove off the main corridor and cautiously retreated from the growing mob.

Many birthing units displayed open hostility toward them, blaming biotechs for the misery and complications caused by carrying six embryos. The crowd's wild eyes and extended claws were all the biotechs needed to convince them to leave. The chanting echoed after them as they weaved their way through equipment access conduits and ventilation ducts that they had learned to traverse as Resistance soldiers.

25 - Resistance

Bill leaned against the wall as he watched Teela sleep. Her twitching and mumbling indicated it was not a very sound sleep. Concerned for her health, he placed food and water nearby so she could eat when she woke up. By using pantomime, he was able to get the guards to lower the lights. He felt hungry, but had found the biscuits unappetizing since Beth showed him they were made of worms and beetles that reanimated when soaked. He sipped on a flask of water in the hopes of appeasing the grumbling in his stomach. When the door cracked open, the green light from the corridor beyond seemed bright in comparison to the dim room. The soldier outside spoke briefly with the guard inside before a figure slipped through the opening and the door closed. From its silhouette, Bill could see it was a Korlah. Without pausing, the Korlah walked over to Bill and knelt next to him, speaking softly yet urgently in the purring and clicking language that he was just beginning to understand bits and pieces of.

In the low light, he recognized the tattoo on her cheek. It was the symbol worn by those he had come to know as the doctors; those who had healed him and had been collecting his semen. He pressed the plugs in his nose deeper and blushed as he felt himself stir. Absent, however, was the small case they usually carried their collection vials in, and this one seemed to be trying to tell him something. When she reached for his hand, he nervously withdrew it and adjusted the glasses he still hadn't grown accustomed to.

Her hands dropped limply onto her knees and she knelt before him silently. Bill had listened closely when Teela explained that body language was an essential part of the Korlah's communication, but this was not among the gestures she had described. He was concerned that he was committing some sort of social blunder by avoiding contact.

"What's wrong? What are you trying to tell me?" Bill asked softly, enunciating clearly and scooping her hands up into his. She began to speak slowly and Bill recognized the basics of what she was saying. She repeated the sentence several times. Bill understood enough to know she was describing something, something about herself. He had heard the word used before and understood it to mean something like big or fat. Withdrawing one of her hands from his, she pointed to Bill's groin and then to hers. She slid her hand over her abdomen and brought her arms together to form a cradle.

"Uh oh!" Bill groaned.

Before Bill could fully react, the door to the chamber flew open and a soldier rushed in. She turned the lights up at the control panel, rushed over to Teela and began to shake her. Bill stood up, pulling the Korlah up with him when she held firmly onto his hand. Teela rolled over and sat up. She blinked and slowly stood. She leaned to one side, braced herself against the wall, and dry heaved several times.

"What the hell ya doing?" Bill shouted, pulling his hand free of the biotech as he charged across the room. Bill grabbed the soldier and threw her back toward the door, causing her to tumble to the ground. The two soldiers at the door energized their pulse rifles, and the one Bill had thrown did the same as soon as she got to her feet. Bill placed himself between Teela and the soldiers, wishing he had the pulse rifle that was lying on the floor where he had been sitting. The biotech jumped between Bill and the soldiers and was shouting something at them when Teela stumbled around Bill, using him as support.

"I am Teela . . . Teela 101 . . . Teela 1012 . . . 7," she mumbled in Korlah, looking first at Bill and the biotech and then at the soldiers at the door. Bill said something, but the sounds meant nothing to her.

"Sick, needs rest!" Bill shouted in Korlah at the soldiers as he bent protectively over Teela, putting his arm around her teetering body to brace it.

"Ya gotta rest, Dade, or you gonna die or something. You ain't slept more than a hour or so," Bill said as he swept Teela off her feet and sat her down.

"Dade?" Teela mumbled, recognizing the word amongst the foreign sounds.

"That's right. You know it. I know it, Ruth know it, and Beth know it, even though she won't say so."

"Bill. Bill!" Teela said, weakly placing her hand on Bill's shoulder. She could remember the name and that it belonged to this human, but she could not find the alien words that she needed to talk to it.

"Have you claimed this male as your mate?" the biotech hissed from where she stood behind Bill.

"What? No . . . no! He is my . . . my friend," Teela stammered in Korlah, completely unprepared for the question.

"Then I claim first rights as his mate by the ancient laws," the biotech stated. She turned to the soldiers behind to acknowledge their presence as witnesses of her claim. Teela slowly removed her hand from Bill's shoulder, avoiding eye contact with the biotech whose glare was clearly challenging her.

The soldier Bill had pulled away from Teela moved as close as she could to Teela while remaining out of Bill's reach. Interrupting the exchange with a clawed salute, she addressed Teela.

"Afron's forces are moving, Your Eminence. They have broken through the blockade at the access to the health section. They are moving quickly. We need to leave now."

"How long until they reach us?" Teela asked, using Bill for support as she pulled herself onto her feet. She released her grip and rubbed her aching temples with the palms of her hands, teetering.

"You gotta sleep, Dade, or you gonna git sicker an' most probably die," Bill said as he reached to steady her, only to find his hand intercepted by the biotech's.

Teela knew this human was speaking to the essence that should be within her, but there were no whispers in her mind to help her understand what was being said. She closed her eyes, clenched her fists, and strained to force the essence to return.

"Your Eminence!" the soldier interrupted again with added urgency. "They are heading directly for the assault pod and will be there in fifteen or twenty bits. We are the only forces in this area. We cannot stop them, and even if we leave right now, I am uncertain we can reach the assault pod before them."

Teela fought the urge to vomit. Choking back a dry heave, she stumbled to the communication panel by the door. She entered the message she feared would be needed and sent instructions to Challmara at the address Shyron had given her. Leaning on the console for support, she desperately considered what she and the few soldiers with her could do.

"Take whatever forces you can gather and secure the vessel defense systems in the arms and warrior sections. You need only to secure the areas that could be used to attack the departing assault pod," she ordered.

"Did you say they broke through the health section blockade? Oh no!" Teela cried in Korlah. Afron's forces would be moving through the very area to which she had sent Beth and Crystal.

The console began to flash with a reply from Challmara. Teela read the message and quickly inserted a log bar into the panel's receptacle. Once the information had been recorded,

Teela removed the bar and slipped it into her pocket. She turned from the console and saw that Bill had picked up his pulse rifle and was ready to accompany her. The biotech stood next to him, maintaining a proximity and contact that demonstrated her claim of first rights.

"This unit does not understand your claim," Teela said to the biotech. "You will need to take the time to explain your intentions while considering the long-term implications of your proposal. I am not able to interpret for you at this time, and I have other matters of greater significance to deal with. He is to remain in this room until I return, at which time we can resolve the situation." Her commanding tone and eye contact, combined with the backward tilt of her head, told the biotech that this was not a challenge, nor was it a request. The biotech broke eye contact with a subtle growl of acceptance.

"The Council will not refuse the demands of the Resistance," the biotech retorted with haughty confidence. "I command a significant cooperative within the health section, and once legal authorization to operate as a cooperative has been obtained, we will be able to deal with whatever 'long-term implications' this proposal demands."

Teela had heard rumors of the illegal activities of the cooperatives, but she had never heard an outright admission like this. To make such a statement could land an individual before the Council, where her right to exist would be evaluated against the collective needs of the whole. The entire complement of the campaign vessel was the one and only legally recognized cooperative. To claim participation in another would be considered blatant disloyalty.

"The Resistance has made many demands. Until you are certain of the outcome, be cautious of what you say," Teela said quietly, genuinely concerned for the welfare of the biotech. Teela turned away and headed for the door.

"The uprising in the population section is spreading into the adjacent sections. If the Council does not agree with the demands, it will cease. There is no longer any doubt as to the outcome," the biotech cried defiantly at Teela's back. Teela turned, stunned.

"What? What uprising in birthing?" Teela demanded, using the common term for the population section.

"Last shift, a group of birthing units demanding food and water were attacked. It is said that many ceased. When word of the attack spread through the section, the mothers, already angered over the interruption of food and water, became insane with anger. They took the weapons left by fleeing warriors and began to attack fortified barricades, taking the existence of all who resisted. They have swept through population and training and are currently engaging Afron's forces in the health section. While in transit here, I passed a barricade where a battle had been fought. There were hundreds of casualties. By now, there must be thousands. They are doing things—things you would never think birthing units would do."

The image of her section sisters swollen to near term with implanted embryos and fighting battles against warriors proved incredible. Teela dismissed the report as too fantastic to take seriously.

Leaving the room without Bill at her side was difficult. After a long, exasperated argument in pantomime, Bill finally acquiesced to Teela's demands when he saw the argument contributing to her exhaustion. Confident that he would be safe in the hidden room, Teela left the chamber and headed to the nearest transit tube.

Shawaugh and Shyron conferred while a lead Resistance soldier apprised them of the strengths and locations of assets, soldiers, and weapons. They were waiting for the arrival of the reclusive Resistance Leader, who had not yet committed to their plan, when two armed soldiers appeared at the door. Shyron's security guards blocked their entry. One of them approached Shyron and Shawaugh and began to speak without bothering to wait for permission.

"Your Eminence," she said to Shyron, "the Resistance Leader has arrived, but she insists on bringing in four armed soldiers."

"Allow them in immediately, as many soldiers as she wishes. Remember that we owe them honor. We owe them our existence," Shyron stated loudly enough for those outside to hear.

The guards didn't wait for the message to be relayed; they backed away from the door and motioned for the Resistance Leader and her entourage to enter. Between two pair of armored soldiers, a thin, nervous-looking Korlah in a basic worker's jumpsuit stripped of rank or identification markings entered the room. Her identifying sabat, like that of the soldiers with her, was obscured by a dark, greasy smear.

"You have nothing to fear. Identify yourself!" demanded Shawaugh, incensed by the subterfuge.

"We have everything to fear," the worker said softly, moving around Shawaugh and taking a seat on a square crate. A soldier stood to each of her sides with swords, and the two behind held pulse rifles at the ready. "If you pry into my mind, I will leave you to negotiate with Afron," she cried, holding a hand up toward Shyron as if to block the invisible probe.

"You are a first!" Shyron exclaimed, finding the Resistance Leader lacking telepathic ability. "I expected—"

"You expected the Resistance was being led by one of the Council. You thought it was Afron, and Afron thought it was you. You're wondering how a first of less than forty cycles has managed to amass the loyalty and resources necessary to avoid detection and capture. I don't have to be a mindtalker to know what you or the Council are thinking. I am what you least expected, and, therefore, you looked in all the wrong places. At least for now, I must insist on protecting my identity. I apologize if that causes you or your assistant any problems." She shot a disdainful glance toward Shawaugh, carefully avoiding eye contact.

Shawaugh leaned across the makeshift table that separated her from the Resistance Leader, narrowing her eyes to study her hands and features. The leader nervously pulled the sleeves of her loose-fitting coveralls over her hands and pressed them between her knees.

"You have made demands, and I assume the purpose for this meeting is to demand a favor as well?" Shyron asked.

"Yes, Your Eminence," the Resistance Leader responded quickly, releasing her hands to make a respectful palm display. "You have transferred to the birthing unit, Eemela. She had aborted the shells she carried and was damaged. With no spares available, you—"

"I am well aware of my shell's origin and history," Shyron snapped. Her mottled face darkened with anger and she narrowed her eyes in a piercing glare. "What do you want?" she hissed.

"I mean no disrespect," the Resistance Leader apologized. Her voice twanged with an edgy whine. "You must now understand why there can no longer be forced reclamations, and why there must be equal rations. You know now that having the genotype of a birther didn't prevent Eemela from becoming a functional warrior. The right to pursue cross-section job assignments must be available to those who want it. Cooperatives and trade have existed for many cycles, long before my existence. They must be recognized as lawful. These are not unreasonable requests, and mine is not an unreasonable favor."

Shawaugh bared her teeth and grimaced with disgust. Not at the Resistance Leader's words, but rather at her whine. *Like a Non begging for a biscuit,* she thought, and with that thought came recognition.

"I know *who* you are!" Shawaugh declared, pointing an accusing finger. The leader recoiled with fear, as though she expected Shawaugh to attack her. The soldiers around her took defensive postures.

Silence! Shyron commanded Shawaugh telepathically. The intensity of the command felt like a slap in the head.

Shawaugh swung her head to face Shyron. Her eyes flashed with anger.

It is unimportant who she is, Shyron declared. *Our sisters are dying while we debate demands and favors. Your expertise, Shawaugh, is campaign, and mine at present is negotiation. Do not interfere!* Shyron demanded telepathically.

Shawaugh turned her head back toward the Resistance Leader, and she slowly closed the hand with the pointed finger into a tight fist. Her joints popped and claws grated across the coarse fabric of her glove. She turned her back to the Resistance Leader, marched to the door she and her entourage had entered through, and stood squarely in its center, blocking the others from leaving.

"You request a favor?" Shyron asked. Her impatience was thinly veiled.

"When the new campaign vessel is—"

"There will not be a new campaign vessel. We will achieve final victory or end our existence trying," Shyron interrupted.

"A position on the Council?" the Resistance Leader whined, her distress evident.

"A first on the Council of Leaders? No!" Shyron barked, glaring. Her crown tendrils had grown thick and engorged with anger. "You take pleasure in thinking you are clever. You believe you have outwitted me. For cycles, I have diverted Afron from discovering your identity." Shyron kicked a box over to the table and took a seat, leaning well into her adversary's personal space. The Resistance Leader's guards, who should have moved to prevent such an invasion, made no effort to stop her.

"I have known who you are for some time. I learned of you when you formed a cooperative with your birth section sisters at sixteen cycles, and I observed you when, at twenty, you developed a lucrative trade in the off-shift manufacturing sector. But it was after you were assigned to assist with repairs following the Kahshinki attack that I really took interest. You used your experience repairing the monitoring and log record system to develop a trade in record logs. Then when the birth section director was murdered, the log that recorded it was reproduced and distributed, creating the myth of an organized resistance—a myth you eagerly perpetuated and profited from. The myth grew, and you continued to feed the rumors and profit from their popularity, never imagining you would actually have to assume the role of Resistance Leader." Shyron paused, letting the impact of the insult register, then she stood and turned her back, following one insult with another.

"The Council has given me complete autonomy to grant the demands of the Resistance. I therefore offer to eliminate forced reclamation and restore equal rations. Cross-section assignments will be permitted on a voluntary one-for-one basis, or as needs permit. Cooperatives will be permitted as long as they don't interfere with individual or section productivity. Trade will be lawful; however, it needs to be evaluated and implemented in a way that will serve the interests and goals of the entire vessel.

"For your limited role in securing the safety of the Council and relaying the demands of your Resistance sisters, I offer you a subordinate directorship and transfer privileges contingent upon performance, provided you successfully release leadership of the Resistance soldiers to the Council. Do you accept this offer, Meezra?" Shyron asked, turning suddenly around. It was clear that her offer was not a request.

"Done!" Meezra cried. The relief of closure was apparent in her voice.

"Done," Shyron concluded, making the agreement a binding contract.

Projecting her thoughts, Shyron gave the order she had been waiting to deliver. A slight shudder, barely noticeable at first, moved through the vessel, growing in intensity but slowing in frequency. Fluctuations in the area's gravity fields created waves like traveling over dips in a road, and a low rumble began to reverberate through the ship. Meezra's eyes grew wide and she grabbed the edges of the box upon which she was seated. Shyron threw her head back and extended her hands and arms above her head, as if reaching to drag the ceiling down.

"Ney Hippa Ankah!" Shyron cast the Korlah battle cry up to the ceiling.

"By fang or by claw!" the Council Leaders and Shawaugh echoed.

"Victory and honor!" Shyron wailed, carrying the last word until the Council and Shawaugh joined in and all were wailing in unison. The stunned soldiers around them did not. Having been born in transit, they were unaware of the significance of this moment.

Shyron's telepathic message had ordered the mighty vessel's flux accelerators secured. With the compressed light plasma no longer accelerated, the vessel began to slow, marking the commencement of campaign.

"Director Shawaugh, coordinate with Subdirector Meezra, locate Teela, and restore order. I ask that this be done quickly with the preservation of existence. Meezra, I expect the results of this meeting to be communicated to all Korlah throughout the vessel."

"Yes, Your Eminence!" Meezra cried, jumping to her feet and heading out. She stopped in front of Shawaugh, who blocked the door.

"Ney Hippa Ankah!" Shawaugh replied to Shyron, giving the warrior's clawed salute. "Come, Subdirector Meezra. It is time for you to prove your existence worthy of transfer privileges." Shawaugh growled and motioned for her to follow with a claw-extended finger. She turned on her heel and marched out of the chamber with Meezra following closely behind.

Challmara read the message from Teela. Now that she knew which com panel Teela was using, she sent the final version of their contingency plan, then recorded Teela's message into the vessel's log. She paused and looked around at the odd mix of Korlah who would comprise her crew. Young Korlah sat alongside those much older. Their eagerness was born of inexperience and contrasted sharply with the sober concern of their elders. She had been concerned that she would not be able to find anyone willing to join her on this mission of madness, but she was surprised by the enthusiasm and overwhelming number of volunteers that met her clandestine requests.

She wondered if the crew would be as enthusiastic if they knew Teela would not be with them, that she could not communicate with the nine aliens they were returning, or that the planet they were going to was known to be hostile. She wondered if anyone would risk her existence if she knew it was for the birthing unit that had once cleaned her quarters. She smiled weakly, knowing why. Placing her fists on her chest one atop the other and touching her chin to the top fist, she closed her eyes and prayed to Toma and Nas. She called on the essence of all who had given their existence to the campaign mission for guidance, strength, and honor.

Challmara ordered the workers modifying the vessel's exterior to bring their materials and tools inside it. The work would have to be finished in transit while they waited for Teela at the rendezvous point. Since she had not planned for a delay, they would be departing on a five-shift journey with barely two shifts' worth of provisions. And now, with four more technicians joining the contingent, their supplies would be stretched even further.

"Release transit tubes, secure access openings, and bring the grav drive on-line," Challmara ordered the pilot once the last technician was inside. "Blast shields on. Divert weapons system power to the compression drive system. Prepare to back out and perform a full-power departure toward the stern using the campaign vessel's field flow as a launch booster."

"Director, to do so could put us in contact with the plasma stream," the pilot said calmly, referring to the concentrated particle discharge that propelled the massive vessel.

"I am aware of the risks and am confident your skills will keep us clear. Pray that my calculations of our rate of acceleration are correct, or we will end our existence in the pulse wave of hull cannon," Challmara replied.

The pilot nodded gravely. Her fear that their departure was unsanctioned was confirmed. They would draw fire from the campaign vessel's lethal grid of hundreds of pulse cannons, each thousands of times more powerful than the ones mounted on heavy fighters. To be hit by even one blast would disintegrate the pod, dissolving the debris of its molecular composition into its subatomic components.

"Director, I recommend bringing the crews into the pod's central corridor during departure," the pilot requested, concerned that a near miss by a pulse cannon would incinerate her sister pilots in the vessels now manned and attached to the assault pod.

"The crews are to remain in place," replied Challmara, who quickly added, "If we are hit or broach the plasma stream, the pod will break up. Each vessel will stand a better chance of survival should that occur."

The pilot acknowledged Challmara's statement with a shake of her head, indicating that the decision and its consequences belonged to Challmara.

"Prepare for departure," the pilot announced, leaning down to speak into the new device that had been installed for spoken communications. The communication officer keyed the command as usual and the information dispersed to visual displays throughout the assault pod and its vessels. The pilot and communications officer glanced at each other; they silently agreed that the old way was better.

Why the director had insisted on adopting all these modifications discovered on the damaged human fighter, they could not understand. Certainly the single sticklike control improved maneuvering capabilities, but the new communication methods seemed archaic. If misunderstood, a communication would have to be repeated. Speed for clarity seemed an inefficient trade-off. But despite her inflexible insistence on the new devices, not to mention the political risks involved, they were eager to accept this assignment. Challmara was the best subdirector they had ever worked under, and with her advancement and this Mission, they were in a position to share the favors of her success.

Inside the cargo vessel, Ruth and Margaret watched with concern as the windows they had been peering through suddenly went opaque. Moments later, they heard a low hum that grew in intensity and was followed by several dull thumps.

“We’re leaving! Everybody take a seat,” Ruth shouted, recognizing the distinctive sounds of the ship’s engines and the impact of pulse weapons.

“What about the others? We can’t leave without them,” Margaret whispered, gesturing furtively at empty seats.

“I don’t know. I’m sorry . . . I don’t know,” Ruth said, burdened with the responsibility of answering this question and guilty that she could not.

A bright flash illuminated the corridor outside the biotech facility where Khranga and Beth were being treated for injuries. Khranga leapt from her table, stumbled and nearly fell when the next flash impacted a warrior just outside the door. A warrior inside keyed the doorway shut as more blasts struck the area.

Beth slid off her table and brandished her energized rifle next to Crystal’s gurney. Shouting orders, Khranga and the warriors with her took up defensive positions behind the equipment and gurneys in the chamber. Beth scanned the room to determine whether the biotechs who had been treating them moments before were hiding or gone; she hadn’t noticed them leave.

Crystal sat up, wakened by the cacophony around her. Slabs of nutrient gel fell off her burned and swollen face and landed in her lap.

"What . . . what's happening?" she croaked breathlessly. Her chest and throat ached. Although they had been repaired to a degree that would have taken weeks without Korlah technology, she still needed time to heal.

"Don't know. Can you stand?" Beth asked, putting one arm around Crystal to guide her off the table, keeping her energized pulse rifle leveled at the door that was now being pounded with pulse blasts.

With Beth's help, Crystal stood. Together they made their way into a narrow alcove at the back of the room. Equipment and materials were neatly stacked from the floor to the ceiling on each side of the aisle.

"There's no way out," Crystal gasped. The short journey made her labor to suck air into her bruised lungs.

"Gotta be," answered Beth.

Handing Crystal the rifle, Beth began to examine the exposed walls of the narrow aisle, certain the biotechs had exited this way. She searched around and behind everything but found only smooth, seamless walls. At the end of the aisle, she found a thin sliver of exposed wall approximately twelve-inches wide. When she tapped it with her fist it seemed solid enough, but when she felt with her hand, she detected the seam of a door like the one on the cargo ship. Exploring further, she found the indentations that acted as the controls and pressed one and then the other until the panel melted away, revealing only darkness beyond. Flashes of light and screams in the outer room alerted Beth that the chamber door had finally failed. Whoever was attacking was now storming the room.

"This way!" Beth cried. Grabbing Crystal by the arm, Beth spun her around and shoved her through the narrow opening. Crystal screamed in pain. Pushing in behind her, Beth turned and fumbled for the controls to close the panel just as a warrior appeared in the alcove and pointed a weapon at her.

Beth managed to press one of the indentations as the glowing end of the warrior's pulse rifle flashed. Anticipating the impact, she turned her head and closed her eyes as the panel materialized, the blast heating it to a white-hot glow inches from her face. The light illuminated the narrow passage just long enough for Crystal to see that the passage went both right and left. She began to move to the left in the darkness.

"No, go right," Beth said, nudging her from behind.

"Why right?" Crystal questioned.

"Go! God damn it, before I shove this rifle up your ass," Beth screamed. She prodded Crystal with the heated tip, knowing the warrior that had shot at her would soon be opening the panel.

"Left would take us back to the hallway outside the room we just left," Beth said.

Crystal stumbled forward into the darkness with one hand out and one hand on the wall. Beth repeatedly bumped into her as she walked backward with her rifle energized and aimed at where she expected the panel to open. After about ten meters, Crystal suddenly stopped and Beth bumped hard into her.

"It's a dead end. I knew we should have gone left," Crystal cried.

"There's a panel. Look for the controls halfway up one side or the other," answered Beth, unwilling to turn and leave the passage behind them unguarded. Her caution was immediately rewarded when the glowing tip of a pulse rifle appeared near the panel down the passage. Beth fired without hesitation, her accuracy evident in a shower of sparks and the disappearance of the weapon's visible glow. Feeling air movement behind her, she knew Crystal had opened the panel.

"It's open!" Crystal cried, pulling Beth into an arched entryway just off a wide corridor.

"Shut the door!" Beth ordered, firing into the darkness for good measure. Crystal obeyed. Beth turned and poked her head out of the entryway, looking first one way and then the other. Dimly lit, like most of the corridors, the passage to the right was more brightly illuminated and stretched off into the distance as far as she could see. To the left, it quickly disappeared in darkness.

"This way. Stay against the wall," Beth whispered, moving down the corridor toward the darkness.

"Teela said they could see in the dark," Crystal whispered back hoarsely, limping closely along behind Beth.

"The darkness is our friend. Fear and *noise*, our enemies. So shut up," Beth growled.

After a short distance, they came to an intersection. They turned right and followed the corridor to another intersection, where they turned left down a much narrower corridor. After proceeding for some time without encountering another intersection, they approached what appeared to be the end of the corridor. A light shone down from an opening in the ceiling. Approaching cautiously, they looked up into a large chamber with a bright, transparent orb in the center. The floor at the end of the hall curved up gradually into the wall and then, about eight feet up, curved away and into the chamber above.

"What is that? Are we going in there?" Crystal whispered. The sound of footsteps and the rattle of armor and weapons meant they would not be able to go back, and there were no entryways in this corridor.

"Come on, I'll give you a boost." Beth moved up the curved floor. She stopped halfway and looked at Crystal, who was now standing at a 30-degree angle to her. Where Beth now stood at the center of the lower curve, it felt to her as though the room had moved and she was standing vertically. She moved up further until she stood on the center of the wall perpendicular to where Crystal stood. Looking over Crystal's shoulder, Beth could see the glowing tips of pulse rifles bobbing in the darkness behind.

"It's a gravity thing, sort of like those elevator tubes. Let's go!" Beth shouted, realizing whispering was no longer necessary.

Crystal followed Beth into the chamber above as pulse blasts began to strike the area where they had been standing.

26 - Spectacle

Afron's forces entered the cavernous hangar as the assault pod began to pull away from its mooring. Realizing that their prize was escaping, the warriors began to fire, but their blasts were dissipated by distance and atmosphere. They watched impotently as the vessel moved past the rows and rows of fighters until it was no longer in range. Having failed to capture the pod, they headed for the weapons defense center, where they hoped to make a final stand.

Challmara guided the assault pod toward a series of large hexagonal chambers, shaped like the cells of a beehive; the openings were armored transit locks that jutted from the ship's hull. The pod slowed to enter the portal that would take them through the campaign vessel's thick outer shell. It flipped end over end at the last moment and backed into the lock. Like a shell in the chamber of a revolver, the Pod was carried into darkness as the lock rotated. Once the chamber had passed through the hull, dark melted away to a dull, star-streaked space. Powerful gravitational fields centered the pod in the chamber as the pilot matched its engines' output to that of the campaign vessel's in preparation for launch.

"Director, we are overloaded," the pilot warned. "We are at full reverse and still have a twenty percent mismatch. We can use it for launch, but the inertia suppressors may fail to compensate."

Challmara didn't need to do the math. The deceleration from hyperlight speed would throw every unfixed object against the forward bulkheads and crush all organic life into biological soup. Her intimate knowledge of the equipment's design, function, and failures told her they were playing Russian roulette. Aware that Afron's forces were likely manning fighters ready to destroy them if they attempted to return to the interior, she stood to deliver the order that could well be the last she would ever make.

A rippling shudder passed through the assault pod, causing her to stumble forward. She braced herself on the back of the pilot's chair and watched as they shot backward out of the launch chamber. The pilot adjusted the speed as they reversed rapidly, making them slingshot forward again. Although the sudden directional change and stressed power demands did not cause the inertia suppressors to fail, they could not fully compensate for the change in course.

Without the grip of her seat's gravitational restraints, Challmara was thrown backward. Her head and shoulders struck the back of her command chair as she somersaulted over the top before crashing into the wall behind. Realizing that they would soon hit the edge of the launch chamber they were rocketing toward, the pilot veered away from the hull. The pod's dynamics were designed for controlled forward travel—not for precise handling in reverse. As the pilot fought the controls, the pod was thrown sideways into the campaign vessel's magnetic wash. They went into an uncontrolled spin within the electromagnetic field that would carry them toward the plasma stream of the larger ship's engines.

The pulse cannons of the campaign vessel were arrayed in a series of rings and strips that ran the diameter and length of the ship. Normally, they were retracted into blisters that acted as articulating turrets, but when they were needed, they extended and made the hull appear to bristle with hairs. The cannon deployed automatically when they perceived the assault pod as a threat. Ten-feet in diameter and thirty-feet long, they emerged from their blisters with amazing speed and swiveled to take aim.

As it neared the stern of the campaign vessel, the spinning assault pod struck the end of a cannon that was swiveling into position. In that fraction of a second, the cannon impaled one of the pod's cargo ships. The momentum wrenched the cannon over the axis of its articulation, vaulting the pod out and away from the vessel and ripping the much smaller cargo ship from its moorings.

The impact interrupted the pod's spin just long enough for its pilot to regain control. She accelerated past the campaign vessel's stern and rode the wake of the plasma stream out of reach of the hull cannon. The ruined cargo ship tumbled out of control and was vaporized by the simultaneous blast of three cannon. The sparkling ionic dust that remained was drawn into the plasma stream like wisps of crematory smoke into the darkness of night.

Shawaugh followed Meezra through the labyrinthine passages that twisted and turned through the energy section. Deep within the vessel, they stopped outside a door with heavy bracing and reinforced panels. Meezra turned to Shawaugh and made a conciliatory palm gesture, her apology for what she was about to say.

"A group of Nons has instigated a situation in the birthing section. They have taken up weapons and are attacking all who oppose them. We tried to contain them, but they are without reason."

"What do they want? Have you tried to negotiate?" Shawaugh demanded.

"They have a leader who calls herself the Oracle. She claims to follow the orders of Shawlmon. It's not just birthers; they are conscripting all they encounter. They call themselves the Claws of Shawlmon. Those who survive an attack must swear allegiance to Shawlmon and the ancient laws of Korlah or cease to exist. They are searching for where Shawlmon is being held, believing she will lead them to victory."

"Does Teela know of this?" Shawaugh asked, unsure that she could trust Meezra's information.

"After the bio section battle, she collapsed in transit to the vessel being prepared for her departure. I sent word when Afron's forces broke through our blockade, but my efforts to contact her since have been unsuccessful."

Shawaugh grabbed Meezra's jumpsuit. "How badly is Teela damaged? Is she being repaired? How many other casualties are there?" she demanded.

Meezra recounted the last few shifts as accurately and honestly as she could, then led Shawaugh into the armored room.

Packed with communications and monitoring equipment, both traditional and experimental, the large room felt claustrophobic. Each of eleven stations was manned by two technicians that monitored, received, and relayed spoken and visual information. This was the secret nerve center of Meezra's illicit activity. As Meezra and Shawaugh entered the room, a technician leapt from her seat to meet them. The din of activity and flashing panels indicated an organization in crisis.

"Meezra! The leader is not answering. The Claws have pushed through the education section. The students have joined the mothers, and together they have taken the supplies section. Our forces are dissolving in their path, either to join them or because they are unwilling or fearful of resisting. Afron is aware of their advance and has fled the security section. Her forces have split. A small contingent is moving through the health section and the remainder has moved into the outer levels of the arms section.

What should we do? Where is the leader?" The technician was panicked and dismayed.

"Our leader is here!" Meezra bellowed, pointing to Shawaugh when all heads turned.

It had been a lifetime and many cycles since Shawaugh was in a crisis that demanded adept leadership. And although nothing in her memory compared to the disarray of this situation, she put aside her burning desire to rip Meezra's head off and instead gave the group before her a resounding and inspiring warrior's salute.

"Order all forces to avoid contact and conflict with the Claws of Shawlmon. Relay the message throughout all sections that the Council of Leaders has agreed to all Resistance demands. Inform all personnel to return to their assigned sections and duties immediately. I want to know where the unit calling herself 'the Oracle' is located. Find her!" Shawaugh ordered.

The technicians immediately returned to their stations. The noise in the room rose to an unprecedented level as they began to carry out Shawaugh's orders; no one questioned their content or validity.

"You have just ordered your army to disband! There will be no one to stop Afron," Meezra whined.

"The Resistance has done what was needed to get the Council to grant their demands. Now we must communicate this to everyone. When everyone knows what has happened, Afron will be defeated. Have the technicians give the repair of com stations top priority. Keep repeating that the demands have been met. List what has been granted."

"Where are you going?" cried Meezra as Shawaugh turned toward the door.

"There!" Shawaugh said, pointing to a monitor that showed birthing units and warriors engaged in a firefight in a corridor of the health section. "You are in charge of this communication center, Subdirector Meezra. Monitor my location, and message me as needed." Shawaugh marched out the door.

Moving as quickly as their bruised and battered bodies would carry them, Beth and Crystal entered the spherical chamber. The illumination brightened with their entry. Overhead, a transparent sphere thirty feet in diameter floated without any visible means of support. The room itself was about 150 feet across, with four evenly spaced identical entrances. Aisles separated viewing sections with reclining seats that gave a comfortable view of the floating sphere. At two points across from each other, two nine-foot high cylinders with archways like transit tubes pointed at the sphere like the barrels of cannon.

"What . . . is . . . that . . . thing?" Crystal wheezed between labored gasps as she stopped to stare at the floating sphere.

"Get down!" Beth shouted, throwing Crystal to the ground an instant before a pulse blast flashed where they had been standing. The superheated air in its path expanded to create a hot gust of wind.

"Kahshinki moo pah!" Beth spat out the insult, followed by the best growl she could manage, hoping to shame her attackers to restrain their assault as Teela had instructed.

"Moo pah! Moo pah!" Beth screamed as more blasts pounded around them.

The last time she'd called a warrior a coward in its own language, she was looking for a fight. Not because it would improve her reputation, as Teela had implied, but rather to exact revenge for the attack in the Nursery. During that encounter, Beth had knocked four warriors senseless in relatively short order before her exhaustion and minor injuries had slowed her down. In the end, she couldn't block the kick to her abdomen that sent her to the floor.

Now, as then, she pulled off the loose-fitting gown the doctors had given her and flung it into the air before standing up to face the warriors naked. Long purple lines on her arms, back, and abdomen attested to the repaired lacerations inflicted by Korlah claws that day. The Korlah's weapons were poised and a strained silence filled the chamber. Only the sound of boots and the rustle of armor could be heard as warriors shifted their positions.

Emerging into the chamber from three of the entrances, warriors with energized pulse rifles moved to surround them. Beth turned around slowly, meeting their eyes and attempting to utter the challenges Teela had taught her. The warriors began to shout and growl. At first, Beth thought they were directing insults at her, but she quickly realized that an argument had erupted among them and an armed standoff was taking place. The argument stopped as quickly as it started and the room once again became silent. The two warriors at the center of the argument de-energized their weapons and set them on the ground before beginning to strip off their armor and clothing.

"Damn the bad luck. I think they're gonna fight each other," Beth said sarcastically.

"No, they were arguing over who will get the honor of killing you. The big one is Ruwaugh; she fought you in the Nursery and beat you. They weren't supposed to hurt us before, but now . . . they're going to kill you . . . but . . . not me," Crystal said, pressing her temples with her palms as though the strain of translating hurt her head.

"How the hell would you know who they are and what they're saying?" Beth asked.

Crystal stood up and scanned the ring of armed warriors around them. She counted at least twenty, but she doubted Beth could beat that many, even one on one. She pulled her gown off and tossed it out with Beth's.

"What the hell are you doing?" Beth growled.

"I've been in a few fights. I can hold my own," Crystal said.

"You're in no condition to fight! Get dressed, lie down, and play dead. That's an order!"

"Too late. Look," Crystal said as the two warriors approached. The one in the lead gave Beth a clawed salute and challenging glare before walking past them with a loud growl. The other did the same, focusing on Crystal.

Walking the perimeter of the spherical room, the warriors approached one of the two arched cylinders. The first warrior stepped in and floated up and into the transparent sphere through an opening Beth had missed earlier. The second warrior followed close behind. Once they were both inside, the opening disappeared again.

The warriors on the floor gestured to the other cylinder. When the women didn't move, one of the warriors shouted, "Moo pah!" The others echoed the cry.

"You stay here," Beth said calmly, turning and marching toward the cylinder.

"Like hell! We challenged 'em, and they accepted. I must fight now or lose my honor," Crystal said stiffly in a mechanical monotone.

"Screw honor!" Beth shouted.

"They murdered Eepalla," Crystal shouted back. "I realize that to you she was just another spaghetti head, but she was my friend! When someone screws with my friends, they screw with me. I'm gonna hurt these assholes. It's something I have to do! Can you understand that?"

"Yeah, I understand. But you better understand this; they will hurt us, real bad, maybe real permanent," Beth yelled. She remembered clearly the events of what couldn't have been more than a day ago, when she found herself lying on the floor of the Nursery trying to hold her intestines in place as they dragged her out by her feet.

She wasn't sure how much blood she had lost. She was already weak and light-headed. Whatever magic the Korlah doctors had worked to put her back together, it couldn't be a good idea to take herself apart again. The lacerations seemed securely fused, and although her severed muscles had somehow been reattached, they were sore and stiff. The thought of repeating the painful experience weighed heavily on her mind. Crystal had been knocked senseless and stayed that way throughout the repair process. Beth, on the other hand, recalled with sharp clarity being sliced and slashed until she fell to the ground and waited for death in a pool of her own blood.

Beth turned and scanned Crystal's naked body. Much of the hair on her head had been burned off, leaving the matted remains hanging in disarray. Heavy bruising on her face, chest, and shoulders were evidence of the nonlethal blasts she had received when she charged through the Nursery window to avenge Eepalla's death. Intense determination was forcing its way past her swollen eyes and lips. But it was her lower abdomen, including a portion of her right hip, that bothered Beth. What was yesterday a charred hole through her upper pelvis and waist was repaired with what must have been Korlah bone and tissue.

Seeing Beth's glances, Crystal looked down and for the first time noticed the repair. She let out a short, high-pitched whimper and reached down, stopping just short of touching it.

Beth spoke, more to interrupt Crystal's panic than to continue to dissuade her from fighting. "Last time they wanted me alive, but I don't think that's the case right now. If we get lucky and beat these two, they'll send in two more, and then two more after that. They won't stop until we're dead. Stay here. You're still pretty banged up. Don't give them a reason to kill you, and . . . maybe they won't. There's no shame in trying to stay alive."

Recovering from her initial shock, Crystal rubbed her hand over the hollow on her side. Her fingertips lingered at the junction of mottled alien skin and her own smooth flesh. She marveled at the seamless attachment of two visibly and texturally different skins. Her hip ached and burned from exertion, the spliced and freshly attached bone and muscles wailing for time to heal. She looked up and glared at Beth.

"Teela will come back for us, just like before. They want me alive, so we need to stick together and buy time—whatever it takes. Anyway, they got a piece of me. Now it's my turn to get a piece of them."

"It's your funeral, kid. I warned you, and now I'm telling you: stay out of my way, and stay out of theirs. Distract and delay, but do not engage them. When I knock one down, you move in quick and keep it down. These are some badass bitches, and you need to understand that if you fight one, you're gonna bleed—guaranteed. One false move and they will gut you like a fish! You sure you're up to this?"

"Fucking-A! Let's rock and roll!" Crystal shouted, her enthusiasm jarring.

Beth gave her a grave nod and hoped she had made an impression. It was difficult to understate the seriousness of battle with a clawed and fanged opponent who was skilled and experienced in hand-to-hand combat. Her penchant for fighting had been replaced with an uneasy dread. She was unaccustomed to defeat, and under the circumstances, she could not foresee a victory.

Beth stepped through the arch and was lifted suddenly off her feet. She felt as though she were upside down and falling; she fought the urge to throw her arms out and flail like she had during her first transfer tube ascent. She looked up instead to see her opponents waiting at the opposite side of the sphere. The warriors too were closely following the women's entries.

As she entered the sphere, Beth felt the sensation of falling dissipate. She leaned forward to move out of the invisible force that held her in midair and stepped inside. The surface felt cold and slick on the bottoms of her bare feet, and she was immediately concerned about traction. She twisted and stepped a few times to check her footing. The Korlah walked on the balls of their feet; she had at least the advantage of superior stability.

Crystal rose into the sphere as Beth had. Once they were both inside, they watched the opening vanish as material from the surrounding area flowed in to seal it. Beth tapped it with her foot to verify its solidity.

"We wait for them to attack. Stay clear of their claws. They're razor sharp and will cut you like a knife. They also bite—those fangs make for some nasty puncture wounds. Oh, by the way, they use the claws on their feet too, so watch for kicks."

"Shit! Why didn't you tell me that when you were trying to talk me out of fighting? It might have worked," Crystal joked.

"Sorry, kid." Beth's apology was sincere. "Just stick with the plan. I'll knock 'em down, and you keep 'em down. Here they come!" She was dead serious as the Korlah warriors began their attack.

Moving in opposite directions, the warriors approached them from two sides. Beth crouched perpendicular to their approach. Seemingly staring away from them, she watched them with her peripheral vision, shifting and turning around suddenly as they moved to get behind her.

Crystal watched the approach from Beth's right, unsure of what to do. Seeing that they were focused on Beth and meant to trap her between them, she feigned an attack, backing away at the last second and dodging to one side. Sensing Crystal's intention, Beth turned her full attention to the other warrior and pressed a determined attack, using offensive blows with a conservative tact to avoid the warrior's claws.

The warrior proved to be worthy of her title, blocking Beth's aggression and meting out a severe raking of Beth's left forearm. Beth dodged out of range of the Korlah's sweeping blows and claws. The other Korlah had broken off its pursuit of Crystal, who had, much to Beth's relief, run away when the warrior came after her.

The two Korlah approached side-by-side, arms extended and high stepping so that with each step, Beth faced three clawed limbs from each. With their thumbs tucked into their palms and the remaining fingers spread and claws extended, they presented their favored means of attack; however, as Beth had painfully discovered, the clawed toes on their feet were quite capable weapons as well.

Beth was convinced this was the Korlah she had fought in the Nursery. It seemed to anticipate her moves, defending, rather than attacking. Those warriors had lost because they expected her to fight like they did, with sweeping, raking, clawing actions. But she had kept her limbs close to her body, deflecting their blows and protecting her throat and abdomen from their slicing claws while moving in close to jackhammer punishing punches into their bodies and heads. Her heavy-fisted attack, wholly different from the rapid sweeps and slaps of the Korlah, had provided an element of surprise that was apparently no longer a surprise.

Shifting her weight constantly in a battle dance that marked her fighting style, Beth felt the greasy slickness of blood dripping from fresh wounds on her arm, which threatened the traction she needed on the slick surface of the sphere.

Beth could see Crystal moving to get behind the warrior on her left. She knew the warrior would turn; anticipating that, Beth sidestepped to her right and then back, drawing the warrior on her right forward. As the one on her left spun to meet Crystal's advance, Beth purposefully stumbled backward, dropping her arms as though to brace her fall and mimicking the fatal mistake she had made in the Nursery, the mistake that had nearly disemboweled her.

The Korlah took the bait. She raised her leg and lunged at Beth's exposed abdomen. Dropping her right shoulder and swinging her fisted arm up in a tight body-hugging hook, she caught her attacker's foot and drove it up and over her shoulder, the claws grazing her neck and ear. Using the full fifty square inches of traction her feet afforded, she drove herself forward. Swinging her arm down with all of her weight and body strength, she slammed into the soft notch of flesh just below the kneecap of the leg supporting the warrior's full weight. With a pop like a muffled gunshot, Beth drove the ulna, the thick bone of her forearm, between the bones of the warrior's leg. She felt the bones separate and come apart at the same instant she felt the sting of claws drag across her naked back and heard the now familiar scrape of the sharp tips creasing her ribs as they severed her trapezius muscles. Beth rolled away and jumped into a crouch, quickly appraising the situation.

The warrior she had struck was on the floor, her right leg hyperextended at the knee and obviously broken or dislocated. The warrior was on her side, hissing and sucking, her eyes so wide with pain that Beth realized for the first time that their eyes had whites like humans'. The thin white ring made the iris, at least twice the size of a human's, look even larger, and the look of pain all the more intense.

A wide smear of blood covered the floor between them. Beth could feel blood running down the back of her legs. Unable to raise her left arm, she realized that this small victory had been costly. She slipped in the puddle of blood forming at her feet and moved cautiously to meet the advance of the second warrior, who had abandoned her pursuit of Crystal after her companion went down.

Circling each other cautiously, the two sized each other up. Beth noted bruises and swelling on this warrior's face. When she bared her fangs, as Korlah do when angry or challenging another, she saw that one had been cleanly broken off at the gum line.

"I kicked your ass once, and I'm gonna kick it again," Beth growled, recognizing her as the first Korlah she had fought in the Nursery.

It had taken less than a minute to knock her out, sending her two-inch fang flying across the Nursery floor with a hard right hook. Seeing the missing fang gave Beth the strategy for this fight. She kept her distance and pantomimed fangs in her mouth with her fingers, first breaking off one and then the other. The warrior, its mane of spaghetti-like tendrils bright red and fully engorged, made a blood-curdling shriek with her arms and claws extended. Beth shot back the extended middle finger of her right hand.

"Try this with two fingers," she taunted, beckoning with her middle finger. "Can't do it, can ya? I'm gonna kick your ass, you two-fingered freak!"

The Korlah on the floor was trying futilely to push her leg back into joint when Crystal, fearing that she might get back up, ran up and kicked her deftly in the back of the head. Screaming curses in Korlah, she twisted onto her side and used both arms to lift herself onto her one good leg. Crystal moved in again and kicked her in the side. The Korlah grabbed her by the ankle, embedding the claws of her two thumbs between Crystal's heel and Achilles tendon.

Crystal shrieked in surprise and pain as she fell onto the floor. The Korlah grabbed her with its other hand further up the same leg, digging its claws into her muscles before releasing the other hand and finding another hold further up, climbing Crystal's wildly writhing body. Kicking in panicked desperation, Crystal tried unsuccessfully to escape. Grabbing the ridges of Crystal's hips with both hands, the Korlah pulled itself up and reared its head back, mouth wide and fangs exposed, before driving its head down toward Crystal's abdomen.

Abandoning hope of escape, Crystal drove a hard right hook into the warrior's head, snapping it to one side before it could plunge its fangs into her flesh. Rolling on top of the Korlah, Crystal put her full weight onto its chest. She grabbed one of the warrior's hands with both of hers and yanked it from her hip, feeling the scrape of claws on her pelvic bone. She forced the arm down and pinned it with her knee. The Korlah drew its bloody claws from Crystal's other hip and struck at her face. Crystal jerked back to avoid the blow and felt the hand pass under her chin. With both hands now free, she grabbed the warrior's hand and pinned it beneath her other knee.

As Crystal shifted her weight, the warrior strained forward to unseat her attacker. Crystal released the struggling arm while driving her elbow down hard into the pitted area between her opponent's eyes. With a sound like crunching potato chips, her elbow sunk half an inch into the face and the warrior went limp. Blood began to cover the warrior's face, but it was jetting in spurts that fell to the floor, first on one side and then the other.

Crystal sat up and her hands darted to her throat. The blood was not coming from the warrior, but from where the warrior had raked the soft tissues of her throat. Unable to swallow, Crystal tried to draw air and choked on the blood filling her trachea. She coughed a violent crimson cloud and covered her mouth; bubbles erupted between her fingers.

It doesn't hurt. It can't be that bad, Crystal thought, coughing again. When she opened her mouth to clear her throat, a thick stream of blood poured onto the face of the warrior beneath her. Suddenly weak, she tried to call Beth, but numbness paralyzed her. The sphere seemed to close in around her as she fell forward onto her hands. Between the blood-slicked floor and her fading strength, her arms slid slowly out to each side and she slumped forward until the top of her head rested on the floor and her face touched the top of the Korlah's head, trapped beneath her. Blood flowed from her mouth, nose, and throat and filled her eyes. Her vision blurred and her thoughts faded as she surrendered consciousness.

Beth felt the prickly flush and noted her tunneling vision, and knew the blood loss was taking its toll. She was concerned about blacking out, but it was Crystal's screams that convinced her to attack first. She put her head down to protect her face and throat and stormed forward, her fists clenched in tight balls in front of her, slightly below her face. Her warrior raked first one arm from shoulder to wrist and then the other as soon as Beth charged. Now in close, Beth made her move. Her shredded left arm gave a feeble uppercut to her opponent's jaw. The warrior blocked the hook, as Beth expected she would.

But the warrior never saw the right hook that Beth delivered with all the power and strength an adrenaline-drenched act of desperation could produce. It caught the warrior on the side of its face, snapping her head around and back with the crack of a major league home run. The Korlah's last fang was shattered and flew up into the center of the sphere, where it hung suspended, trapped in the heart of the gravitational field. The warrior's arms dropped limply as she fell to the floor, sliding across the sphere on her head and shoulders in one of many puddles of blood until she came to a stop.

Beth turned her attention back to Crystal and the other Korlah and found them both motionless. The warrior was on her back in a spreading lake of blood, Crystal slumped over her head. Slipping and sliding through the puddles, spatters, and pools of vermillion that coated the inside of the sphere, Beth ran to Crystal. She dropped down on her knees and gently lifted Crystal off the warrior and turned her over. Crystal's blood-soaked head fell back heavily, opening two deep gashes across her throat, above and below her larynx. Pulling the slack body tightly against hers, Beth screamed in anguish, forcing the air from her lungs with her friend's lifeless body. She sobbed deeply and drew Crystal into her lap, and began to rock her like a child. For the first time in her life, she cried without shame.

The room beyond the sphere began to flash, drawing Beth from the hypnotic trance of her grief. Through her tears, she saw activity and the flash of pulse weapons. She wiped her eyes with the back of her hand and focused. A group of Korlah wearing the light blue gowns of the Nursery was charging into the fire of pulse weapons. As quickly as one group fell in the warriors' well-aimed blasts, another would replace them, leaping over the bodies or dropping behind them for cover. The birthing units fired wildly, some blasts striking the sphere. Within seconds of their initial attack, birthing units charged in at all four entrances, often firing into their group, now caught in the crossfire.

After gently laying Crystal down, Beth moved to an area that wasn't as thickly covered with blood to gain a better view of the battle outside. The twenty or so warriors had been quickly overrun by the mob, but not before killing and wounding several hundred of their attackers. A scene of horrific carnage was covered with a pall of blue-gray smoke, the wounded writhing in pain or hobbling about with missing limbs while the remaining birthing units exacted their revenge on fallen warriors. Some continued to blast into the lifeless bodies while others hacked at them with long blades, holding up heads and arms as trophies. Eventually they settled down to tend the injured. Some dipped their hands in the entrails of their enemies and made bloody handprints on each other's gowns.

Inside the sphere, it was quiet. The only sounds were Beth's labored breathing and a low moan from the toothless Korlah, who was regaining consciousness. Beth rose painfully and stalked over. The Korlah rose up on one elbow and Beth knocked it back to the floor, her knee crushing its throat as she dropped down with her full weight. Grabbing Beth's knee weakly with both hands, the Korlah kicked several times before once again passing out. Beth looked over at the other Korlah. In an instant, she decided its fate. She rocked back onto her feet and moved toward where it lay next to Crystal.

A hissing noise drew her attention away. It grew louder as sounds from outside spilled into the sphere through the reappearing entrances. Beth could see armed birthing units rise from both of the arched cylinders, their energized weapons pointed toward the openings in the sphere through which they were about to pass.

The adrenaline rush dissipated and Beth sat down, exhausted. Depression and apathy overwhelmed her. She looked at the deep lacerations on her arms with detached interest, amazed that despite the severity of her wounds, the bleeding had nearly stopped. Her head wobbled in slow circles and the room began to spin around her. Her eyelids felt unbearably heavy and finally closed, despite her strain to keep them open. She shivered uncontrollably.

No longer remembering why she wanted to keep her eyes open, she fell backward. Her head hit the floor with a dull thump, yet the hard surface of the sphere felt like a thick feather pillow to her. The sounds around her muted to near silence, and through it she was certain she could hear Crystal's voice.

We kicked their asses, didn't we, Beth?

Beth wanted to answer, but her mouth would not comply. She managed one nod of affirmation before succumbing to the embrace of oblivion.

27 - Shawlmon

The gravitational forces generated by the chairs kept the humans from being thrown out of their seats when the assault pod made its haphazard departure from the campaign vessel. However, the pulse rifles sitting on the floor by the seats had nothing to restrain them. When the pod crashed into the hull cannon, rifles were hurled about the compartment.

Two of the tumbling guns hit passengers. Ann was struck in the back of the head and began to bleed profusely, but it looked worse than it was. Rebecca suffered a severely fractured collarbone, but since she usually screamed and ranted during a crisis, everyone ignored her.

The passenger area of the cargo vessel was a cacophony of screams and shouts. Having removed the bindings from his wrists earlier, Captain Ramsey took advantage of the confusion. He stepped from his seat the instant it released him and picked up a nearby rifle. The moment the pulse chamber registered a charge, he fired it squarely into the center of Ruth's chest where she sat ten feet away. Marsha charged her rifle, but before she could use it, Ramsey shot her in the lower abdomen. The blast threw her against the wall and she collapsed onto the floor. Ramsey confiscated Ruth's and Marsha's rifles and went about collecting the remaining weapons, moving them to the forward end of the passenger area. He pulled the gag from his mouth, threw it at the group, cleared his throat and spit on the floor.

"I will kill anyone that leaves their seat," he announced calmly.

He slowly swept his weapon across the group at head level, gauging the remaining women for threats. Seeing only terror, he turned to the front of the vessel and disappeared around the corner. A moment later, the sound of three pulse blasts in rapid sequence shattered the silence.

"He's going to get us all killed! We have to stop him," Catherine whispered.

"He said he wants to take us home," Ann countered weakly.

"Bullshit! He couldn't care less about us; he's just trying to save his own ass. We take him back, and he's a war criminal. He takes us back, and how much you wanna bet we disappear. This is shit the government is gonna wanna cover up or, more likely, bury. You know what I mean?" Catherine cried angrily, her voice rising.

"Shhh! We need a plan, and we need it fast," Margaret whispered, leaving her seat and moving stealthily toward the edge of the partition that separated the front of the vessel from the rear.

Keeping a wary eye on the rear of the cargo ship, Ramsey pulled the unconscious Korlah from their seats and piled them to one side. He examined his rifle more closely and found another setting; he pressed the indentation and noted the crackling increase in the weapon's electronic signature.

Haven't seen this before. What is this? A kill setting? Ramsey considered the differences from the pulse weapons he had been trained on.

"Don't shoot! They're planning to rush you," Ann cried, stepping out from behind the partition, her arms raised over her head.

"You frigging traitor!" Catherine screamed.

Ramsey fired a crackling, lethal flash into the bulkhead between Ann and the partition. The blast left a smoking indentation in the smooth gray surface.

"My weapon is now set to kill! You rush, you die!"

"I just want to go home," Ann sobbed, bending over and holding her bloody head in her hands.

A shoe flew out from behind the partition and struck Ann on the top of her head. More shoes followed, hitting the wall and floor around her.

"You're never going home, bitch! If he doesn't kill you, we will!" Catherine screamed, hurling another shoe.

"Get over here!" Ramsey ordered.

Ann scurried over, her slight frame seeming even more diminutive as she crouched and cowered. "I just want to go home," she sobbed again softly, stopping several feet short of Ramsey.

"If you do exactly what I tell you, I promise I'll take you home," he said with all the sincerity he could muster. He'd overheard what Catherine said about government cover-ups. He knew she was right; these people would disappear, and he wouldn't ask why or where. He had helped make people disappear before; that's what had gotten this assignment, and surviving it was now his primary concern.

"Okay," Ann whispered, blowing her nose on the sleeve of her bloody gown.

"Sit here," Ramsey said, pointing to the seat next to him, the Korlah crew sprawled unconscious on the floor nearby.

It would be difficult, if not impossible, to pilot this ship while fending off an attack from its passengers. Ramsey weighed his options. He considered stunning the remaining humans and breaking their necks, but it seemed easier to kill them with this weapon. He had killed many times in the past, but always from a distance. He pushed the button that sent the bomb or missile to a predetermined location, and it did the killing—not him. Many times, many people, and he had never asked why or whether it was right or wrong. He had been trained in hand-to-hand combat; his psychological profile said that if ordered, he would kill without hesitation.

Ramsey studied Ann's blood-streaked face. The bleeding from her head wound had stopped. Her eyes, although red and puffy from crying, seemed clear and lucid. She was obviously a coward and craved his protection. Cowards made good defenders. If they were convinced that surrender was not an option, fear would give them the courage they needed.

"You know how to use one of these?" he asked Ann, gesturing with the pulse rifle he was pointing at her chest.

"I just want to go home," Ann sobbed pathetically, shaking her head.

"If your companions get hold of you or, worse yet, the noodle heads, they're gonna beat the hell out you or, more likely, toss you out an airlock. If you really want to go home, you're going to need to help me. Now pick up one of those rifles," he commanded, pointing with his energized rifle.

Ann went to the pile of weapons and picked one up. Holding it awkwardly in her arms, she faced Ramsey with her head down. Her eyes nervously searched the details of the rifle's construction as though trying to fathom its function. One of the Korlah moaned and moved slightly, drawing Ann's attention.

"Put your thumb into the lower indentation on the stock, just above the trigger area, and hold it there until you hear the weapon energize," Ramsey ordered.

Ann obeyed and the weapon whined to life as its pulse chamber charged. Ramsey carefully repositioned his rifle so that, although it was not directly pointed at Ann, it could be quickly brought to bear if needed.

"The noodle heads are waking up. If you really want to go home, use your weapon to put them down."

"What? What do you mean?" Ann stammered, looking up at him.

"I need you to prove whose side you're on. They are the enemy and represent the greatest threat to our escape. Press your thumb into the upper indentation to raise the weapon to a lethal charge, point it at the enemy, and shoot. Do it in the head. Do it now!" If she made it over this hurdle, he may actually be able to rely on her. If she refused, he would have to kill her and the others.

Ann looked at the Korlah lying on the floor, then at Captain Ramsey, and finally at the rifle in her arms. Turning the rifle on its side, she began to fumble with the controls, first de-energizing it and then re-energizing it, but failing to switch it into the lethal mode.

"I . . . I don't know. I'm not sure how," Ann mumbled. She fumbled and nearly dropped the weapon.

"Good God, woman!" Ramsey exclaimed, cradling his rifle and stepping toward her.

Before he took his second step, Ann shouldered her energized rifle with fluid ease and fired into the center of Captain Ramsey's chest. The blast lifted him off his feet and sent him flying backward onto the control console. He rolled off and his rifle tumbled out of his reach.

"I got him!" Ann screamed. "I got him. I got him good. I think I heard some ribs snap. He's not moving. I . . . I . . . might have killed him."

"Fucking-A! We can always hope," Catherine shouted as she and Margaret charged out from behind the partition, collecting Ramsey's rifle.

"Ann, check on Becca," Margaret said, bending over to grab Ramsey by the feet. "She's hurt too. She's bleeding, not bad, but the bone by her neck where she's bleeding looks funny, kinda dented. She's a lot whiter than usual, and, oh yeah, she stopped praying. I think she might be in shock." Catherine jumped in to help Margaret drag Ramsey toward the rear of the ship.

Before heading back to check on Rebecca, Ann stopped by the Korlah crew members, who were now sitting up, awake but dazed.

Repeatedly making the apologetic hand gestures she had seen Teela use, Ann hoped for understanding, if not forgiveness, for the attack. Once one of the Korlah acknowledged her apology with a shake of its head, Ann hurried back to check on Rebecca.

Tiffany was sitting in the chair next to Rebecca, leaning over the thin woman who lay back in the chair and stared up at the featureless ceiling. Her pale green eyes were sunken and red-rimmed; they were fixed on a single point, no longer darting nervously. Ann had grown accustomed to the constant muttering Rebecca made as she mouthed her prayers, trying to avoid the others' ire. Ann had listened to her pray for each of them individually and as a group; she had prayed for their salvation, for the salvation of Earth, and for the Korlah. She thanked God or Jesus for every meal, she prayed when she woke up and before she went to sleep. Ann's annoyance had slowly evolved into acceptance, and at this particular moment, Ann realized that she had gained a level of comfort knowing that Rebecca believed she was in touch with God. A belief or faith she herself had longed to experience and yet had never been able to achieve. She found herself thinking that if Rebecca were to die, there would be no one to talk to God on their behalf.

Ann examined Rebecca and concluded that she had a broken collarbone and was in shock. She put the affected arm in a sling and secured it to Becca's chest with a wrap. With donations of clothing from the others Ann provided a make-shift blanket to treat her for shock. Without medical supplies, there was nothing else she could do. Ann checked her pulse and was satisfied. She began to comb the mats out of Rebecca's hair with her fingers, talking calmly and trying to soothe her companion. Looking at the inch or more of natural gray hair between Rebecca's scalp and the hair dyed bright red, she wondered how long they had been gone. How many days? How many months? How long did it take hair to grow an inch? She knelt next to Rebecca, took her free hand, and held it in hers. She prayed for Rebecca, something she'd heard Rebecca do many times for her.

Teela tried to run but lacked the strength. Stumbling along as quickly as she could, she traveled the length of the accoutrements section and entered the aft access to the energy section. Her heart was racing and she was out of breath. She took the transit tubes for equipment and materials in the aft-most area of the energy section, right up against the back of the plasma compression chamber. The freight tubes there dropped her much more slowly than the ones at the transit hubs. Her intention was to avoid meeting up with Afron's forces, and so far she had not seen anyone. Her choice seemed to be a wise one.

Straining to hear over the drone of the massive engines and the pounding of her own heart, Teela could hear shouts coming up the tube as she approached the midlevels of the health section. She stepped off the transit and searched the equipment and conduit spaces until she found an access shaft where she could climb down the last few levels. Once she finally reached the level Beth and Crystal had been sent to for repair, she cautiously made her way to an alcove off the main corridor by the repair chamber.

The smell of blood, burned flesh, and worse permeated the air, growing stronger with every step Teela took. Fighting the urge to turn and run back to the safety of the hidden room, she forced herself to go on. She peeked into the corridor and was shocked. It was littered with the bodies of birthing units and the mutilated bodies of warriors, identifiable only by their shredded uniforms. Looking in vain for signs of life, she darted across the corridor and into the repair chamber, sliding to a stop on the blood-slicked floor.

The entrance to an alcove in the back corner was piled with bodies. Vivid memories, the recollections of a child torn, damaged, and left for dead in a pile of bodies such as this, poured into her mind and an involuntary scream poured from her mouth. She waded into the bodies, desperately searching for life in this pile of death. Pushing and shoving at warm corpses slick with blood, she uncovered each body until she was convinced there was no one to be saved. Near the bottom of the pile she found Khranga, dead from a pulse blast to the center of her chest.

At the sound of voices behind her, Teela spun around and attempted to draw her swords. She drew her blades out halfway, but was unable to lift them any further, as if they were made of lead. Two birthing units stood just outside the door. Their tahs were spattered with blood and they had energized their pulse rifles and pointed them in her direction.

"Where are they? Where are the two . . . beasts?" Teela asked weakly, dropping the blades back into their sheaths.

One of the birthing units dropped her rifle. The other spoke quickly in a voice pinched with fear while the other pointed aft with a trembling arm.

"Spectacle. They fought Ruwaugh and Apoulauh. They fought with fangs and claws. Two have ceased, and the other two may cease also. They are attempting repairs near the chamber."

"Take me there!" Teela demanded, stalking toward them.

The armed birthing unit de-energized her weapon and stared intently at Teela's blood-smeared face and the swords dangling from her hips.

"You are Shawlmon?" she asked in a whisper. Her companion lowered her arm and stared with her mouth agape.

"I am what I need to be. Now please take me to the humans," Teela asked as calmly as her impatience would allow.

"Hu mons?" the birthing unit asked, the word strange in her mouth.

"The beasts! You said they fought spectacle. Take me to where they are being repaired," Teela screamed, her flimsy composure shattered.

"I—I'm sorry . . . Your Eminence. I—I'm so stupid. Of course . . . Hu-mons. Yes, I will take you there," the birther stammered nervously, clumsily trying to hold her weapon under one arm so she could make an apologetic palm display.

In that instant, Teela saw herself in this birthing unit. This was what she was like before transfer. This was how she had behaved when confronted by Afron. To this child, her own genetic twin, she was an intimidating superior to be respected, not for merit or reason, but out of fear for her existence.

"No, little sister, you are not stupid," Teela said, softening her voice and pulling the surprised girl into a quick embrace as if they were section sisters.

"Sometimes I forget who I was . . . who I am," Teela said, quickly correcting herself, unsure whether it was in fact a correction or an admission.

The birthing unit bowed deeply before heading down the corridor, looking back several times to ensure that she was not moving too fast for her sister. Teela felt the excitement and hope her presence seemed to bring these two tattered youngsters. They were so haggard and filthy that it was difficult to guess just how young they were, but she was certain they were old enough to have participated in this birth cycle. And yet it was still many shifts until this cycle would deliver, and they were both obviously not carrying embryos.

"How is it that you didn't participate in this cycle's birthing?" Teela asked.

The lead birthing unit suddenly slowed and her head dropped to her chest as her crown tendrils blanched. Shuffling to a stop, her head twisted first one way and then the other. Her mouth moved, but no words came. Her sister quickly moved to console her with a hug. They stood silently in the corridor.

"This birth cycle has failed, Your Eminence," she whispered, turning a moist eye toward Teela. Speaking weakly at first, the birthing unit began her explanation, her voice growing stronger and more fervent as she told the story.

"The birthing started four shifts ago. Nearly all the shells have been born without existence or ceased shortly after. Many mothers have also ceased during birthing . . . or were damaged. Damaged units are being reassigned to the warrior section, but . . . we . . . we did not report. The Oracle found us. She told us of Shawlmon. She told us you had risen, and that you would lead us to victory. She tells us of your words, and we act on your commands. All who oppose you will be destroyed!"

Teela looked into her eyes, now wild with anger and passion. Teela resisted the urge to question this Oracle's credibility; this unit was deeply committed and clearly fragile.

"Where is the Oracle now?" she asked instead.

"She is with the Hu-mon. She told everyone that you were coming. We were sent to meet you, to guide you. She says you are preparing to go on a journey that will bring an end to campaign and a beginning to a new Korlah existence."

"Take me there," Teela said. She felt suddenly as though her inner thoughts were exposed, and sought to dampen their intensity; it was possible that this Oracle could hear them.

Glancing at the bodies littering the corridor, she hoped that her thoughts had not been used to justify this carnage. She concentrated on that premise and filled her mind with displeasure that violence was being wrought on her behalf.

The birthing units led Teela to an area two levels out that was unmarred by conflict. The cylindrical shape of the vessel gave the circumferential corridors the illusion of always dropping off, so at any point it appeared as though you were at the top of a crest. During their transit, other birthing units armed with pulse weaponry or swords ran out in groups of two or three to join them. As Teela passed, they would stop and genuflect, then fall in behind her. Before long, Teela and her escorts were being trailed by several hundred armed birthing units.

As they came over the rise, the fifteen-foot-wide corridor was filled with armed Korlah of all assignments. The crowd stretched back for as far as Teela could see and parted to let her through; she walked past thousands of Korlah before they approached a repair facility like the one they had left. In the corridor outside the main chamber, the crowd had formed around a cloaked figure that stood with her head down. Teela's escorts stepped to the side and motioned for her to enter the circle. The crowd was quiet, speaking only in a whispered hush.

The cloaked figure held a defensive stance, and the folds in its gown allowed the possibility of concealed weapons. Teela crossed her arms at her waist and reached for the blades that protruded from her splayed scabbards. She mirrored her opponent's posture and tipped her head down, straining to project her thoughts from beneath a furled brow.

You are the Oracle? she demanded.

The Oracle straightened slightly and unhurriedly drew a long blade from the folds of her garment. Teela clumsily unsheathed her swords with a metallic hiss. Their sharpened edges danced with static electricity.

The circle opened wider as those on the periphery stepped back. The crowd drew a collective breath. Shakily holding one blade above her shoulder and the other across her midsection at arm's length, Teela held her stance. The Oracle knelt and laid her sword on the floor. Turning to one side and pushing the deep hood back from her face, she offered Teela her exposed neck.

Teela immediately recognized the grizzled Non she had fought in the abandoned section after receiving Shawlmon's robe. The old warrior's eyes were downcast as she held her gnarled hands over her head in the humblest of apologies.

"I am the Oracle, Your Eminence. I live only to serve Korlah and to serve you. Since my enlightenment, I have listened to your words above all others. You called for help, and I came. You restored the rank and status of those forgotten, and we are grateful. Your words come to me, and I repeat them. Those who have heard the words have joined to become one. A voice without claws would not be heard, you said. The mothers of us all heard these words and knew them to be true. They begged for food and water while their sisters and unborn shells were dying. Now they scream your words of honor and equality while proving that they can destroy as well as create existence. You are the voice of Shawlmon, and we are your claws."

"I did not . . . I would not ask the birth mothers to fight this battle!" Teela cried. "The corridors are filled with their lifeless shells. They have ceased for something I would have done with words." Her voice squeaked, pitched high from a throat tight with guilt.

With eyes wide, the Oracle turned her head to look at Teela from her kneeling position. "I heard your words. Your words! Your words come to me above all others. I have seen your memories of Korlah before the Kahshinki—expansive lakes and mountains, valleys covered with lush vegetation. I heard your words of anger. I've seen how you plan to wield your swords, cutting your enemies to pieces. Fight! You said fight! Kill before we are killed. To fear death is to fear freedom. Our existence means nothing without freedom. These were your words," the Oracle cried, her voice rising to a shrill scream.

The iteration of her innermost thoughts struck Teela like a fist in the gut. She took a step back, and with arms that suddenly felt weak, lowered her swords until their tips rested on the ground.

"Thoughts are not words," Teela gasped. "I have many thoughts that should never become words, never be taken to action. My thoughts . . . the thoughts I have had lately have been filled with anger, yet I restrain from action because I would harm those I care for. I care deeply for my Korlah sisters, and it brings me great sorrow to see what has happened. *These* are my words," Teela said, her voice trembling.

The Oracle turned her head to one side and gestured to the auditory duct on the side of her head. A thick scar covered the channel.

"I am a deaf fool, Your Eminence. Thoughts are the only words I hear. They are the most meaningful of words. Speech is filled with lies and inaccuracies, but thoughts provide the purest sense of what the speaker is saying. You tell me with words that we should not kill for our freedom, yet with thoughts you proclaim your willingness to kill and die for me—for all of us. Can we not by action proclaim our willingness to bring thought to reality? You think I am an enemy. You think I am insane, and you fear that I will reveal the thoughts you struggle even now to hide."

Rising to her feet, the Oracle extended her arms out to her sides and tipped her head back. "I did not believe the words at first, but their power became apparent when all who heard them found hope where there had been only apathy. When the words came to me, I relayed them to all who would listen, and all who listened wanted to hear more. Ten followers became hundreds, then hundreds became thousands, all within a few shifts. Word of your rising blew through this vessel like the hyperlight plasma stream on which we ride. The purpose of my pitiful existence became clear. Your words lit my path, and I have followed in utter obedience what I hear. You spared me once; if that was an error, if the dream I chase is only a dream, end my existence now, for I am not worthy to serve you or Korlah." The Oracle sobbed, her body shaking from head to foot, making her cloak flutter.

"No!" A cry from the circle became a roar of no's as the crowd chimed in.

"Teela, the Oracle saved me, saved all of us!" a birthing unit cried as she pushed her way into the circle. Her head was ravaged in a pattern of burns that had shriveled her crown tendrils to blackened stumps and rendered her face unrecognizable. She tilted her head to study Teela with her one good eye; the other was a burned and blackened empty socket. "It is you. My little Teela, you have returned," she sighed, reaching out to touch Teela's face.

Teela recoiled and averted her eyes, examining instead the unit's soiled and bloodied tah. She read the crude stencil on the breast and gasped in disbelief. Her eyes darted from the unrecognizable face to the stencil again.

"Nerhala?" she cried, her revulsion apparent.

Nerhala slumped and withdrew her hand. Fumbling to sheathe her blades, Teela pulled her into a soft embrace and gingerly pressed her cheek to Nerhala's, careful not to hurt her.

"I will take the existence of whoever did this to you. By the blood of my existence, I swear you will be avenged!" Teela hissed, her tendrils engorging with rage.

"Their existence has ended. I cut them to pieces with the Oracle's blade while they were still breathing. It was not an easy thing to do the first time, but it is becoming easier," Nerhala said, almost offhandedly. Teela pulled her adopted mother closer. She could not recall a time that Nerhala had raised a hand in anger against her or any other child. She could not picture her taking a life or understand why anyone would want to harm this gentle woman.

"Why, Mother? Why would they do this to you?" Teela cried, hugging her more tightly. Nerhala began to cry. The Oracle lowered her arms and moved her face in close to Teela's. She whispered softly.

"Afron sought information about you. She did not understand how a birthing unit of such a diminutive status could know and interpret ancient laws. She called for Nerhala, knowing her to be the one who had looked after you since the discovery of your . . . damage. She wanted to know who taught you and what you had learned. But neither pain nor the threat of death brought forth answers from your friend. It was by chance that I interrupted her reclamation. I am sorry I did not find her or the . . . humans sooner."

"What has happened to the humans? Where are they?" Teela asked. She broke Nerhala's embrace but held tight to her hand and followed the Oracle's gaze to the entrance of the repair chamber.

Pulling Nerhala with her, Teela pushed her way through the crowd into the repair chamber. It was many times larger than the others she had seen, efficiently arranged with hundreds of tables, gurneys, and devices the functions of which she could not imagine. Biotechs clustered around a dozen tables that held injured prepped for repair. Salvaged body parts and tissues lay neatly on nearby counters, and damaged and unusable bits were piled onto hover carts waiting to be moved to a reclamation portal where they would be shoveled into grinders.

Teela led Nerhala down the center aisle, scanning the tables. She picked up speed and ran down one aisle and then another, searching for Beth and Crystal. From between two carts crammed with tall flasks, Teela spotted a patch of unmottled human skin. Apprehensive, she slowed down and rounded the carts.

Beth sat on the edge of a table with her naked back to Teela. Dark lines crossed her well-defined muscles, the marks of fresh repairs. On the table beyond, Crystal lay with a blood-spattered tah draped from her neck to her knees. Beth stared at Crystal's lifeless body, pressing her palms tightly together between her knees. She swayed silently from side to side and her jaw tensed in anguish. Teela froze. She feared that approaching Beth at this moment would solicit another attack. Teela whispered her suspicions to Nerhala and waited while she moved away a safe distance, then turned back toward Beth.

Hearing the exchange, Beth stood and turned with her fists clenched at her sides. Her pale blue eyes were swollen and red.

"She said—" Beth stopped to clear her throat, "you'd be back," she whispered hoarsely.

Teela did not understand her. Moving cautiously around her, she stopped alongside the gurney where Crystal lay. She stared at her ghostly pallor and longed to cover her face, but she refrained, fearing that it would offend Beth. Instead, she smoothed and patted the shroud, unable to convey to Beth the grief she felt.

"You look like shit. Not as bad as your friend, but bad enough. You have another spell, like before?" Beth asked, her voice an awkward mix of bravado and concern.

Unable to understand, Teela assumed it was another verbal assault, that she was being blamed for this. Perhaps the blame was well placed. In anguish and frustration at her inability to communicate, Teela removed one of her thick gloves and dug her claws into her forearm, hoping the pain would bring out the memories she needed. Her face twisted as her claws burned their way into sensitive wounds.

Beth thought Teela was punishing herself and reached over to pull Teela's hand from her bleeding arm. "Don't do that. It's not your fault. I wanted to blame you for this—*all* of it. But you weren't here, I was. I had to make the tough choices, the ones that have no right answers, the ones where people die. I don't blame you for this; I blame myself," Beth said.

"I also blame that bitch over there," she continued, her voice becoming acid as she gestured toward a nearby table.

On the table lay a heavily muscled warrior. One leg was bent awkwardly at the knee and her face was distorted and swollen, the sensitive area between the eyes crushed. If it weren't for the slow rise and fall of her chest, Teela would have thought she was dead. The sabat on her face identified her as Ruwaugh, Afron's lead assassin and Shawaugh's archrival. This was Apoulauh's adjutant, the warrior that had challenged Teela to spectacle. Teela suddenly realized that if it had not been for the events of the last few shifts, it could well have been Shawaugh and she that faced Ruwaugh in the spectacle chamber.

"If she doesn't die, I'm gonna kill her. I'm gonna cut her throat like she cut Crystal's. The last thing she's gonna see is me—spitting in her fucking eye," Beth growled.

Even without speaking the language, Teela knew that Beth's intentions toward Ruwaugh were violent and lethal. She realized that revenge would have to wait if she wanted to lead Beth to safety. She took the human's hand and gestured toward the door, gently pulling her in that direction.

"You don't seem to understand. I'm not leaving until—"

The room rumbled with distant thunder. A shudder beneath the floor shook the room, rising and falling with the fluctuations of the gravitational forces that gave the room stability. Several of the injured rolled from their tables, and screams began erupt everywhere. Slowly, the rumbling dissipated into a steady thrum that seemed to come from all around them. The Oracle shouted in the corridor and a hush fell inside the chamber as everyone strained to hear her.

"We have to go. Now!" Teela exclaimed to Beth in Korlah, her tone and wild gesticulations indicating the urgency of her request.

"I'm not leaving Crystal, and why the hell can't you speak English anymore?" Beth grumbled, pointing at Crystal before crossing her arms in defiance.

Teela went to Crystal's table. Like a mother lifting a sleeping child, she drew Crystal from the table and moved her onto a gurney. She began to float Crystal toward the corridor. Nerhala stepped in and put her hand onto Teela's, offering to push the cart.

"Honor me with the privilege to serve you," Nerhala murmured, her eye downcast in submission.

Teela turned to Nerhala and dropped onto one knee to meet Nerhala's gaze before dropping her eyes to the blood-spattered floor. "Mother, it is I, Teela, who serve you. It is my shame that harm has come to you and my sisters, and it is my obligation to end this madness."

Rising to her feet, Teela took adopted mother into an embrace. She pressed her cheek gently against Nerhala's and spoke softly into her ear duct. "Stay here Mother, and let them repair your damage. When you return to our section, assign a bed for me next to yours, and when I return we can work together like we did before. I have missed you, and I have missed the little ones."

"Teela? You are so different. Is it really you who speaks?" Nerhala whispered, cupping her daughter's cheeks in her hands and searching her eyes.

Nodding her head in confirmation, Teela took Nerhala's hands in hers and pressed the backs of them against her forehead as she had so many times in the past. She led her mother by the hand to an empty table, and despite Nerhala's objections, directed a biotech to expedite her repairs. With a final press to her cheek, Teela turned back to Beth.

Beth waited with Crystal, ready to go; she nodded toward the door, cueing Teela to take the lead. Teela glanced back at Ruwaugh and verified that she was still breathing.

"I'll take care of it on the next trip," Beth rumbled, guessing Teela's thoughts.

I'm not dead! a voice shouted from everywhere and nowhere. Teela spun around, expecting to find the source standing behind her.

"What? Who said that?" Teela cried out in English, the words erupting from her subconscious, sounds without meaning that left her with a feeling of fear and urgency.

"Said what?" Beth asked.

Beth's words were unintelligible grunts to Teela; the connection between her Korlah and human memories was lost. Teela paused for a moment to scan the chamber for the source of the voice, then she gripped her swords to hide the shaking of her hands and headed for the door, Crystal's gurney on her heels.

Outside the chamber, the Oracle stood where Teela had left her. As Teela emerged from the chamber, the Oracle raised her arms over her head, and the crowd that had filled the corridor as far as she could see roared.

"SHAWLMON!" the crowd shouted in unison.

When the Oracle dropped to her knees and put her palms up in supplication, the crowd followed, creating a wave that rumbled down the corridor in both directions. Teela stopped abruptly and Beth ran the gurney into her, bumping her into the Oracle's circle.

"Shawlmon has risen!" the Oracle cried. "Campaign has begun! As it was foretold, so it has come to pass. Shawlmon will lead us in this campaign to final victory!" The Oracle jumped to her feet and shrieked the last word.

"Victory!" the crowd echoed.

"We are your servants. Lead us and we shall follow. We are your claws! We are the Claws of Shawlmon!" the Oracle cried, her head thrown back, her voice fervent.

"Shawlmon! Shawlmon! Shawlmon!" the crowd chanted as Teela glanced down the crowded corridors at thousands of Korlah.

28 - Truth

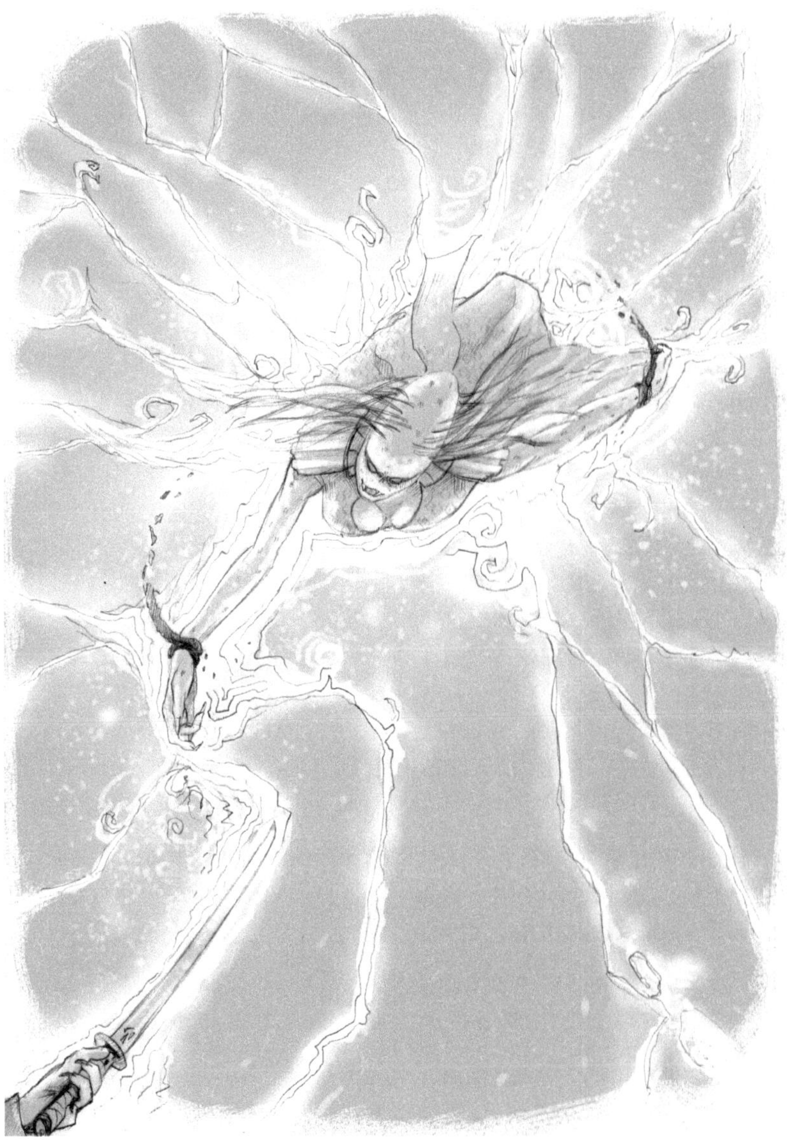

Shawaugh stepped out of a tube adjacent to the bio section. It was here that she had observed the battle on Meezra's monitoring panel. She headed up a corridor toward the thick bulkhead and heavy door that separated the two distinctly different sections. A communication panel next to the access door displayed the Council Leader's peace message; as Shawaugh approached, it suddenly went dark, then lit up with her name, as if it were a private comstation with a personal message.

Shawaugh reached for the panel to acknowledge the message, but before she touched it, the message appeared on the screen. Shawaugh cursed, scanning the area for the monitoring device that Meezra was undoubtedly observing her with. Seeing none, she turned her attention back to the screen.

> DIRECTOR SHAWAUGH,
>
> TEELA, TWO OF THE BEASTS, THE ORACLE, AND SEVERAL BIRTHING UNITS HAVE DEPARTED BIOREPAIR LEVEL 35 ON AN OUTWARD TRANSIT CUBE AT COORDINATE 2. AFTER THEIR DEPARTURE, A MESSAGE WAS SENT FROM THE REPAIR FACILITY TO THE ARMS SECTION, WHERE AFRON'S REMAINING FORCES ARE CURRENTLY CONCENTRATED. A GROUP OF WARRIORS IS MOVING AFT THROUGH THE ACCOUTREMENTS SECTION. I BELIEVE THEY INTEND TO INTERCEPT TEELA AT THE OUTER LEVEL TRANSIT CUBE EXIT. THERE IS A SERVICE TUBE IN THE ENERGY SECTION NEAR YOU THAT CAN TRANSIT THE ENTIRE DISTANCE AND DELIVER YOU TO COORDINATE 3, LEVEL 1 OF ACCOUTREMENTS. I WILL SEND WHATEVER RESISTANCE FORCES ARE STILL AVAILABLE TO MEET YOU THERE.

Shawaugh scanned the corridor in vain for a transit tube and reached for the keyboard. Again, before she touched the panel a message appeared on the screen.

> "SECOND CROSS-CORRIDOR AFT. TRANSIT TUBE WILL BE ON FORWARD SIDE, CENTER OF COORDINATE 3."

With crisp precision honed over three lifetimes as a soldier and a speed and grace that belied her lumbering appearance, Shawaugh spun and sprinted toward the spokes that ran outward from the quadrant designated section three. The centermost spoke would take her one hundred and twenty levels out, where she hoped to intercept Teela's group that Meezra reported was transiting on a much slower cargo cube. Approaching at a run, she slid across the smooth floor into the transit tube, and immediately plunged outward at an unanticipated velocity. Falling headfirst at such speeds challenged even Shawaugh's steadfast calm.

Express velocities were reserved for emergencies, and those using them were normally prepared. Shawaugh was at the mercy of whomever controlled this tube's gravitational fields. She tilted her head back to look up the tube she was now hurtling through and the air stung her eyes. As her body shot past the air compression valves, the pressure pulsed with a rapid fhup, fhup, fhup. The tube ahead in the distance disappeared into a black dot that would soon end at the underside of a grav-plate. Fighting the urge to slow her ascent by clawing at the sides of the tube, she watched the darkness fade and the end of the tube rush toward her. She stared up in defiance and awaited impact.

The rapid deceleration caused her crown tendrils to stand straight up and would have likely caused her to disgorge the contents of her stomach had she eaten anything recently. By the time her ascent was arrested, the grav-plate was three-feet above her head. Hanging in stasis before an exit, she leaned forward to move her center of gravity. She glided out of the tube and stepped into the corridor. A young, low-ranking energy tech at a nearby panel bowed respectfully as she emerged. Shawaugh took a deep, calming breath and acknowledged her with a crossed-fist salute.

"There has been weapons fire nearby. I have been informed that Resistance soldiers will be here to assist you in ten or twenty bits," the technician said.

"How far is it to the transit bay?"

"Two corridors forward of here. It will be the first transit station you see." The technician's eyes were respectfully downcast but she examined Shawaugh's face with her peripheral vision.

"Is your weapon charged?" Shawaugh asked gruffly, irritated by the way this unit was staring without staring, a consummate talent required by Korlah protocol. This unit lacked subtlety.

"Yes, but the soldiers are expecting to meet you here," the technician responded.

Shawaugh snatched the weapon and marched away. The transit hub was much closer than she expected. Turning into the corridor, she slid to a stop and quickly backstepped around the corner.

Warriors in battle armor filled the corridor. They were moving away from Shawaugh and didn't see her. She waited until their rattling armor and footsteps faded before peering around the corner. When she was certain they were out of sight, she turned the corner to follow. The corridor reeked of burned flesh and oxidized armor. Stopping at the transit hub, she found the source of the stench in the open cube Teela's group had taken.

Three birthing units and a cloaked Non lay on the floor, their garments still smoldering from lethal blasts. Shawaugh could tell from the size of these units that none was Teela, but she still knelt to see if any were alive.

"Shawaugh . . . help me, sister," the Oracle wheezed.

Shawaugh lifted a dead birthing unit off the Oracle and helped her sit up before she pushed back her smoking hood.

"Dooaugh! You old fool. I thought you could see the future. How is it that you did not see this coming?" Shawaugh growled.

"I was listening to Shawlmon. Help me . . . remove this . . ." the Oracle gasped, struggling with the fasteners of the armored breastplate she was wearing beneath the cloak.

Body armor was effective from a distance of thirty to forty feet; anything closer than that was usually fatal. From the size of the crater in Dooaugh's armor, Shawaugh knew she had been shot from less than six-feet away. She ripped the cloak open and deftly unfastened the breastplate. She lifted it away expecting to find charred flesh beneath, but instead she found another breastplate.

"I can't be expected to hear everyone's thoughts," Dooaugh said, smiling slyly.

The smile turned to a grimace as Shawaugh lifted the remaining breastplate. Patches of skin had fused to it, exposing raw flesh. Shawaugh examined the blistered skin, wondering if Dooaugh truly possessed the ability to foretell the future.

"Your existence will not end today, old friend. And Teela . . . was she . . . ?" Shawaugh hesitated, expecting the worse.

"No. Their purpose was to take Shawlmon and the humans alive. They expected our arrival; a traitor, I'm not sure who, told them. Hit us with nonlethal blasts. Finished those they didn't want . . . with lethal. These warriors . . . they had no honor . . . no honor," the Oracle wheezed.

The late afternoon sun turned the dull, scratched Formica blood red. Daedalus stared at the edge of the table where a piece of the metal edging was bent out at the seam. *I could fix that,* he thought, but what he couldn't fix was the pile of bills, the centerpiece of which was an eviction notice. He looked down at the shotgun cradled in his lap. The barrel had spots of rust and the stock was dry and peeling from years of neglect. He would have preferred a pistol, which would have been much easier to conceal, but for twenty bucks you get what you can. The tequila helped him decide that this was his only choice. The last of his cash helped him buy the tool that would fix the problem, because if it wasn't, by tomorrow he'd be on the street, homeless. He had been homeless before, a long, long time ago, and he could not, would not, accept that option.

"I'm not a thief!" he shouted at the eviction notice, his liquor-drenched breath fluttering it to the far side of the table. He slammed the empty tequila bottle down on it.

The apartment, even though it was dingy, dark and rundown, was home, his last bastion in a war against the world he had been waging since childhood. The battles he fought, some won, most lost, only served to feed his anger. He'd thought the military would be a good career choice since he couldn't hold a job for longer than a few months, but he was dishonorably discharged shortly after boot camp. He destroyed his marriage and spent two years in prison for assaulting his wife. And now, after losing yet another job, he was out of money, out of friends, and out of time.

"Loser. Yeah, a fucking loser, that's what I am." Shame and despair roiled deep inside him. Taking a shuddering breath, he put the barrel of the loaded gun in his mouth, stared at the bills pinned under the tequila bottle for a few moments, closed his eyes, and pulled the trigger.

From his earliest recollections after realizing he was an abandoned child, he had focused on being independent, never giving up, never giving in, and fighting anybody and everybody that stood in his way. To be beaten, to give up, to commit suicide—he knew with the very fiber of his existence that this was the ultimate statement of his failure. So when the weapon didn't fire, his failure was complete.

The taste of oil and rusty metal filled his mouth during the slow seconds that followed the snap of the firing pin. He watched tears and saliva drip onto his shaking hands as he surrendered to the fact that his life was an exercise in futility.

Teela quaked with an anguished sob, coughed, and gasped loudly as she regained consciousness. The dream left a foul taste in her mouth that she tried to spit out. The room was moving past her at a rate that caused her aching head to spin. When she tried to put her hand to her head, she found that her arms were bound tightly to her sides; she opened her eyes to see two warriors dragging her by the feet down a corridor. Her eyes throbbed from the pulse blast that had caught her in the center of her chest the moment the transit cube opened Armed warriors surrounded her, their feet raising dust that set off a coughing fit. Realizing that the situation was out of her control, she relaxed, closing her eyes to block out the light of the glowlamps.

"Where do you want them?" a voice in the distance asked as the warriors turned a corner. Her shoulder struck the threshold of a door as they pulled her through the narrow opening.

"Bring me that one and put the others there," someone answered. The warriors released her and then shoved her with their feet to the wall.

Struggling from the awkward position and unable to use her arms, Teela managed to sit up. Warriors blocked her view of the room. Six-feet away, Beth was lying face down against the same wall, not moving. Teela stared until she saw Beth's chest rise and fall at regular intervals.

"Find out how long until the pods will be ready to depart. The rest of you take positions outside," someone said in a voice that Teela couldn't quite place. The warriors marched out of the room and the door closed behind them with a hiss.

The room was round, twenty-feet across with a domed ceiling that blended smoothly into the walls. The very surface of the dome seemed to glow, providing light much brighter than Teela was used to. She squinted and strained to see who was standing over the gurney that held Crystal's body.

"Who are you?" she demanded angrily in English. The Korlah by the gurney went to her. The bright light cast the person in silhouette, and it wasn't until she knelt in front of her that Teela was able to recognize who it was.

"Gremensh? What are you doing?" Teela asked, this time in Korlah, her surprise apparent.

"Oh, little mother, my sweet, sweet little mother. I have thought of this moment for so long, even in my dreams. I wish . . . I had more time," Gremensh murmured, her eyes trailing across Teela's breasts.

"Support for Afron has crumbled. Your only hope now is to surrender," Teela growled, twisting away as Gremensh began to unfasten the clasps of her vest.

"Afron has ceased. Ironically, it was you who caused it. You interrupted her transfer to this human. Whatever part of her that completed the transfer was lost when its existence was taken during spectacle," Gremensh said, grabbing Teela by the vest and dragging her to her feet.

She pushed her against the wall and brushed her face gently against Teela's as she continued in a soft, ominous tone. "Your plan for alliance with the humans is a waste of time. The entire campaign has been a waste from the beginning." Spinning Teela around to face the wall, Gremensh shouted, "Look around you! For hundreds of cycles, no one could figure out what this room was for, what these symbols meant. Many believed that it was a map, but no sense could be made of the markings. The room went unused, a curiosity to some, but mostly forgotten. Forgotten, that is, until the last campaign when our studies of captured Kahshinki discovered the hidden meaning within the language of their eyes.

"Korlah can see only a fragment of the light spectrum that Kahshinki see. This is why we could never completely understand their communications and had to manually bypass many of the ship's control systems. They weren't protected by codes, as we had thought. Once I discovered the invisible light, Afron's technicians began decoding the entire Kahshinki language. We have discovered much in the last few cycles alone.

But this room . . . it has both shattered and bolstered our hopes and dreams for a future."

Gremensh withdrew an oblong device about the size of pocketbook from her robe and flipped it open to reveal a keypad. Deftly typing with one hand, she held the back of the open cover toward a circle on the wall. The cover flashed lights as iridescent as the eyes of a Kahshinki. The wall went slightly translucent and the circle next to Teela lit up, becoming a three-dimensional, slowly rotating planet. Gremensh kept typing, and Kahshinki glyphs began to appear next to the circle in columns that scrolled from top to bottom.

"Planet mass, atmosphere, gravity, populations of indigenous species, and the populations of the farmed species. Harvest quantities by species, genetic codes, and modifications made to select species since the previous harvest. These are just content headers. The information for each subject is extensive and the detail intricate. The planet you are looking at has been harvested twenty-one times in the last 250,000 cycles. The planet is Korlah! Now watch," Gremensh said, making another entry on the device before pulling Teela away from the wall by her collar. The circle that represented the planet Korlah illuminated, as well as a line to its left.

"Campaign planet one: the mountain world," Gremensh said just before the next line and circle illuminated, then another and another.

"Campaign planet two: the jungle world. Three, four, five, six, seven, eight, nine, the one the Kahshinki are at now, and the last one is the planet of the humans. The route continues in a circle leading back to Korlah. Every one of these planets is being harvested approximately every twelve thousand cycles. According to the Kahshinki records, neither Korlah nor humans are indigenous to their planets; both come from the same genetic origin, albeit modified considerably by the Kahshinki. The beasts, it would seem, are our sisters."

"Then as their sisters, we must, by obligation of honor, help them defeat the Kahshinki," Teela said weakly.

Gremensh threw her head back and laughed. "You and your incessant prattle about honor! Korlah honor is a myth created to control the masses and perpetuate the belief that we intend to end the Kahshinki harvests. There is no hope that we can end the Kahshinki harvests. Look!" Gremensh shouted as she made another entry. The walls and floor dissolved into star-filled space. Lines connected a group of stars.

"This is the harvest route of this vessel. And these . . ." Gremensh tapped the controls, "are the rest of the harvest routes in this galaxy." Immediately, lines formed thousands of rings, connecting hundreds of thousands of stars to thousands of planets.

"There are hundreds of Kahshinki base planets coordinating the harvest of thousands upon thousands of worlds in this galaxy alone. We have found hundreds of galaxies mapped just like this, and records that date back over three million cycles. How can we hope to end this?" The room returned to normal. "There is no hope!" Gremensh closed the star chamber's controller, dropped it on the floor and kicked it into the corner.

"We must try to prevent this harvest. We must," Teela said.

"Must we? Do you realize that in nearly one thousand cycles, we have not been able to prevent a single harvest? All we have done is capture their cargo ships and convert them to campaign vessels. Do you know where we have sent those campaign vessels?" Gremensh asked, knowing what Teela would say.

"They are sent in pursuit of the Kahshinki vessels that seek to harvest other planets," Teela answered, as all Korlah were taught.

"Shyron has always ensured that her vessel, this campaign vessel, pursued the Kahshinki vessel that first made contact with Korlah and each planet thereafter," Gremensh said. "That was no chance decision. She knew that the cargo ships were returning to the Kahshinki home world, and she hoped her vessels would destroy or conquer their planet as the Kahshinki had done to ours. To Shyron's disappointment, we have been unable to determine the outcome of those efforts. The distances exceeded the capacity of our long-range scout craft—until now.

"From this room and these maps, we determined that we were close enough to the base planet of this harvest route to send a scout ship. What it discovered confirmed our worst fears. Not only have we failed to destroy or conquer their planet, the Kahshinki know we are coming, and they are preparing for our arrival."

Gremensh moved up close and put her arms around Teela in a gentle embrace. When Teela tried to pull away, Gremensh pulled her back roughly.

"This vessel and the planet of humans are doomed. The Kahshinki are sending three campaign vessels against us. This will be a very short campaign, one battle, a massacre." Gremensh sighed almost apologetically as she turned Teela to face her.

"We've found a suitable planet that will not be harvested for another twenty-four thousand cycles. It will be a long and difficult journey by small craft, but it can be done. Afron prepared four assault pods to take those who recognize the futility of this campaign. The humans have given us what we need to survive without duplication.

"We can start over, Teela! Not as duplicates, but genetic originals. I can repair you and you will be able to bear young. Your own children, Teela—not duplicates, not shells. My young will not die for a cause that cannot be won. They will build a new planet of Korlah and rule it! You have gained great popularity on both sides of this struggle. Join me, little mother. Together our clan, our collective, will be unchallenged as long as we exist!"

"I have given my blood oath to return the humans to their planet to negotiate an alliance and to fight this campaign. Your offer is . . . the dream of all Korlah. But not all Korlah are willing to defy the judgment of the Council. I cannot and will not."

"You will not be able to negotiate an alliance, now that your precious humans and their escorts have ceased," Gremensh sneered.

"You lie!" Teela shouted, charging toward Gremensh, who sidestepped and tripped Teela, sending her sprawling onto the floor.

"That is the last human of your group that retains its existence," Gremensh said pointing to Beth, still prone on the floor. "Do you really think it will speak on behalf of the good intentions of the Korlah that ended the existence of all its companions?"

"You lie. They escaped," Teela moaned, praying it was not true.

"It was by no act of mine or Afron's that they have ceased. It was Shyron. She secured the hyperlight drive at the very moment

Challmara and the humans attempted to depart. The shift from hyperlight created a gravitational wash, as she knew it would. Your dear friend Challmara could not control her craft and was disintegrated along with the humans by three automated hull cannons. You need only check the hull cannon's visual log. If you like, I will display the record for you. It's quite clear," Gremensh said indifferently.

"Shyron . . . would not do that," Teela rasped, wishing Gremensh was lying. But she remembered the timing of the engine fluctuation and believed it could be true.

"You don't know what Shyron is capable of!" Gremensh shouted. "How could you? Shyron has been using you since your damage was discovered. She created the myth of a Resistance, a myth that became a reality. That exquisite costume you are wearing—who do you think had it made? Challmara? Hah! Even I, with all the influence and power of my section, could not afford to commission such a garment. Shyron had the robe and vest made for herself, for the purpose of resurrecting Shawlmon. As Shawlmon, Shyron would be free of interference from Afron and the Council. Afron prevented her from transferring and assuming the ancient persona, so Shyron had the robe sent to you. You were intended as nothing more than a distraction. It was no accident that she has taken a mature birthing unit as her shell. How hard do you think it will be for her to pull that robe off your lifeless shell, change her sabat, and assume the role of Shawlmon?" Gremensh asked.

"I was at Shyron's transfer. The choice was . . . random. It could not have been staged," Teela responded, her doubt evident.

"Nothing with Shyron is random," Gremensh retorted. "Everything is carefully planned and executed. The intended shell became hysterical at Shyron's projected thoughts. Eemela agreed to transfer only because Shyron was controlling her. You are behaving like a warrior because Shyron has made you believe you can actually be one. But you must realize that as a warrior you serve her purposes, not yours, and most certainly not the humans'."

Gremensh stormed over to Crystal's gurney, gesturing wildly. "Nearly one thousand cycles ago, with the help of the Kahshinki, the Ron Clan controlled all of Korlah. All of the competing clans had been defeated and subjugated. Teyron, the matriarch of the Rons, worked with the Kahshinki, providing all of the Korlah slaves they requested. It was not until the Kahshinki had taken all of the remaining clans and demanded more slaves that Teyron attempted to organize a rebellion against them. She had her clan-mate, the most fearsome bladesman Shawlmon, lead the campaign against the Kahshinki, utilizing every remaining adult and adolescent male. With the weapons the Kahshinki had given them, Shawlmon believed his army was invincible. In less than a single rotation of the planet, the Kahshinki had exterminated Shawlmon's campaign force and delivered his battered body to Teyron, alive, but without arms, legs . . . and that which made him male.

"Teyron and her blood sisters, the cowards that they were, went into hiding, taking Shawlmon with them. But Shawlmon was dying. It was then that the first unsanctioned transfer occurred. Breaking the last and most sacred law, Teyron stole the secret of transfer from the priests of Korlah and took the essence of Shawlmon. She has renamed herself Shyron to bury the shame of her past. Yes—the same Shyron you serve is a traitor to all Korlah."

Gremensh paused to study Teela, trying to gauge the effect of her words. "Shyron seeks revenge, not for the people or planet of Korlah. She seeks revenge against the Kahshinki for betraying her." Gremensh lifted one of Teela's swords from where it lay by Crystal.

"Come with me, Teela. There is nothing here worth losing your existence for," Gremensh said, drawing the crackling blade from its sheath.

"Take your followers and leave. I will convince Shyron and the Council to let you go. Please, Gremensh, let me return this human to her planet," Teela pleaded.

"No!" Gremensh snapped. "I will need both of these humans. Their ovum will be harvested for the genetic diversity to develop a suitable breeding pool on the new planet. I don't need Shyron's or the Council's permission to leave, and since you refuse to join me, you have no utility to me." Gremensh pointed the blade at Teela and stalked toward her.

"Please, Gremensh, with an alliance we will have access to all the genetic material you will need. There is no profit in taking my existence, no honor," Teela pleaded, frightened by the cold intent on Gremensh's face.

A low moan drew Gremensh's attention from Teela. Beth was trying to sit up, which was causing her considerable pain. Gremensh turned the blade toward Beth and grinned maliciously at Teela before sliding her thumb up to trigger the sword to fire a pulse blast at Beth.

"No!" Teela screamed in English, shoving off the wall to charge Gremensh.

With a crackle and a thunderclap, the sword discharged. The pulse struck Teela high on her left side, vaporizing the bindings around her arms and hurling her, spinning, through the air. Her robe and armor flashed brilliantly from the absorbed charge, illuminating the room and throwing flashes of static as she pinwheeled through the air. Gremensh was encased in the same halo of light and energy that crackled like thousands of firecrackers as it dissipated into the floor through her feet. Beth could barely raise her aching arms in time to cushion the impact of Teela's body as it slammed into her.

The firing of the weapon took only a fraction of a second, but the static charge coursed around the room for several seconds before it was absorbed. Once the charge had settled, Gremensh slumped forward and tumbled stiffly to the side. Her sandals remained fused to the floor. Thin plumes of blue-gray smoke rose from her charred hand and her feet, filling the room with the stench of burnt flesh.

Beth stifled a reflexive scream as Teela's hot armor seared her legs. She rolled and kicked her way out from under Teela's dead weight. Fully awake and adrenaline-charged, she leapt to her feet and scanned the room for threats. She tried to kick the sword from Gremensh's grip and ended up prying it from her smoking hand; it was surprisingly cool. She glanced at the gurney that Crystal was on and then at Gremensh, but her eyes stopped on Teela.

Teela's limbs were splayed awkwardly at her sides and she showed no sign of life. Beth looked down at the gown covering Teela's legs. The designs embroidered on the rich garment had burned into the thin blue cloth. Cold swept through Beth, leaving butterflies in her stomach and a fist in her throat.

"Oh shit. No! No . . . God damn it!" she croaked, dropping the sword. She fell to her knees and rolled Teela onto her back. She had been trained in emergency cardiopulmonary technique more than a decade ago, but had never had to use it. She fixed upon Teela's glazed eyes and checked for a pulse and respiration, but found none. She prayed that memory, instinct, and luck would guide her.

She unfastened Teela's armored vest and moved it aside, then tilted her head back and paused. Since there was no nose to pinch shut, she placed her palm on Teela's forehead and her mouth over Teela's and delivered two quick breaths. Teela's emaciated ribcage was visible even through the embroidered fabric of her robe. Beth positioned her hands to begin the chest compressions that would restore circulation.

A breath followed by twelve compressions; Beth repeated the cycle over and over, stopping periodically to check for a pulse. The adrenaline rush over, Beth could feel the collective weight of her injuries and exhaustion. She felt again for a pulse and screamed in frustration, slapping Teela hard across the face. She grabbed her by the vest and jerked her into a sitting position. Teela's head sagged to the side as Beth raised her hand to strike her again. She stopped in midswing and pulled Teela into an embrace, cradling her head on her shoulder.

You took this hit for me. Why'd you do that? Why? Beth thought as she began to cry, rocking Teela as she had held Crystal.

"Dade! Was that you, you smug little prick? If it's true, you dodged the reaper once, and you can do it again," Beth said as she dropped Teela roughly to the floor.

"Dade! Wake up, you asshole," Beth shouted before administering another breath.

"Dade—wake —up—Dade—wake—up—Dade—wake—up—Dade—wake—up," she panted, compressing Teela's chest with each word. She delivered another breath and repeated the process, determined to chant and compress until she dropped from exhaustion.

Losing track of time, slowing, and repeatedly losing count, Beth teetered on the brink of passing out. With her eyes closed, she continued to administer closed-heart massage. As sweat dripped from her nose to the back of her trembling hands, she felt something close around her wrists. She opened her eyes to see Teela's hands clasped loosely over hers, her face contorted in pain.

"Jesus, Beth, you're killing me!" Teela gasped in clear English.

"Save . . . saved . . . you . . . You . . . jerk!" Beth panted breathlessly before falling over. Laughing softly between breaths, she took Teela's hand and gave it a squeeze. Teela squeezed back, and Beth's laughs turned into quaking sobs of relief that she fought to control.

Teela's vision was blurry. She forced herself to sit up and began to cough violently, each cough sending spikes of pain throughout her body. She rested her head between her knees and concentrated on not coughing, trying to make sense of the thoughts that raced through her mind. *Who am I?* she thought, remembering a suicide attempt.

A loud thump, then a series of louder thumps, drew Daedalus to full consciousness.

"Damn! God damn it! What is going on?" he muttered. The pounding helped him call his memories forth. The memory of transfer and everything afterward flooded into his mind.

"I died! Oh shit! What the hell?" he cried, looking down at his alien hands. *Teela, Teela! Where are you?* he shouted with his mind.

Raising his head, he forced his eyes to focus on the room. In black and gray, he saw Gremensh lying on the floor near the gurney with her arm outstretched, as though pointing to an adjacent wall, her sword nearby.

Aw Jesus, not a dream. Shit, shit, shit. Reality sucks! Daedalus pulled his hand from Beth's grip. Beth watched in shocked silence as Teela struggled to stand.

His legs were shaky, and he felt dizzy and faint. Teetering on the verge of collapse, he braced himself against the wall for a moment, drawing a few painful breaths before stumbling drunkenly to pick up the sword. He leaned on it like a cane, then doubled over with another violent coughing fit.

"Teela, are you all right? What are you going to do?" Beth asked. The loud thumps coming from just outside the door had a sobering effect on her fractured composure.

"I'm never going to be all right. I'm screwed!" Daedalus muttered, his eyes focusing on his pale, mottled feet.

"I'm gonna need both swords," he said. Swaying unsteadily, he leaned on the gurney and reattached the scabbards to his belt.

"I don't know how safe those are. One shot turned your pal there into a crispy critter," Beth advised, eyeing the swords in Teela's hands.

The door made a loud metallic clang a second before the wall adjacent to it began to glow red-hot.

"Get behind me," Daedalus said softly. He crossed his blades in front of him and watched the door apprehensively.

With a loud crack and a tortured squeal, the door slid open. The corridor outside appeared empty, but the growling barks of Korlah came from either side of the opening.

"Aren't you going to answer them?" Beth whispered.

"I . . . I don't have a fucking clue what they're saying," Daedalus replied.

"What? They're telling us to surrender, or give up weapons, or something like that. Even I can understand that much of your fucking language. What's wrong with you, Teela?" Beth asked, unwilling to acknowledge what she was thinking.

"Teela's not home. All you got is me," Daedalus answered from between clenched jaws.

"What? What the hell is that supposed to mean?" Beth asked.

"She runs the body. I'm like an adviser, and we talk. I remember doing a few things, but it was only instinctive reaction. When I'm not needed, I wander—dream, I guess. I was gone, lost, sleeping, dreaming—hell, I don't know where I was. I thought I was dead, lost in black nothingness. I couldn't find my way back. You called me. I followed your voice, Beth! She's usually in front, like . . . like I'm looking over her shoulder, or through her eyes. She's always been there, but she's gone. And right now, I'm alone. You can't imagine how this feels! I am sooo screwed!" Daedalus wailed.

"That's all right. I . . . I know a few words," Beth stammered. She wanted to say his name, realizing for the first time that, perhaps, what had happened to Daedalus was something more than memory theft. For the first time, Beth actually believed she was speaking to the person she had known as Dade.

"Ney hippa ankah. Kahshinki moo pah, kah riz oomach rachnich." Beth growled her complete collection of Korlah words, unconcerned and unaware that she had just said, "By fang or by claw. You Kahshinki cowards, fight with gloves in mouths hungry."

A moment later, a large, unarmed but heavily armored warrior stepped into the doorway. Making a clawed salute, she stepped into the room and raised the visor on her helmet.

"Rouche Hah!"

"Rouche Hah!" Beth returned the honored greeting for Teela.

"Teela, this looks like Tiny, the big sucker that—"

"Shawaugh. I know her. Her name is Shawaugh, Beth . . . ?" Teela asked weakly.

"Yeah, okay. Her name is Shawaugh. I remember," Beth answered.

"Beth, I'm fading fast," Daedalus whispered.

"What's wrong? I'm right here," Beth answered.

"Teela is back. Thanks, Ms. Porter. Later," Daedalus whispered as he released control to Teela.

Slumping forward slightly, Daedalus slowly lowered the swords to the floor and surrendered the body. Beth put her arm around Teela's waist to keep her from collapsing.

Teela took a deep breath and straightened. She sheathed one sword, and gently pried Beth's arm from around her waist so she could sheath the other.

"To my honor," Teela said in Korlah, returning Shawaugh's greeting while making a trembling palm display.

Shawaugh studied the room suspiciously, circling the gurney before stopping at Gremensh's body. "Shyron sent me," she stated as Resistance soldiers entered the room.

Teela stiffened. She placed her hands on the grips of her swords and slowly backed up so that she and Beth would not be caught between Shawaugh and the soldiers.

"Your eye has been repaired. And your honor . . . restored?" Teela asked stiffly, her eyes darting nervously between Shawaugh and the soldiers.

"Yes!" Shawaugh growled angrily, irritated that Teela would ask.

"And the price? My existence, and that of the humans?" Teela asked.

"Yes, that and—" Shawaugh began, not realizing that Teela believed she had betrayed her.

Upon hearing the word "yes," Teela drew her blades, pointing one at Shawaugh and the other at the soldiers.

"These are more than blades," Teela cried defiantly. The blades crackled with static charges, lending credence to her words.

"Your mind is damaged! We have been sent to protect you. Why do you turn your weapons on us?" Shawaugh growled, making a gesture of surrender.

It is time I separated truth from lie. Shyron's thought came to Teela as a voice. Turning to the door, Teela saw Eemela, or more appropriately, Shyron in Eemela's shell, wearing a common birth section tah. Making a clawed salute, Shyron bowed deeply before speaking.

"By fang or by claw, by the blood of our existence, if Teela and her human companions are harmed or fail to achieve an alliance, our existence shall be terminated and command transferred to the next ranking leader," she swore. Then she directed her thoughts to Teela alone.

There are no dishonors greater than those of my existence. No shame deeper. Much of what Gremensh has told you is true. All we ask is that you give us a chance to explain while we walk to the pod that will return you and our human friends to their planet.

Soothing, comforting feelings coursed through Teela. She knew that Shyron was projecting them, she knew she was being manipulated and she wanted to resist, but she was involuntarily relaxing. She lowered the swords and returned them to their sheaths.

"Afron's forces have surrendered. You are free to go, little sister. Honor me by letting me walk you to your vessel," Shyron said, offering her hand to Teela. After a moment's hesitation, Teela reached out and took it.

Two Korlah holding hands would not have been an unusual sight aboard the ship, had it not been for the human pushing a gurney behind them and the column of Resistance soldiers, warriors, and guards that flanked and followed them. Shyron tried to walk close at first, but the scabbard of Teela's sword kept slapping her leg. Shyron was obviously leading. Her head was erect and she glanced around as they walked, but it was apparent that she was focused on Teela. Teela walked slumped over with her head and eyes down. Shyron spoke to her as they walked.

"Afron did not reveal the secrets of the map room to the Council until after the human had transferred to your shell. She, along with many others, was filled with a great sense of hopelessness when it was discovered that the origin of our existence is nothing more than a Kahshinki farming enterprise," Shyron said. She glanced at Teela, who was unresponsive.

"Are you hearing my words?" Shyron asked after a moment.

"Yes," Teela answered in a hoarse monotone.

"The long-range scout sent out after the arrival of the humans brought back disturbing news: the Kahshinki are prepared for our arrival. We will be facing not one campaign vessel, but three. The two unexpected vessels we believe were sent from the Kahshinki base planet. Communications monitored between a campaign vessel and a patrol of fighters has led us to believe they are manning their fighters with Kahshinki, rather than duplicates. Afron and Tooron made it clear to the Council that even if we were at a state of complete readiness for campaign, there is absolutely no chance for victory against three enemy campaign vessels.

"Afron proposed that we abandon our pursuit of the Kahshinki and change course for a remote planet that is only harvested every twenty-four thousand cycles. It would take another four cycles' travel by campaign vessel, but could theoretically be reached now by taking long-range assault pods to their limits and then traveling the remainder of the distance in troop transports. Either way, the journey would be difficult and challenging."

"Gremensh said that four pods were preparing to go there . . . to the new planet," Teela said.

"Yes, that is true. We have temporarily blocked their departure. The Council has agreed that any who wish to flee to the planet, this New Korlah, will be permitted to do so. Those who were being taken against their will are being removed from the assault pods and will be replaced by any who wish to fill their vacancies. Do you want to go with them, Teela?" Shyron asked.

"No!" Teela cried, emerging from her trance to flash angry eyes at Shyron.

"Teela, this vessel cannot protect itself, let alone the planet of humans. Without an alliance, the humans will not be able to protect their own planet. You are physically and mentally exhausted. You will need to rest and take nourishment on your journey if you hope to succeed," Shyron said as she led Teela into a transit cube.

While Beth, Shawaugh, and the others of the immediate party filled the cube, Shyron and Teela stood in silence.

We sense a great distrust. A distrust of the Council—of us, Shyron said with her mind as the cube moved upward through the warrior section.

"You've been using me. Haven't you? From the time my damage was discovered," Teela said in a whisper that was barely audible over the hum of the transit cube.

"If we did not fear your ability to read our thoughts, we would lie. We would lie to you about our past, about our shame, about doing the things that were necessary to prevent Afron from seizing control of this vessel. What we did was without malice. You lacked utility as defined by our doctrine, so we created utility. The events since your transfer have been . . . most unusual, and far outside our control."

"This robe, it wasn't made for me. You had it made for yourself. Didn't you? Do you still intend to claim the role of Shawlmon? Do you?" Teela demanded.

"It was originally intended for us. We hoped the image of Shawlmon would be able to unite this vessel for campaign. When we had Challmara give it to you, it was because we had given up, and we were ready to embrace the peace of nonexistence. Your . . . actions . . . the events that followed were quite unexpected."

"Challmara knew of this! She was your spy? Wha—wa—" Teela stuttered, pulling her hand free of Shyron's. "Has there been any part of my existence that belonged to me?" Teela tried to back away, pressing against the dense crowd around them.

"A reluctant observer, your Challmara. She would never have assisted with anything that would have brought you harm," Shyron quickly responded, palming her apology. "Challmara's affection for you is genuine. We did not contact her until after Afron had used you for the unauthorized transfer. Her loyalty to you is . . . unprecedented. It was her descriptions of your stories, your infatuation with our past that gave me hope for the future. You need to understand, you are an enigma, a freak occurrence that has no precedence for me to draw upon.

"Challmara told me of your infatuation with the sculpture of Shawlmon and that you dreamed of being a warrior. She said you wanted to feel a blade in your hand and experience the excitement of battle. We remember what it felt like to wear that robe. Or at least, that part of us that was Shawlmon remembers. We told ourselves we gave it to you to grant your wish, but the truth is, we were afraid. To wear the robe meant that we would assume the role of Shawlmon. But we had no plan for victory, as we are faced with certain defeat. You, however, as preposterous as it seemed, actually believed in victory. You, a damaged birthing unit, proposed an alliance that, although unlikely, allowed us to reject despair and cherish our continued existence. A vision from the past, a vision of victory that has motivated us for a thousand cycles, in you we could see a future.

"We didn't give you the robe expecting you to become Shawlmon. We gave it to you because it is designed with a new form of pulse-absorption armor. It was our hope that in addition to letting you feel like the warrior you dreamed of becoming, it would protect you and provide a symbol of rank and authority."

The door to the transit cube opened and the occupants exited. Shyron took Teela by the hand and motioned the others away. When the cube slid shut, Shyron moved Teela so she could see herself in its highly polished door. Weaving her arms with Teela's, Shyron drew her close and leaned down until their foreheads touched.

"Look at the reflection and tell me what you see," she said.

Teela glanced up and froze. She and Shyron were the mirror image of the ancient sculpture she had meditated upon for so long.

"The sculpture. But that was my dream, my fantasy. It felt good to dream. This is not how I imagined I would feel. It doesn't feel good," Teela whispered, averting her eyes and withdrawing from Shyron.

The first time we saw you in this robe, we knew the choice we made was the right one. You are a warrior. You are no longer Teela, nor are you the human Daedalus. Once you have rested, you will know who you are. We would be honored if you took the name Shawlmon, but whatever you decide, whenever you come to terms with your new self, remember that who *you are will shape* what *you are. We believe you can accomplish this task. Now it is time for you to believe it.*

A technician walked up to Shyron and waited to be recognized, then passed her a message board. Shyron read the message and passed it back, sending her on her way.

"Shawaugh, have your warriors take their positions. The other human will arrive momentarily, and you may then begin the ceremony," Shyron announced.

"What ceremony?" Teela asked apprehensively, glancing at Beth, who stood stoically alongside Crystal's body, and at the armed warriors that were forming a ring around them.

Great deeds demand great honors. You have nothing to fear. You will not be late for your rendezvous with Challmara, Shyron answered with her mind.

Teela's head jerked up and she stared at Shyron.

"No, Challmara has not ceased," Shyron said, surprised at the clarity and strength of Teela's projected thoughts.

"Gremensh said her vessel was destroyed by hull cannon," Teela said, wanting to hear that it was a lie. She hoped Shyron was not the evil entity Gremensh had painted her to be.

"One of the pod's transports broke off during launch and was destroyed by a hull cannon. Analysis detected no biological debris. The main body of the pod and all of its remaining vessels have disappeared off our sensors, obscured by the plasma stream of the campaign vessel. Challmara and your human companions will be waiting for you as planned," Shyron said.

The words instilled her with invigorating relief. Teela put her head back slightly and closed her eyes as the words flowed through her, washing away her guilt and trepidation.

"Dade!" Bill's voice boomed, as he passed into the ring of warriors and saw Teela.

Teela straightened up. Closing her eyes, she rotated her head on her shoulders to loosen her neck while her mouth moved to speak. She opened her eyes and looked at her open hands before closing them into fists at her sides. She looked at Bill and grinned, exposing her fangs in what would otherwise be perceived as a threat display.

"Glad to see you could make it," Teela said in perfect English.

"You feeling better now?" Bill asked, offering her his hand.

"Not really. Bad, bad headache. What I would do for some extra-strength aspirin. But I'm okay for now, and I'll feel a boat-load better once we're heading home, which, by the way, will be really soon. You ready to rock and roll?" Teela asked, taking Bill's hand in a two-handed shake.

"Well . . . I kinda wanna talk to you about that," Bill said, pulling his hand free. He put his hands in his pockets and looked around nervously, his eyes settling on Beth. "Hey, Beth," he said with a nod, loud enough for her to hear but much softer than usual. Beth nodded in return.

"What's the matter with Crystal? She still hurt?" Bill asked.

"She's dead, Bill," Teela said softly.

"I'm real sorry," Bill said in a detached, mechanical voice.

"Yeah, me too," Teela replied, both curious and concerned by Bill's lack of interest.

Bill turned his head away from Beth and whispered, "I don't wanna go back. Think maybe I'll just stay here. If it's no problem, I mean."

"Are you frigging nuts? You may not get another chance. Jesus, Bill, why?" Teela asked.

Bill didn't respond; instead, he looked over his shoulder and scanned the crowd. Spotting his new companion, he motioned fervently for her to join them. Reluctantly, the biotech walked over, followed closely by several warriors. She stood next to Bill.

"This here's Rahfoon. We're gonna git married and stuff. Have kids an' all. We been working real hard at trying to understand each other. Maybe you could see if I understand right. 'Cause it's what I want. I mean, I'm fine with it. Ain't nothing back home for me," Bill said nervously, glancing sidelong at Beth.

"Kids and married? Are you shitting me? Bill, this is an experiment. They're trying to create a hybrid; a cross between humans and Korlah. I heard it's possible, but Jesus Bill, you don't really want this do you?"

The biotech began to speak, but Dade could not understand what she said. He held his hand up for her to stop. He closed his eyes and called the essence within, trying to access the memories that would allow him to understand what Rahfoon was saying. When nothing happened, he rotated his head, this time stamping his foot twice and clenching his fists tightly, and again called to Teela. Taking a deep breath that was almost a gasp, Teela coughed and cleared her throat before slouching forward slightly. She looked up at Bill and ignored her throbbing temples that pulsated with each deafening boom of her heart. Nodding respectfully, she turned from Bill and addressed Rahfoon.

"What do you want with this male? Teela asked.

"I have told you!" Rahfoon hissed. "I claim first rights as his mate by the ancient laws. Cooperatives have been legalized. This male will ensure the sovereignty of our clan, and ours will be the first clan free of duplication. I carry the first embryo from natural procreation since the onset of campaign. He has already agreed to join our clan. We are blood bound!" She growled and bared her fangs.

"If this human stays, it will be under conditions bound by blood oath," Teela said quietly, her aching eyes meeting Rahfoon's challenge.

"State your conditions," Rahfoon hissed, her eyes narrowing.

"This unit will stay on this vessel only as long as it chooses to. It will not be permitted to challenge or be challenged. It will not engage in physical conflict inside or outside the spectacle chamber. It will receive full rations, even if its utility is lost. When its existence ends, it will be without assistance. And if it breaks any laws, you and your collective will assume responsibility. These conditions are not negotiable and must be accepted as stated or my offer is rescinded," Teela said.

"How can you make such demands? You have already stated that you have no claims on this male," Rahfoon hissed.

In matters concerning our human guests, Shyron interjected telepathically, *Teela, Assistant to the Potentate, speaks with the full authority of the Council. As acting Potentate, we will bear witness and will see to the enforcement of the conditions.*

Rahfoon's mouth dropped open as she realized that the unit in birther's garb behind Teela was in fact the Potentate. Rahfoon fell to her knees and sank her head nearly to the floor, presenting an apologetic palm display.

"Your Eminence, I . . . did not . . . know you were here. I apologize for my ignorance," she cried.

"An apology is not required. Since our transfer, we have enjoyed a fair amount of anonymity. We realize it will not last much longer. Rise, Senior Technician Rahfoon, and respond to the conditions presented to you."

Rahfoon stood to face Teela. This time her eyes were downcast; whatever plans she had to skirt Teela's authority had evaporated. She wrestled with Teela's demands and considered the plans of her collective.

"What is your decision?" Teela pressed after a long pause.

"By fang or by claw, by the blood of my existence, I accept your conditions," Rahfoon managed through the knot in her throat.

"Done!" Teela and Shyron said together.

"Done," Rahfoon repeated, slipping her arm through Bill's.

Teela turned to Bill and opened her mouth to speak, then closed it again. She closed her eyes and rotated her head in a slow circle, trying once again to relieve the stabbing pain at the base of her skull as she called to Daedalus for help. Her face twisted and she lurched backward as if she were kicked in the chest. Shyron grabbed Teela's arm, easing her collapse onto the floor. Shyron knelt over her and cradled Teela's head in her hands with her forehead against the crown of her head.

We warned you of this, Shyron said with her mind. *Your memories have divided and the strain of accessing them is disrupting the relationship between minds and body. Do not try to force a shift again or you risk permanent physical and mental damage. The disruption you have caused may heal with rest. You cannot continue like this, one essence must be expelled or your shell will cease to function.*

Daedalus slowly opened his eyes. Although his pounding head was making him nauseous, his perceptions had never been this clear before. The fog over his transfer had lifted, leaving no doubt that he was in a body that was not his. He saw in high-definition and sharp contrast, but could detect no color, which gave the skin of the Korlah around him a surrealistic sheen. He opened his hands and stared at the four digits and brightly glowing palms.

"Oh . . . my . . . God!" Dade groaned, holding his hands before the face that was nothing like his face.

"Dade, you had another spell. You gonna be all right?" Bill asked, kneeling next to him.

"No, hell no! I'm never gonna be all right!" He groaned, moving to his feet with Bill's help.

May your Mission bring you honor and victory, Shyron said telepathically to Teela. *We have briefed Shawaugh on the actions you need to take once you have negotiated the alliance. Concern yourself only with rest and repair. I will coordinate your departure.*

Dade looked at Shyron. He marveled at the way her thoughts seemed to have a sound but transferred meaning without language.

"If you can communicate telepathically, you don't need me. You never needed me," Daedalus said to Shyron. "Why the mind-swap? Why didn't you just let me die?" He pressed his palms to his temples to contain the pressure that made his eyes ache and his skull feel as though it would explode.

Shyron tilted her head. She tried to make sense of the chaotic thoughts that came with the alien words. Unable to read human thoughts and concerned that she would try to force another shift if pressed, Shyron bowed deeply and turned away.

Dade watched as Shyron and her guards left in the transit cube.

"Whad she say, Dade? Did Rahfoon tell you what she been trying to tell me?" Bill asked, breaking Dade's trance.

"Yeah, pretty much what you thought. Except maybe you don't know about the others," Dade said, directing his full attention to Bill.

"What others?" Bill asked innocently.

"Rahfoon already considers you married, if you can call it that. You have been selected as her clan-mate, as in the ancient histories. Having accepted her as a mate, you not only married her, you married her entire clan. They consider you more like a business partner than a husband. Rahfoon is the matriarch of her clan. On behalf of her clan, she has offered you a job, a job for life. She seems to think you have accepted her job offer. Have you?"

"I've had worse jobs. This one's just fine with me. Rahfoon and her sisters wanna learn English. I'm gonna learn Korlah and teach um English."

Beth began to laugh loudly, drawing a fierce scowl from Bill.

"Great idea, Bill. Really, I mean it," Beth said, chuckling.

"I am perfectly capable of speaking proper English if I so choose," Bill said with crisp precision. "Syntactical conformity and rigid adherence to the mid-Atlantic dialect have no particular value to me. I will leave proper English, or white English, as dey calls it in mah hood, fo' bitches like yo'."

"You're right. Yeah, I think you're right. The gangsta sound is much better," Beth said with a smirk.

"Bill, I won't force you to come with us," Dade said, "but we're a team and I need to hear that this is what you really want."

"Listen Dade, there's no team. No offense, but I ain't your boy; I never was. I screwed up during our escape and it cost me mah face. I know where these eyes of mine came from, an I backed you cause I know you would of backed me. Nothing against where this new face a mine come from, but if I go back, I'm gonna be a freak. Anyhow, the government won't let this story get out. The only thing Beth an me agree on is that they gonna put a bullet in each and every one of your heads. I am gonna stay, and I don't need your permission."

"You're right; I didn't mean it like that. Bill, without each other, we never would have made it. I will be forever grateful for your friendship. I wish you and Rahfoon all the best. Good luck, sir," Dade said, shaking Bill's hand. "Now, if you'll forgive me,

Beth and I have an appointment to keep. Beth! Oh, excuse me, Ms. Porter! Shall we go?" Dade asked, making an exaggerated sweep toward the transit tube that would carry them up to the hangar that housed their assault pod.

"God, I hope so!" Beth cried as she turned the gurney and followed Dade. As they progressed down an aisle of Korlah, the warriors on each side saluted; Dade soon realized the salutes were specifically directed at Beth. Three warriors took up positions in front of them. The large warrior in the center gave a clawed salute and the others each carried a bundle topped by a long cylindrical object; it became clear that they had no intention of moving out of their way. Recognizing Shawaugh by the scar across her face, Dade returned her salute.

"Now what?" Beth muttered.

"Ah . . . some kind of ceremony. I don't know what it's about. Can't remember just now," Dade said.

Shawaugh and the warrior to her left marched past Teela and to Crystal's gurney. Shawaugh spoke loudly to Crystal and took the cylinder from the warrior, then withdrew a meter-long blade with a snap of her hands.

"What the?" Beth growled between clenched teeth as she stepped back from the gurney.

"Don't be a knucklehead," Dade said to Beth. "It's some kind of ceremony. It's okay. This is our friend—Shawaugh. Don't interfere." Although he sounded calm, his heart raced.

Shawaugh pointed the sword at the floor and shouted, then pointed overhead and shouted again. She moved around the gurney repeating the motions, pointing the blade away from Crystal at each of the four sides of the gurney and shouting the same words. She held the blade and sheath over Crystal and reunited them with a loud snap, and the congregation of warriors shouted in unison. Shawaugh laid the sword on Crystal's chest. She held up a belt for all to see and draped it over the sword, then unfolded the bundle and held it up high. It was the ceremonial tunic of a warrior, black with gold embroidery around the high collar. A large Mission emblem with a Korlah glyph at its heart was centered on its front and back. Shawaugh draped the tunic over Crystal and pulled it up under her chin before stepping back and giving a clawed salute.

“Roche Hah Crystaugh!” Shawaugh shouted.

“Roche Hah!” the rows of warriors repeated in chorus.

The warrior assisting Shawaugh marched to join her peers and the other, holding a similar bundle, took her place. Shawaugh took the tunic first. She held it up as she had before, calling and the group responding. When she held it out to Beth, Beth looked at Daedalus.

“Take it and put it on,” he said, acting on a vague recollection.

When Beth started to put the tunic on over her gown, Dade interjected.

“No! It has to be all that you wear.”

“Oh man, you’re kidding, right?”

“It’s important . . . I think,” Dade answered.

Shaking her head in mute protest, Beth pulled her own gown over her head and, much to Dade’s surprise, took the time to neatly fold it before setting it at the foot of Crystal’s gurney. Dade couldn’t help but stare at the dark lines that streaked her arms, shoulders, and abdomen, from the recent lacerations by the claws of Korlah warriors. He admired her coolness before these hundreds of warriors, genetic duplicates of those who had inflicted injuries that nearly took her life.

Beth pulled on the tunic and straightened it, surprised at how well it fit. “Nice threads. Thanks,” she said to Shawaugh, bowing slightly.

Shawaugh lifted the belt and handed it to her. Beth put it on without instruction, fumbling at first with the clasp. Shawaugh waited patiently for her to finish before taking the sword and holding it high over her head with both hands. While Shawaugh froze with the sword over her head, the warrior that had delivered it returned to her place. Pulling the blade from its sheath, Shawaugh stepped up to Beth and slid the sheath into the ring on her belt. She stepped back, pointed the blade at Beth, and shouted in Korlah.

“Hold your hand up,” Dade said. “No, the other hand.”

As Beth reached up, Shawaugh stepped forward and nicked Beth’s wrist with a deft flick of the blade just below the pad of her palm. Beth didn’t flinch; she made a tight fist as a thin rivulet of blood trickled down her forearm. Her eyes locked on

Shawaugh's, flashing the unpredictable anger that Teela had come to dread.

"Don't do anything stupid. This is almost over," Dade whispered to himself.

As Shawaugh laid the tip of the blade in her own left hand, Dade noticed that she was not wearing the coarse gloves that, along with her scarred face, were features he had come to expect. The large thick-fingered hand, creased with scars and thick calluses, closed on the blade. Shawaugh drew the blade from her clenched hand. When she raised and opened her hand, she let a pool of blood spill in a thick stream into the sleeve of her tunic.

Shawaugh moved face to face with Beth and wrapped her bloody hand around Beth's pricked wrist. With a practiced snap, she flipped the blade in midair and caught it by the blade, then held it to Beth's closed fist. When Beth understood, she opened her hand and accepted the grip of the sword. Shawaugh carefully guided the blade into the sheath before snapping it down with force. The instant the hilt hit the scabbard, Shawaugh released Beth's wrist and stepped back with a clawed salute.

"Roche Hah Bethaugh!" Shawaugh shouted.

"Roche Hah!" Dade and the warriors shouted together.

The chamber became deathly silent.

"What am I supposed to do?" Beth hissed between clenched teeth, her hand still on the grip of the sheathed sword.

"Oh . . . I'm sorry. Ah, you return the salute . . . I think," Dade said.

"Roche Hah!" Beth shouted, mimicking Shawaugh's salute.

The chamber roared with cheers, and then activity in the hangar recommenced. Half of the warriors marched three abreast toward the transit tubes, and the other half began funneling into the tube that led to the assault pod. Beyond the warriors in the tube, Dade could see a platform about twelve-feet across floating down from the pod to land by Crystal's gurney. Two laborers jumped over the platform's rails and maneuvered the gurney onto it. Beth made no effort to intervene. She jumped up after them and resumed her position alongside Crystal.

"See you on board," she said with a faint smile, leaning over the rail as the skiff rose silently up to the pod, suspended high above in the cavernous hangar. Dade watched in amazement. As it approached the composite craft, the platform suddenly tipped sideways and Beth threw her arms up in reflex, expecting to plunge to her death. Instead, gravitational forces contrary to earthly logic allowed the laborers to transfer Beth and Crystal into a cargo craft attached to the pod at a perpendicular angle. After the women were inside, the opening in the craft disappeared and the loading platform drifted down to a stack of large rations cubes.

Dade followed Shawaugh into the transit tube that would take him up to the pod. As he floated slowly upward, he closed his eyes and tapped the heels of his boots together.

There's no place like home, Daedalus thought, wishing he would wake up from this dream. He realized that whatever home he'd once had was gone, or at least, it was no longer within the grasp of the alien hands he clenched into tight fists. The pain returned him to clarity and to Teela.

We will need each other to succeed. You will stay . . . with me? Teela asked.

You know that I will, for as long as you want me. Will you help me get my message to Julie?

Yes! Teela shot back, anticipating the question and angry that she could not hide her emotions from Daedalus.

So all we need to do now is win a war and save a world. The odds are against us. But hell, that's been the story of my life . . . and death.

29 - Illation

Night faded to the milky gray twilight of dawn, coloring the blinds at the kitchen window with a warm glow. For a little more than twenty minutes the alien had sat staring at Julie. Neither had moved or spoken a word as the two agents shifted nervously. The alien's expression softened. She took a deep breath, exhaled slowly, and touched a small recess on the side of the silver box in front of her. The box opened like the aperture of a camera and she pushed it across the table toward Julie. The alien broke eye contact and closed her eyes before bowing her head slightly. She spoke quietly in a raspy voice.

"These are your husband's personal effects."

Julie took the box with a trembling hand and tipped the contents onto the table. A wallet, a pocketknife, and a thin chain holding a St. Christopher medallion and a wedding band spilled out.

"These objects arrive with a message. Dade wanted you to know that he greatly regretted parting without telling you how much he loved you."

Julie's face twisted in anguish. She lifted the chain and scooped the ring and medallion into her fist, releasing a choked cry. Tears welled in her eyes and flowed down her cheeks when she clenched her eyes shut, falling onto the fist that held the two things her husband had carried with him every day of the twenty years of their marriage. Sensing Julie's distress, the dog jumped up and licked her wet face, trying to console her. The alien and agents remained silent.

Julie's sobs turned to deep breaths as she fought to control her emotions. She raised her head to look at the alien.

"What's going to happen now? What about Earth? Can we win this war?" she asked, sniffing and blinking tears from her red-rimmed eyes as she smeared fresh mascara across her cheek with the back of her hand. The alien's color paled to bone white.

"There's a place, another planet. If you want, if it is your wish, you would be welcome there. It is my belief that anywhere will be safer than this planet."

Julie stared at her for a moment before looking back at the objects in her hand. She stirred them with the tip of her finger.

"You don't have to decide right now. I have a device. It's like a phone," the alien said, tapping the thin black briefcase on the table with the tip of her clawed finger. "Open it and speak. Your message will be sent, and I will respond as quickly as I can. If you decide to leave, you can. If you wish to talk, you don't need a reason. We can just . . . talk."

Julie was unresponsive. After several minutes of silence, the alien rose to her feet. She donned her clock deliberately and slowly. With the hood back in place, her face was once again hidden in shadow. As she passed Julie on her way toward the front door, Julie reached out for the hand that had earlier seemed hideous.

"Is that you, Dade? Is it?" Julie stammered, holding tightly with both hands.

"No, but like Teela, I have also received a human transfer. I'm just a messenger, nothing more."

"I don't believe you," Julie whispered.

The alien tensed, grasping Julie's hands with enough force that Julie tried to pull away. The alien held on firmly, took a deep breath, and let it out slowly before speaking.

"I am neither of the individuals I once was. They no longer exist. I am new, reborn. I am acutely aware that I cannot return to either of my past lives. I'm truly sorry if this is not what you were hoping to hear." She gave Julie's hands a gentle squeeze before releasing her, and moved toward the door.

"Wait!" Julie cried. "Then what happened to Teela, Beth, and the others? What about the alliance?"

The alien stopped and turned, looking down. She wrung her hands. "The journey back was difficult. Teela is missing and presumed dead. Some of the humans were returned, but a few were not, and never will be. There is still much work to be done to negotiate an alliance. Dade's commitment to the others has been met and his message has been delivered. I have told you all that I can for now. Be patient, Julie. As soon as I can, I will tell you what I know of Teela's final journey." She offered Julie an apologetic palm display.

"Take this . . . please." Julie removed the wedding band from the chain and pressed the St. Christopher on its chain into the alien's palm, closing the clawed fingers around it.

"I gave this to Dade a long time ago. It had a difficult journey during our life together. I don't believe that journey is over yet."

"Thank you. I will keep it with me always. Good-bye, Julie," she said, moving quickly to the limousine.

Julie stood in the doorway, holding the wiggling boxer by its collar, an odd smile on her tear-streaked face. She remained there long after the cars were gone. Eventually, she sat down on the step in front of the open door. She watched the sunrise through the morning clouds with a new reverence for her planet's fragile beauty.

Glossary of Humans

Bourke, Jimmy. Abducted; student at USC, physical education major.

Clarke, Marsha. Abducted: musician, drums, member of the band Metal Maidens; Seattle, Washington.

Heckart, Margaret. Abducted; elementary school nurse: Southeast Oregon.

Jacks, Bill. Abducted; security guard at Mill Valley Industrial Center; Central California.

McCabe, Rebecca. Abducted; self-described missionary of the Christian faith.

Moore, Ann. Abducted; day care center manager; Northern California

Porter, Bethany. Abducted; ex-Marine, undercover federal agent working as a bank manager.

Purcell, Catherine. Abducted; musician, bass guitar, member of the band Metal Maidens.

Ramsey, Jason, aka Hollywood, Captain USAF, asteroid outpost fighter pilot.

Rimes, Daedalus. Abducted; maintenance supervisor at Mill Valley Industrial Center; Central California.

Rimes, Julie. Wife of Daedalus.

Santos, Crystal. Abducted; musician, vocals and lead guitar, member of the band Metal Maidens.

Steiner, Tiffany. Abducted; student at USC, performing arts major.

Tuman, Ruth. Abducted; electrical engineer.

Glossary of Korlah

Afron \ˈaf-rän\ Strategy Section leader, tactics and navigation.

Apoulauh \ap-ˈol-ə\ Warrior; Spectacle pugilist; assassin working for Afron.

Balron \ˈbäl-rän\ Education Section leader; instruction, records, and xeno-studies.

Challmara \ˈchäl-mä-rä\ Senior technical unit; Arms Section, assigned to weapons maintenance, research, and development.

Dooaugh \ˈdü-ə\ **also "the Oracle."** Warrior; designated for reclamation; outlaw Non.

Eemela \ē-ˈmel-ə\ Resistance soldier; birthing unit, damaged during first-cycle implantation.

Eepalla \ē-ˈpäl-ə\ Birthing unit, first-cycle implantation; assists humans to learn the Korlah language; friend of human Crystal Santos.

Fezron \ˈfez-rän\ Supplies Section leader, food, water, and raw materials.

Gilron \ˈgil-rän\ Population Section leader, shell generation and distribution.

Gremensh \ˈgrə-mench\ Director of Biological Repairs, Health Section; performs memory transfer experiments for Afron.

Khranga \ˈkran-gä\ Director of Warriors and Pilots, Warrior Section; conspires with Afron to seize control of the Campaign Vessel.

Krron \ˈker-rän\ Security Section leader, information and communication.

Lahsoon \ˈlȯ-sün\ Senior Resistance soldier; laborer; soldier genotype that was never apprenticed.

Manalla \mȯ-ˈnäl-ə\ Birthing unit; birth sister assigned to same shift and section as Teela.

Meezra \ˈmēz-rä\ Laborer; Accouterments Section; involved in illicit black market trading activities, particular area of expertise being visual logs.

Mesron \ˈmes-rän\ Arms Section leader, weaponry and shielding.

Molron \ˈmäl-rän\ Energy Section leader, propulsion, life support, and power generation.

Nerhala \nər-ˈhäl-ə\ Senior birthing unit; Teela's Birth Section mother; friend and mentor who cared for Teela when she was injured.

Ohhron \ˈō-rän\ Accouterments Section leader, fabrication, food processing, maintenance, and repair.

Ohmensh \ˈō mench\ Minor maintenance technician; Accouterments Section: works for the Resistance.

Pelnaugh \ˈpel-nȯ\ Commander; Warrior Section; leader of ground assault on human-Kahshinki asteroid base.

Plefauna \ˈplȯ-fä-nä\ Senior guard; Security Section; officer in charge of Teela's security following transfer.

Rahfoon \ˈrä-fün\ Biological Technician; Health Section; leader of cooperative interested in acquiring Bill Jacks as their mate.

Ruwaugh \ˈrü-wä\ Warrior; Spectacle pugilist; archrival of Shawaugh; mercenary willing to work for the highest bidder.

Sethron \ˈseth-rän\. Health Section leader, biological maintenance and repair.

Shawaugh \ˈshä-wä\ Warrior; deposed director of Campaign Warrior Forces; "living shame of the Warrior Section"; blamed for failing to prevent devastating Kahshinki attack; found Teela in wreckage following attack.

Shawlmon \ˈshȯl-män\ Famous arbitrator and bladesman of ancient Korlah; Korlah legend states that Shawlmon will rise to defeat the Kahshinki in the final battle for those that cherish life and reject despair.

Shyron \shī-rän\ Potentate; Campaign Vessel Council leader; one of the original survivors of the Kahshinki holocaust; essence passed down from shell to shell for over one thousand cycles (Korlah years).

Teela \ˈtē-el-ə\ TEELA20.10127; T series, Group E, Ela clan, generation 20, unit 10127, birthing unit damaged during Kahshinki attack, designated for reclamation;-reassigned to Health section for memory transfer experiment;- received the essence of Daedalus Rimes.

Teyron \ˈtā-rän\ Matriarch of the Ron Clan; Korlah leader at the time the Korlah home world was harvested by the Kahshinki; consort of arbitrator and bladesman Shawlmon.

Tooron \ˈtü-rän\ Warrior Section leader, soldiers and pilots.

Glossary of Terms

assault pod. Cylindrically shaped spacecraft transport vessel. Fitted with twenty recessed docking bays for smaller craft; each bay provides access to the mother craft. The smaller craft are comprised of five heavy fighters ringing the forward end, five troop carriers ringing the center, and ten light fighters filling the back. When joined together, the craft appears to be one vessel. The mother ship provides the means to travel the vast distance to the target so that the attached fighters could be built without the large and bulky plasma conversion components they would otherwise need for long-range travel. This allows the fighter craft to be more compact and maneuverable, an especially important consideration for planetary atmospheric activities.

birther. (derogatory). Birthing unit; usually taken to be offensive; genotype assigned duties of surrogate mother for clone embryo gestation.

bit. Measure of time; one three-thousandth of a Korlah planetary rotation; 100 bits = 1 set.

bladesman. Mercenary warrior skilled in the use of bladed weapons; associated with ancient Korlah tradition for settling armed disputes and clan warfare when arbitration fails.

braddle. Small rodents similar to mice or rats, possessing a long snout and prehensile tail; food source of Korlah; prepared for consumption by removing fur and purging the digestive system; served live.

cease. 1. To cease existence; to die. **2: ceased.** Dead; without honor.

crown tendrils. Olfactory organs that project out in long strands from twelve patches around the crown of the Korlah skull. They swell with blood when the individual is agitated or in a state of heightened sensitivity.

cycle. Measure of time; one Korlah solar revolution.

duplicate. Of or relating to clones or groups of clones and clone genotypes.

grav-reflector. Gravitational reflection amplification generator; sublight form of propulsion. Also used with gravity reflection plates (grav-plates) for personnel, material and equipment handling devices.

hisnah. 1: Organ that provides a form of thermal vision. **2:** A series of pits located in the center of a Korlah face where the nose on humans would be.

hyperlight. Transit stream propulsion capable of achieving up to three hundred times the speed of light.

Kahshinki. 1: The race that enslaved the Korlah and is the current target of their quest for revenge. **2:** Blood-sucking parasite found in stagnant pools on the planet Korlah.

log bar. Record-keeping device that stores written and visual records.

non. 1: Measure of time; one one-hundredth of a bit. **2:** Something without merit; inconsequential. **2: Non.** (derogatory). A unit that has been slated for reclamation.

Pulse-rifle. A shouldered Korlah weapon that discharges an energy pulse.

reclamation. The collection and processing of organic materials for reuse.

riz. Devices used in lieu of fangs and claws during Spectacle events that deliver localized pain and debilitating paralysis, depending on the force with which they impact the opponent.

Rouche Hah. 1: Warrior greeting or farewell; to my honor, to your honor. **2:** Battle cry to honor those who will cease.

rouk. Aquatic snakes. Food delicacy. Care must be taken to remove paralyzing slime that the creature exudes. Consumption produces a form of intoxication.

sabat. 1: Tattoolike marking of the face of all Korlah that is used for individual identification. Indicates the genotype, birth cycle, and production number. **2:** Stenciling or embroidered or embossed markings on Korlah uniforms and equipment to identify the individual wearing it, especially when it hides or obscures the facial marking.

scrum. 1: Scarab-like beetle that consumes decaying organic material. Used in reclamation digesters. **2:** Food source comprised of ground scrum beetles and grubs that is made into protein bars. **3:** Someone that is dirty and disgusting. **4:** Someone that is dishonorable.

scrum worm. Grub of the scrum beetle.

set. Measure of time. One-thirtieth of a Korlah planetary rotation; 10 sets = 1 shift

shell. The physical body without regard to the individual's essence. An individual is not considered to exist until they have been assigned rank and status.

shift. Measure of time. One-third of a Korlah planetary rotation; 1000 shifts = 1 cycle.

Spectacle. Pugilistic honor dispute involving unarmed combat, historically using only fangs and claws, nonlethal methods involve the use of riz.

tah. Loose-fitting floor-length gown or robe, usually worn without a belt. Standard apparel of the birthing units.

tenth. Measure of time; one-tenth of a cycle.

transfer. The act of moving the essence and memories of one individual into the mind of another.

transit-spoke. Portals for access and egress within the Campaign Vessel that utilize gravitational adjustment to allow falling up or down through the conduit at controlled rates.

wave compressors. Light speed propulsion devices used to gather and compress light into a stream of plasma energy.

COVER / CHAPTER ART

By Oliver Wetter

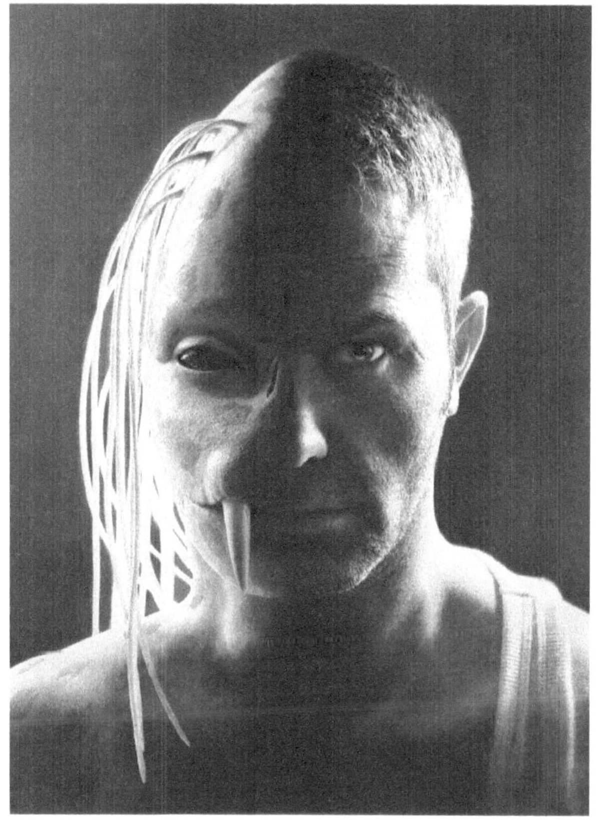

The Essence of Daedalus Rimes
2011, Commissioned Work

Oliver Wetter aka Fantasio was born and raised in Trier.

He passed an apprenticeship to become a painter and later studied at the arts-center IBKK in Bochum/Germany.

After graduating in Airbrush-design 2007 at the Arts Center IBKK in Bochum / Germany he has specialized in creating compelling book cover art, editorials & genre art, preferable character driven and portrait related.

Since then he has worked for large publishing houses and enjoys collaborating directly with authors and other creative individuals.

Oliver is published in magazines like Heavy Metal and ImagineFX, annual artbooks from Ballistic publishing & Ilex press, and in his spare time he runs a successful blog about art marketing.

Currently Fantasio fine Arts is located in Germany, but virtually connected with international talent to collaborate on projects if required. Oliver is experienced with conducting working relationships via phone and email, his mother tongue is German but he speaks and writes English fluently.

He is a networker and creates worlds out of briefings, his solution oriented work attitude leads to great visual appeal.

His diverse body of work is the result of different demands and the conviction that boredom hardly leads to remarkable results.

Visit Oliver Wetter's Web site: http://fantasio.info

www.ingramcontent.com/pod-product-compliance
Lightning Source LLC
Chambersburg PA
CBHW030822310726
48980CB00006B/598/J

* 9 7 8 0 9 8 8 7 5 0 4 2 5 *